"With its linguistic razzle-dazzle, *Mr. Timothy* is a mock-Victorian tourdeforce: a shilling-shocker that touches the heart and makes it race." —*Wall Street Journal*

"There isn't one throwaway sentence in this fabulous Victorian mystery. . . . Shimmering, knock-your-socks-off language . . . a subtle character examination and a page-turning plot, one truly engaging book." —*Entertainment Weekly* (Editor's Choice)

"[A] divinely crafted novel. . . . It is impossible to avoid being caught up in caring about the story." —*Denver Post*

"What a terrific book." —*Detroit Free Press*

"Soaring language, memorable characters, splendidly atmospheric settings, and a heartrending theme of parental love and loss. . . . In scope, in setting, and in heart, Bayard proves to be a worthy successor to Charles Dickens." —*People*

"Inventive and amusing. . . . Bayard elaborates so commandingly on Dickens. . . . Far from being cowed, he is confident enough to turn this story on its head." —*New York Times Book Review*

"This mix of thriller and literature is as rich as a Christmas cake. . . . A spirited adventure." —*Atlanta Journal-Constitution*

"A fantastic Victorian thriller. . . . The ending is as much Edgar Allan Poe as *Mission Impossible*, a plot with enough trapdoors and false bottoms to show just how much fun a ripping thriller with eggnog can be. But what's particularly satisfying is that beneath these waves of adventure rests a truly moving meditation on grief and reconciliation." —*Christian Science Monitor*

"Sink into a fireside chair with Louis Bayard's stellar *Mr. Timothy*. . . . Bayard's remarkable imagination is rivaled only by his elegant, mordant wit. Somewhere, Jonathan Swift and Oscar Wilde are applauding. Tim's droll, insightful narration is as side-splitting as it is poignant, and deftly interwoven into the plot are his meditations on the burden of potential, on loss, and on the often discordant kinship between fathers and sons."
—*Orlando Sentinel*

"Richly imagined, deeply compelling. . . . A tense, rollicking ride with more bumps, twists, and hairpin turns than a hansom cab yanked down a winding cobblestone street by a team of wild horses."
—Salon.com

"An audacious and triumphant entertainment. . . . With surprising but plausible twists, and a visceral, bawdy evocation of Victorian London, Bayard has crafted a page-turner of a thriller that is elevated beyond its genre by its endearingly flawed hero for whom nothing human is alien."
—*Publishers Weekly* (starred review)

"Inventive. . . . Bayard drenches the reader in the underbelly of 1860s London and, in true Dickensian fashion, makes us care passionately about the fates of his characters. . . . A first-rate entertainment."
—*Booklist*

"A clever premise and smartly detailed prose." —*Kirkus Reviews*

"Bayard creates several clever ligatures to Dickens's original text, but it would be wrong to consider *Mr. Timothy* a sequel: its intent is not to show how characters turned out but rather, at least in part, to meditate on the question of identity and loss, and redemption as well, drawing on *A Christmas Carol* for a few founding precepts. When it evokes the original, it's with a sly twist." —*Washington Post Book World*

"This *Christmas Carol* for the new millennium is highly recommended. If you have not had your fill of ghost-ridden heroes, needy orphans, and foggy nights in cobblestone streets, this sequel—with its break-neck plot, colorful characters, and the reappearance of Scrooge and the Cratchits—will fill the bill." 　　　　　—*Library Journal*

"Poignant. . . . Makes the always-valid point that families can be formed wherever there is trust, generosity, teamwork, and a little Christmas magic." 　　　　　—*San Francisco Chronicle*

"I read gleefully and full of admiration and pleasure—a total delight. The voice and intelligence behind the book are a real marvel." 　　　　　—Sena Jeter Naslund, author of *Ahab's Wife* and *Four Spirits*

"Imagine a latter-day Victorian thriller with all of the moral passion of a Dickens novel but none of the quaint sentimentality. *Mr. Timothy* is an exciting read, a rich historical re-creation, a literary meditation on character, and, most affectingly, a spiritual ghost story about the long, broad, and all-encompassing reach of family." 　　　　　—Gary Krist, bestselling author of *Extravagance*

"*Mr. Timothy* is a spirited and absorbing thriller, and Louis Bayard is a very talented writer." 　　　　　—Kevin Baker, author of *Paradise Alley*

"Timothy Cratchit, now a twenty-three-year-old making his living teaching a madam to read, has to confront not only horrifying murders but also his own powerful ghosts, his relationship with his father, and the specter of his own goodness. Bayard crafts a satisfying, gruesome thriller and a moving meditation on fathers, sons, and the making of a family." 　　　　　—Sarah Smith, bestselling author of *The Vanished Child*

"God bless us, yes indeed. What a terrific book." 　　　　　—*Philadelphia Inquirer*

"A first-class historical thriller. . . . Despite its dark undertones, *Mr. Timothy* is filled with optimism and the strength of the human heart, much as the original to which it pays homage."

—*Ft. Lauderdale Sun-Sentinel*

"A real page-turner."

—*New Orleans Times-Picayune*

"A rowdy . . . thrilling ride."

—*Courier-Post* (Cherry Hill, N.J.)

"Thank heavens for Louis Bayard. . . . [He] has crafted a book of which the inimitable Boz himself would be proud. Adopting a neo-Victorian prose style, the author peppers his pages with Dickensian wit and, above all, memorable characters."

—*January* magazine

"Like Dickens, Bayard plunges us immediately into the whirling cauldron of this great, awful metropolis, replete with a narrative that holds more curves than Hyde Park's Serpentine River, odd, funny characters, sinister villains, and pathetic child victims. . . . This novel . . . [is] authentic and flavorful: a solid, old-fashioned, tucked-into-bed kind of book."

—*Frontiers* magazine

"A brilliant starting point of an idea, a richly evocative setting, a panoply of hilarious, menacing, and heartbreaking characters, and *two* brilliant authors, one working at the absolute top of his game."

—*Metro Weekly*

About the Author

LOUIS BAYARD is a novelist and reviewer whose work has appeared in the *New York Times*, *Washington Post*, Nerve.com, and Salon.com. He lives in Washington, D.C.

ALSO BY LOUIS BAYARD

Fool's Errand
Endangered Species

Mr. Timothy

— A NOVEL —

LOUIS BAYARD

Perennial

An Imprint of HarperCollins*Publishers*

FOR SETH

Special thanks to Christopher Schelling for nurturing this book from its infancy. Thanks also to Marjorie Braman and everyone at HarperCollins. Additional help came from Jeffrey Hunter, John Edwards, Helen Eisenbach, Abby Yochelson of the Library of Congress, and Roberto Severino of Georgetown University. Of the many historical references I consulted, I should single out *The London Encyclopedia* (edited by Ben Weinreb and Christopher Hibbert), Peter Ackroyd's *London: The Biography*, and Donald Thomas's *Victorian Underworld*, which had the additional benefit of introducing me to Dickens's great contemporary Henry Mayhew.

The usual stream of gratitude to friends and family . . . and to Don, above all else.

He had no further intercourse with Spirits, but lived upon the Total Abstinence Principle, ever afterwards. . . .

CHARLES DICKENS,
A CHRISTMAS CAROL

Mr. Timothy

Chapter 1

NOT SO TINY ANY MORE, that's a fact. Nearly five-eight, last I was measured, and closing in on eleven stone. To this day, people find it hard to reckon with. My sister Martha, by way of example, wouldn't even meet my eye last time I saw her, had to fuss at my shirt buttons and stare at my chest, as though there were two dew-lashed orbs blinking out of my breastbone. Didn't matter I've half a foot on her now, she still wanted to be mothering me, and her with a full brood of her own—six, last I counted—and a well-oiled husband gone two nights for every night he's home, why would she want more bodies to tend? But she does, and old habits, and let the woman have what she wants, so on this last occasion, I dropped to my knees and looked straight at the sky with that look I used to have, it comes back in an instant, and I sang "Annie Laurie." And Martha laughed and boxed my ear and said Out with you, but I think it pleased her, remembering me smaller, everything else smaller, too.

The iron brace was bought by a salvager long ago, and the crutch went for kindling shortly after—quite the ceremonial moment—and all that's left, really, is the limp, which to hear others tell it is not a limp but a lilt, a slight hesitation my right leg makes before greeting the pavement, a metrical shyness. Uncle N told me once to call it a caesura, but this produced looks of such profound unknowing I quickly gave it up. I now refer to it as my stride. My hitch-stride. A lovely forward connotation that I quite fancy, although I can't honestly say I've been moving forwards, not in the last sixmonth. But always better to leave that impression.

I never think of the leg, truthfully, until the weather begins to change. I'll know it's spring, for instance, by the small ring of fire just under the right buttock. Fall is the dull, prodding ache in the hip joint, and winter is a bit of a kick in the knee. The whole kneecap sings for three or four days solid, and no amount of straightening or bending or ignoring will stop the music.

It's winter now.

The twelfth of December, to be specific, a date I am commemorating by staying in bed. I can't say bed rest does the knee any better, but if I lie still long enough, the knee merges with the rest of me and dissipates. Or perhaps I should say everything else dissipates; I forget even how to move my arm.

Many years ago, a doctor with violet nostrils and kippery breath informed my mother that the paralysis in my leg would, left untreated, rise through me like sap, up the thigh and the hip, through the lower vertebrae, the breastbone, the lungs, to settle finally in the heart itself, little orphan bundle, swallowed and stilled forever. Being just six, and possessing an accelerated sense of time, I assumed this would happen very quickly—in three or four hours, let us say—so I made a special point of saying good-bye to Martha and Belinda because they were rather nicer than Jemmy and Sam, and I told Peter if he wanted my stool, he could well have it, and that night, I lay on my pallet, waiting to go, pinching myself every few seconds to see if the feeling had vanished yet. And I suppose after all that pinching, it did. Only a matter of time, then, before the heart went. I lay there listening in my innermost ear for the final winding-down, wondering what that last, that very last beat would sound like.

Well, you can imagine how alarmed I was to awake the next morning and find the ticker still jigging. Felt a bit cheated, if you must know. And perhaps by way of compensation, I've been dreaming ever since that the long-awaited ending has at last come. I dream I'm back in Camden Town, except now I'm too big for everything: the stool, the bed, the crutch. Even the ceiling crowds a little, I have to stoop or lean against the wall. My feet are rooted to the ground. The sap is rising. I've already lost the feeling in my hands, the last draughts of air are being squeezed from my lungs, and my heart is thumping loud enough to wake the dead——and I realise then that the heart doesn't shut down at all, it keeps beating long after everything else has stopped, it's a separate organism altogether, and in a fury of betrayal, I grab for it, raking my fingers along the rib cage, and my lung squeezes out one last accordion blast of air, and that's when I cry out. I'm never sure whether I've actually cried out or whether it's part of the dream, but it always leaves me feeling exposed in some deep and irreversible fashion, so I must spend the next five minutes inventing plausible excuses for the neighbours who will come pounding on my door any minute, demanding an explanation.

The neighbours never come, of course. I have the great fortune of sleeping in an establishment where loud cries are part of the ambience. Indeed, in Mrs. Sharpe's lodging house, one might scream "Murder!" several times in quick succession and elicit nothing more than indulgent smiles from the adjoining rooms. Murder here being simply another fantasy, and fantasy being the prevailing trade.

The only person within earshot of me most nights is Squidgy, the droop-shouldered, hairy-eared gentleman with a tonsure of white hair who comes three times a week to be punished for the infractions he committed in public school half a century ago. Squidgy normally takes the room next to mine, which gives me the confessional privilege of hearing his sins, delivered in a high, breathless quaver.

——And then I gave Podgy a page out of my Latin copybook because he's quite hopeless at indicatives. And I saw Bertie Swineham sneaking out to the grange to bag squirrels, but I swore not to peach. I'm quite keen on the riding boots Simon Bentinck's mother sent him last term, and I've half a mind to pinch 'em. And Willie Robson took me down to the boathouse and showed me his pee-pee. . . .

The lashes come between each sentence, unless the instructress is over-hasty with her whipping, in which case whole predicates may be sheared off. Fortunately, Squidgy is usually paired with Pamela, a young woman who combines Prussian efficiency with Hindoo patience. It is rumoured she was once governess to the family of a deputy cabinet minister, by which personage she was seduced and shortly thereafter traduced. This may well be a fiction created for the benefit of patrons, but she surely *sounds* like a governess when she's locked in that room with Squidgy.

—Somebody hasn't learnt his conjugations!

I'm atremble just listening. Imagine poor Squidgy, having to croak out the day's lesson.

—*Amo, amas . . . a . . . ama . . .* ah, no! Please, no!

One night, I got back particularly late and found Squidgy ambling down the corridor, his sins already whipped out of him, his body as naked as the day it came into the world. He was carrying a glass of port and smiling at me like a fellow clubman.

—Evening, Timothy, he drawled.

His head was inclined with a suave deference, and as he passed, I could see Pamela's long red stripes running from the knobs of his shoulders to the backs of his knees, the new lacerations already melding with the old in a raised carpet of livid purple. And in this way I learned that Squidgy had no one waiting home for him, no one who would ever remark on the condition of his backside or even entertain suspicions.

—And a good evening to you, sir, I said.

The honourific tumbled out quite naturally. A testament, perhaps, to the dignity in which men like Squidgy are naturally clothed. And a sign that I am, like Pamela, an employee of Mrs. Sharpe's.

Certainly that is how Squidgy regards me. Many's the time he has nodded my way, commented on the weather, commended me on my peg trousers. We are the best of acquaintances, and we both know full well that if we ever ran into each other in Mayfair, he would cut me dead. Which is to say that even if I did cry out in the night, and even if Squidgy did manage to hear me through the crackings, he'd feel no obligation to interrupt his joys on my behalf.

But then who would? My few surviving relations, to the extent they are able. Uncle N, of course. Captain Gully. Beyond that, silence.

Silence, yes. A fine reason to quit your bed on a December evening, even with the knee still singing, even with the night air catching your breath as soon as you lose it. Keep moving, Tim. Towards the noise! Towards the light!

And no town has more of same than London in the year of our Lord eighteen hundred and sixty. London waits for you at every interstice. Come down the stoop of Mrs. Sharpe's any time of day, turn right, and the human traffic of Regent Street sweeps you into its tidal embrace. You dodge a twopenny bus and fall into a coffee stall. You scrape horseshit off your shoe. You hear the clocks in the church towers striking the hours and quarters. You see the season's first sprigs of holly gleaming from the storefronts of poulterers. You walk past the plate-glass windows of Oxford Street, the sweet-shops and linen drapers and tobacconists, all shining like glazed hams. You jostle with silk-hatted toffs and ladies in crepe de chine and sailors and financiers and shoeblacks and jugglers and lurkers and nostrum vendors.

And oh, my eye, do you meet some gay ladies. From five in the afternoon to three in the morning, from Langham Place to St. John's Wood. A fellow can't even pass from Piccadilly Circus to Waterloo Place without having his virtue fairly laid siege to. The lacquered hand on your hip, the breast against your shoulder. The thirteen-year-old in pigtails, the bald crone with a moth-worried purple cowl. None of them so nicely dressed, I should say, as Mrs. Sharpe's retinue, but all of them ready to do in a pinch. They come from Sheffield and Birmingham and Belfast and Brussels and Amsterdam. They squawk, they coo, they whisper—a great symphony of sex—and we men, we passing men, are just the staves for their winding melodies.

—Ooh, ain't he handsome? This un's mine, girls!

—Give us a kiss, love.

—Be a sport, Old Sal needs a lick of gin.

I've often thought a blind man could find his way through London simply by gauging the changes in innuendo: mild through Trafalgar Square, less veiled towards the river.

—Care for a fuck?

—Shall I show you my cunt?

Hear enough of these offers, it becomes almost an unpatriotic act to refuse. And look at me! Mostly able-bodied citizen of twenty-three, organs in working order. As good a candidate as the next fellow. But apart from the occasional back-alley groping, I haven't felt much up to it of late. Astonishing, really: the closer they get, the colder grows the cockatoo. And so I'm torn between hurrying on and staying to apologise because, you see, I do want them to know it's not their fault.

—No, truly, you look smashing. With your pretty yellow hair and your lilac garter . . . a man would have to be mad not to go home with you.

But by then, they've moved on to the next one. And I am left to wonder what has come over me.

What *has* come over me?

Not half a year ago, my loins were on military alert. I couldn't breathe a woman's scent without swelling. And now! Can't even get hard with my own hand. My fingers clamp on like limpets, but no divine spark issues from them. I might as well be making sausage.

Some nights, looking for inspiration, I land at Kate Hamilton's Night House, just a few blocks from Mrs. Sharpe's, or better still, at the Argyll Rooms in Great Windmill Street. On the books, Argyll is a dancing academy, but in fact, dancing is merely the thing that happens before the next thing. I'm not much for capering anyway, what with the leg, so if I have spare change, I treat myself to a beer and sit at one of the outside tables. I watch bankers and solicitors in frock coats whirling with beautiful young birds. The band in the far corner is playing a waltz—Vienna by way of Leeds—and the women, still holding glasses of champagne, rustle their satin dresses and lean their heads theatrically on their escorts' shoulders. The attitude of their necks, the droop of their gloved hands—everything conveys the same message: Oh, it's never been this nice with anyone else! Not Mr. Seven-Ten, nor even Mr. Eight-Thirty! And the men seem to believe it, as I would, too, probably, in their place. There's an arousing conviction to these women. The very stillness with which they carry themselves across the floor becomes a form of copulation. And it all makes me intolerably hungry, without giving me the means to feed.

It's a goodly amount of work, you can imagine, being a voyeur. That's why, on Saturday evenings, I suss out a different sort of sensation: I wander over to the New Cut to catch the Lambeth street market. You want light, do you? Not even Heaven has this much light. Every coster in England has his stall here, and every stall has a light: a lamp, a candle, a stove, a brazier. The whole sky aflame with humanity, and a righteous din to match.

—Who'll buy oranges? Sweet, sweet oranges!

—Kerchief for threepence!

—Flounder three-a-penny!

Here, more than anywhere else, your classes converge. Buyers, sellers, thieves, gulls. Here is where the day's fog retreats, and the frost drips from the store eaves, and the smell of broiling chestnuts fills the air, and someone's snuff missile whistles past your ear.

And then I see my father grabbing a pair of apples from a barrel.

For a second or two, I'd swear to it on a Bible. That long, wizened body, bending at a hundred joints. Pipestem legs, elbows pointing in wrong directions, narrow ribbon of fat along the hips. Hectored air of attentiveness. It's him.

I shouldn't be surprised. Wherever I go these days, I see my father. Swinging a billy club. Laying out meat pies in a shop window. Driving a brougham down Petticoat Lane. Cadging for coins outside the Lord Mayor's house. Most often, I see him from behind, which allows him to sprout a stranger's face by the time I get to the other side. Sometimes, though, I stumble across his actual face, staring at me from a brand-new body, looking, if anything, more surprised than I. His eyes glimmer with foreknowledge, his mouth begins to form my name. And then he passes on, this banker, this linen draper—whatever new trade my father has taken up, he takes it up again.

I was standing by the bedroom door when he died. Standing with Uncle N, both of us, I think, itching to leave but not quite able. Perhaps we had a pre-sentiment, I think it was more likely boredom that dug our heels in. That's the sad fact about vigils: they can be terribly boring. Father's had been going on for six weeks now, and there was no sign of its ending soon. That partic-ular evening, I had just about made up my mind to leave when, from his chest, a sound jerked free. A bellows-draught of air, no different from the others except in how it ended: the quick tapering hiss of a hot iron lifting off a trouser leg. I rushed to the bed, but Uncle N never moved. Didn't have to.

—Don't be sad, Tim. He's gone to his rest. Gone to your mother and the rest of the angels.

And at the time, that looked to be the only possibility. There was about as much life left in Father's nightshirted stalk as in a tailor's dummy. Whatever he *was* had slipped out the door while we were looking the other way.

But now I'm not so sure Father had the proper passport for the next world. Why else would he be pushing coster barrows, floating on river ferries, sell-ing cures for corns? Why else would he be looking for me so diligently, even as he pretends not to see me?

I left it to Peter to sort through his possessions. The one thing I took was the comforter. I can't say why. Father used to wear it to the office—long ago, in the days of one-coal fires. Wore it in the streets, too. Till the end of my days, I shall remember how he looked coming down Bayham Street with the ends of that bloody scarf swinging round his knees. Like a deposed king in an ermine robe, I think in my more charitable moments; like a blithering madman, I think other times.

The comforter was blue in its original incarnation, but years of street liv-ing eventually dyed it a pigeon grey. Mother was always offended by the sight of it, and so I had assumed it'd gone the way of other family belong-ings until I found it again, stopping up a hole in the back of a cupboard. I didn't tell anyone, just stuffed it in my bag and left. Now it lies across a cov-erlet on the second floor of Mrs. Sharpe's establishment. And it does keep out the cold, I will give it that, even where the threads have pulled away.

Some things it can't keep out. I find them on my pillow when I wake, little lozenges of memory. My mother's voice, perhaps, calling me down to dinner. Or the dark lily of my brother's body, wafting down the canal. Or things of a more recent vintage.

One girl in particular—she visits my dreams quite often. No more than ten or eleven, I'd estimate, although guessing her age is difficult because when I saw her, she was lying on her side in an alley off Jermyn Street, stretched out like an artist's model on a chaise. Fully at her ease, I thought, until I drew closer and saw the hands, not flexing as I had imagined but frozen in place— *talons*, smeared with blood. And her head had been ratcheted back and . . . and what else? Grey-blue lips. And grey-brown eyes, staring back down the alley, as though they were following the progress of her recently absconded spirit.

Two constables stood one on either side of her. Voluble, blithe chaps in swallowtail coats and specially reinforced top hats, waiting for another kind of reinforcement, perhaps, or just passing the time, and preoccupied enough or bored enough to admit company, even if the company was you, silent, bending to study the uncovered form on the ground. Their patter settled like foam on the back of your head.

—Fancy, though, the neck's clean.

—Hundred to one it were a pillow.

—Come, now, Bill, blood on the hands? Fighting a pillow? Don't be daft.

—Look who's calling who daft.

You'd seen strangers' bodies before and never once stopped. Why should this one have been different? And why this tender scrutiny? Your eyes lapping up everything, the dingy black stockings (torn and bloodied round the feet), the black woollen folds of the skirt, the shreds of petticoat. The *face*: white as sugar, and everything on it flung open like the windows on a cuckoo clock, mouth, eyes, even nostrils all dilated as far as they could go.

And something else, too. A square of skin where the sleeve of her dress had torn away, and through that aperture, the most remarkable sight, strangely accented in the gaslight. Not a tattoo, nothing so mild as that. A *brand.* The skin not dyed but blistered, *seared*, like the flanks of a Jersey. And what did you read there? A letter, that was all, an inch and a half in diameter.

G

Except there was more. Beneath the upper loop, a pair of eyes had been likewise burnt into the skin. And those eyes had the strange effect of turning the letter into something quite palpably alive.

A bird of prey, that was your first thought. And yet you might have read anything there: a jack-o'-lantern, a cloud-soaked moon. Nothing else, though, explained the animal intelligence with which this single letter quivered.

It was two months ago I saw that girl, and I don't think a day has passed but that she hasn't exacted some tribute from me, some revolution of my brain. I don't even need to dream her. All it takes most days is closing my waking eyes, and I see everything again, freshly minted: the two constables, and the alley with its livid purple shadows, and the rumble of a passing dray, and this girl, opaque and anonymous. And I see *that*, too, the black G with its ravenous eyes and its orifice. And it seems to me the orifice has the power of speech, but only for people with the power to hear. I am not yet one of those.

Chapter 2

—FIRST . . . I MADE HIM KNOW that his name should be . . . Ffrigh. . . .

Mrs. Sharpe crumples her plucked brows. Her eyes shrink to coin slots, and her lips encircle the errant sounds.

—*Fffriday*. Like the day, does he mean?

—Yes, exactly.

—*. . . which was the day I saved his life.* Oh, yes, I see. *I likewise . . .* mm . . . tawt . . . *taught him to say, "Master," and then let him . . . let him know that was to be my name.*

—Good.

—*I also taught him to say . . . "Yes" and "No" . . . and to know the mee-ning of them.*

She holds the book very close to her face, like a priest with a missal. The candlelight softens the rather florid henna of her hair, the powdery steppes of her face.

—I kept there with him all that night, but as soon as it was day, I took him away with me.

—Very nice.

We meet every afternoon at three-thirty. We sit in the one place where we can't be heard: a small back room just off Mrs. Sharpe's bedchamber. Bare walls, bare floor. Just the two of us and a table and a tallow candle and an open book. And in this spartan setting, free of any obligation, Mrs. Sharpe greets the English tongue with the raptness of first love.

—So that's how they write *drawers*, is it? Nothing at all like *doors*. Ooh, it's a silly language, it's frantic!

There is something so undistilled about her in these moments. One would never guess what heights of artifice she can otherwise scale: the buns and swags and tendrils of synthetic hair, the wreaths of imitation pearls, the Chinese brisé fans. The giddy, affected lilt that flies up from her throat every time a patron walks through the door, a voice like a drunken piccolo—high and girlish, but with no foundation—crashing down every few seconds in a raucous scrape.

—Sir Edgar, it's too ecstatic! I don't think I've ever seen you looking so well. And there was I, thinking marriage would be the ruin of you, when here you are, ripe as a peach and handsome as a church. Your wife is to blame, I think. Oh, someone else? Well, whoever it is deserves a medal and a citation and quite possibly sainthood. Now as I recall, you and Sadie had the loveliest chat when you came by last. . . .

This is the public Mrs. Sharpe. But here, cocooned in this dark, unventilated office that smells faintly of attar and night soil, she is illuminated in a different way. She runs her finger down the printed columns, she licks her lips clean of each word, and a smithy fire burns inside her. It taps something molten inside me. I think this must be how a father feels around his child.

And then the inevitable, the tectonic shift occurs, and I find I *am* the father of a child. I am the father of *that* child. I am bending over her still form in the alley, I am trying to wrench her bloodstained fingers back to their natural shape, but the rigor mortis has frozen them into claws, and as I tug on them, they snap like icicles, and I leap back, but it's too late, someone is screaming . . .

—Mr. Timothy? Are you all right?

—Fine, thank you.

—You look like someone walked over your grave.

—I'm fine, thank you.

That's what comes of my trying to imagine myself a father. Absurd! When not six months ago, I was myself something of a child, uncompassed, wandering nameless streets, looking for who can say what. So much of it dissolves in the memory now, but I do recall strolling quite merrily down Charing Cross Road and stopping before a padding-ken in Seven Dials and deciding that here I would stay the night. The mistress of the house wouldn't hear of it.

—You'll find no private rooms here. Best try over by Drury Lane, there's a good man.

I told her I wasn't with the police. I told her my tuppence was as good as anyone else's. I told her I wouldn't leave until she gave me a bed, and I never once stopped smiling. A disturbing figure I must have cut, because the good woman did find a place for me, in a room already crammed with a dozen others. I slept on a rag bundle. Fifteen minutes after I set my head down, a boy with no shirt tried to pick my pocket; fifteen minutes later, he went for my hat; half an hour after that, I found him very calmly unlacing my shoes. And sometime in the middle of the night, I was awakened by the strenuous sounds of human congress, punctuated by a man's gruff voice:

—Here, that's my wife you're fucking.

—It's *my* wife, ain't it?

They argued for several minutes, until the woman in question screamed:

—Christ, will you shut your holes! I got three more in the queue!

I left early the next morning, without my watch. I wandered into and out of public houses in St. Giles and was fleeced of a couple of pounds by a magsman. Most of that afternoon is lost to me now, but I do know that at just past eight in the evening, I was standing on a street corner in the Haymarket. A tiny girl with no shoes and a great black orb round her eye was pulling on my sleeve, demanding sixpence, and a hansom cab was swerving past me, spraying up a spume of mud, and a troop of gay ladies was passing by, in bonnets and gloves and white silk stockings and dresses turned up just slightly at the bottom, and in this context, they were as beautiful as daylilies. Seraphim lowered by heavenly wires.

I felt a clap on my back. A slope-shouldered bald man with theatrically guileless blue eyes swung his head round to meet mine.

—Sir, if I may ask, what's a discriminating personage such as yourself wanting with these hags? Seems to me you'd hanker after a more refined class of gal. A woman with *je ne sais*, you get my drift. Here.

He handed me a card.

MRS. OPHELIA SHARPE
Rooms for Gentlemen

No. 111, Jermyn Street

—— *Referrals Required* ——

—Comfy beds, sir, you can't go half wrong. Just tell 'em George sent you.

I don't know which was more startling, being offered a houseful of women or being mistaken for a gentleman. I stood there in the middle of the sidewalk, examining myself with a new interest. And it was then that I realised I was still dressed for a funeral. Black top hat, black crepe frock coat, black gloves. Black bluchers. (Someone must have polished the shoes: they were too clean to have borne me on a week's pilgrimage through London.) Father, it seemed, had gone to the furthest possible extreme to make me a gentleman.

I sniffed at my sleeve: kitchen grease, rat droppings, spit-laden gin. The smell passed all the way through me and then out again, and it took all my concentration not to retch on the spot. I bought a vial of toilet water off a vendor and splashed it behind my ears, beneath my arms. For the breath, I bought a tin of mints from a confectioner, and then I ducked into a pub for a tankard of hot lemonade and gave my hair a quick dousing, parted it again as best I could, and clamped the hat back on top. By the time I reached Mrs. Sharpe's, I was giving off a great cloud of spurious scent.

The house was easy to find. A quick right off Regent Street and there it was, rearing up from the pavement with an almost comical respectability, a three-story Georgian with ideas above its station, taking on airs as it rose: small cornices over the ground-floor Palladian windows, more elaborately reticulated pediments over the first floor, trumpeting gargoyles over the second, and finally a great gaudy mansard roof, patched with strumpety green and yellow tile and pierced by two breasty dormer windows with lime-green sashes.

It was a warm evening in June, and all the windows were open and blazing with candles, and the day's last expirations filled the toile curtains and gave them a quicksilver human shape, a teasing dancing odalisque motion. The curtains curled their painted fingers and beckoned me in, and it was such an insinuating gesture that I had half a mind to scale the building, grab the nearest gargoyle, do anything to shorten the distance between us. I settled on the door. A timid *rat-a-tat*, and within seconds, the oaken slab was being dragged open by a plump, beet-haired woman in a black lace collar. She was panting from the effort, but her sound was lost in the bull-like moaning of the door.

—Mrs. Sharpe?

—Yes, sir.

—George sent me.

In the ten seconds she took to look me over, all my last-minute toilet seemed to be for naught. A rill of impure sweat bled down my temple, a monstrous itch spread across my scalp. . . .

—Very well, said Mrs. Sharpe.

The door scraped shut behind me. We passed through a cramped vestibule and down a long, dimly lit hall, unfurnished but for a fist-sized looking-glass, missing a frame, and a small wine table on an empty porcelain pitcher.

—I will say I'm surprised, Mrs. Sharpe said.—You're a little younger than what George normally sends our way. But I daresay we can find someone to answer.

We came at last into a parlour. The first sounds I heard were the peaceful murmurs of a parrot, calmly yanking out one of his breast feathers—he had evidently been most industrious, for he was already half bald. A cat was stretched snakelike along the swag of a divan, and sitting on a camelback sofa were three women in flounced crinolines. One of them was darning a pair of stockings; the other two were playing a languid game of Pope Joan. Such a domestic effulgence! It spoke of maidenly comforts—trousseaus and hearthside prattle. Even the smears of red on their cheeks were like archetypes of innocence. What cruel bowman was I to disturb this palisade of nymphs?

The darning girl took one look at me and averted her eyes. As luck would have it, this was the girl Mrs. Sharpe fastened on.

—Iris?

The girl froze for a second. Then, with her mouth set in a grim line, she laid down her needles and stood. A vacant, lopsided smile slid across her face and then off again, like rainwater.

—Iris, please make our guest welcome. Your name, sir?

—Timothy.

—Mr. Timothy, she said, landing lightly on each syllable, as though it were the airiest of fictions.

As we climbed the stairs, Iris trailed her hand along the banister. Two steps shy of the first landing, she wheeled on me.

—D'ye hurt your leg?

—No.

—You was limping a bit, is all.

The room faced the back alley, and a thick sandalwood scent was pouring through the open window, but from the look of Iris's quivering nostrils, it was *my* smell she was trying to fix.

—It's ever so hot, isn't it? she said.

She stifled a yawn and sat down on the edge of the chintz-covered four-poster. Her hand, working almost independently of the rest of her, wriggled through the folds of her skirt and gave a yank. A great silent commotion of rings and cords, and then, like a gathered drape, the skirt began rising . . . rising . . . revealing first a measure of magenta stocking and then the embroidered hem of a single petticoat, even more brilliantly magenta.

—Ever so hot.

A fine-looking lass, I could see that. Eyes perhaps too given to starting—as though someone had just swatted her on the back of the head. In her late twenties, very likely: no longer ripe but retaining some of her original juice. Thin in the arms and shoulders, with a compensating fullness below—the kind of plenitude a man could lose himself in. I lowered myself onto the bed next to her. I took off my hat. I fingered the top button of her bodice, and just as the button pulled clear, I felt a drop land on my knee.

And then another. And another.

I didn't understand at first where they were coming from. I had to rule out several possibilities before my hand at last flew to my face and came away wet. And just then, my chest coughed out a sob so large my throat couldn't contain it. It caught halfway up my windpipe and then exploded out again.

Iris leapt from the bed.

—Bloody hell! What's got into you?

I couldn't answer; I was too busy. So many tears, a factory's worth, and no one but me to cry them. My head dropped into my hands, my chest shook, my eyes blurred into darkness. I had never done anything quite so thoroughly.

And still I tried to speak.

—I've got the money. I can make good.

In fact, I was already reaching into my pocket, feeling the familiar press of Uncle N's change purse, but Iris was having none of it. She had already thrown open the door. Yelling, she was. Loud enough to scare rats from the walls.

—Mrs. Sharpe! We've got us a weeper in the Regency Room!

The entire house broke into alarum. A cavalry of footsteps thundered up from below, and the light from the hall dimmed and flickered around me as body after body passed into the room. I had become, in the span of thirty seconds, a blood sport. And recognising all this, I yet persisted in grief's offices. My arms wrapped themselves around my chest, my head lolled between my knees. The sobs came vomiting from my chest.

—Lookit him.

—Third weeper this week.

—Must be the lunar cycle.

Iris cried out:

—Shit, he's no gentleman! He's got crawly nits in his hair.

I heard a quick hot slap. And then Mrs. Sharpe's voice, cool as licorice:

—Miss Iris, you will kindly watch your fucking mouth.

And then a few seconds of edgy silence before Mrs. Sharpe said:

—Everyone else can clear off.

I had assumed that losing my audience would come as a relief, but this feeling was somehow worse. Like being hauled up before God's throne.

Mrs. Sharpe cupped her fingers under my chin, raised my face until it was looking into hers. She had great rings of kohl round her eyes—a parody of mourning.

—You remind me of someone, she said.

—Who?

—No one.

She went to the window, brushed a layer of dirt off the sill.

—He'd be about your age now.

Her hands made a soft *tum-tum* on the pane, and when she turned around, they were still drumming the air. She stared at them, half disenchanted.

—Do you have anywhere to go, Mr. Timothy?

I thought about that one.

—I suppose I do. I just don't want to go there.

—Money?

—I've an uncle who's been very generous. But I can't take any more from him.

She chewed on her lower lip. Another minute passed. Two, perhaps.

—Look here, she said. You know how to read, don't you?

—Yes.

—I mean different sorts of things. Newspapers and novels and racing forms.

—Of course.

—And write, too?

—Yes.

—And it's not difficult, is it? It's quite easy once one gets the hang of it?

—I expect so, yes.

She nodded once, smoothed the front of her dress.

—Well, then, you may have yourself a position. If you've a mind to it.

I made my debut next day at dinner. Mrs. Sharpe had lent me a new shirt with a starched collar two sizes too big. I felt vaguely like a box turtle, emerging from a hard young shell. My eyes blinked and welled in the new air.

The girls scarcely noticed me; they were immersed in a platter of Mary Catherine's corned beef. Breakfast didn't exist here, and the evening meal came and went depending on how busy things got, and so the girls tended to be quite peckish right round the middle of the day. All the decorum that Mrs. Sharpe had drilled into them was forsaken during these moments. They leant over the table like brigands, jammed their knives into their plates, wrestled with enormous chunks of beef, swallowed with the barest minimum of chewing. Most of them hadn't washed off their cosmetics, so when they wiped their mouths, their hands came away with hard brown crusts of rouge and powder, which, in their zeal, they often mistook for food.

The man who had directed me here the night before had already finished his meal. He was leaning against the mantel, reading the *Pall Mall Gazette*. He might have been mistaken for a particularly tenacious client but for his unbuttoned collar and his rolled-up sleeves and his air of quiet entitlement. A man at home.

—Afternoon, George, said Mrs. Sharpe.

He began nodding in her direction, then he caught sight of me, and his head briefly arrested itself before finishing its motion.

Mrs. Sharpe made two quick raps on the table.

—Mary Catherine, we'll need another place setting.

At this, the girls broke off their chewing. Gazed at one another with a wild surmise, as the poet writes. Mrs. Sharpe must rather have enjoyed the effect she was creating, because she provided no explanation just yet. She helped herself to some boiled potato. Took a few sips of her claret. Dabbed her lips: once, twice. Only then did she speak.

—Girls, I wish you to know that I have hired Mr. Timothy as my book-keeper.

Another sip, another dab.

—For the time being, he will be staying with us. I have installed him in Nell's old room, next to the dungeon of unspeakable horror.

Their heads were bowed now like schoolgirls'. Only their eyes, furtively meeting and then swerving away, betrayed any sign of independent thought.

—You are to treat him as you would any other employee. That is to say, trifle with him, and you will answer to me.

It was then that Iris, propelled by her neighbour's nudge, emitted a snort louder and bawdier than any I had ever heard. Such a snort! It described a visible, almost classical arc from her mouth and nose to the table.

—Miss Iris, am I to take this as dissent?

Mrs. Sharpe's voice was at its most fluted and grandiose. Her finger was pointed like an arrow at Iris's heart.

—Not at all, ma'am.

—And you, George?

George folded his newspaper. And then, for good measure, refolded it.

The education of Mrs. Sharpe was rough going at first. Apart from George's daily journals and some bound ledgers, the only literary works in the estab-lishment were *Buchan's Domestic Medicine* and a copy of *Sartor Resartus*, left behind by a Kings College student who had jumped out the second-story window in the belief that a police raid was afoot. (It was just Mary Catherine banging pans in the scullery.) Mr. Carlyle proved a touch abstruse for both of us, so next morning I bought a children's primer from a bookseller in Charing Cross Road. It was titled *Beauteous Betty Butterworth*, and it played out its tale in a world of *b*s. *Betty baked biscuits. . . . A bee bit Betty on the bottom. . . . Betty bawled and bawled.*

—Now, when you see that letter, that tells you the sound will be "buh."
—Buh. Buh.

And as we passed from letter to letter, from word to word, through skeins and skeins of sentences, how could I not relive the pilgrimage I had once made with my mother? I wasn't supposed to learn as early as I did. Mother was teaching Sam at the time—he was sitting in her lap, with the book cradled between his legs—and I was quite put out that they were playing a game that excluded me. I kept wandering into the room, and it was only a matter of time, really, before Mother craned her head in my direction.

—Tim, would you care to learn, too?

And so, for me, it began as a lark and became, at some juncture, deadly earnest. For Mrs. Sharpe, it was the reverse. She took it so very seriously at the start that I wasn't sure we would ever get anywhere. The sounds lodged in the base of her throat; releasing them was like breaking an unpickable lock. We spent a full week on *gh* words alone because she couldn't see why the same combination of letters should produce such radically different sounds, and I myself could not explain the wisdom behind these divergences.

—It's just . . . it's how it is. It's how people say it.

But the more sounds she absorbed into her repertoire, the more animated Mrs. Sharpe grew, until our sessions together became simply a vehicle for her joy. These strange hieroglyphics, no longer mysterious, no longer terrible, cannonading from her chest, ricocheting up her throat, exploding in the air around us. Marvelous sounds! *Fowl. Powder. Parcel. Handle. Axe. Gudgeon. Turf. Barley*. They spilled from her mouth like fruit pulp, masticated but with a trace of their original sweetness. *Ladder. Stalk. Rum. Beeswax. Providence.*

Weeks' and weeks' worth of sound and sense had to go by before Mrs.

Sharpe began to rise above the individual words, to feel the shape of a sentence and the deeper pull of a paragraph. At times, she has even surprised me by stepping outside the written word altogether and offering her own supratextual commentary.

—Oh, he should never have let the one savage go, Tim. Mark my words, he'll regret it.

Or else:

—Isn't it amazing when you think on it? Hasn't poked a woman in twenty years! I shouldn't wonder if he buggers Friday before long.

In the face of such a discriminating intelligence, there is less and less for a tutor to do. Mrs. Sharpe's brain works largely independently now. The letters whir in and out, the cogs grind them exceeding fine. Her writing has come along nicely, too: she now produces a handsome, if tentative, cursive. And so my interventions are now confined to correcting the occasional pronunciation or defining the overly latinised adjective. Dr. Johnson, I tell her, might serve her purpose just as well as I, but she won't hear of it. Insists I have a calming influence on her.

I suppose a bit of calm might be a fair exchange for room and board. Although it does occur to me that, as Mrs. Sharpe's official bookkeeper, I might try to bring some order to her finances. The very idea is abhorrent to her.

—Christ, that's why I keep George around! You don't want to deny a man his employment, do you?

George is, in fact, the only one who knows the true nature of our arrangement. Which is not to say he approves. Whenever he sees us passing into Mrs. Sharpe's back room, he twitches away from us, as though we were the despair of England's future. At other times, he is more vocal. During one of our sessions, he opened the door on us, as if by mistake. Stood there in a transparent attitude of surprise, the candlelight flickering in the open chasm of his mouth.

—Oh, my, look at us. Will it be Shakespeare next?

He dropped his head to one side.

—A fine Romeo and Juliet you'd be. Brings tears to my eyes, just imagining it.

At which point, Mrs. Sharpe, reverting to the child she must once have been, squealed:

—George, d'you know Shakespeare had an *e* at the end of his name? Just like *moi*!

This, I believe, is the mark of a true scholar: to be unfazed by the world's skepticism. The one thing she can't abide is the thought of her girls finding out. She fears it will cost her some of the sovereignty she has built up over the years. Of course, she's perfectly capable of enforcing that sovereignty when the need arises. I once saw her box the ears of an employee who had refused to lick a vice admiral's scrotum. And when she learned that one of her girls was privately blackmailing a married barrister, Mrs. Sharpe sent the girl packing before another half hour had passed:

—If there's any extortin' to be done, it's I as will do it!

And yet she can be very good to her girls. She will not allow them, for instance, to be punished for anyone else's pleasure (although they may freely inflict punishment when called upon to do so); whenever a customer indicates such a preference, she refers him to Mrs. Lee's on Margaret Place. I am told that one gentleman was so very persistent on the subject that Mrs. Sharpe herself agreed to be spanked with a pillow—but only while clothed, and only while standing. As soon as the gentleman had taken five passes at her, she snatched the pillow from his hands and informed him that he owed her five pounds.

Thus, between Mrs. Sharpe's general good nature and her occasional royal edicts, none of her girls would ever dare cross her. Or even speculate openly about what she and I do during our daily sessions. They assume, probably, that I am Mrs. Sharpe's concubine. At least, I have seen them wink at one another as they ask me leading questions. Iris is the boldest in this regard. She will open her eyes wide and inquire:

—Have you seen the madam's cherries about?

Iris has never truly forgiven me for that first night—I can see I was a pique to her professional pride. She wastes few opportunities to get her own back.

—Mr. Timothy, wasn't Lord Byron quite the swordsman?

On this occasion, I was lulled, I confess, by the sound of a poet's name emerging from Iris's mouth.

—Yes, I suppose he was.

—And is it true he had a club foot?

—I think so, yes.

—Then there's hope for you, isn't there?

No one else generally rises to the bait, and in fact, most of the girls are quite lovely to me. Pamela, for instance—the former governess—always has a kind word. And Sadie, too, sweet little thing, tiny of bosom, tiny of voice. Mrs. Sharpe tried to fatten her up in the beginning, then headed full steam in the other direction, with the result that Sadie is now known to patrons as Wee Lucy, a twelve-year-old milkmaid with extravagant ringlets and flimsy peasant bodices that rip very neatly down the middle.

And then there's Minnie, a plump Christmas goose of a girl, with stately carriage and a heavenly coral complexion and two toffee drops for eyes. Quite the catch, is our Minnie. It's rumoured that the second son of the Bishop of Exeter has larger designs on her: he sees her three nights a week and has lately broached the possibility of introducing her to his mother. Minnie knows better than to believe a boy's promises, but everyone agrees that if ever a girl was marked for rapid social promotion, it is she.

And lest I forget, there is Mary Catherine, boiler of beef and maid-of-all-work. Nurses a dream of someday becoming a top-of-the-bill attraction herself, although it must be acknowledged that her chances in this regard are slight. Tenterhook hands, pachyderm elbows, turnip nose, and potato chin . . . she is not built for love's work. She is, rather, one of those people who spread love as they go. Even the act of cleaning water closets becomes, through her good graces, a ritual of devotion. On her hands and knees, scrubbing deep veins of grime from the front staircase, she is yet able to lift her head and toss you a smile as you step over her.

Yes, all things considered, they're a fine mess of humanity, my fellow employees. I can't say I fancy any of them in particular—excessive proximity has a way of ruining that—but I do hold them in the highest regard. I have seen them go out of their way to drop coins in a beggarwoman's apron. I have seen them squeeze spare shillings from a tightfisted customer to help a friend pay his rent. I have seen them comfort men in every degree of affliction. I have been one of those men.

Sometimes just coming home to them is a comfort. I walk up the stairs of a December evening, and the sounds of Mrs. Sharpe's boardinghouse come floating up to me. The phantasmal whispers and elongated moans. The creaking of a floorboard, the thumping of bedpost against wall. A shriek, brief and genderless. I feel strangely welcomed in these moments. Embraced.

And this feeling follows me all the way to my room. I give my face a quick scrub from the basin. I blow out the candle by my bed. I throw off my clothes and pull Father's comforter over me. I rub my bare limbs to get them warm.

Some evenings, I even receive a parting benison. Tonight, for instance: the litany of Squidgy and Pamela, resounding from the adjoining room.

—What is thy duty towards God?

—My duty towards God is to . . . to believe in him . . . to fear him and . . . and . . .

Thwack!

—*Love* him! Oww, love him with all my heart!

And then I remember: it's ten days till Christmas.

Chapter 3

I SCARCELY NOTICE IT AT FIRST. The courtyard behind Mrs. Sharpe's boasts so many other late-night attractions, each making its own claim upon the eye. At this very moment, I can see, from the vantage of my bedroom window, a torn-off playbill from the St. James Theatre, a troop of rats gnawing on soup bones, crates and bins, an abandoned spittoon, and a long trail of cracked gin bottles ending in the crumpled heap of an old sot, sleeping off many yesterdays.

Amidst such a rich tableau, why pay any special mind to a tarpaulin, bunched and creased and billowed, its corners tucked in? Flung, probably, from some neighbouring window. I wouldn't even look at it twice were I not so struck by its whiteness—the absence of any paint or glue. A purely spotless tarpaulin, left for rubbish.

Even stranger: it begins to move.

Almost imperceptibly at first, by the barest of degrees. And then either my eye becomes attuned to its motion, or its motion accelerates, for it begins to pulse with a restless intelligence. It *wafts* down the alley, the most graceful of ectoplasms, with no definite point of attachment, no obvious axis, just a clear line of intent. And even when it jars against a refuse bin, retracts its border and adjusts its alignment, its movement is so deliberate that it seems somehow to have accounted for the bin in advance, and incorporated it.

A pantomime spirit. That's my best explanation. A children's pantomime, rehearsing well past midnight, and now one of its lead goblins has wandered offstage, stumbled out the side door, and headed down the wrong alley. The other cast members must even now be giving chase: "Have you seen our little goblin? Yea high? Moving rather slowly?"

And so I'm not surprised, not truly surprised, to see the tarpaulin drop away to reveal a child's uncovered head. And yet the effect of this head against the white of the cloth and the near-extinguishing black of the alley is so intense, so cauterizing, it stops the breath in my throat. I step back from the window, and my hand jiggles the candle on the sill. The barest flicker of light, that's all, and yet it might as well be the infusion of a thousand torches, because the child's head jerks towards my window, and in the ensuing second, her face—for the child is a girl—stands strangely segregated from the rest of her accoutrement. And in the next second, she has taken flight.

No longer a slow parabolic line but a clean, straight trajectory, accorded a special geometric purity by its sheer haste. She wants very much to be gone. Very soon she is.

Next morning I find the tarpaulin, snagged on the corner of an ash bin, three houses down. Cast off like the skin of an enchanted snake.

That night she colonises my dreams. We pick up almost exactly where we left off. The girl is running—running hard. Her tarpaulin streams behind her in a long, resplendent wake. Jermyn Street has disappeared, and the buildings have pulled back, and there's nothing now but a long track of pavement, wide enough to hold all of London's carriages. The girl is running, a blur of light and steam, and above her, a shadow gathers. A shuddering blue shadow that expands until it covers the entire track. I hear the beating of wings and a high, strangled call—a sound from the furthest aeries of Asia. The shadow parts, and through the vent, a head emerges, eyes hard and unblinking, beak pointed like a butcher's hook at the running girl.

The girl never looks up; she knows what's there. Her hands, flying before her, assume the guise of talons. An act of desperate cunning, I can see that: she wants the predator to think she's one of its own. But the creature is under no such illusion. It contracts itself into a bundle, a bale of infinite density, and, with one last burst of terrible power, flings itself towards earth . . .

—There! cries Mrs. Sharpe.—What think you?

From across the breakfast table, she slides a torn piece of green paper towards me. It's the backside of an empty ledger sheet.

Your Presents Is Most Humbly, Awflly Beseeched
By Mrs Ophelia Sharpe
For an Our of Yule-tied Cheere

—The lettering is very fine, I say.

—Oh, do you think? I'm feeling very glum about my *f*'s; they keep curling back on themselves. I think they must secretly want to be *g*'s.

—Everything looks very nice. Shall I correct the spelling?

—Please.

I work in silence for a few moments, waiting for Mrs. Sharpe's voice to fill the void round us. It soon does.

—The whole party is George's idea, isn't it? Competition being what it is, tooth-and-nail, dog-eat-dog, what's a genteel operation to do? Why, find some way to thank its most loyal customers, that's what. Nothing awfully grand, just some eggnog and negus. Christmas crackers. . . .

—Sounds delightful.

She waves an admonitory finger.

—Expect no trees!

Christmas trees are closely allied in Mrs. Sharpe's mind with Prince Albert and hence with Germany, a country that arouses in her the most pronounced animus. No one quite knows why. There's talk she was swindled many years ago by a Prussian arms merchant, and the wife of the local baker says she knows for a fact that one of Mrs. Sharpe's earliest and most bestial husbands was a Bavarian pastry maker.

—Oh, and Mr. Timothy? I should like to read a poem for the occasion.

She's hunched over now, stammering like a child.

—I'm, of course, I'm aware . . . this poetry business . . . not exactly in my line, is it? P'raps you could proffer a few suggestions? Something with a lovely holiday spirit.

—I will certainly think on it, Mrs. Sharpe.

—Nothing too wordy, dear. Seeing as I'm only now getting my sea legs. . . .

—Short would be best.

—And nothing too gruesomely moral. We don't want to be spoiling anyone's fun. Oh, and you're certainly welcome to invite someone, if you . . . if there's *someone* and they're willing. . . .

—Thank you, Mrs. Sharpe.

She worries, I know. I speak very little of family (although I still wear my black crepe hatband). I don't bring any friends home. I go off alone, come back alone, never take even a complimentary poke at one of the girls. It can't be healthy.

But I do have company—all the company a fellow could need. Girls in alleys and a dead father and mother and a dead brother. A sister buried somewhere in Nova Scotia. Another sister dropped out of view. Yes, a whole vanished history, crowding round me wherever I go. I would venture to say I am one of Her Majesty's more haunted subjects.

Then again, how am I to know? Londoners give so little away. They stride past you in their black dresses and black lounge coats and black mackintoshes, keep you at bay with their black umbrellas, do anything to avoid the human gaze: tug at their gloves, study their watch chains. Who's to say they aren't all communing with invisible attendants, expending vast logistical powers on behalf of their spectral households?

Therein the virtue of walking down a crowded London street: everyone's spectres draw away, and the living are left unaccommodated. It makes you feel quite liberated, even on mornings like this, when the wet, knuckle-scraping cold works up through the feet, clusters in the knee. I have to walk just to keep my leg from locking up. I wander down Regent Street (unconscious gentleman, collapsed atop unconscious lady). A nod to the Athenaeum, a left onto Pall Mall. Before me, the freshly washed dome of the National Gallery and the ugly steeple of St. Martin-in-the-Fields and the poised arses of Lord Nelson's lions. Down Northumberland, past the turn for Scotland Yard— and the whole way, that slanting feeling beneath my feet, that sense of being decanted into the river like a long-lost tributary.

This is where I come most mornings: Hungerford Pier. Up the hill, there used to be a market—plumpest chickens in town, Mother always said—but that's gone now. From its ashes rises a great six-platform railway station, not quite finished, and stretching to meet it, a nine-span wrought-iron lattice girder bridge, not quite finished. And up from the pier, earth for a new embankment garden is being laid (per Prince Albert's orders) over the remains of rotting sewers and wharf shops. The garden isn't quite finished, either, but that's Progress for you.

And what better occupation for a man than to observe Progress unfold? Me, I'm a natural watcher, anyway. Most comfortable with other watchers, like the silent watermen who share the pier with me. Lord, they do nothing *but* watch. Little call for their services, even now, with the river steamers stowed away for winter. It was different, of course, in the old days. A landlubber like me couldn't have cleared the arches of London Bridge without some stout oarsman poling him through. But then came the new London Bridge, and then came the steamers. And now the watermen sit. The same sons of Neptune who used to shoot London Bridge are huddling for warmth along the Hungerford Stairs and breaking one another's noses over three-penny fares.

One of them catches sight of me now. An old man, sun-stropped, in a pilot jacket and canvas trousers. For the barest of seconds, his rheumy eyes spark and glint, and then he remembers: I am the fellow who comes here every morning, bringing nothing but his own body.

—Morning, sir, he says, grudgingly.

—Morning.

We return to our separate vigils, and mine may well be happier, for if there's a better vantage point on the river, I don't know of it. Sit and watch the sun lighting up Waterloo Bridge, scrubbing the face of St. Paul's pink. Watch the seagulls circling an empty coal barge. Feel the slow rocking of the jetty, the lapping and slapping of water against the piles.

It's a little shy of ten in the morning. The sky is cold and clear, crisp as a carrot, the river's summertime stink is just a memory, and the woollen tangle of the fog is holding off for now—a mercy in December—waiting until late in the afternoon to press its chloroform compress to your nostrils. And such is the beneficent influence of the weather that my leg, for the first time in a week, has ceased its throbbing. It courses with a new life. Oh, the possibilities of me! I could run from Hyde Park to Southwark. I could do handstands across Blackfriars Bridge. I could swim to Dover, if I had ever learned to swim.

What is this but a sign of grace? And as I cast my eyes about, the benediction spreads across the entire scene. It sweeps a gentling hand over the plane trees, hurriedly shedding their skins. A pair of sailors, feet intertwined, sleeping off last night's toot. A coffee shop, pregnant with day labourers. A blacking factory, long abandoned. Everything is at peace, and the calm extends even to my father, sitting quietly on the end of the pier in a broad blue coat, whittling a pipe from a block of planed wood.

How could I have missed him? The tight, narrow ridge of the shoulders. The hands at once panicked and resourceful. The whole fidgeting, funnelling way of him. *Waiting* for me, not twenty yards off.

It would take me perhaps half a minute to cross the distance between us— enough time for him to escape, certainly. I would be tapping some strange man on the shoulder and mumbling an apology, and the stranger would be shrugging me off like a midge, and if I were quick about it, I might whirl round just in time to see Father flying down the river, disappearing over Westminster.

No, approaching him is out of the question; better to speak from where I am. But Father, I am dumb in your presence. If you would but turn and rest your eyes on mine, it might jar a word loose, and then everything else would surely follow. My new situation and two or three of the more disreputable friends I've made and what happens when a fight breaks out in the gallery of the Old Vic and what a dead horse looks like when it's pulled from the Thames. And I could bring you all the latest news! Uncle N yet breathes, can you credit it? Peter's wife is still barren, more's the pity, but the salon (as Peter calls it) pulls along nicely. No word of Belinda—I've nearly given up hope on that score. And Martha . . . well, I haven't seen her since your funeral. That lout of a husband won't let her out of doors, I imagine. Or perhaps it's just too hard for her to look us in the eye any more.

Oh, I would tell you everything, Father. I'd write it down in a letter if I could be sure of your reading it. I would tell you how sorry I am for not knowing you while there was still time. That part would be either very brief or very long, I'm not sure which.

And look! The audience I wished for is about to take place. The man on the pier is turning his head. Revolving it into profile. And it will be only a matter of time, surely, before our eyes connect and speech pours forth and whatever comes after speech. And who can say how long this moment will last? Who dares predict?

But the profile that reveals itself in the morning light is altogether foreign. Ruddy and blotched and hairy, with the brine-cured features of a lifelong sea dweller, a man who's sixty if he's a day, and squinting so hard his eyelids nearly curl over on themselves.

Such a strange medium for Father to occupy! But perhaps he had no choice.

In any case, he's gone. Only his enchantment lingers after him. It muffles the sounds of the tugboats and the coal waggons and the omnibus making its cumbersome way down the hill from Camden Town. It diffuses the light but also sharpens it in peculiar ways, so that the passengers shivering on the omnibus's top tier blur from view even as a familiar figure flattened against a peeling grey building flares up like a cathedral cherub.

An odd sort of building to choose as a refuge: a naval outfitter's store, the Rollicking Tar, slated for extinction but with its inventory still intact. In the front window sits a large teak model of a man-of-war, the kind that once chased Napoleon's navy across the main, and no doubt every other item in the store dates from the same era: tarnished quadrants and sextants, mottled chronometers and unwieldy compasses, chapped oilskin jackets. And biscuits hard as hawser hooks, one of which she is now clutching in her hand. Collected it from the rubbish, very like, and in God knows what state of petrifaction, but she's making it do, gnawing it down from every corner.

Even from this distance, I can see more of her than I could the other night, when she was draped under that tarpaulin. I can see the oval face and black brows and patrician nose. A pair of bare twiggy arms, poking through the muttony sleeves of a plain black woollen dress. A white apron, filthy, drooping down to her knees. Battered leather shoes, the tops yawning away from the soles. And a canopy of black hair, tied back with a large bright-red ribbon.

The ribbon is what makes her interesting.

Because she needn't have bothered, do you see that? Hurrying though she must have been, she yet took a moment, wrenched a still interval from her chaos, to reimpose order. Didn't just slap the thing on, either. Wound it very carefully several times round, placed and tied it with great intention. Perhaps even inspected her effort in the glass of the shop window. An aesthetic impulse—an *aristocratic* impulse.

She yawns. Wipes her hand across her mouth. And before I'm even on my feet, she has disappeared.

I run down to the store as fast as my stiffened legs will take me, but I might have flown for all the difference it makes. No sign of her. No tarpaulin chrysalis, not even a crumb of the biscuit she was eating. Just me and that lavishly fitted man-of-war in the storefront window, sailing off to meet Napoleon.

Chapter 4

IN MRS. SHARPE'S ESTABLISHMENT, I am reckoned something of a toff. The girls see my double-breasted worsted lounge suit, my peg-top trousers and braces, my silk hat, my front-laced half-boots, my double albert with fob . . . they see a gentleman who has wandered off course—an *haut bourgeois manqué*. But here on Threadneedle Street, gathered into the cold bosom of the Bank of England, subjected to the lizard gaze of a captain of finance named Otterbourne, I am revealed as something else: a climber. Worse: a climber with his feet already slipping off the rungs. The light from the ground-glass windows calls my deficits to attention. Boots streaked and cudgelled by hard use. Worsted a little worse for the wear. The debauched stripes of my braces, the hothouse wilt of my shirt collars.

Mr. Otterbourne's collars, by contrast, do not wilt. They stand as inviolable as chalk cliffs, and over his shoulder leans an equally inviolable clerk, bending his body like the arm of a drawbridge and gesturing almost sublim-inally towards the small, square document three inches from the Otter-bourne elbow.

—Ah, yes, says the captain of finance.

Around us, black-coated clerks pass in stately measure. A damp newspaper hisses from a fender. The smells of leather and mahogany fill the air, and a young boy ladles lumps of coal, one by one, into a coal box, pausing over each lump as though he were performing unction.

New boots, I am thinking. *This month's installment goes to new boots.*

—Thank you, Greeley, says Mr. Otterbourne.

The clerk bows and, without changing posture, melts imperceptibly into the distance. Remarkable effect: if I didn't know better, I'd think *I* were the one falling soundlessly away. Do they teach that in clerk school? I wonder. Was it in Father's bag of tricks as well?

—Mr. Cratchit.

With a damp finger, Otterbourne smooths each of his thin, ruddy eye-brows.

—I am obliged to tell you that your uncle has attached a new condition to your stipend.

—Yes?

—According to this most recent proviso—may I read it?—"before mak-ing any additional draughts on this account, said beneficiary must, at his own convenience and on his own recognisance, pay said benefactor a personal call, in the nature of an at-home visit."

—At-home visit?

—Yes.

He looks up from his paper. His head tilts delicately to the left.

—I am authorised to supply the address, Mr. Cratchit, if it has escaped you.

Deep inside my chest, a bubble of heat escapes through a wrenched-open grate. I feel it shimmering in my voice.

—And once there, Mr. Otterbourne, am I to beg? Am I to get down on my knees?

—I'm afraid the proviso says nothing one way or the other about begging. Or knees.

Smiling is something of a foreign language for old Otterbourne, and so once he has made a token stab in that direction, his face realigns itself into the shell I have to come to know tolerably well. He is the sort of man who absorbs light without ever imparting it.

—And you mean to say this is my only option? I ask.—No other capital at hand? No investments?

—As best as I can determine, Mr. Cratchit, you have a small sum in the consolidated annuities, to which you will have no access for some years to come. The rest is housed in government-backed funds, and in order to draw on these, lamentably, you would need the approval of your countersignatory, said countersignatory being in this case—

—My uncle.

—The same.

I settle back into my chair. My hands form a screen over the ridge of my eyes, which offers the dual advantage of shielding me from Otterbourne's gaze and allowing me to study my boots in all their disrepair.

—When must this visit be paid? I ask.

—Whenever you wish.

—And until I do . . .

—Until you do, yes.

He strokes the blotting pad on his red-pine desk.

—If it's any comfort, Mr. Cratchit, I have known far more onerous conditions to be attached to the disbursal of funds. Just last week, one of our account holders was required to hop two hundred paces about Leicester Square. Grew dizzy and fainted dead away. The stories these walls could tell, Mr. Cratchit!

—Stories, yes.

To think that only six months ago, I swore I wouldn't take another shilling from him. Swore it up and down.

Beneath me, a blue pattern swarms across a Persian rug, coils its back, darts its dragon tongue towards my heel. I pull my foot away. I give my boots one more turn of the eye.

—Tell him I'll come when I can. As soon as I can.

—I have no charge to tell him anything, Mr. Cratchit. He waits. That is all he wishes you to know.

Threadneedle Street is a good distance from my usual haunts, so by the time I've made it back to my spot at the Hungerford Stairs, it's nearly noon. The tide is out now, and where the river has retreated, a tribe of young nomads has advanced. Amphibious creatures, scavenging the foreshore for coal, for wood, nails, chains, files, hinges—anything, anything at all. They're a small species, mostly, but in their robes of mud, they look quite ageless: one can't be sure whether the boy digging a key chain out of the riverbed is six or eighty-four. Some of the more adventurous are swimming out to the barges and knocking off lengths of rope or iron scales. A kind of etiquette prevails here: the mudlarks don't consider anything their property until it's touched water. If a bargee interrupts them before they can make off with a cask, they leave it unmolested. Once it has left the safety of the deck, it belongs to them. They swoop down on it with an animal cry, hug it to their breasts, and paddle to shore with the shouts of the bargees trailing after them like steam from a whistle.

Not a bad afternoon's entertainment, although it does make me feel older than I am, if only because it reminds me that London is a city of children. Any day now, I expect the proclamation that makes it official. Her Majesty's subjects, behold: children on every side of you! Stealing nuts from a barrow. Swiping brooches and combs from a stall on Mile End Road. Pulling panes off sweetshops in Oxford Street, snatching rolls of calico from a linen draper in Spitalfields. Wrestling with dogs for two-day-old apple cores.

Indefatigable, these creatures, and proliferating at an insane rate. I shouldn't be surprised if they all rose up one day, stormed Whitehall and the Lord Mayor's palace and the royal apartments, slashed our white quivering throats, plucked out our gibbering tongues. There would be no pity, I can tell you.

Look into their eyes if you don't believe me. Something missing, you see? Something that doesn't come back.

I remember stumbling across a whole colony of them one night. I was coming off the ferry at the Adelphi Stairs, and they were crouched beneath the arches, the very poorest of the poor—not even a penny for lodging. So little clothing left on their bodies one had to wonder why they bothered with clothing. Their eyes had vanished inside great dark planetary orbits, their faces *glowed* with hunger. Watching them lick their lips, wipe their hands in mad, endless cycles, I knew, with the force of revelation, that they wanted to eat me. And if I hadn't been surrounded by fellow passengers, and if two of the older lads hadn't been busy lifting hankies, who can say what my fate would have been? I think I might have tasted all right.

Of course, the Adelphi colonists are the children of darkness. The children of early morning are a brighter, nervier lot. With their avian industry and their high, coded calls, they create a distinct musical idiom, and there are times when I wish I still had an ear for it. But today I'm all eyes.

Although I don't know, honestly, if I will recognise her if I see her again. She strikes me as the kind of vision that can only be granted, not sought, and it may be that the mere act of my seeking will just drive her further from view, until finally she is nothing but a residual warmth.

And then, through the day's vapour, I *do* see her.

Exactly where she should be—crouching once more by the Rollicking Tar—and virtually the same as when I saw her last. Gnawing on the now-familiar biscuit—the same biscuit as yesterday, for all I know—wearing that misshapen apron, the red ribbon in her hair. Only two changes to her ensemble, at least so far as I can detect: a woollen scarf, distractingly blue, wrapped around her neck like a beehive; and something less tangible, a slight jiggering of attitude, perhaps, a reorientation of the internal compass. Yesterday, she was a product of the haste that had brought her here. Her posture, the way she ducked her head round corners—everything suggested conditionality. Now she lounges against the storefront like a discharged midshipman, waiting for the next ear to bend. Twenty years on, who knows? She may still be slouched here, assuming she can find warm places at night and stay away from the wrong people and find a few of the right ones and escape the cholera and scrounge up food even when the holidays have passed.

But fate doesn't always allow, does it? Someone needs to tell her that. Things *happen* to girls like her. One day chewing on biscuits; next day stretched out in an alley off Jermyn Street, constables on either side of you, strangers bending over you. . . .

And that's all it takes. That vision. I'm on my feet: climbing the pier steps, stepping gingerly along the embankment wall. Every tread is calm and measured, and as I walk, I am risibly conscious of the symbolic freight I carry. I am Society's civilising impulse. I am England's outstretched hand.

And then she sees me, and I'm just one more man.

Does she remember me? Did she even *notice* me in that brief flurry of candlelight the other night? All I know is that her face has stopped like a watch; even her eyes have ceased their blinking. She pulls her scarf tight round her and steps carefully away—one step, two steps—feeling her way along the front of the building like a blind seer. Refusing to let me either out of her sight or any nearer. Her mouth falls open as if to scream, but no sound emerges, only—I imagine—the slow . . . leaking . . . of air.

—Wait. It's all right.

And what a sound comes from my mouth! High and weak and bleating, a dying fall. And somehow this sound has a greater effect on her than if I had bellowed. She whips her head away.

—It's all right!

And now she's running, running almost as quickly as she did in my dream. And my own feet, as in a dream, cling stubbornly to the earth, drag behind me like anchors. Helpless, I watch her clamber to the embankment wall, perch on the edge, and then, after the briefest of backwards glances, pitch herself over the side.

How terrible the silence is. As I dash to the wall, I have to fill it with my own calculations: *Fifteen-foot drop. Nothing more. Twenty feet, perhaps.*

But when I peer over the edge, I find something I haven't calculated. A body not broken but stilled. Tipped forwards onto its hands and knees, crouching in the riverbed, squelched in Thames mud, while shoeless children sprint heedlessly past.

And then the hands twitch into life, the torso levers upwards. Her face lifts to the sky—no, not to the sky; to *me*. She slaps the mud from her hands and knees, readjusts the ribbon in her hair, hoists herself to her feet—and the entire time, her eyes refuse to part from mine. I can half believe she is waiting for me to say something. And so I do.

—I won't follow you.

But she knows that already. I wouldn't dare. Which affords her all the time in the world, really, to saunter downshore: no sign of twisted ankles, bruised knees, her gait almost insolent in its ease. And as I reverse direction, as I run back along the embankment wall, back to the stairs, the receding glimpses I have of her are like schoolyard taunts. *Catch me*, she is saying. *Just bloody try.*

By the time I lower myself from the pier into the riverbed, she is gone, once again. No amount of searching will bring her to earth this time. And even so, I wander down the shoreline she followed. I track her footprints in the pebbly grey sediment, curiously dainty outlines except where the heels of her boots have sunk in, and round me echo the hilarious chants of children, other children, too rapt in their frenzy even to notice this intruder from the upper world. How absurd I must look to them anyway, in my top hat and lounge coat, the very image of the gentleman slummer. And that absurdity is almost enough to send me back, but then a flash of red, ten yards downshore, calls me on.

Strangely unanchored at first, hovering in the air. Only when I come nearer does the ribbon attach itself to the embankment wall, and only when I'm actually touching it—reassuring myself as to whose it was—only then do I realise it's not the wall that has snagged it, but an opening in the wall. An opening perhaps three feet across, lined with crumbling bricks and tunnelling away into blackness. As I lower my face to the opening, the blackness breathes back, a squall of fumes that has me diving in my pocket for a handkerchief.

I press the white silk to my mouth, and as I wait for the next wind to clear my head, it occurs to me that in the midst of all those other effluents, I must have smelled fear.

What else could have made her leap twenty feet? What else could have plunged her into a sewer hole?

I won't follow her; I made her that promise. And how easy it is to keep, now! Hard, too. Hard to think that within a few short hours, the tide will come in, and the river will rise up and swallow everything in this noisome tunnel, from here to the far side of London. Everything and everyone.

—Here! What d'you want with her?

It comes at me from behind. A high, radiant, runny-nosed treble, like a congested bit of cloud falling to earth. I turn round slowly, pivoting on my heels, and my eyes fasten on a boy, not skyborne at all but earthbound, standing in the riverbed like a tiny pugilist, one foot thrust forwards and one hand balled in the other. Barely into his teens, by the look of it, with a wild scruff of black hair pulling away from a high, almost intellectual brow. A blackened smile behind an avidly protruding lower lip. Shoes easily two sizes too large for him, and a cap missing its bill, and pinning everything together, that street attitude, worn like a vest. Cheek and affability and pugnaciousness, all mixed together, as though he were spoiling for a good fight and a good laugh and didn't see much to distinguish between them.

—Well, you see, I thought she might be hungry . . . thought I might fetch her some food. . . .

—And you done a good job scaring her off. Bit clumsy at this, ain't you?

—I'm not, if you must know, this isn't something at which I normally practice.

—At which you prak-tiss, he says, slapping my consonants silly.—Normally prak-tiss.

A chafing spirit sweeps across my face. It lingers only a moment, but it's enough to make him even bolder.

—I know some other poppets, if that's your line. . . .

—Quite all right.

—Plumper gals. Quite athletic. One of 'em does this *trick*, sir, most alarming, the Hungarian cartwheel. . . .

And in fact, just hearing the words "Hungarian cartwheel" does the trick. I no longer feel obliged to take any tone at all with him.

—Don't be disgusting, I say.

And as I turn away, I hear his voice blow in a new direction.

—Didn't mean to offend, sir. Heaven forfend, sir.

—You don't offend. You would have to do much more to offend.

So saying, Mr. Timothy Cratchit takes his leave. Observe him now: promenading along the embankment, stately as a dowager in a sedan chair, social position intact, dignity restored.

But the boy keeps interfering with the dignity. He runs alongside me now, his feet breathtakingly agile in their outsize shoes, his hands providing an extended accompaniment, sawing and circling and planing the air, never quite touching me, just wrapping me round in gossamer thread—a folk dance, improvised on the spot and gibing with thousands of other dances being performed at this very moment by legions of boys just like this one.

—Sir, it was an awful, a terrible misunderstandin'.

—Apparently.

—I see now, it's this gal in particular, ain't it?

—Go away, please.

—Old acquaintance, sir?

—No.

—'Course not! Silly monkey! Family member, is what I'm guessin'. As has run away from home. . . .

—I don't see that it's any business of yours.

—'Course not, sir, but I'm a man of business, ain't I? Anyone's business'll do.

He almost breaks my stride with that one. It's maddening to feel that twitch of humour in my cheeks.

—You may run along now.

—How about a song, then?

—No.

—A few bars, sir.

With a small grunt, I thrust myself forwards, and for a moment, I could swear I've broken free, but then something calls me back. A voice, that's all. Much like the one I've just been listening to, except this one really does fall from the sky. All the defiance, all the glottals and sinus obstruction that marred the boy's speech have been cleared away, and there's nothing left but sound, pure and lustrous, rising and swelling with no discernible effort.

> *Oh, the summertime is comin'*
> *And the trees are sweetly bloomin' . . .*

I used to sing this very song for my family. A retired Scottish hussar from round the corner taught it me, and I could reproduce his exact burr to charming effect when I sang it after Sunday dinners. My brothers and sisters would sit round the table in peaceful, half-enforced attendance, and as I sang, I could see my parents' eyes widen in response to certain tremolos and cadenzas. I knew precisely how to elicit these responses, how to break off phrases, when to raise the volume. I could stand outside myself and watch it all happen.

> *Will ye go, lassie, go?*
> *And we'll all go together . . .*

But even at my best, I never sounded like this boy. Never held myself like him, either: so calm and still, so respectful of his muse. Cap pressed against his chest, gaze fixed on some rewarding vision in the middle ether.

> *To pluck wild mountain thyme*
> *All around the bloomin' heather*
> *Will ye go, lassie, go?*

And just like that, the sound ends, and the boy stands quiet, almost estranged from what he has produced.

—There's two more verses, sir. If you're willin'.

I move a few paces towards him. A flush of slyness steals back into his eyes.

—What's your name? I ask.

—Colin. Colin the Melodious, as I'm known professionally.

—Thank you, Colin.

My hand is already closing round a coin, and as I draw it from my pocket, the sun's rays set it smouldering in my palm.

A half sovereign. My last gold piece.

Colin flinches with surprise.

—Thank *you*, sir.

I nod and turn, but the boy isn't about to let it rest now. His limbs jig back into life, and the harder I press on, the more nimbly he trots alongside me. After a few yards, he spins himself about and pedals backwards, so that the two of us now resemble a pair of amorous paddle wheels, pulling against each other.

—See here, sir. You and me ain't done, is we?

—I think perhaps we are.

—Oh, sir, you break my heart, you really do. Here you are, a gentleman in need of service, and here am I, a young cove ready to supply it.

—What are you going on about?

Still facing backwards, he darts ahead a few paces, then stops suddenly and leans into my chest. It's the first time he has allowed himself to touch me.

—I knows people, sir. Me and my mates, between us we got eyes 'cross town, all 'long the river. You want that gal found, sir, depend on it, Colin's your man.

—Who says I want her found?

—No one, sir, no one. I was purely speculatin'.

—And what makes you think I can't find her myself?

—Well, you frighted the bollocks off her, didn't you? She ain't never goin' back *there*. And what with the, what with the little catch in the old locomotion, you won't be runnin' her down, sir. Not so's anyone'd notice it right off, sir. You carries yourself right elegant.

It doesn't exactly turn my head, but it does stop me in my tracks. I have to wipe my face clean of any pleasure.

—How old are you, Colin?

He doffs his cap. His cheeks puff with vanity.

—Half a month shy of eleven, sir.

—And you're not in school? You have no other pressing business to occupy your time?

—Depends what you mean by "pressing," sir. Got my career to think of, naturally, but being a nighttime artiste and all, why, I've got packs of day-light time. Eternally at your service. Beck'n Colin, that's me.

The wind has whipped up now. The piers sing, the water shushes beneath Hungerford Bridge, and a patch of twigs and leaves—the remains of a bird's nest—rolls down to sea. But, as far as this boy is concerned, none of this is happening. He has eyes only for me.

—Thank you, Colin. I'm afraid I cannot accept your generous offer.

—Reasonable terms, sir, if you're—

—I've no doubt you're reasonable. The answer is no.

—Ooh, sir!

—Sorry.

—Ooh, you're killing me, sir! You're *murdering* me!

—I hope you get better.

By the time I reach the top of the hill, the sound of him—his dancing feet, his mercantile panting—has faded away. And even so, how surprising to turn and find him gone. I squint hard, as though I were trying to spy a ship, and there, at the bottom of the hill, he stands, his cap leaping almost autonomously from hand to hand, his head thrown back like a cock's as a raucous crowing swells the reedy column of his throat:

> *Buffalo gals, won't you come out tonight?*
> *Come out tonight?*
> *Come out tonight?*

Chapter 5

SHOVING OFF WITH HIS ONE GOOD HAND, Captain Gully wobbles and weaves in the trough of the boat. One foot lurches forwards, an arm rears back, but soon enough, he has found his equipoise, and his tiny figure, squarer than usual in a dreadnought pilot coat, rises and drops so serenely it seems to have absorbed the river's rhythm straight into its sinews. His eyelids fold down, he takes a single long drag from his pipe, and as he pushes the smoke back through his lips, his nostrils widen to receive the latest intelligence.

—Someone's out there, Tim. We can *smell* it.

Another draught of night air. He screws the stem of the pipe into his ear canal.

—We're never wrong, you know. Not when the bones get a-gnawin'.

Now is the time, perhaps, to compliment him on his intuition, but the only gnawing I feel is in my hands. I've been rowing half an hour straight, through blankets of brown fog, past invisible wharves, under drooling, frost-stained bridges, rowing north and south and east depending on how the river crooks, rowing with the tide, against the tide (one is hard pressed sometimes to tell the difference), in full view and beyond the reach of gaslight, rowing where the only illumination is the moon. Rowing all the way to Gravesend, for all I know—isn't there a lick of salt water in the air?—but more likely Wapping, yes, very likely Wapping, if those are the old stairs I see up to the left. Difficult to say. The fog throws one back into a geography of the mind. From reading my maps, I could say that the Docks lie just to the north. I could say there are hundreds of ships laying by, thousands of slumbering sailors, goods and wares from every continent. But for now, all I can say for sure is that it's me and the captain and the amber light of a lantern. And the water, always the water, slurring and lapping against the keel.

And perhaps because we are so functionally alone, Captain Gully has chosen this moment to turn voluble.

—Off to starboard, Tim! It's bloody Rotherhithe, ain't it? Can you believe the luck? Just yesterday, the papers was saying as how a stoker in Jamaica Road had gone missing, an' here we are, Tim: bloody Rotherhithe! We find this sod, it'll fetch us five and six just from the inquest money, never mind the pockets.

So absorbed am I in my work that I tend to forget about the medium-sized trawling net that drags beneath us. Not for the customary aquatic harvests, no. Captain Gully and I are fishers of men, and I get half the take.

—It's enough rowing, lad. Reckon the tide'll take it for now.

The oars drop from my hands and rattle in their locks, and as I loosen my shoulders, a cramp seizes me round the small of the back. I have to bend forward again, all the way over, just to unclench, and the unplanned movement stirs new protests in new regions. Every muscle in my body is husbanding its own tenacious flame, but on a night such as this, any warmth is welcome. Bitter chill it is, as the poet says: slashing lines of sleet, stinging pellets of frozen rain. A scarifying wind from the southeast, and the moon winking in and out of view in the blackness, and no other light save for a small fire in another boat fifty yards off. A purlman's boat, I'd wager, carrying malt kegs to some famished pub in Limehouse. As it wafts downriver, it bleeds into the fog, until there's nothing left but a single levitating light.

—Cold, Tim?

—Just a bit, Captain.

—Let's us have a nip, then.

I think this must be why I row so hard. So that I may have the satisfaction of seeing Captain Gully take the box-end wrench that has replaced his left hand, twist it round the cap of a metal flask, and then, clamping on to the flask as gingerly as a Belgravia hostess, pour a jigger of brandy into a small pewter cup. I never tire of it. I remember asking him once—this would have been when we first met—why he'd been rigged out with a wrench instead of a proper hook.

—'Twas the only thing in reach, Tim. Hundred knots off Barbados, we got ourselves snarled up in some rigging. Freakish business, lopped the hand right off us. Ship's surgeon shook his head, said, Gully, you has your choice. You can waits till we reach land, or you can make do with what's to hand. Why, sir, we said, you calls that a choice? Give us a lick of rum, fit us out with the nearest implement, and have done with it, we said.

Whatever Gully may have lost in menace, he has made up for in rather astonishing dexterity. I have seen that wrench of his toss an anchor, lower a jib, thread mooring ropes around a pier, even uncork a rather musty bottle of Madeira. And now, under the generative influence of brandy, that same appendage is very deftly turning the winch that lowers the trawling net. One might think his right hand would do just as well for such tasks, but as Gully is always the first to point out—and with great forbearance, considering how often the subject comes up—he has been left-handed from the day he met the midwife.

That idle right hand is now making a slow circling motion in the wind. The mouth has opened into a checkered smile, and through the gaps in his teeth, Gully's hard, uncannily piercing voice delivers its Delphic pronouncement:

—Make no mistake, Gully and Tim'll be receiving guests tonight. By God, they will. Set the table, lad, we got us company!

Kind of him to think so. To tell the truth, our partnership has not been notably successful. In three months of sporadic searching, the only bodies we've dredged up have been quadrupedal. A pair of hogs—enormous, marbled black and green, swollen with mud—not even the knacker would have taken them. An emaciated goat, staring wildly to each side. And one memorable night, a gelding, so heavy it actually tipped us over. I remember the razor slash of panic as I flew from the boat. My hands scrabbled for purchase and came back with nothing but air and water, and my eyes burned shut, and I might well have sunk like a boulder if the net hadn't caught me round the wrist. The river that night was so cold I quickly lost all sensation below the chest, and suddenly, I was back in my dream, my old dream. The killing sap was rising through me, paralysing my feet and legs, wrapping me round the waist like a lover, licking my ribs into numbness. . . .

It was Gully who, having righted the boat, thrust out one of the oars and drew me back in. I'd never seen him so put out.

—Why'n't you tell me you couldn't bloody swim?

Well, that was a different night—a different river, as Professor Heraclitus would say. Tonight, the job of evacuating London's bowels has given the water a costive restlessness, and on its grumbling belly, Captain Gully and I rock, scalded by brandy, scorched by wind.

—Little squeezed for money, are we, Tim?

At such moments, Captain Gully unfailingly finds some island on the horizon on which to fasten his gaze. Doesn't matter, of course, that there's no island, and no horizon; he's still staring for all he's worth.

—That's norm'lly when we hears from you, is all—when you're short. Not that we mind. Always glad for a spot of company, ain't we?

He pours himself another shot, and, without asking, pours me one as well.

—That uncle of yours getting tight with the purse strings again?

—Not exactly.

—Now, now, we're chums, ain't we, Tim? Blast him all you like. Defame away.

—No, it's just that he's laid down a condition. He wants to *see* me before he parts with another shilling.

—Well, damme, then! Pay the fellow a visit! What would it cost?

—Very little. Possibly nothing.

—Oh, Lor', look at you! Pride, is it? Listen to me, lad, pride is all well and good in its place, but it don't plug up the old bunghole, do it? People like yours truly, Tim, we can't afford pride, can we? You think yours truly'd be working nights if he had any puh-ride?

We, you, yours truly—it can be wearying, honestly, this confusion of pronouns. I feel at times there must be at least three Captain Gullys, all badgering and quarrelling. The boat fairly founders under their weight.

—Tim, it's the Yuletide season, now ain't it? Why, yes, it's a time for buryin' them hatchets and beatin' the . . . the ploughshares into swords and reflectin' on Jesus and warn't he good to get himself all nailed up and—

—No, not yet, Captain.

—How's that?

—It's only Advent. He's just getting round to being born. He hasn't had time for the rest.

At moments like this, he may perhaps wonder why he bothers using me to man the sculls. He has considerably better luck with the boys he hires off the Hungerford Pier, though they have a disconcerting habit of running off with the corpses' pocket change—a risk that is significantly reduced in my case.

Leaning back, Captain Gully sucks the last fumes of incense from his pipe. His left foot beats out a dance jig as the fingertips of his right hand trail absently in the tea-brown water. The symptoms of reverie.

—Yes, my boy, a night such as this . . . well, it gets a chappy to thinkin'.

—Mm.

—The way we figgers it—and correct us if we're wrong, Tim, coz Gully ain't no accountant—

—Mm.

—The way we figgers it, a few more rounds of dredgin', a few more investments comin' clear . . .

—Mm-hm.

—Why, we'll have saved up all we needs. Majorca bound, that's what we'll be.

It was thirty years ago that one of Gully's ships moored off that remarkable island for a week's worth of repairs. Thirty *years*, and in Gully's mind, it might as well have been yesterday, the memory is so dripping and fresh. In his mind, I think, he's already back there, dozing away the afternoons in olive groves, scrambling down ravines, climbing hulking stone towers older than man. . . .

—Sun all the bloody day long, Tim. Nary a scrap of fog nor frost. People runnin' 'bout in their naked God-given *feet*, Tim. And the women! Gully ain't never seen such a display of pull-chritude in his livelong days. Holds your eye, they do, holds it so long you're ablush. Not ashamed to be *women*, you see. Lor', did we ever tells you about that gal, plays gee-tar with her ankles? We did? Thousand pardons. Gully's an old bird, keeps flyin' back to the same nest. . . .

A fresh wind drives up from the south, but the tide draws us eastward. The water slaps and kisses our boat; the cold air scratches our knuckles. Gully's wrench traces the outline of a woman's leg.

—You'll come, Tim. You'll see. Changes a man forever.

Sweet old buzzard: can't bear to conclude a reverie without including me in it. And why not Majorca? I sometimes ask myself. Why not? I've never been out of England, rarely even set foot outside of London. A brief rainy sojourn in Brighton, that hardly counts, and when I was still quite young, an expensive week of hydrotherapy at Bath, subsidised by Uncle N. Six glasses of Pump Room water a day, and many hours in the Cross Bath, cooed over by yeasty-thighed matrons. It was fall, and the sun had turned the soft limestone walls to butter, and the water made my skin tingle in a most pleasant fashion, and I remember remarking that this water had first rained down from the skies a thousand years ago and was only now filtering up through the earth's crust, and how remarkable to think it might be carrying messages from the Romans who had built this place. And that was when the urge to travel first seized me—an urge that has yet to let go of me, though I've done nothing, *nothing*, to indulge it.

Why not Majorca?

—We'll gets there by Holy Week, Tim. That's the time. The whole place a-rippin' and a-rantin', and such cos-*tooms*. Colours such as you never knew existed, colours God went 'n' forgot He made, that's what they say.

Here is one good thing about reveries: they always leave you a little warmer than they found you. Or perhaps it's the brandy, perhaps that's why the palsy is draining from my limbs. I find I can lie back in the boat now, with my legs thrust out, my hands cradling my head, a pose almost as indolent as Gully's. And even though the fog has sealed off the sky—not even the moon can break through now—I can imagine a sky in its place. See the stars, even.

And then, all round us, the gush and plash of water are stilled. And in the splinter of silence that ensues, I see Gully's good hand instinctively wrap itself around the winch, and I start to brace myself, too, but the boat is already bucking, lurching back and rolling me to the side and tossing Gully to his knees. And then it lurches once more, and once more, and each time we're thrown about the flat bottom of the boat like matches in a phosphorus box, and a vagrant thought forms in my head: *an earthquake . . . in the middle of the water. . . .*

Gully is sprawled on his belly now, but his face has the ecstatic smile one associates with martyrs. And as soon as the boat has rocked to a stop, he is up on his feet, shaking his clenched fist and howling to the sky.

—Ohh, we knowed it! We *knowed* it!

Breathing in short, greedy rasps, he crouches over the winch and then, after a moment of ceremonial silence, sets to cranking. But after about a dozen turns, the resistance on the other end grows so strong it threatens to snap the wrench clean off his arm.

—Well, don't just a-lay there gogglin', lad. Give us a hand!

Even with two of us cranking, it's heavy going. The boat is listing sharply to port, and we have to throw our bodies all the way to starboard just to keep it from tipping. I grit my teeth against the burn in my shoulders, and the winch groans and screeches and drives needles into my blistered fingers, and I think it must be a giant we're hauling to the surface.

When I look over the edge of the boat, I can see, rising through the brown water, the first inklings of net, no longer limp but taut with intent. And as the winch draws it higher and higher, I understand why it has cost us so much labour: stones. Stones and river sediment and dead fish, packed together in a great black bale, dense and loamy and dripping something like whale oil.

Dragging the river bottom. That's all we've been doing.

I understand now that I've been ready to give up, ready from the moment we began pulling. I've been waiting only for Gully's signal, but his eyes are still glazed with avarice, and his wrench is rotating for all it's worth, and I don't have the will or reason to stop on my own, so we keep cranking. And then, after another minute, Gully does stop, quite suddenly, but only to shout in my ear:

—Grapplin' iron!

I grope for it in the darkness—a cold, scabbed hook resting on a coil of rope. Heavy brute: I have to rest it on my shoulder before I can swing it, and it takes me three swings before the hook catches in the maze of the net. And just as it does, our cargo pulls away, pulls so hard it's all I can do not to be dragged over the side.

—Hold 'im, Tim! Hold 'im!

By now, at least two or three gallons of water have swamped the boat, and the line between us and the river has dissolved. My toes swim inside my boots, and the boots themselves gasp and swell with water, and the heels of the boots slide by slow, aching degrees along the planks below.

—Shit, it's too much mud, Tim. Shake it out! Shake it out!

But our haul is too heavy to be shaken; I can barely keep it from sinking. With a cry of muffled rage, Gully flings himself towards the net. His wrench pierces it like a lance, and the shock of the contact makes me flinch and stagger backwards, but when my eyes spring open again, I see Gully, stretched like a footbridge between the boat and the cargo, plunging his good hand into the net's cavity and scooping out great fistfuls of streaming black mud. There's nothing anchoring him to the boat but those two mite-sized feet of his, and my stomach clenches when I imagine him dropping into the water, dropping face-first and then sinking like marble, and me unable to follow, and I'm just about to let go the grappling iron and rush to his aid when I hear Gully snarling over his shoulder.

—Lever him up, lad!

Acting purely on instinct now, I lower the iron until it's lying athwart Gully's bench, and with that fulcrum in place, I throw all my weight to the far end. The handle creaks with the strain, and the boat lists back to port and swallows another couple of gallons of water, and the water ices my hot, chapped hands, gnarls and welds them so completely to the pick I don't think I could let loose now if I tried.

And after perhaps half a minute, our great bundle, with an almost human groan, climbs above the surface. And with it rises a measure of hope, for with each new second, the bale sheds weight, coughing up shards of fish, plumes of half-solid water. And there! Projecting from it like a buttress: mad Gully. Still anchored by his feet, still clawing his way to the prize. The mud has smeared his face, soaked him all the way to his shoulders, but he can't be deterred, keeps pumping his arms into and out of the cavity like a furious midwife, sending up storm clouds of rock and sediment and grease.

And just then a lathe of wind catches the shrunken bundle and swings it sharply to the bow. And Gully swings with it. Torn from his perch, kicking like a spider, the great dredger disappears into the fog and then, with a roar, reemerges on the other side.

—Captain! Are you—

But I cannot finish the question. My fist, you see, is crammed in my mouth to keep me from laughing, for Gully resembles nothing so much as an out-raged crustacean: his upper limbs pinioned in the net, his bandy legs adangle, his red mouth sluicing out streams of oaths.

—I'm sorry, Captain, I can't hear you.

It's only when he stops to draw breath that I notice that his right arm is curled around something, some knob or appendage, rendered nearly amor-phous by its silt coating. I realise now what Gully's been yelling.

—A foot! God damn you, a foot!

Snatching up the iron, I fling it one more time at the net and drag the bundle and its human barnacle back to stern. And Gully, once he's clear of the water, loosens his grip and, with a short, satisfied grunt, drops into the boat. The impact triggers only the slightest bend in his knees, and as he once again rears up to his full five feet, he looks unaccountably large, as though transfigured by Nike.

—D'you see that, Tim? Now was *that* a bleedin' horse's foot, I ask you? By God, it bloody well warn't.

No, indeed. But as Gully and I open the net's cavity, my eyes keep flicking back to that protruding appendage—that strange bare peninsula, extending from its still-dark continent—and the more I study it, the more clearly I see something that Gully has, in all his excitement, missed.

I see how tiny it is.

A human foot, no question, but too small, surely, for a stoker from Jamaica Road. And when I try to imagine who could own such a foot, my mind stops me from venturing any further.

Gully, though, soldiers on.

—Who's to say, Tim? Sod may've been carrying two weeks' wages in his pockets. On his way to the pub, like. Oh, we'll shake him head t' foot, Tim. Such a Christmas it'll be! And with luck like this, why, we'll be in bloody bleedin' *Majorca* by Holy Week, can you doubt it?

And just then, our cargo, stripped of its swaddling mud, plunges into the boat with the muffled, otherworldly force of a meteorite. The boat lowers to accommodate the new weight, and Gully and I, acting on the same sacerdotal impulse, remove our caps and sink to our knees. In lieu of prayers, the captain begins muttering instructions.

—Don't pass over the shoes now. Amazing how many on 'em keeps banknotes next to their feets. And mind, if there's a watch, you leave it be. Just the sort of thing they trace, ain't it? And no breakin' the fingers, the coroners can't abide it. If he's got hisself a ring on, Gully has a special grease, slicks it right off.

I don't think he's even addressing me in particular. I think it must be the litany he goes through each time.

—And don't be goin' and gettin' any of them *screw*-pulls. You think the

police'd have any? Gorr, they'd be doin' the same as us, and it'd be them
gettin' rich 'stead of us, is the only difference.

And now, through its vestments of mud, our haul begins to assert some of
its original identity. The crook of a knee, the swoop of a buttock, an arm
bent at the elbow—all of these point synecdochically to a larger whole, a life
once lived. Funny how long one can carry on before fronting such a basic
fact. Even Captain Gully seems daunted by it: his voice has dropped to an
awestruck whisper.

—My, but he's a little un, ain't he?

Like the boy pharaohs, I want to say. The ones Mr. McReady used to show
me in the British Museum. Except that instead of being fitted out for the
afterworld, this one has his knees drawn up to his chest and one arm flung
behind his head and a torso so contorted it seems locked in eternal recoil.

And something else: a pair of hands, curled into the form of talons.

I don't remark the transition. All I can say is that one moment I'm
crouched next to Gully, and the next I'm sprawled headlong in the boat,
grubbing through the mud, wiping the dead face clear. In the dim nimbus of
Gully's lantern, I see two distended eyeballs, bleached grey and jellied over.
Then a pair of water-bruised lips. And as my hands smear away the clay
remnants, the bladders of the cheeks emerge from a field of purple-blue skin,
skin of an ancient pallor, like the frontispiece of a medieval romance.

—Bollocks!

I turn and find Gully straddling the torso, gesturing bitterly at something I
can't quite make out—a bare leg, perhaps? a telltale declivity? I can guess his
import even before he declares himself.

—A bloody *girl*, ain't it?

Sore disappointed is our captain, and I should be the last to blame him.
Someone of such a young and female persuasion—from such a low aquatic
vicinity—how likely is *she* to be carrying coin or valuables? Tuppence at
best, for butter and potatoes (her mother still wondering, weeks later, where
she's made off to). No, it's a fair waste of good net, as far as Gully is concerned. Small wonder the fire has gone out of him.

—Dunno, dunno . . . maybe got a, a bag tied round her, like. Got a, got a change purse, p'raps. . . . Could be lots of places for secretin'. . . .

But his heart's not in it. He's written her off, hasn't he? Whereas to me she has become steadily more engrossing. Holding the lantern just above her head, I examine with great interest the short, blunt object that is her nose: a speckled mushroom cap, frozen in the act of tipping upwards. Nothing like the dark, aquiline version I saw on the Embankment yesterday.

My hands travel to the hair, which after a week's immersion in the Thames, clings stubbornly to its original curl, and which, even in its owner's lifetime, could never have reached her shoulders. Nothing like the lank black hair I saw yesterday, done up with red ribbon. Nothing at all like that.

How strange! To stare into a dead girl's face, to study it as intently as one would a rune, and to feel at the same time such a curious lightness, as though one had just saved a life.

—Come away, Tim. There's no use worryin' it.

And I want to tell him I'm not worrying—not at all—but already, I feel the lightness in me filling up with something else.

It's the hands.

Tiny, brittle talons, exotic and also familiar, doubling and redoubling in my mind until they rhyme like a bad pun.

I reach for the shears. Working with great method now, as metronomically as a carpenter planing a table, I scissor away the cloth from the girl's right shoulder. And as the scissors round the last corner, I wait for the sounds of Gully's protest, for "What in God's name are you a thinkin' of," but I think the calmness of my demeanour must be disarming him. And it may be the calmness is no pretense, for when I pull away the swath of cloth, my fingers show not the slightest sign of trembling. And my eyes refuse even to blink when they behold the letter G rising from the purplish-white skin, glaring outward with raptorial eyes.

Behind me, I hear Gully's piercing, irascible voice.

—Christ almighty, has you ever seen such a botched tattoo in your life? It'd been our mother, we would've got what for, take our word, gettin' ourselves all carved up as that. You all right, Tim? Lookin' a bit green roun' the . . . if you don't mind us . . . well, never fear, there's bound to be some inquest money, 'less she's a foreigner, and hospitals is always a-wantin' bodies, ain't they, and tomorrow we'll have us another go downriver. So keep the chin up, that's the spir—oh, it's *that*, is it? Not to worry, boy, just lean the head over the water. No, downwind, *down*wind, there's a good lad.

Chapter 6

I WAS SIX THE FIRST TIME I CAME TO THIS HOUSE. It was a Sunday in March, a volatile day, variously spitting and smiling, and I remember thinking as we arrived that the Maker had not yet decided what sort of day he wanted to make. But it was the rooms inside that I was most struck by. Three months into the new year, and they were still decorated for Christmas. A half-eaten Yule log in the grate, a brace of empty stockings on the mantel. Sprigs of holly dangling like aged coquettes from the door lintels; the wattled remains of a bough of mistletoe swinging disconsolately from the hall lamp; and all round us, overwatered poinsettias, sapped of their red and collapsed like Bedouin tents.

The candles, at least, were new, and the air was quick with oranges and cloves, and there on the hearth, beneath a garland of bay leaves, stood a half-sized Father Christmas, almost sinfully hearty in his purple ermine. But much as he glowed, he could not compete with the efflorescence of our host, who, as soon as we arrived, informed us with a cackle that he had given his housekeeper the day off so that he might personally minister to his guests. It was with some trepidation that we realised we were the guests in question. Mute we sat, in our starched Sunday finery, while this twiggy, animated man in slack breeches danced attendance on us.

—Come now, Martha, more eggnog, don't be bashful. And if I'm not mistaken, there's a boy who needs another helping of wassail, is that not so, Sam? And behold yon Master Tim! Not a crumb left on his plate. Oh, it cannot continue, it cannot. He must have plum cake.

Some consciousness of our situation, of the strangeness of being served wassail in March, made me resist initially, but not too long, for the cake proved delicious, very much like Mother's but with a new flavour that my tongue tried in vain to isolate. Not so chewy as currants, not so pungent as grapes. Pulpy and sweet and very slightly bitter, giving up its juice reluctantly at first, yielding only after additional acquaintance. A *sultana*, I later learned, and something of that name's exoticism must have come through even then, for I found myself suffused with an equatorial warmth, and tingling with gratitude towards the man who had, in one stroke, so altered our climate. I said:

—Thank you very much, Mr. Ogre.

I am to be faulted, I know. But in my defense, we were just a few months into The Change (as Mother called it), and we had been so long in the habit of referring to him as Ogre that it seemed only natural to attach a business address to it. I didn't recognise my error until I saw Mother's face crumple and dive from view, and then I noticed Father running his hands up and down the arms of his chair, as though he were trying to propitiate the furniture. A dank silence fell over the room as one by one the Cratchit children set down their plates and cutlery and waited. I closed my eyes to the terror, and then I felt myself being borne aloft, and when I dared to open my eyes again, Mr. Ogre's face was three inches from mine, and an irreducible grin was pushing through his scraggly lips.

—There, there, you've nothing to fear, my boy. But you know, surnames will no longer do for us. From now on, you're to call me Uncle.

He paused for a moment, as though to make sure he had heard himself right, and the realisation that he *had* said it seemed only to embolden him. He swept his gaze round the room until he had caught the eye of every Cratchit child.

—All of you! You're all to call me Uncle, if you please.

It took some practice, getting *that* salutation and *that* name to come streaming from our mouths. Peter (always a bit of a wag) insisted on shortening it to Uncle Neezer. Even built a mnemonic chant around it—"Uncle Neezer's a frightful old sneezer"—which he illustrated with a rather elaborate pantomime that ended with his bowing his face all the way to the floor. Imagine his alarm, then, when he rose from this comical salaam one morning and saw the very object of his parody standing in the doorway. In no way outraged was our Uncle. Simply stood there, abristle with gifts, smiling like a country curate.

—What a charming boy it is. Very well, then. Uncle Neezer it shall be!

I don't recall how the name came to be shortened still further—hard usage, most likely—but very soon, we were all addressing him as Uncle N. An algebraic symbol, whose value would change quite markedly through the years.

One thing else I remember from that long-ago day: the glances my mother kept casting towards the front door. Anxiety, I now think, mingled with resignation, as though any minute the *real* guests would arrive, and the Cratchits would be sent scurrying through the scullery—the harmony of our respective social spheres at last restored. But the minutes bled into hours, and it began to dawn on us—on me, at any rate—that we were the only guests expected, and *still* Mother kept looking at the door, waiting for the sound of that enormous, deathly knocker.

The knocker is still in place. I find that oddly reassuring: to arrive a little after eleven in the morning, to pass through this black gateway and find this same tarnished-silver gargoyle glaring back at me, like some chivalric test. I need hardly lift it from its resting point, for I know what a reverberation it produces inside. And indeed it is only two or three seconds before the door opens to reveal yet another gargoyle, of a slightly more ancient variety. Feminine once, but now simply a fortress, with lancet eyes and a battlement nose and a mouth more unyielding than any portcullis.

—Good morning, Mrs. Pridgeon.

—And to you, *Master* Cratchit.

Well, she is old, I remind myself. Nearly as old as Uncle N. Won't remember I came into my maturity five years ago. Probably wondering where the other Cratchits are, all those whey-faced, runny-nosed brats in their third-hand clothes, trailing mess and clamour. . . .

—Is my uncle in, Mrs. Pridgeon?

—Would he be expecting you?

—That's a very good question. He is not expecting me today, perhaps, but he *is* expecting me. He has even demanded me.

—Very well.

The door swings open to its fullest compass, with Mrs. Pridgeon standing just off to the right, the enigma of her head tilting ever so slightly towards her shoulder.

—You'll have to wait.

Not a further word or gesture from her, and so I move to the sitting room, where I pause on the threshold, briefly nonplussed to see three other men ahead of me in the queue. Two of them are huddled by the fire: plump, bearded burghers in worn frock coats and high-buttoned waistcoats, indistinguishable from the mob of other supplicants who have been ushered into this very room almost daily for the past fifteen years. As I lower myself onto the divan by the window, I make a little game of guessing which particular charity they represent. Mission to Discharged Prisoners? Distressed Gentlefolk's Aid Society? Guild of the Brave Poor Things? One could fill scroll after scroll, drain a dozen inkwells, and still not have enumerated all the receptacles for Uncle's flying farthings.

The room is, as always, decorated for Christmas: tall, cherry-red beeswax candles on the occasional table; a wreath of rosemary and privet just above the mantel shelf; a small fir tree (look away, Mrs. Sharpe!) in a wooden tub, trimmed with golden balls and clumsy gobs of cotton wool, too large by half for the snowflakes they are meant to impersonate. A first-time visitor, however, is likely to be struck less by the decor than by the prevailing aroma, which comes not from nutmeg or cinnamon but from rotting grapes. For as long as he has occupied this suite of rooms, Uncle N has rented out the downstairs apartment to a wine merchant, and with each passing year, the exhalations of that merchant's casks have grown only more and more redolent, until the very air of the upper rooms has become a kind of advertisement for the business below.

Inhaling that air is, for me, like being whisked straight back to the past, and I find myself feeling almost sleepy from the journey. I think I would give in to it—close my eyes and let the sounds of my snoring fill the ears of those two astonished gentlemen by the fire—but for the sudden awareness of *other* eyes resting on mine.

Through my half-shut lids, I can just make him out: a tangle of savage hair and an unkempt shawl of greying beard over a still-full, still-sensitive mouth. His frame quivers with a barely contained histrionic quality: an actor, very like—Prospero and Lear on alternate nights—seeking emergency funds to stave off his company's ruin.

But it's the eyes I keep coming back to. They pierce and retire at the same time, and they are so limitless in their sadness I can't be sure whether they are looking outwards or in.

And how odd! I have barely registered his presence until now, but already he seems more than conscious of mine. I feel myself straitened by an unguessed obligation. I rear up in my chair and give him the briefest of nods, and when I address him, I make sure to speak through my nose.

—How d'ye do?

Perhaps he smiles at me; it is hard to tell, for the only movement I can detect is a small, satisfied shake of the head. But his eyes refuse to part with mine, and so my only recourse is to look out the casement window, into the arms of a maple tree, where a few fatigued orange leaves still cling, whirling like feathers on a lady's hat.

—*Master* Cratchit, he will see you now.

Here she is with the "Master" again! My face steams with the usual shame, except that this time the shame gives way to a gush of silly pride. Barely a sixpence to his name, and young Timothy is given primacy over these honourable gentlemen? It is rich, my friends. It is very rich.

I get to my feet very slowly. Mustn't let people think this is anything out of the ordinary. My hat dangles from my left hand, and I take long, indolent strides across the rug, picturing in my mind the looks of bottled rage on either side. But when I glance back, I find the two charitable gentlemen gazing into the fire, and the only one who has even been following my triumphal march is the third man, whose eyes are awash with a strange and all-knowing pity. It exerts an almost backwards pull on me, so that leaving this room finally is like pushing through a twenty-knot headwind.

I make for the study, my uncle's usual room for welcoming visitors, until I spy, out of the corner of one eye, the gargoyle's squat and dogged figure tramping up the wide staircase.

—Has he taken to bed, then, Mrs. Pridgeon?

Not a sound. Nothing but the laboured music of her lungs as she hauls each foot in turn to the next step.

—I can find my way there. You needn't trouble yourself.

But her stooped shoulders are already shrugging me off. Obediently, I start up the stairs after her, and very quickly, I have matched my pace to hers, until we are locked together in a pallbearer's stride.

Taken to his bed so early? Or never left it?

Ah, the privileges of the very old. Lie abed all day if you like, and no one to cuff you round the ears and call you a filthy beggar. I shall have to get very old very soon.

But when at last I cross the threshold into Uncle N's bedroom, I feel I am peering across an insuperable chasm, and I find I can no longer imagine being as old as the figure sitting before me, propped up in bed. A single tasselled pillow keeps him erect—that and the bedpost, which he grips like a rifle. He has thrown off his nightcap and wrapped a plain cambric gown round his nightshirt, but the gown and nightshirt have both fallen open to reveal a shrunken, hairless, chalky chest and thin, slack cords of neck, wobbling under the exertion of speech.

—Merry Christmas, Tim.

—And to you, Uncle.

Not six months ago, he had the look that belongs to men of a certain age, that querulous air of having missed too many appointments with Death. *Tiresome fellow, when will he get here?* None of that now. Uncle N has shed all superfluities of flesh, and what's left is strangely magnified: the nose more acutely angled than ever, the eyes redder, the lips bluer.

From behind me sounds a vulcanic *crack*. I whirl into a blast of heat. A large and well-tended fire rages in the bedroom grate, and as the smoke sears my nose, and as my ears tune to the crackle of the oak logs, I am transported back to Father's room, those last lingering days. Back to that other fire, which was Father's most constant companion and his last, having sprung into life only on the day he took ill and burned without lapse until he died.

—Sit you down, Tim, you must be tired.

For a visiting room, there are surprisingly few places to sit: just a cabriolet, set arbitrarily a few feet from the bed and upholstered in something that looks like moss.

—Would you . . . I could have something fetched for you . . . Mrs. Pridgeon has made some cider, I believe.

He's actually reaching for the bell rope—I have to put out a hand to stop him.

—I've just had tea, Uncle.

—Ah.

—And you have three other gentlemen eager for an audience.

—The usual mendicants. I'm not clear on . . . not clear on *who*, exactly. . . .

His hands fall into his lap. He draws a long, stertorous breath and then, after a suspenseful pause, releases it.

—You must . . . you must forgive an old man his stratagems, Tim. Short of taking up residence in the bank, I knew of no other way to find you.

—Well, you have found me, then. Not that I was ever really lost.

The slightest flash in his eyes.

—Lost to *me*, Tim. No word, no forwarding address. Not a sign of you since the funeral. What were we meant to think?

I wait a few moments, and then his voice comes back again, more softly. As I knew it would.

—I understood, of course, that you were grieving for your father.

—Of course.

—And your mother, too, no doubt.

—No doubt.

He coughs—just once, initially, to clear his throat. And then the cough takes on a life of its own, wracks his shoulders, drives his chest back. And finally releases him in an oddly chastened form.

—A hard time we have of it, Tim. A hard time on this earth, but we know that coming in, don't we? Your parents have gone to their reward, and that must be our consolation. Let us speak now of obligation. You have *other* family, Tim, you . . . you have people who care very deeply about your welfare. Who want to know you're in good hands.

—I'm in good hands.

He peers at me unguardedly as the hall clock ticks away the seconds.

—Your brother has been asking after you.

—Oh, yes?

—He says he hasn't run across you in months. Says he's quite keen to show you his, his *salon*.

—I've seen it.

—He says it's changed since you saw it. You'd hardly recognise it.

Peter. Peter and his damned shop. If I'm not careful, my mood will lighten.

—Well, *you* haven't changed too much, Uncle. You still look well.

—Ah.

He waves me off. I believe this is the only thing that can make him cantankerous now: empty words.

—Tim . . .

—Yes, Uncle?

—I wanted to see you because . . . I thought there might be some way, you know, I could help. . . .

I shake my head, very slowly.

—You've helped us enough for many lifetimes, Uncle.

—And still it is not enough.

—It is more, sir, than we had any right to expect.

—You had every right. What right had *I*?

—The same as any dutiful and loving benefactor. You are too hard on yourself, Uncle.

Something surprising then: a look of slyness, of almost entrepreneurial cunning.

—And yet I believe that given half the chance, Tim, you would be still harder on me.

—That is not true. I have never blamed you—how could I? If anything, I blame myself.

—For what, Tim?

—For many things. Nothing at all.

He smooths a section of bedspread just to the left of his knee.

—You know I've always tried to do well by you. By everyone.

—I know that, Uncle. And I try, too. In my fashion.

Another slow intake of breath . . . but this time, no apparent release. The air simply expires inside his chest, and his shoulders bow, and his head lowers, as though he were bracing for a punch.

—Tim, would you kindly fetch my little casket?

No additional instruction necessary. I glide across the room to the secretary, reach into the upper-left-hand drawer, and feel for Uncle N's miniature vault with its mother-of-pearl veneer. I take it back to the bed, as smoothly and unthinkingly as a trained pony. And then I retreat a few deferential paces, almost to the doorway.

Ward of the state.

That's how Mother once referred to me. Not to my face. She was complaining to my father about Uncle's habit of disbursing monthly remittances.

—If he cares for their welfare, Robert, if that is truly his prime consideration, why not settle a sum on them once and for all and be done with it? Why make them come begging the first of every month?

Can't recall now what Father said. Something, I'm sure.

I do remember, though, the day Peter made his break. He had me follow him over to the changing house for reinforcement, but he never needed it. Never once looked my way, never spoke for anyone but himself.

—Listen, Uncle. You mustn't think me ungrateful, because I'm not, and I could never be, but from here on out, it will have to be just me, I'm afraid. That's how Annie wants it, that's how *I* want it. It's the only way it can work.

I'm atingle just recalling it now, and for a moment, I wish Peter were actually standing alongside me, filling my ear with jests. But there's no sound now save for the soft rustle of Uncle's bank-notes. The quiet must be a kind of itch under his skin, for he begins chattering in a way that doesn't really suit him.

—Dreadful weather, eh? . . . T'rifically biting. . . . Must tell you, wonderful organisation, had the honour of endowing them just last week . . . Society for Something T'Other . . . blankets for the destitute . . . I believe nothing quite so lovely as a blanket, is there?

He looks up suddenly.

—Oh, and Tim, I've asked some guests for Christmas Day. Your brother and his wife have done me the honour of accepting. I've sent an invitation to Martha, as well, but . . .

—Yes.

—That husband of hers . . .

—Yes.

—Well, there you are.

—I will see if I can come, Uncle. I'll do my best.

—I only thought I'd mention it, you know. So you'd have a few days' notice.

—It's most kind of you.

He's been so busy chatting he seems to have forgotten why I am hovering there. With a kind of infantile surprise, he raises his arm and finds the bank-notes protruding from the crevices of his fingers. The hand is moving autonomously now—a flirtatious fanning motion—and as it moves, the fingers loosen their grip, and the notes work their way free, fluttering to the floor on a rocking cradle of air.

—Terribly . . . sorry. . . .

They're on the floor for only half a second before Uncle N's beneficiary snatches them up, tucks them inside his shirt pocket, and mumbles a curt prelude to the more elaborate thank-you still to come. But he interrupts his beneficiary:

—No. Please. Listen to me, Tim. I am certain you have your own reasons for remaining apart, and I will do my best to honour them, I promise you. All I ask in return is that every now and then, when it crosses your mind, you send a little word to me, by whatever means possible. To let me know you are well.

He laughs just then, a rueful hiccough.

—That I may cross you off my ever-lengthening list of worries.

—I will do that, Uncle.

—And you know you are always welcome here. At any time.

—I know that.

It is the moment, I know, for my gracefully understated exit, but I've lost the knack somehow. I stand there fidgeting and irresolute, and I can't think what can be keeping me, and then I hear myself ask:

—Do you believe in ghosts, Uncle?

—Ghosts.

The word catches in his chest. He has to speak it again to jar it loose.

—Why do you ask, Tim?

—I'm not sure. I do seem to see Father everywhere I go, but I imagine that's quite common when you've . . . when someone has been lost. I'm sure it happens quite often, really. Curious though, I haven't seen hide nor hair of Mother since she passed on. She was only too relieved to be gone, I expect.

—And is that all? Your father?

No, Uncle, that's *not* all. I have seen young girls—dead, mostly. I have been stumbling across them at regular intervals. No, that's not quite right: they have been stumbling across me, or rather, *seeking* me. And I am convinced they are trying to communicate something, and perhaps it's the same thing Father is trying to tell me, but I cannot be sure because I cannot divine it. There is no interpreter to be found, and no one to apply for the position. No one but me. And I'm not certain I'm up to this line of work. In fact, I'm almost certain I'm not.

—Please tell me, Uncle says.—If there's anything at all.

I go to him now. I lower my face to his and press my mouth against his forehead. My lips linger there for a second or two, and they seem to absorb something from his skin, from the very fibres of his body. It has a taste: acrid and tart. Like fear. And from the look in his eyes, I can't tell whether I have received it or imparted it.

———ο‰ο———

18 December 1860

Dear Father,

Having failed to waylay you during our last encounter, I find myself obliged to communicate the way I know best: by post. A spectral post, to be sure. You will find no postage attached; indeed, you will find no envelope, for I am committing my message to the stationery of the air, in the hope that you may stumble across it during your peregrinations. A ghost, I imagine, needs quite as much entertainment as the next fellow, and if my words can add a bit of pigment to your day, so much the better.

How few letters I sent you, Father, while you were alive. It's a bitter thing to reflect on—nearly stops me in my tracks outright—but I stay the course, for no other reason than that I wish us to come to an understanding. Or something perhaps better than understanding.

I was going to ask you first of all what you think the letter G might stand for. But there are so many possibilities, I think it would take us many lifetimes to sort through them all. And so I will pose another question to you.

Who shall be the narrator of us?

Of you and me, I mean. Of all of us.

As a narrator, of course, I'm still feeling my way, but I do have quite a lot of practice being narrated. The holiday season always calls one particular instance to mind. You may yourself remember. I was six at the time, and it was Christmas Day, and I was sitting in the next room when you told Mother what I'd said to you in church. Let me see if I recall aright. Let me see.

—O, Father, I hope the people in church see me, because I'm a cripple, and it might be pleasant to them to remember who made lame beggars walk and blind men see.

It was still novel then, that feeling of going over ground I thought familiar and finding nothing I could recognise. Everything had been transformed by an alien sensibility. Yes, I could remember going to church with you. I could remember saying how cold I was and why couldn't they get on with the service and why must Mrs. Groundley wear such a frightful bonnet with all those dead pansies. But I couldn't recall even thinking the words you assigned to me.

But those were the words I was assigned, and so they became my words, and you became my teller.

There were more words, I know, more narratives, but they tend to merge into a single strict mythos, a unitary tableau. You and I returning from our ramble, coming through the front door, and Mother there to greet us—always there to greet us—and before you had even removed your scarf, you'd have launched your latest narrative.

—Oh, my dear, I must tell you what this boy of ours said. Right as we were passing the canal, we saw an old woman with a missing leg. And Tim said to me, "Father, I wish I could make my crutch a thousand times longer, so that I could share it with everyone in the world who needs one. . . ."

It was a bit like a serialised novel. By which I mean that I was always eager for the next installment. What was it Tim had said today? Of course, I knew that certain formulae applied: the pious, improving cadence, the little grace note of hope. Although if I might step outside the story for a moment—allow me, if you would, this textual insult—I was never particularly hopeful in those days. If you must know, I was absolutely convinced that I would die . . . very soon . . . and the only thing I ever really hoped for was that death might come quickly and not leave my heart fluttering in my chest like a bird trapped in a chimney. That was all.

In any event, it was a complex business, Father, this dual imperative of being primary character and audience. There were times, I admit, when I found myself bouncing between the ontological poles—bouncing so hard it smarted. Well, of course it did. Those tales of yours came complete with implicit morals, didn't they? Little barbs of reproach for the things I hadn't thought to say, the things you had been forced to say for me. Why else would you go to such lengths of invention?

Or was it the mere act of inventing? Did that carry its own reward?

Because there truly was a rapture about you, Father, in those moments of telling, more than I could stomach, for if you weren't reproaching me in disguise, then you were believing. All those words, all those stories were being dredged up from some secret and inaccessible well, drawn up through your head and into my mouth, and what was that if not faith? The substance of things hoped for, the evidence of things not seen. . . .

Well, it's only proper, I suppose. Every storyteller must have faith in his story. And so must his audience. And so I did, a bit—and then a little bit more. And if I never believed wholeheartedly, I was moved at least to become a part of your story, which is close to the same thing. I wanted to be the boy you told Mother about.

And if I couldn't quite manage that—not every minute—I could at any rate take a turn at narrating him. And so when you bore me through the streets on your shoulders, I did my best to speak in his voice.

—Look at that poor lad on the corner selling buttons—how happy is my lot compared to his!

Even then, it was too obviously theatrical for my tastes, but your tastes were different. And whenever the family was gathered, I could never be obvious enough. A dewy look at Sam when he carried me to the table. A dewy look at Belinda when she slid me some of her potato. Prayers at pregnant intervals. And then, when the plates had been cleared, songs: lovely maudlin songs, full of tremolos and cadenzas.

And Lord help me, how I smiled. Which came in handy, Father, because I soon learned that, going out in public as often as we did, we could no longer keep our text private; we would have to contend with rival interpreters. They had no compunction about calling after us.

—Lookit! It's the two-headed beast! And the top un's the ugliest!

—Sir, you got a wart comin' out your hat!

Critics.

You never heard them, Father, I'm convinced of that. Faith was your stanchion, and more power to you.

The mistake I made in those days—pardonable, I hope, in one so young—lay in thinking that by occupying your narrative, I might exert some authorial power over it. But in fact, the more thoroughly I inhabited it, the more completely it became your story. It took me many years to scribble out my own, which, I shouldn't have been surprised to learn, was rather different from the one you and I created. (I claim coauthorship only on corporeal grounds.) This boy . . . this new boy . . . well, he was much angrier, for one thing, terribly angry. And funnier, too: that was a surprise. I remember sitting in the British Museum and telling Mr. McReady about the religious enthusiast Uncle N sicced on us one summer, that Welsh Congregationalist with the walleye and pitted nose and the extraordinary breath.

—Like rotten ham soaked in turpentine, I said.—I think I shall have to get well so as never to inhale him again.

And Mr. McReady got that look on his face, that strange halfway condition between laughter and outrage. And over time, such remarks created in us a state of mild but chronic alarm, as though I had daggers secreted in places neither of us knew about. And I came to realise that those daggers were nothing but the proddings of me, desperate to emerge.

But I never made amusing remarks around you, Father; I couldn't. They would have been out of character.

Mother, though, might have appreciated them. I've always suspected she was closer to me in spirit than she ever let on. The week before she died, she said:

—You know, Tim, I wish we hadn't got rid of that crutch of yours.

I asked her why, thinking perhaps she'd gone a bit soft on the old artifacts. She said:

—It was the best back scratcher I ever had, wasn't it?

There was a wag for you. I wish I'd known it sooner.

Do you remember what you told Mother right after The Change?

—I think, my dear—no, I am absolutely sure of it. Things will never be the same.

And on this occasion, you were right, Father. They weren't.

Chapter 7

—MR. TIMOTHY?

Timid and sore flustered, Mary Catherine twines her head round my bedroom door.

—Mr. Timothy, there's a . . . there's a Colin the *Melodious* here to see you.

—You're jesting.

—No, sir, he's . . . I left him in the—

She is cut off by the sound of her own squeal. The visitor in question has followed her up the stairs, crept up behind her, and made his presence unequivocally felt. And even as she reaches back to swat the offending hand, he ducks under her arm, darts into the center of the room, and stands there in diamonds of morning light, his shoulders thrown back like a barnyard cock.

—Filthy little . . .

—It's all right, Mary Catherine. Leave him to me.

She retreats with all the pride she can muster, but he ogles her all the way back down the hall. Very serious about his work. Robed in abstraction by the time he turns back to me.

—Nice rollickin' bum on that one. Spoken for?

—I'm afraid I can't say.

—Not that I got me room for any more. You can guess, my line of work, I'm always a-havin' to beat 'em off like rats. Someday, though, a cove's got to settle down, eh? What then, I ask you? What then, Mr. Tim-o-thee?

There's only one chair, which he quickly seizes for his own, swinging it round so that his chest presses against the chair's back. From my perch on the bed, I have the precarious sense of being a visitor in my own room.

—How did you find me, Colin?

—Followed you straight home the other mornin'. A right easy mark you was, sir, don't mind my saying. Any child coulda done it.

He leans back and casually studies the room, in all its fourteen-by-ten-foot splendour. The sloping floor, the thin fault line in the ceiling above. The patternless carpet. Tiny table, tiny washing stand, tiny wardrobe—everything seems suddenly pitched to his scale.

—Wouldna guessed it of you, sir. Livin' in such an establishment as this. Shameful.

—Well, I don't . . . it's not as if I were reimbursed. . . .

—Oh, no, sir. Nothin' in *coin*. I got ya.

His tongue slides with agonizing slowness around the oval of his mouth.

—Do you go out of your way to offend, Colin? Or is it just like breathing for you?

—Listen to him! When I'm the one as should be offended. You ain't even asked why I come.

—Then tell me and be gone.

—I *found* her, sir.

And now the excitement of his errand finally overtakes him. It roils his carefully composed face, sets his hands to dancing on the frame of the chair.

—Found whom?

—*Whom*, the man asks. *Whom.* That gal you was takin' on about, that's whom.

—Where?

—Oh, now he's risin' to it! Wants to know, don't he? Well, I'm afraid, sir, this being highly confidential intelligence, I cannot part with it on account of I am unremunerated.

—*How much?*

—Well, it all depends, sir. On one's eagerness to possess the aforementioned—

—How much?

—Half a pound to say where. Another half to take you there.

—Done to both.

And simply for the pleasure of checking his pleasure, I add:

—Payment upon completion.

—Oh. Well, speakin' frankly, sir, we were . . . we were hopin' for a bit up front, just to tide us over. . . .

—You'll get the full amount when you lead me to her.

Frowning, he bangs his cap against the back of the chair. For the first time in our brief acquaintance, he is acting his age.

—Drury Lane Garden, he says.—By the churchyard. It's no good goin' now, she only comes first thing in the morning. And it's no good goin' on your own, you'll never find it, not in a million years.

—Well, then, I look forward to your enlightened escort. Meet me tomorrow morning at Covent Garden, by the blind woman's cabbage stall. Eight o'clock, shall we say?

He gives me a tetchy shrug, which I take for consent.

—Honestly, sir, don't know what you wants with her. She's a bit touched, if you ask me.

—Touched how?

—Well, she don't . . . she don't speak the language, do she?

—And how would you know that?

—Seen her chasin' down some cove as stole her scarf. All in a righteous fury she were, a-screamin' and a-hollerin'. Didn't understand a bloody word she were sayin'.

—And would that be the same scarf you have wrapped round your neck?

His hands fly to his throat, bury themselves in the blue woollen folds. His eyes form great cracked moons.

—Why, so it is, sir. Acquired it, I did, from the fellow as took it.

—And would that fellow be you, Colin?

—Sir, you wound me, truly you do. I mean the very . . . to even think you'd—

—It *was* you.

—Bloody hell, I had to have *somethink*, didn't I? So you'd know it were really her. Had to be sure you'd trust me, sir.

—Trust you. Let me see, you steal scarves, you beg for change, you extort money. How could I fail to trust you, Colin?

—Well, I'm glad you sees it that way, sir. For an instant there, I was concerned.

It takes some doing to get Colin out of the house. He is hell bent on sampling the local merchandise, and it doesn't matter that the girls are all asleep in their beds and won't be stirred for love or money, he wants me to sound the morning reveille, send them all running into his welcoming arms. Only after I have slipped him a few shillings and promised him introductions at a future date does he agree to vacate, and just in time, for not half a minute after he has slipped out the back, Mrs. Sharpe comes charging through the front, laden with festive petticoats, bottles of brandy, and, pinned between the crumbling chalk cliffs of her teeth, a frond of maidenhead fern.

—There you are, Mr. Timothy. You have found me in shocking dishabille. A poor, wretched woman, ready to throw herself at your feet. Tell me! *Tell* me that your circle of acquaintance numbers at least one professional musician!

It is startling, I own, to be addressed in the same manner as her patrons.

—Musician, Mrs. Sharpe?

—I have just learned—and with the greatest *chagrin*—that the harpist engaged for our *petite soirée de Noël* has come down with catarrh. Why this should prevent him from strumming his damned stringbox, I cannot tell you, but our little holiday function teeters, teeters on the precipice, and so I must repeat, Mr. Timothy: Do you know of anyone? With the slightest inclination to carry a tune in any direction?

At such moments, I find it always best to simulate thought: peer at the ground, wrinkle the brow, shut the eyes halfway. This time, against all odds, a thought emerges, actually stamps its feet in my ear.

—I know a young boy. With a fine voice.

Sniffing speculatively, Mrs. Sharpe strokes her temple with the fern frond. The public madam drops away.

—You vouch for him?

—Oh, yes. I have heard him.

—And what would he need by way of accompaniment?

—None, I believe. He prefers to work a cappella.

—So much the better! We won't need to get the piano tuned. Now, he's not one of those beastly little altar boys?

—Very much not.

—I only ask because one of our guests, I won't mention names, has come within a whisker of being defrocked on at least three separate occasions. We don't want to be throwing the wrong kind of temptation his way.

—Of course not.

—Boy singer, eh? He might be charming. Invite him, by all means, and let me know if he's free. We can discuss his fee at today's session. Oh, but I must tell you, Mr. Timothy, I've been all in a stew over Mr. Crusoe ever since he promised to return Friday to his native land. All those dreadful *cannibals* and bearded Portuguese and whatnot, what can he be thinking? But hush, I'm a foolish old woman, keeping a well-dressed young man from his appointed rounds. Confess, you scoundrel! Which lucky *jeune fille* will be receiving a caller this afternoon?

—No girl. Just my brother.

This information produces a small puff of surprise in Mrs. Sharpe's cheeks, and I can't say I blame her. All these months behaving as though I had no relation in the world, and now alluding to one as casually as if he were a greengrocer. I think I must be taken in by my own nonchalance, for as I stroll up Great Windmill Street, I feel soft and half-attentive, as though I really were shopping for apples. Or women. Passing the shuttered-down face of the Argyll Rooms, I feel a prick of longing for the gay ladies who will be gathering there tonight: the whispering dresses, the fumes of champagne. And it is with a start that I see the newly erected edifice of St. Peter's Church rearing up before me—its very name a prod and rebuke.

Casting my eyes down, I hurry on towards the other Peter's. Up Poland Street, then a quick left just shy of the Oxford Market . . . walking at such a clip and dodging so rapidly between carriages and hansoms and growlers and omnibuses that I have to stop myself after a stretch to make sure I haven't gone too far.

And that's how I discover I am just where I need to be. The very block. There's the draper's with the misspelled placard. There's the fruiterer's, its barrels of oranges cursorily inspected by a wandering heifer.

And there's Peter's store. The thyme-coloured awning and the golden scrawl: Cratchit's Salon Photographique.

And there's Father in the window.

No mistake this time. Really him. Glazed and enamelled in a brass frame, frozen a few weeks shy of his forty-ninth birthday. Peter had told him not to move for a good two minutes, and he took this admonition so seriously that his body went quite rigid from the effort—I remember it took us several minutes afterwards to uncoil him. The exertion is still visible in the portrait: he has the strained, fatalistic look of someone desiring only to please.

You won't find any pictures of Mother here: she couldn't abide cameras, hated the way her smile went crooked on her. Nor will you find one of me, but that's only because I was one of Peter's first subjects. By the time he took the glass out, the image was almost completely black. *Give it a few hours*, he said. *It'll brighten as it dries*. It never got an ounce lighter, and I was too young then to attach any symbolic value to it.

Peter soon realised, of course, that on sunny days, he needn't let his plate stop quite so long. And as his understanding of the medium improved, so did his clientele and his surroundings. A shilling portrait gallery in Whitechapel, followed by a half-guinea photographic saloon in Old Kent Road, and then this last, most spectacular leap: a plate-glass storefront in Oxford Street, swarming with London luminaries. Even *I* recognise a few of them: a twice-widowed marchioness; one of the generals charged with stamping out the sepoys; a sporadically infamous actress, recently decamped from a cotton plantation in Alabama and rumoured to be plotting a return to the stage. Unimpeachably correct portraits, all of them, propped on tiers of red velvet or hanging from wires, unmoored and isolate, like warring satellites.

And then, from deep in the heart of this galaxy, a planet emerges—a living, breathing head. Just the crown at first (poignant little bald track) and then the face, tilting upwards. A contented sort of mug, all of its adolescent excesses planed away, and a new bourgeois fullness swelling its jowls. Only six months since I last saw him, and already the scraggly black hair has started to recede, and a new beard has rushed to fill the vacuum—a tentative growth, much lighter than the hair and rather too carefully trimmed to be fashionable, but strangely hopeful all the same.

He doesn't notice me at first. Too much to do. Has to adjust the angles of the frames, doesn't he? Swipe specks of lint off the velvet, primp a garland of mums . . . only then can he look to see who's on the other side of the window.

I see his mouth form my name: a quick drop and then a resealing of the lower lip. The pure shock of me. I'm surprised he can even make it to the shop door, but he's there when I walk in, clapping me on the shoulders, grabbing my elbow, feinting a punch to my jaw—and then, for a few seconds, doing nothing at all. Only looking.

—Christ, Tim, where in hell have you been keeping yourself? God above me . . . Annie! Annie, look who it is!

From an adjoining room, a cool voice answers:

—I'll be there presently.

—Oop, says Peter, winking.—She's *with* someone, I half forgot.

—Duchess? Empress?

—Somebody's aunt, that's all I know.

I take a few interrogative steps into the shop, rest my fingers on a tortoise-shell and mother-of-pearl visiting-card case. Always the trinkets, isn't it? The *petits objets*, shouting the big news of success.

—A long time you've been, Tim.

—Yes. Well.

And rather than incriminate myself further, I jerk my thumb towards the front window.

—Nice to see Father in such good company.

—Yes, I thought he'd quite enjoy it.

—Still can't believe the nobs let you hang them out like this. A bit vulgar for that crowd, isn't it?

—Ah, but they get the portrait for free. You'd be amazed how cash-poor some of them are.

—Shake 'em by the heels next time.

—Doesn't make for a good likeness, I'm afraid. Ah, here she is! Say hello to your prodigal brother-in-law.

No hanging back for our Annie. Once she spots you, she takes the shortest possible route there—you feel as though you were the very terminus she had in mind entering the room. Such a ravishing directness in such a small, muscular figure. Jutting out her chin like a train bumper, opening her steam-whistle mouth.

—Oh, he's thin as gristle, I *knew* it. Didn't I say? I told Peter, "He's starving half to death. No woman to cook for him, no one to sew his buttons on."

—Annie, I was waiting for *you*.

—He doesn't look half bad, says Peter.—All things considered.

—Half bad? He looks a fright. You're to stay for dinner, there's no arguing.

—Who could argue?

And having swept the field of me, Annie turns her full arsenal on her husband.

—Darling, listen. The session is over, but Miss Ashbee's still inside. She's under the impression we're mesmerists, and she won't leave until she's sure the spell has been broken.

—Perfect! We can give her any picture at all, she won't know the difference.

—No one ever does. The point is she's already paid up, so if you see her wandering about, just push her nicely through the door: "Have a lovely afternoon, mind the step." Do you think you're up to it?

—I believe so, my love.

—In the meantime, gentlemen, I have refuse baths to empty, and you two have *mouths* to empty, I'm sure. You'll pray excuse me. . . .

She backs her way into the adjoining storeroom and, at the last minute, aims a quick wink in the general direction of her husband. It leaves Peter dazed . . . *still* dazed! . . . after three years of marriage.

—The brains of the establishment, Tim. I'm just . . . I'm towing along in her wake, that's all.

—Do you object?

—I do not. Come, though, we've got—oh, hang on, we can't pop into the studio just yet, but do please note the furniture. It's nothing like what you'd find at Sarony's studio, not exactly Louis Quinze, I mean, but it's all new, except for the fire screen, that belonged to Annie's grandmother. The souvenir case, we picked up in Guildford. And the seashells—well, we just plucked 'em right off the shore in Portsmouth. I don't know, it all seems very cluttered to me, but Annie says it's just the right note of romantic *disarray*. Says it's expected of an artist. Imagine, Tim, me an artist! When I couldn't even draw a window, remember?

I do remember. But Peter's covered some distance since then, and for the last three years, he's done it without Uncle's money. And as I follow him through the lanes of professionally arranged bric-a-brac, past the rows of oxyhydrogen gas lamps, as I absorb his sloping, unhurried gait and his foreshortened gestures—an open palm, a casually raised finger—I think: *Yes. Yes, this is what it looks like. To be a man.* And I want to embrace him right there, in the middle of his damned shop. Or throttle him.

—'Course, Annie's the *real* artist. No one like her for tinting out the faces a bit, bringing out the blue in someone's coat. Ah, and here's a little theatrical trickery on our part: painted scenery, Tim. The young gentlemen love it. We've got backdrops of Mont Blanc, the Parthenon, Colosseum—they can tour the Continent now without ever leaving home. Oh, and you must look at these.

He gestures towards a wine table, laid over with pocket-sized prints on thin paperboard mats. The prints are still slightly damp from their recent immersion. They exhale clouds of nitrate of silver, and smelling them is a bit like mashing one's face into an old woman's hair.

—The newest thing, Tim. *Cartes de visite*. I ask you, likenesses like these, who needs tiresome old calling cards?

—Who indeed?

My fingers flutter across the image of an upright, swarthy man, on the far side of forty but dressed like a smart twenty-fiver, in a full-sleeved frock coat and a crossed tie and high collar. Nothing behind him but the recumbent swag of an organdy drape—as fraudulent as Mont Blanc, for all I know, but the impression is authentic. To think it is with personages like this that my brother, who once threw rocks at constables on Camden High Street, now spends his days. The contrast with my own circle is almost too much; I shall have to invite them all to Mrs. Sharpe's party.

—Not to paw the merchandise too much, Tim.

—Sorry.

—If you like, I'll make a card for you. Free of charge.

—I can't think when I'd ever need it.

I say it simply for something to say, but it casts a strange pall over us. He steps back a pace, fiddles with his watch key. I stroll another loop around the room. Then another.

—See here, Peter, I know it's an odd thing to ask, but I was wondering if you might enlighten me on a particular point.

—Certainly.

—Well, you remember how . . . in the old days . . .

—Which old days would those be, Tim?

—When you . . . when you got around a bit.

His dark eyes twinkling, he lowers himself onto a settee.

—Bless me, Tim, where can this be leading?

—Well, I was thinking how you used to know a certain class of person. Not that you . . . any more, I *know* that. . . .

—Go on.

—Did you ever hear talk of girls being . . . you know, for any reason, branded?

—Like cows, you mean?

—Like that, yes.

—*Hoomm*. I can't . . . no, I can't really . . . *Tattoos* now and again, that goes without saying, but brands. . . . It's what they do to slaves, isn't it?

—Yes.

His eyes squeeze down into slits.

—Someone you know, Tim?

—No. No, it's not even anyone alive.

A hiccough of laughter escapes me. Most disconcerting. I keep talking simply to cover my embarrassment.

—Well, you'll be glad to hear I saw Uncle N yesterday. Quite filled my ear with all my obligations: *A hard time we have of it in this world.* . . .

—Yes, I've had that one.

—*But we know that coming in,* he said. And that's—that's where I can't follow him. We *don't* know that coming in, how could we? And if we could, would we even bother?

—You're in fine holiday fettle.

—I can't help it. I can't. One sees things, Peter. Young girls dead before they've even bloody lived. You think *they* didn't wonder, with their very last breath, why in God's name they'd been put to all this trouble? I don't have an answer for them, do you? There's no answer. There's no reason to bring any child into such a world.

And then Annie's icicle voice comes scraping through the air:

—Pardon me.

How long she's been in the room, I can't say, but she's making great haste to leave it. Peter is halfway out of his chair, but she's too quick for him, the darkroom door is already slamming after her, and as he slumps back in his seat, he gives his head a slow scratch. His mouth twists into a grimace.

—Well, it's . . . you mustn't mind her, Tim. We're still . . . God hasn't seen fit to bless us yet, but we're still hoping, you see.

My head drops into my hands.

—Ohh, Christ.

—You weren't to know.

—I damn well *was* to know. I'm just a great fat idiot, that's all.

—Not so fat.

I love that smile of Peter's: soft and reproving all at once. Judgement and then permanent amnesty.

—I tell her all the time, Tim, if God means it to be, it'll be. But that's not enough, she *feels* it so. Can't get around it. I think it's to the point now she'd take any baby at all.

He snorts at the floor.

—Even branded on all sides. And shod by the local smith.

Suddenly, over his left shoulder, a strange and ephemeral vision: a woman, tall and straight and ancient, under a nest of strawberry curls. Drawn by some magnetic field all her own, too insensible, perhaps, to notice the slow, inexorable slide of her bonnet towards her left ear.

—All right, Miss Ashbee?

—Oh, yes. You know, while I was being mesmerised, I had the most charming dream.

—Is that so?

—I'm afraid I can't recall a moment of it now.

—Well, that accounts for its charm, perhaps. Shall we send on your portraits when they're done?

—That would be lovely. And do say good-bye to the other gentleman, if you would.

—Other gentleman, Miss Ashbee?

—Yes, he was standing very still and quiet in the center of the room. Three legs and one large glass eye.

Chapter 8

Swinging his head round, Colin the Melodious fixes me with a basilisk stare.

—Christ, is that the fastest you can go?

Until now, he has been the most admirable of guides. With his low-slung gravity and busy feet, he can navigate any puddle, skirt the most treacherous morass, and he has a keen inner eye for the sheets of black ice that crop up every ten yards or so. A good thing, too, for it's the dreariest, drizzliest of mornings—sleet and ice and rain sloughing down in a great numbing soup—and Drury Lane's courts have never been mazier. Only fifteen minutes ago, we were in Covent Garden, surrounded by oxen and sheep, handbarrows and donkey carts, costers bawling for all they were worth: the holy din of the market. Now we might as well be in another hemisphere. The streets have vanished under drifts of mud. The houses charge at us like bellicose dart throwers, or else lean drunkenly on one another's shoulders, and from their chimneys, parabolas of soot rain down on us in hard black flakes.

—Lord bless me, Mr. Timothy! You must have a week's worth of shit up your bum!

It's half past eight, but the morning hasn't quite taken hold here. The street lamps still smoulder through curtains of sleet. Candles flicker from barely discernible windows. The sky holds far off, and the only sound is Colin's occasional whistling—as lovely, in its way, as his singing—and even this dies away as the streets taper into tunnels and the houses close down on our heads. We step over shattered, frothing cisterns and wrenched-off water spouts, still clogged with black ice, and it seems to me we no longer have any location to speak of. We are off the human map.

A few more minutes, and we have passed into a small court, even darker and colder than the one we just left. We sidestep a recumbent, bloodstained man . . . thirty? sixty? . . . He opens one eye to us, then slowly, regretfully closes it again. From off in the distance come the sounds of a German band warming up for nobody.

—Ssst.

Colin puts a finger to his lips, motions me to stop.

—Over there, sir. That's the churchyard.

I will have to take his word for it. Through the haze and sleet, all I can see is a large blotchy archway, with a listing iron gate and, above it, a single lamp, still burning. The rest is intuition: a row of crumbling, unevenly laid bricks; an inscription; wrought-iron tracery.

—I don't see her, Colin.

—What'd you expect? She'd be waitin' there with a pie for you?

We ford the muddy street and come to a halt by the gate. From the blackness on the other side, a dank sulphurous gas billows forth, but this is less terrible than the sheer unmitigated dampness of the place. I wouldn't have imagined we could be any wetter than we already are, but standing here, I think we must have stepped into a great panting, oozing mouth.

Through the bars, I can just make out isolated heaps of stones and markers, and as the haze slowly lifts, I begin to see the true method therein: grave piled upon grave in promiscuous confusion. As unhallowed a ground as one could wish for. Even Colin sounds awed by it.

—Fearful spot to be dead in.

The gate, deprived of its hinges, has managed to cling to the outer wall through some stubborn oxidation, and so the only way to enter the enclosure is to squeeze through the crevice between the gate and the archway. Colin takes less time about it than I do. By the time I'm through, he is already leapfrogging over the gravestones, dropping into handstands—and then stopping suddenly, his body poised and quivering like a pointer's. And when I come up alongside him, he is indeed pointing—to a small grey figure twenty yards off, kneeling before one of the stones.

—It's her, sir.

—Are you sure?

—'Course I'm sure.

But before we can take another step, a titanic howl sets us back on our heels. A large black-whiskered dog has darted from cover and crouches now before us, snarling and bellowing to beat Cerberus, slashing the ground with its forepaw and spitting drool. I take a step back, but Colin, with truly alarming aplomb, picks up a fragment of crumbled stone from the nearest grave and shies it at the dog's head.

In that instant, the dog ducks its snout, lowers its ears, and dashes past us in a most un-Cerberal fashion, squeaking where it once howled, scrambling through the gap of the gate and making off down the street with nary a backwards look.

Its flight serves at least one function: it rouses the hooded figure in the distance. Rising to her feet, she wraps herself round with a cloak—a new addition, that—and glares through the mist. Locked in her sights, I grow as still as if *I* were the quarry, and it seems she is under the same impression, for she shakes off her own stillness and comes hard on. *Running*, she is. Charging with such ferocity I find myself virtually helpless before it. She dodges grave markers without even seeing them, so merciless is her intent, and the closer she gets, the greater her velocity, until at last she is almost airborne, flinging herself not at the sky, as I half imagined, but at the boy standing frozen next to me. I hear Colin's startled cry:

—*Goomf!*

And down he goes. Kneeling on his stomach, the girl rears up in a towering rage and rains down punishment, blow after blow to Colin's face and shoulders and chest, as he squirms and grunts beneath her. I grab her round the waist and pull as hard as I'm able, but she won't budge, just keeps raking and pounding. I pull harder, harder still, and at last she gives way, but only of her own volition, I know that much, and when I have dragged her a few paces away, I understand the reason for her acquiescence: the blue woollen scarf has been wrenched from Colin's neck and hangs now from her still-clenched fists—a conqueror's tribute.

—Christ almighty! says Colin.

He wipes a smear of blood from his lip, climbs to his feet with a long, dissipating groan, and stares at me with glassy eyes. I hand him his cap, grab him by the shoulders, and turn him round until he is facing the girl.

—Young lady, you must excuse my friend Colin. He would like you to know how very sorry he is for stealing your scarf.

It takes a poke to the ribs to jar the necessary words from Colin.

—Very. Awf'lly.

Still glaring, the girl slowly winds the scarf round her neck, taking special care, I notice, with that last dangling fringe, draping it just so between the folds of her cloak, so that the two articles of clothing form a single continuum.

—We only wanted to be sure you were all right, I tell her.—You mustn't be crawling about in sewers, you know, it isn't safe.

She takes a step back. Another step.

—We won't come any closer.

Another step.

—You needn't be afraid.

She's not afraid. That much is clear. The simple act of plying her fists has stiffened her spine, pushed her chin into a promontory.

—If you . . . if you wish to leave now, we won't follow. I can't run very fast. As you know.

I make a quick little running motion with my arms, then frown and shake my head: *No runny runny*. And strange to say, this desperate pantomime manages to reach her—elicits the barest ghost of a smile. Or am I imagining it? Colin, at any rate, is ready with a translation:

—He means he's a bloody cripple!

And whether it is his mode of expression or the reaction it produces on my face, her smile does draw a little wider.

Here is Drury Lane's gift. Standing in this tenement of the dead, this girl and I at last approach some degree of ease together. If ease it can be called, both of us coated in rime and soot and fixed in place, several yards separating us and not even the glimmer of a conversation on our horizon.

It will have to do for now. It is enough, at any rate, to embolden me towards something that only a minute ago I would not have attempted. I point to the place where she was lately kneeling, and I ask her:

—Is that someone you know?

A shade comes rolling down over her eyes; she turns away. Not the retreating motion I remember from our first encounter, but a slow, graceful circling, almost flirtatious in its delicacy. And in that moment, the very arc and style of her movement become a form of permission, and so, taking Colin by the elbow, I make for the graveside she has just vacated.

The stone is new, but it might as well be a century old, for all the care that has been taken with its carving and placement. It leans back at a crazy angle, almost kissing the turf, while a small bouquet fans across its base. A paltry collection, given the season: flowerless dandelions, a couple of pansies, the snipped-off heads of chrysanthemums. Snatched from curbs and refuse bins, no doubt, and so ragged I'm not sure even a flower girl would try palming them off, but a gentle hand has slapped them back into life, interwoven them in such a way that their old identities have reemerged.

Colin is kneeling now, tracing the letters on the stone, and as he traces, the syllables seem to bleed from the marker and rise up through my mouth before I'm even sure of them.

—Serafino Rotunno.

I had meant only to whisper it, but I see her head whip around and her body plant itself in a defiant straddle, as though preparing for a new outrage.

—Did I pronounce it correctly?

No yielding. Not a smile, not a frown.

—Is he related to you?

And now she begins to circle us—moving faster and faster as she spins farther away. Despairing, I call out to her:

—Do you speak English at all?

A slight tilting of the head, the barest shrug of a shoulder.

—My name is Timothy.

And still she keeps marching in her steadily expanding circle. Marching us out of her head, very likely.

—And this, as I mentioned before, is Colin.

Nudged once more in the ribs, the boy doffs his cap, lowers his head. But even this piece of decorum fails to move her. Her circle grows still wider . . . extravagant apiarian loops . . . she'll have reached Lincoln's Inn Fields by the time she's done.

Half frantic, I dig through my trouser pockets for the article I took from Iris's wardrobe this morning, and for a few grisly seconds, I think it must have tumbled out somewhere back in the wastes and been tramped down into the deepest geological depths, and I have just about given it up for lost when my hand at last closes round it . . . and raises it carefully into the half-night of morning.

A ribbon, that is all. Scarlet and satin. Burning off the grey light like a tiny volcano.

—I thought you might like this.

She has stopped now.

—Your old one . . . was a bit torn, I'm afraid.

One hand plunges into the mess of matted black ringlets. The other rests apprehensively on her belly.

—You may pick it up whenever you like. I'll leave it here, shall I?

My first instinct is to drape it over the headstone, but the crazed angle defeats me: unanchored, the ribbon slides earthward, catches on a chrysanthemum. I point towards it, vaguely, but she's not looking at the ribbon, not looking at anything.

I whisper to Colin:

—Time to go.

He whispers back:

—Where's my bloody remuneration?

—You'll have it when you lead me back.

That's all the assurance he needs. He claps his cap back on his head and gallops for the gate . . . trips once over a sunken marker but rights himself quickly and keeps moving, and it seems I am moving as well, for I am only a few yards behind him when her voice comes.

A huskier voice than I would have thought, but soft, too, as though the abrasion of the vocal cords had served only to plane it down. It blows through us like a wind through rocks, rising on the third syllable and singing into silence.

—Philomela.

And when I turn round, the ribbon is already in her hair, tied in a neat bow without benefit of a glass.

—My name is Philomela.

She clears her throat, swallows twice, and walks towards us. From the recesses of her apron she extracts a discarded cigar box and then opens it, carefully, to reveal a week's worth of secreted treasure: row after row of copper nails, salvaged from wharves and riverbeds and God knows where else. Bowing her head over her luminous currency, she says:

—For ribbon. I pay you.

It's the last thing I would have expected. This proud collegial air! It brings quite the blush to my cheek.

—Oh, well, thank you, but you see, *these* would fetch you . . . oh, my, dozens of ribbons, so it wouldn't . . . and besides, there's no need, really, it's my pleasure.

And it's Iris's ribbon.

For the next few moments, she contents herself simply with searching my face. Whether she finds what she is looking for, I cannot say. All I know is there is one final beat of hesitation before she says:

—Serafino Rotunno is my father. He is dead. He make frames.

Chapter 9

VERY DAINTY SHE IS AT FIRST, freeing the roast potato from its cocoon of whitey-brown paper, peeling back a segment of skin, pausing a moment to let the aroma tingle in her nostrils. And then hunger, as it must, takes over. She plunges her mouth into that warm bank of tuber and doesn't emerge for a good two minutes. I think I can feel each of her senses prickling back into life. She never notices the fork I have proffered, and even I am hard pressed to notice, for I am too busy planning her next meals. Smoked herring and pickled eels at Billingsgate . . . roasted chestnuts from the Lambeth market . . . one of Mary Catherine's famous Christmas cakes, with the currants and candied orange peel and the breath of brandy in each bite. . . .

But there will be time enough for that later. For now, I am content to watch her eat this potato, piece by piece, and chase it down with gargles of ginger beer.

Around us: Covent Garden Market, all joints and jaws. The squawks of
the costers, the brays of the donkeys, squeaking shoes and squealing children
and tipped-over waggons and the haggling murmurs of gentlefolk—none of
it subdued in any way by the day's ceaseless drizzle, which freezes as it strikes
the cobblestones. The only stationary point is a silent man ten yards off,
encased in an advertising placard for the Christmas pantomime at Theatre
Royal. He is grimly dedicated to his profession. Two boys Colin's age have
already given the man a kick in the hindboard, and yet he stands, frowning
and rigid, ever so slowly resolving into ice.

How can his vigil, though, compare with young Colin's? Having already
pocketed his pound, and a few shillings' surcharge, he abides with us still. No
explanation has been tendered, and a credulous soul might suppose it was
loyalty to me that keeps him here, but the evidence points in other directions.
Look, if you please, at the impatient arcs he sketches round the girl's indif-
ferent person. Watch him repeatedly tear the cap off his head and put it right
back on. Listen to his apologetic mumbling, directed, one might think, at
anyone other than the intended object:

—See here. Hope you know. Scarf 'n' all. Strictly business. No harm
meant.

And the only face Philomela turns on him is a blank one—the look a baby
might give a large dog poking its head into the bassinet. For poor Colin, this
is just an invitation to more locomotion. He whirls on his toes, scuffs his
heels in the dirt, and swings his hat in fidgety circles, as if marching in a
sulky and invisible regiment. It's enough, finally, to make me tap him on the
shoulder and say:

—Colin, I think our young friend might still be hungry. Do you think you
could fetch us some pease porridge?

His lips draw back from his teeth.

—I ain't your bloody servant.

—I know it well.

—I don't fetch for nobody. In case you forgot, old brown son, I'm an
artiste.

—Of course you are. And just wait until Mrs. Sharpe's girls get a glimpse of your art tomorrow night.

This reminder of his prospects must stir him down to his tiny loins, for in response, he squares his shoulders, thrusts out his chest, and hurls himself into the market throng. Claws his way past an orange merchant, nearly upends a turnip vendor, pauses only long enough to ascertain that we are still where he left us before charging on.

As oblivious of his departure as she was of his presence, Philomela tears off a strip of potato skin and lowers it suspensefully into her mouth. Then another strip, and another. How good it must taste. No potato, I think, ever aroused such gratitude in its consumer or went to its end more gratefully.

I am grateful myself. Her raptness allows me to study her in profile, the way a sidewalk artist might. The long, slightly arched, womanly nose and the hard, almost mannish chin: two parents happily conjoined, with almost nothing left of girl save for the round, brown, exuberantly lashed eyes and that sleek young skin, darker than its English counterpart but with a clarity and creaminess all its own. No wonder Colin can't see straight.

Which makes it all the more incumbent on me to see straight, or at least true. And so I find myself craving not romance but fact, some shard of hard knowledge to drive into this still life.

—Philomela. I don't know a word of your language, I'm afraid, so we are left with mine. If I were to ask you questions, do you think you might be able to answer? Do you . . . can you even understand what I am saying now?

The chewing stops; the eyes retreat; the face hardens. And here I was thinking we had already surmounted our barrier, but no, this is the real barrier, and it has less to do with comprehension than apprehension. Once she answers the first question, who knows how many more may be in the offing?

The seconds pass, the sleet turns to cold feathery rain, the shoving and squawking carry on unmodulated around us, and yet I feel the two of us becoming more and more isolated, as if the noise were calling down a mantle of silence over us.

And then she nods. Curtly but unequivocally, she nods.

I understand.

—Very well, then. Can you tell me how old you are?

—I am . . . I am ten years.

—And how long have you been here? In London?

She considers a moment, then holds up one of her hands. The fingers spring out like quills.

—Five? Do you mean five *weeks?* Five . . .

—Months.

That *th* sound slides away, leaving a tapering sibilance. Unsatisfied, she repeats it: *Months.*

—And your father . . . Signor Rotunno . . . how did he die?

She looks at me as though waiting for something more. I start again.

—How did—

—Sick. On boat sick. More sick here.

The advantage of speaking tragedy in a foreign language. One concentrates only on the pronunciation. Everything else flies to the back of the brain.

—When did he pass on, Philomela?

—When . . . ?

—Did he die when you arrived? Did he—

—No-vem-ber.

—Just in the last month?

She nods.

—My father died, too, I say.—Six months past.

She frowns a little, absorbing this intelligence. I can't be sure whether it's some spark of sympathy catching inside her or a lingering distrust. She purses her lips and, in a risibly solemn tone, asks:

—His trade?

—Oh, what was his trade? He was a clerk, actually, all his life. He worked in an office. A changing house.

Clerk in a changing house. As though that were all one could say of a man. And indeed, the very sparseness of the description compels me to add more.

—He was very kind. A good man. Was your father a good man?

Another nod, this one slightly aggrieved.

—And he made frames, is that right?

—For the painting. Lovely.

—Did he leave any behind?

She shakes her head.

—And when he died, you were alone? No mother?

Again she shakes her head, more slowly this time.

—I don't . . . she dead when I . . . all dead. . . .

—When you were born?

A nod.

—And there was no one else to take you in? No other family?

—Family Calabria, not . . .

Her voice trails away. Her eyes drift back to that last patch of potato skin, now resting in her palm. To eat or not to eat?

She eats. Claps it into her mouth and lets the earthy undertaste evaporate down her throat, waft into the far reaches of her sinuses. A serene sadness settles over her—a silent obituary notice for that lost tuber.

—Philomela, when I saw you—when I *first* saw you, the other night—you were running. What were you running from?

—River. . . .

—No, no, two nights before that.

—I see you river.

Something so odd, so mulish about her tone. Doesn't want even to acknowledge the possibility of our having met previously.

—It was two nights before, Philomela. You were hiding. Under a tarpaulin.

No response.

—You were running.

Once again I pump my arms in a furious pantomime, but it's not amusement I inspire this time but choler. A head of steam rises inside her. I can see all the signs: the twitching chin, the tightening shoulders, the fingers of her right hand closing and unclosing. With a detached fascination, I wait for the scalding bath of her rage.

—I see you river.

And there we will leave it. That is what she is truly saying. *One more brazen wall, Mr. Timothy.*

Carefully, I fold the potato's old wrapping into a small, compact square. I smooth the section of bench that separates us.

—Philomela, tell me what happened after your father died.

She gives her shoulder an irritable jerk.

—Was there a funeral?

—A little.

—Did you . . . who paid for the burial?

—People.

—Which people?

—The next door.

—Your neighbours?

—Yes.

—And they weren't able to take you in?

A slight softening here. The memory seems to be at work inside her.

—For day. Two day. But poor.

—And what happened after that?

My eyes have now left her face entirely. Untethered, they range freely through the crowd, taking in clowns and conjurers, blacking sellers and umbrella menders, before coming to rest once more on that godforsaken boardman, rusted in place, glistening like bronze.

I hear her say:

—Man come.

The voice different, yes. Quieter.

—What kind of man?

Silence.

—Did he have a trade?

I steal my eyes back towards her in time to see the vigorous, almost distasteful shaking of her head.

No. Nothing so honourable as a trade.

My mind meanders back to our meeting by the river, to the shudder, the instinctive recoil my appearance produced in her. Not a reaction to our earlier encounter as I then believed, but a visceral response, an involuntary chain of association.

—Did he look like me, Philomela?

She rubs her hands together slowly.

—Dress like you.

—How so?

—He have hat, big hat. Boots like you.

Her eyes dart towards my feet, and a streak of amusement creases her brow.

—More nicer boots.

—And what did this man say to you?

—He say you come. . . .

A large bubble of air ripples down her throat. She clamps a hand across her mouth, and whatever it is that has surged up inside her subsides through the sheer force of her breathing, which seems to issue through every pore of her face.

—It's all right, Philomela. We don't have to speak of it any more at present.

Her hand fidgets inside her apron, and for a half-crazed moment, I think she intends to pay me for the food—in fistfuls of copper nails—but what actually emerges is a string of black and white wooden beads, badly chapped and in one section virtually crushed.

—Gor! Why don't she wear 'em round her neck like a normal gal?

So absorbed have I been in our conversation that I have failed to note the return of Colin the Melodious, clutching his bundle closer in mild alarm.

—And what the hell's she *squeezin'* 'em for?

—They're rosary beads, Colin. For praying. Roman Catholics use them.

—Well, it ain't bloody Sunday, is it?

—No, it's not. Some people pray every day of the week.

—Waste o' good air, you ask me. Here, Filly, they was out of porridge, so I got us some pasties.

With a lack of ceremony that may be deliberate, he drops one of his prizes into the trammel of her apron. His reward is a glare of such magnitude as to force him back a pace. He turns an incredulous eye on me.

—Don't they eat pasties in Africa?

—*Italy*, Colin. Italy is in Europe.

—Same difference to me, I'm sure.

We're all of us rather peckish, it turns out. For the next few minutes, we do nothing but eat, verily *brooding* over our viscous pasties, worrying them down like beggars. Philomela, not surprisingly, is soonest done, and as she waits for us to catch up, she undergoes a subtle alchemical change. The girl by the Hungerford Pier reemerges, in all her withering independence. Folding her mouth downward, she jabs me in the lapel.

—Trade.

Even with his mouth full, Colin is ready with an answer:

—Rooster. In a henhouse.

On the whole, "rooster" strikes me as a rather flattering term for it.

—What sort name Teem-thee?

—Well, that's my Christian name. My surname is Cratchit.

—Kra-shit.

—Mm. Perhaps we should stay with Christian names for now.

—Fine idea, says Colin.

Her pasty consumed, Philomela clasps her hands in her lap and looks expectantly around, as though she had arranged this very spot for her next appointment. Around her mouth a thin necklace of crumbs has formed, mysteriously troubling—I have to resist the urge to wipe her mouth clean.

—Philomela, do you have any notion of where you're bound? Or what your . . . your *object* in life may be?

She looks at me.

—I am get by.

—Yes, but you might get by a little easier if you accepted help, you know. If you . . . well, if you came back with me, for instance.

Even as I say it, I gird myself for the recoil. Surely, surely she will pick up and run, halfway back to Italy if need be, so appalled must she be at the very suggestion. And yet there is no hint of revulsion in her face. No response of any kind, in fact.

—I don't mean with *me*, exactly, but you could always stay with Mary Catherine, she's the maid, and I know she has a cot free, and no one would bother you. And then, once you were all settled in, we might, you know, we might think about . . .

About what?

This, finally, is what stops me: the thin gruel of possibilities.

The workhouse. The poor-law school. The training school. An obliging orphanage in Seven Dials or, God help her, some charitable institution with rope-necked spinsters ready to beat Christ into her from sunup to sundown. And all to the end of making her a dressmaker's apprentice by fourteen, so she can pull half that many shillings a week and watch gay ladies rake in twenty quid. How long then? How long before Philomela joins the troop of rouged dollymops catching soldiers' eyes outside Knightsbridge Music Hall, soliciting teen-age boys in Grosvenor Place? Hauled up by the police twice a year . . . treated for the clap once a month at the local infirmary. . . .

I rub my hands, briskly.

—Well, we have time to decide all that, don't we? But for now, we need to put you in the way of food and clothes.

—I have food close.

—Not enough, surely.

—I have food close.

—We can also give you a roof over your head. So you won't freeze to death.

She is so impassive now I think perhaps she is already freezing to death, degree by degree. Colin may be of the same mind, for he leaps to his feet and yowls straight into her face:

—Come, Filly, don't be a daft bitch! Can't you see he's ready to piss money on you? I'm tellin' you, it's a fuckin' entre-pre-noorial opportunity!

The girl's nostrils flare open as her head whips towards mine.

—What he say?

—Nothing worth attending to. Listen to me, Philomela. This is the last time of asking. You may come with us, or you may go your own way. The decision is entirely yours.

In later days, perhaps, I will wonder what it was that swayed her to our side. I will wonder if it was the sincerity of my expression or the violence of Colin's outburst or perhaps just the prevailing weather. But for now, I incline towards the potato. I believe that from deep in her belly, that potato is quietly vouching for us. Because you see, I picked it with some care.

Philomela brushes the crumbs from her mouth, pats the ribbon in her hair, rewinds the scarf round her pale neck. And as she rises to her feet, everything about her conveys the same attitude: engagement without compliance. She will travel down this road a league or two; she will accept us as temporary companions; that is all.

And just to be sure I understand, she pats her apron. From its inner compartment comes a jangling of nails.

—For room. I pay you.

How we must look, our little triumvirate, travelling in a westerly procession down the Strand—three distinct nations in uneasy entente. Philomela holds back a yard, as though to express her grave reservations, and Colin strides militarily forward, gaining several yards on us only to circle back with a look of chaffing obligation. And me? I simply whirl between them, in little orbits of irrelevance. Not really a nation at all—indeed, in my spattered hat and clothes, I resemble nothing so much as those men who cluster every day by Uncle N's drawing-room fire. One more sycophant for charity, dragging along a pair of glamourously dirty children.

The climate here is altogether different from Drury Lane Garden. No drifts of mud, no patches of ice; the street-sweeping machines have been indefatigable, and even the manure has been gathered into discreet, cairnlike piles. Broughams, hansoms, the occasional coach and six . . . gentlefolk may stay gentle here.

Just past Charing Cross Hospital, we come upon a long arcade, ceilinged over with glass domes and bisected by parallel rows of toy shops from which pour great regiments of children. Elegant, almost painterly children, dressed like little bankers and tea-party hostesses, in silk hats and gleaming boots . . . and, for all that, carrying on like a brood of mudlarks, pounding on toy drums, wrestling one another over dolls and wooden horses and tin soldiers. One boy, temporarily toyless, contents himself with shrieking at the pigeons that skitter along the glass.

By unspoken agreement, we have stopped here. Colin and Philomela gaze upon their contemporaries, assimilating every line of clothing, every shape and style of artifact. At last they have found a common purpose. And how gratifying it would be to step into one of these shops and buy them something, even the littlest of somethings. But it seems to me what they most covet are the things I could never attain for them: the genial giants who hover over this scene like deities, indulging whims and adjudicating squabbles and promising to make it up to their darlings next Christmas. No, those particular items come rather dear this time of year.

—Come along now, I say.—We should be going.

I hadn't intended that we should walk the whole way. But somehow the prospect of bundling the three of us into a cab seems fantastical. Then, too, the sleet and rain have stopped for now, although what has taken their place is scarcely better for walking: a hard damp fist of wind, pressing our eyes back in their sockets. It whets itself on the corners of the buildings, then surges down the streets, centrifugal and centripetal all at once, and so human in its purpose that the creakings of the cart wheels and lampposts are like the protests of a beaten woman. As we turn one corner, my hat is nearly blown off my head. I have to clutch it against my chest and press my umbrella to my stomach and bend my torso parallel to the ground, while on either side of me Colin and Philomela assume the same angle, and together we lean into the wall of wind and drive it before us until it seems we are driving all of London. And just as London appears to be on the verge of winning, the wind dies suddenly, and we raise ourselves up and stand in the middle of the pavement, dazed and blinking and startled to find ourselves no longer alone.

The shambling, wide-eyed vision of a beggar woman has materialised before us, and the feel of the wind is still so strong in my bones that the only question she sparks in me is: From which district has she blown? Islington? Stepney?

—The blessings of the Christmas season upon you and yours, sir.

A large woman, tottering and lurching, with a wheedling way of inclining her face towards mine and a high, raspy voice whose educated vowels belong not to a beggar—my error—but to a more alarming species: the missionary.

Ah, yes. The plain white bonnet. The black woollen dress, bunching always in the most unusual places, and the hair parted brusquely in the middle and pinned back so severely that it seems to be taking the rest of her face along with it. And the Bible, of course, almost completely smothered in the recesses of her armpit.

—What a sight is this, sir! You have taken pity on an unfortunate angel, good Christian soul that you are. She is not your own, I think?

—She is no relation, no.

With an agility that surprises me, the missionary lowers herself onto her haunches until her face is level with the girl's.

—Hello, pretty pretty. We have met before. Do you recall?

If Philomela does, she's not telling.

—It was on the occasion of your dear father's funeral, remember? I said you might come with me if you liked, but you ran off, and now look at you! Soaked to the bone and ready to catch your death. When all this time you might have found a warm, toasty bed with us.

She tilts her face upwards and reveals all thirty-two of her formidable teeth.

—My manners, sir! Forgive me. I am Miss Binny, of the Bible Flower Mission. And you are . . . ?

—Mr. Cratchit. Of no affiliation.

—Ah, but you are beloved of us, surely. You have returned our little flower to us. We have been so wretched, wondering what had become of her. I don't need to tell you, we have been praying ceaselessly, and now the good Lord has seen fit to answer our prayers! And just in time for Christmas! What a gift you have bestowed upon us, sir.

She strokes the girl's hair, gathers her ringlets into tight little strands, and begins coiling them into informal braids. Philomela submits to these ministrations rather as a horse submits to being shod.

—I must tell you, Miss Binny, this strikes me as a rather sudden incursion. And since I am unfamiliar with your organisation, I can't be sure what you intend for this girl.

—Why, we offer only the word of the Lord and the company of like-minded pilgrims. We let God settle the rest.

—Yes, well, I think God has been a little off the mark lately. There are many more children where she came from.

—One soul at a time, Mr. Cratchit, one soul at a time.

I wouldn't have thought that smile could stretch much wider, but it does, crawls almost to her ears—not so much a smile any more as an unstitched wound. She rests her large hands on Philomela's shoulders.

—Would you care to come with me, pretty pretty? We've a bed already waiting just a few blocks away, and you'll find many friends your age.

For a second or two, I am convinced that Philomela is actually considering the offer. But it turns out she is simply weighing the appropriate response, which is to prise Miss Binny's hands from her shoulders—first one, then the other—fold her arms across her chest, summon the most penetrating from amongst her large retinue of frowns, and pronounce:

—I will thank you, no.

The smile leaps from Miss Binny's face. She whirls back to me.

—Oh, sir, you must reason with her. She really oughtn't to be wandering the streets like this!

—She is *not* wandering, I can attest to that. And as for accepting your kind offer, I believe she has made herself tolerably clear.

It is left to Colin to underscore the point. Stepping between Philomela and the missionary, he juts out his man-boy chest and feints a punch in the general direction of Miss Binny's head.

—Piss off, you fat cow!

The missionary falls back a step, sends me one last beseeching look and, seeing no softening in that quarter, calmly gathers her skirts. Her mouth forms itself around some parting benediction, but the words never come. She nods to us, once, then totters down the street.

And even as she rounds the corner, I am thinking: *Why did she want just Philomela? Why not Colin, too?*

And then, from my right, a faint clicking sound, like a nest of baby crickets. Philomela's rosary beads, rolling and diving in her palm, dancing themselves into exhaustion.

Chapter 10

WHAT WITH LINGERING before shop windows and buying wassail and stopping for oysters and whelks (coated in the tangiest of vinegar sauces), it is nearly four-thirty in the afternoon when we finally take the corner into Jermyn Street. The wind has blown off the fog and clouds, the sky is scarring over with pink, and Philomela is walking even with me now; for some reason, it is Colin who hangs back, slack and listless, bowing his shoulders as though some new debt were being laid on him with each step.

—Home at last, I say.

The word is out of my mouth before I have a chance to examine it. Home. *Home*.

Philomela asks:

—Which you?

—That house just down the way. Number One-eleven.

—Number . . .

—Now, you mustn't judge it by the exterior, it's more inviting inside. Some rather eccentric characters, but all quite harmless. A parrot, too. Quite an honourable fellow, almost entirely bald now. I think he must be pining for a lost love, he tears out a new feather each day on her behalf. . . .

Doubtless I could keep going, I could yammer us all the way to the doorstep, but she is no longer attending. Having already pushed several yards ahead of Colin and me, she is busy canvassing her new lodgings with a scrutiny that would amuse me if I weren't somehow implicated in it. Observe her now: sampling the native aromas, studying the character of the lamplighter, assaying the sturdiness of Mrs. Sharpe's grilles, even going so far as to inspect the contents of the alley. Who would have supposed that her previous journeys had left her with such very high standards?

—Don't know what she's bein' so snooty about, Colin mutters.—She's gettin' the place free, ain't she?

My response is swallowed up by the bells of St. James's, tolling the half hour: —*Ding dong* ping *dong. Ding dong* ping *dong.*

No matter what time of day I hear them, I am always brought up short by their cadence. One of the set has fallen out of its natural orbit and now produces a high, metallic tingling that weaves through the stentorian chimes and, in subversive fashion, undermines them.

—*Ding dong* ping *dong. Ding dong* ping *dong.*

This errant bell has been my daily, my hourly companion for the last six months. Why, then, should it have chosen this moment to create such an alien resonance in my ear? Under its spell, I feel my senses broadening in every direction, until the contents of this street become a vibration in my skin. Colin growling asides to the cobblestones. The mystical glow suffusing the head of the lamplighter. The agonised leers on the gargoyles over Mrs. Sharpe's second-storey apartments.

And something more: the flash of a black dress slipping down Regent Street and disappearing behind the brick edifice of the corner house.

Miss Binny, unless I greatly mistake. Our old friend the missionary, still bent on heavenly errands.

Some protective instinct jolts my attention straight back to Philomela. I clutch my umbrella, my lips part, I am on the brink of crying out—what? a warning? a joke at Miss Binny's expense?—but I am stopped short by the quick-rising cold front emanating from the girl. From her *eyes*, I should say, which have fixed on mine a look that would freeze a warrior's blood. Dread and anger and . . . and something else . . . a look that confirms and exceeds every awful opinion I have ever entertained about myself.

And then the front shifts once again, and Philomela is gone.

Hitching up her dress and running as fast as the wind, faster than I have yet seen her go, and jerking her arms in midflight, as though someone had fastened himself round her shoulders. Not a moment of hesitation, not a backwards look: she turns the corner and shoots down Babmaes, retracing the very trajectory in which I first witnessed her.

Colin looks at me, incredulous.

—What's got into *her*, then?

Without waiting for an answer, he takes off after her, calling as he goes:

—Here! Filly!

A blur of limbs, is our Colin, dizzying to contemplate. I do what I can to follow, but my own flight is delayed by an unexpected movement on my left flank: Mrs. Sharpe's door swinging open with a gale of vehemence, to reveal the benign figure of George, stepping onto the landing with the air of a workingman on holiday. His collar is open, his sleeves rolled up; he looks to be girding himself for an afternoon's entertainment. Which, by all appearances, is me.

—Mercy's sake, Mr. Timothy! Don't you know your own lodging?

It slows my step, that mock-jovial timbre. Even with my back to him, it drags at my ankles.

—Off again so soon? Without a word?

Waving him away with a flat hand, I hunch my shoulders and press on, but the voice follows me round the corner.

—What shall I tell the missus, Mr. Timothy?

Tell her what you bloody like. And the moment that thought escapes me—the moment he leaves my sight—George ceases to be an active concern, for I am met by a new obstruction: the stilled form of Colin. Such a shocking contrast to his normal restiveness that it is all I can do not to collide with him, and he himself is so strangely silent that he gives off an almost tangible aura of danger. Squinting over his shoulder, I make out at last the sight that has struck him dumb.

Philomela in the arms of a man.

The juxtaposition is too much at first. I'm tempted to look away, as though I have surprised a pair of lovers. But Philomela is not disposed to love, one can see that. Her fists are clenched, and her torso is writhing, and her feet scissor the air.

And her suitor, rather than pressing her body to his, is wrenching her into submission, using one arm to lock her head in place and the other to drag her in the direction of a waiting carriage. It's all too easy. He is short, yes, but strong as a warthog, densely muscled, and his black bowler hat is like a final flourish of muscle, and the only delicacy in the scene is the carriage itself: a forest-green brougham with salmon filigree, festooned with somebody's coat of arms and shuttered down like a manor in winter, except for its door, panting open.

I must run to her. And to my surprise, I find I already have. I am standing just behind Mr. Bowler . . . clapping him on the shoulder . . . using the one word that presents itself:

—No.

Even more surprising: my tone of voice. Can you hear it? Scrupulously polite. *See here, my good man, d'you think you might . . .*

And when Mr. Bowler turns to face me, he appears to be responding in kind. Such a calm air about him, as though he were patiently sorting through all the damage he might inflict on me. The tremble of a smile appears on his clean-shaven face, and with Philomela still pinioned in the crook of his arm, he reaches into his pocket and extracts a knife.

Knife is too elegant a word for it. There is no handle to it, only blade: a gleaming band of steel with two bevelled edges, stropped to a lapidary gleam. A blade such as a wood-carver might use, and when he presses it to my jugular, he has the dispassionate air of an artisan. *Where to cut first?*

The cul-de-sac is empty—save for a coachman, sitting atop the waiting carriage and looking pointedly away—and the sun is falling, and everything has been reduced to that simple question: *Where?*

And as if to complicate the inquiry, Mr. Bowler passes the blade between my neck and Philomela's. Back and forth it goes, hanging as loosely in his hand as a paintbrush, and the thrumming sound it makes as it cuts the air is enough to root me in place. Only two tasks am I capable of performing: inching my left hand towards the girl and peering into Bowler's mild hazel eyes for some sign of his intention.

And then, against all odds, those eyes jolt upwards in their sockets, and the hat sinks like a counterweight, and the next thing I'm aware of is the sound of the blade clattering on the pavement. And after that, the hat, and then the hat's owner following it to earth in a faint echo.

And standing just above me: Colin, pale and unnaturally tall.

Not on stilts, as I first imagine. He has perched himself on the axle of the carriage wheel, and grasped in his uplifted hand is my umbrella—the one I left behind in my haste—its handle now bent and shivered. And Colin's face is frozen in wonder at the feat he has just performed.

I pry the umbrella from his hand and cast it away.

—Thank you, Colin. It wasn't very expensive.

He nods and looks down, abashed.

Below us, the compliant form of Mr. Bowler awakens, rolls onto its back. The mild eyes blink at the sky. One hand reaches for the hat.

—Run! yells Colin.

I grab Philomela by the arm, but she won't budge. She is staring into the cavity of the open carriage, from which a man's head is now emerging. A long-faced, swarthy man in a silk hat, wearing on his index finger a very heavy Spanish ring of carved rose gold, with an inset emerald, large and square and perfect. I might never have noticed the finger were he not using it now to trace a line around his plump lips: a tutelary gesture, as though he were showing us how to smile.

I whisper into Philomela's ear:

—Come away.

Her limbs jerk back into life, and as we round the corner, she is running as fast as I. Colin, not surprisingly, has bested us by several yards and is looking likely to add to his lead, but then stops suddenly and turns to face us.

—I gots me an idea, he says.

Without preface, he whips off his coat and cap, flings them to the ground, and grabs hold of Philomela's cloak. For once, she is too frightened to resist, and it is only a matter of seconds before he has wrapped it round his smaller form. Then he commandeers—once again—her scarf.

—Distraction, Mr. Timothy, you sees where I'm headin'? Now you two make for the park. Me, I'll head straight back to Piccadilly.

—Colin . . .

—Christ, you think I can't outrun them bastards? Get on with you, go!

Philomela has already tucked her long hair under Colin's cap, and is looking at me with such an expectant air I haven't the strength to protest. Colin draws the hood of her cloak over his head, gives us a quick salute, and then dashes in the direction of Regent Street. Some proprietary part of me wants to follow, but then Philomela lays hold of my arm—a surprisingly gentle touch, given the circumstances—and that's all it requires to send us running down Jermyn Street. Or at least, Philomela is running, and I am doing my best approximation: flinging the good leg as far as it will go and then letting the right leg dance lightly on the sidewalk before pushing once more onto the left. Such is the adaptability of the human body, that the motion begins to feel natural, acquires even a pleasing rhythm, and as we turn the corner into Duke Street, I have forgotten why we are running, so absorbed am I in my art, and then out of the corner of my eye, I see a pair of bays emerging from Babmaes Street and a green carriage following close behind, and the vista before me dissolves, and I am back in my dream, the dream of Philomela in flight, except it's the two of us now, chased by talons, dwarfed by blue shadow.

Night is falling with an unreasonable haste. The winter solstice has sucked away the light, and the streets have emptied out as though in preparation for a plague.

The girl glances at me over her shoulder.

—Go on, Philomela. I'll catch up to you.

Her English must fail her, for she insists on measuring her steps to mine. Her nostrils flare, and her hair, no longer bound by the cap, streams behind her like a ministering cloud, and I think she is in her element now, secure in her body and all its evasive powers.

We sprint past a livery stable, past corniced homes lit with twinkling candles—each home, perhaps, a refuge, but for how long? How long before Bowler and his master discover Colin's ruse? And how long before they find *us*, pounding on someone's door, begging to be let in?

No, it's crowds we want. Someplace that will swallow our scents.

And then, through the gloaming, a small, freshly painted signpost appears: The Lion's Paw. Grabbing Philomela by the elbow, I push through the heavy, tawny door, staggering a little before the wall of pipe smoke that greets us: the accumulated exhalations of perhaps two dozen men—professionals, mostly, sublunaries of the banking and mercantile worlds, conjoined with a few mangy journalists, their moustaches wilting beneath ale froth.

How must we look, Philomela and I, tumbling through that door? Arriving from two different stations, as it were, both of us damp to the bone, swallowing roomfuls of air.

It doesn't matter. These are English gentlemen. They look away as soon as they see us.

—Excuse me, sir.

From behind the horseshoe-shaped, zinc-topped counter, a bald publican regards us with a cast eye.

—Afraid we don't serve females in the taproom, sir. Perhaps you'd care to step into the lounge.

—Would you tell me, please, where we might find a constable?

—Why, you need only wait a few minutes. It's Hugh's custom to stop in once he's off duty.

—Thank you.

Cozy sort of place, the lounge. Under better circumstances, I might be more receptive to its charms: casks and cordial bottles and beer-pulls. A parson's table on which sits a copy of the *London Illustrated News*, and by the hearth, a three-paneled screen, seared with soot. The Windsor chairs are wobbly but adequate, and the only sounds in the room are the fire's sputtering and our own breathing.

Reassured now, I collapse into one of the chairs and stare into the flames, and as my breathing subsides, a single question buzzes through my head:

Why, Philomela?

And upon closer inspection, the question turns out to be many questions.

Why did you run in the first place, before you ever saw the green carriage? You had already suffered Miss Binny once today; seeing her again shouldn't have put you out of countenance. And truth be told, you weren't even attending to her, you were looking at me. And with such an expression! What have I ever done to deserve *that*, Philomela?

And that man in the carriage, making that gesture with his finger—more intimate than anything a stranger would venture—what was it about him that stopped you in your tracks? You *know* him, don't you?

But perhaps I should be posing myself the same question. For the strangest thing of all, Philomela, is this: I know him, too.

The face, at least, with its dark skin and heavy lips, its air of calculated youth. I know for a certainty I have seen that face. The only thing I don't know is *where*.

Ten minutes later, the potboy has brought a hot rum for me, hard cider for the girl. We blow away the steam from our half-pint pots, and as the boy pushes back through the half-door, I hear, above the din of the adjoining room, the publican's voice rising clear:

—Sorry, sir, didn't quite catch that.

And then an answering voice, equally distinct:

—I said Deputy Inspector Rollins, from Scotland Yard.

I'm on my feet in a flash, peering over the doorsill. Through the tendrils of smoke, I can just make out the gleaming dome of the publican, saying:

—Off duty, too, eh? Why is it every officer who comes in my pub is off duty? Yes, it was a gentleman and a young miss, stopped in a little while back.

The man he's talking to is hidden from my sight, an obstreperous bagatelle player having blocked the view. All that filters back is his voice, low and pleasant and businesslike, kicking over the traces of old working-class vowels:

—Just the pair I was looking for, the man says.

And as if on command, the bagatelle player leans over to address his next ball, and the way to the bar is clear now, and I see, in perfect profile, the bulky pair of shoulders, the ring of solid neck . . . and the black bowler hat, clamped even more securely onto the head.

And as I leap back towards the fire, I hear the publican remark:

—Odd, they were *asking* for a constable.

I grab Philomela by the arm, put a finger to my lips.

—No, sir, they're still here. I told 'em to wait till Hugh stopped in.

I snatch up the *Illustrated News* and lower it into the fire.

—Oh, I put 'em in the lounge. We don't serve ladies in the taproom.

The embers are dull. I have to shove the paper deeper into the fireplace, and still it won't catch.

—It's just down and to the . . . never mind, I'll take you there.

At last. A flicker and then a flare, and the newspaper becomes a torch. I drop it, still flaming, next to the fire screen. I reach for Philomela's hand, and we dance across the doorway, flattening ourselves against the wall on the other side.

A second later, the publican pokes his bald head round the door frame. The nostrils twitch, and the head swivels towards the hearth, where even now the *London Illustrated News* is sending rivers of flame to the ceiling.

—Awww! Gawd!

Groaning, he flings himself at the miniature bonfire, stamping it down as fiercely as Rumpelstiltskin. Ashes coat his boots and trousers, and flaming shreds of paper fly into his face and hair; he claws them away, groans some more, stamps some more. Quite a little spectacle, all told, and we're not the only witnesses. Mr. Bowler—Deputy Inspector Bowler—is watching, too, his back turned to us, his head so close I could knock off his hat with a single blow.

A second passes; another. I can feel Philomela drawing in her breath.

And then Bowler takes a step towards the fire screen. And then another. And I realise, with a jolt of relief, that he thinks we're on the other side.

Pantherlike he approaches, treading on the balls of his feet, and just as his head peers round the screen, I grab Philomela, and the two of us go flying through the half-door. Bowler whips round, and then he is lost in a sea of bodies, for we have plunged into the heart of the Lion's Paw populace, and our heads are lowered and our elbows are out, and we are hacking a path to the door.

Recoiling heads, loud remonstrances. A dart whistles past my ear, a glass of ale splashes down the back of my coat. I slip under someone's arm and barrel through someone else's, knocking its owner against the bar.

—Steady on, then!

But I'm already clearing away the next obstruction. A shove here, a side-step there, and now we're almost at the door, I can see Philomela reaching for the handle . . . slowly, too slowly . . . I'm egging her on, I'm screaming in her ear—*Turn!*—and then, from nowhere, a new obstacle appears: a pale, bleary-eyed man in a torn jacket, swaying across our path, cutting off our escape.

—Buy us a gin, chappie. They've cut us off.

He folds me round in a clumsy embrace, moans in my ear like a mistress.

—It's *criminal* how they treat us here.

I try to scrape him off, but he seems to grow new arms, and each one clutches more desperately than the last.

—Just the one. I'll go home then, I swear. . . .

From behind me comes a stentorian cry, the voice of officialdom:

—Stop that man! He's wanted by the police!

The bleary-eyed man swings his head round.

—No, I ain't!

His hands form a protective phalanx even as the rest of him goes limp, and when I shove him from behind, he flies even farther than I dared hope, right into the protesting arms of Deputy Inspector Bowler. Down they go, in a thrashing jumble, and as I wrench open the door, I see the man hanging on to Bowler's legs like ballast.

—Buy us a gin, mate. . . . We'll go quiet. . . .

We fly down Duke Street at twice our natural speed. I wouldn't have thought it possible, but the image of that blade, bevelled and honed to a fare-thee-well, is all the spur we need. The buildings pull back, the pavement broadens, and it doesn't even feel like London any more; we seem to be running once again into the old dream. But then up in the distance, I see King William astride his bronze horse, frozen in the act of tripping over a mole-hill. And I know then where we are: St. James's Square.

The very opposite of a crowd. Here are private town houses with pedimented windows and decorative pilasters, all set back behind wrought-iron battlements. Earls and dukes and marquesses live here. The Army and Navy Club, the Bishop of Winchester's home. A great big advertisement for gentility.

And we're on the wrong side of it.

Chased by a Scotland Yard inspector, a peer of the realm . . . it's easy to see where St. James would align its sympathies. And, indeed, as we tear across the square, it feels like enemy terrain: every house, every passing carriage seems to bear down on us. Even William III spins his bronze head round to track us with his falcon eye.

It's all too much. I grab Philomela's hand, and we swerve into Charles II Street, and when I look back I can see Bowler's compact figure perhaps fifty yards off, moving as inexorably as a cannonball, and just as I prepare to accelerate, a new hurdle rises in our path: a large frame hung with green baize, capped by a tiny proscenium bearing a letter cloth—"Punch's Opera," and standing to one side, a man in a many-caped blue coat and a limp old beaver hat, already shaking his head.

—Very sorry, sir, done for the day. Must be home to the missus.

—No, it's not . . . we're . . .

Words fail, don't they? They *flail*.

I lift the baize curtain of the puppet box and motion Philomela inside, as if it were the most natural thing in the world. The puppetmaster's hand slams down on my shoulder.

—Here! Do I look like a bloody hotel?

—There's twenty shillings in it for you.

—Don't matter if it's twenty quid, I don't let no one play with my happyratus.

What would Colin do?

And simply asking myself that question produces the metamorphosis. I whip off my hat, give the man a wink, and in my best Cockney approximation, whisper:

—The peelers is after us!

—Jesus, whyn't you say so?

He shoves me inside, pulls the curtain closed.

—Mind you stand on the footboard, he says.—And keep the feet longways, now. You'll be seen otherwise.

There's not enough room for the both of us, so I must clasp Philomela round the waist and lift her off the ground. It's a hard thing to do when you're gasping for air. Between us, our chests swell so violently I think the entire booth must be billowing.

We hear the footsteps first, decelerating slowly, and then a soft, interrogatory grunt.

And then the puppetmaster's voice, saying:

—Very sorry, sir, done for the day.

Bowler sounds barely winded when he speaks. The working-class vowels have reasserted themselves, and the tone is intimate and confiding: he's undergone his own metamorphosis.

—Yeah, mate, sorry to interrupt. I'm looking for this young bloke, twenty-two, maybe. With a young gal. They was headed this way.

—Hain't seen no one like that, Officer.

A pause; a soft chuckle.

—Oh, no, mate, it ain't like that. See, they peached something from a friend of mine, I'm just trying to get it back for him.

—Have it your way, Officer.

Another pause. And the voice, when it comes back, is a little harder.

—A gentleman and a young girl. You must've seen them.

—We hain't seen nobody 'ceptin' yourself, has we, Punch?

Followed by a high, screeching call:

—Nooy-ey, nooy-ey!

I'd cede a fair amount of my life's income to see the deputy inspector's face right now, but his voice never wavers.

—Listen, mate, there's a reward in it for you.

And there it is. The one word I most feared. *Reward.*

My hands tense round Philomela's waist; my stomach screws itself into a ball. Any second now, those curtains will be torn open, and that will be all, won't it? Every escape route closed off. Destiny bearing down. . . .

And then I hear the puppetmaster say:

—A reward, is it? Well, in that case, ladies and gents, they went that way.

I can't see, but from the tone of his voice, I'm almost positive he is pointing in opposite directions.

We wait there in the darkness, our breath stopped, our ears primed for the sound of travelling feet.

And before long, that sound does come, or at least something close to it. And after it the puppetmaster's voice, murmuring in the night:

—He's gone, but give it a minute.

In fact, it is two or three minutes before the curtain opens once again to reveal our benefactor, extending his hand to Philomela. He helps her back onto the sidewalk, then turns to me.

—Your accent needs work, mate.

I grope through my pockets, I say:

—Let me . . . let me. . . .

He puts out a hand to stop me.

—Just tell me. Did you really pinch anythink?

—No.

—He really a peeler?

—I don't know.

He nods.

—Well, you take good care of yourself, young miss. And a merry Christmas to you both.

Ten minutes later, we are making our way up Regent Street, relieved to feel the familiar press of bodies, London's black-suited throngs squeezing us back into anonymity. But for all that, we are not so anonymous as to escape a tap on our shoulders just shy of Piccadilly.

—Mr. Timothy!

Philomela's cloak hangs rather loosely on Colin now, but her scarf is still wrapped round his neck, and there is about him a barely concealed air of triumph.

—I give 'em a good chase, Mr. Timothy. The coach was a-followin' me a good three blocks, I thought I had 'em, and then the damn cloak catches on a hitching post—ripped a bit, sorry, Filly—and Bowler Boy there, why, he jumps right out, don't he? Hoofs it the other way, so I run back, but I can't find no trace of you, not till now, anyways, so you gave him the shake, did you, there's a treat, and you didn't let him fillet you, there's a good fellow.

—We're fine, yes. Now if you'll help me escort Philomela back to Mrs. Sharpe's . . .

Colin frowns, falls back a step.

—Oh, I wouldn't be in too big a hurry on that score, Mr. Timothy.

—Why not?

—Well, he were just knockin' on Mrs. Sharpe's door, weren't he?

—Who?

—Bowler Boy, who else? Prob'ly been makin' the rounds of the whole bloody neighbourhood. "You seen so an' so?" "*You* seen so an' so?" It were only a matter of time 'fore he got to yours.

Of course: one would expect no less from a dedicated emissary of Scotland Yard. And one could depend on no end of cooperation from the local citizenry.

—Colin, tell me. Who was it answered the door?

—Well, it were hard to see, Mr. Timothy, bein' at pains to stay out of eyeshot and all.

—Man or woman?

—Man. That much I can say. Bit bald, maybe. Oh, and had his sleeves rolled up, real casual like.

George.

I see him now as I last saw him, on Mrs. Sharpe's front stoop, with his middle-class ease, his submerged glee . . . and lying just behind, a bland hostility, ponderously deep. Who more likely to assist the police in their inquiries?

Colin claps me on the arm.

—Don't trouble yourself, Mr. Timothy. Who's to say they'll even recognise you from the description?

—All the same, I think this young lady here will be wanting a new place to stay.

With his index finger, Colin gives my sleeve a caressing stroke.

—And a certain young hero will be wantin' a raise in his salary. Retroactive, like.

Chapter 11

A FLEET OF COAL BARGES is moored at its base, but these days, Craven Street, the Strand, belongs to the law. The limestone fronts wear their attorneys' shingles like so many lesions. Houses that once harboured wood-carvers and poets and doctors are now devoted to the promulgation of paper, more paper, and more paper still—a constipation relieved only by the periodic effluence of barristers carrying their hard-earned paper in bursting octavos as they hustle over to Lincoln's Inn in search of new trade.

At night, though, the buzzing paper factories fall silent, and the buildings empty out into tall and imposing shells, and it becomes all the stranger to find, halfway up the block, this two-storey hunchback, gasping for air, stunted and squeezed by the terraced fronts and, for all that, curiously hardy—a gnarled cypress that finds its own way to the light and promises to outlast all its companions.

Perhaps this abiding quality is what infuses Colin's voice with such respect when he first beholds the place.

—A right shitheap, ain't it?

Hard to quibble there. The knocker swings off its screw, the windows sag in their frames, the walls go concave or convex according to whim—we might as well be back in Drury Lane. And when we open the front door, five shrieking cats burst upon us, slip through our legs, and scatter into the street like minions of Chaos. I smile a little to think that tomorrow, these creatures will be invading some attorney's office, knocking over inkwells, befouling foolscap. Still, I can't be too happy about the prospect, for these same cats are the bane of Captain Gully's existence.

The house, you see, is owned by a corpulent spinster who has dedicated her life to felines and whose daily mission it is to add one new member to her collection. As a consequence, cats do not overrun this place so much as they bleed from every pore of it. Squeezing through the railings, swarming along the gutters, leaping from door lintels, copulating on the landings and in the stairwells—there's not a floor, wall, or ceiling they haven't colonised in some way. Such is their artfulness they can even penetrate the closely guarded fortress of Gully's upstairs flat.

—Don't understand it, Tim, he once lamented to me.—Gully keeps the door closed, stops up the holes in the floorboards, jams the windows shut . . . they gets in all the same! It's diabolic. And don't you think they *knows* how Gully gets to sneezin' round them? Sneezin' his brain halfway out his head? Why, they makes sure to pass under his nose every time, and as soon as he's done with one fit, they makes one more pass and starts another. Instruments of Lucifer, Tim, sure as I breathe.

It is said that every man needs a vocation, and this, I fear, is Gully's: defending his person from the daily—hourly—onslaught of cats. I have seen him sprinkle gunpowder under the door, pour pools of tar along the windowsill. I have seen him hang dummy kitties from the ceiling. Nothing works. The cats keep coming, and Gully takes up his vocation with an urgency that verges at times on the monomaniacal.

Tonight, for instance, he answers our knock by throwing open his door and roaring into the hallway, all five feet of him. Arms swinging, eyes bulging, he looks ready to seize us by our tails and hurl us to Lambeth Palace.

—It's Tim, Captain. I've brought a couple of friends.

He passes his hand across his eyes.

—Tim. 'Course, it's Tim. Well, come in, then. Quick, before they notices.

Ushering us inside, he makes one last reconnaissance of the hallway, then slams the door after him. And for another full minute, he is still and silent, his ears pricked for the slightest whisper of paw on wood.

—Aye, they're gone.

Mindful now of his hostly duties, he claps his hands together and beams all around.

—Well, ain't we pleased as punch, havin' company in this blessed holiday season? Sorry, place is a bit of a stable, as you can see, and we don't have much for the young 'uns, but we can spot you some Madeira, Tim, if you're agreeable.

Freed for the moment of his vocation, he hums a scrap of carol to himself as he wraps his box wrench around a well-handled cork and pops it free. I hear Colin murmur:

—Most buggered excuse for a hook I never saw.

At once, the humming grows louder and more confident, erupting now and then into fits of language: *Herald . . . glory . . . born king*. Gully's head rocks back and forth, his foot keeps the beat, the box wrench follows in time. *Mercy . . . sinners . . . recon— . . . joyful*.

And then, in a burst of combustion, a blur of calico streaks past him, so blinding in its speed it spins Gully round like a top.

—Aaaahh!

He raises a fist to the sky.

—D'you see? D'you *see*? Where'd he fuckin' come from, eh? Bloody fan-*tooms* is what they . . . what they . . .

The rest is lost in a titanic sneeze, a sound so ferocious it sets the whole house to rattling, and it seems to rattle Gully, too, for he forgets that one of the glasses is mine and promptly drains it, then the other. Collapses into his chair and closes his eyes, as though there were no one else present.

—Fiends, he mutters.—Devil's issue.

—Philomela, come meet Captain Gully.

Small wonder she is apprehensive. Has to be dragged part of the way. Doesn't quite know whether she should curtsy or kneel. Compromises by lowering herself onto her haunches and giving her host a curt half-nod.

—Captain, I say.—I would appreciate very much if you would put this girl up for the next few days.

His face opens into a mask of remonstrance.

—Days, Tim? *Days?*

—Not so very long, I promise you.

—But we—you see, we're a bit cramped as we are, Tim.

—I understand, Captain, and I should have been glad to keep her with me, but I'm afraid there were some men lying in wait for us near Jermyn Street.

—Men?

—Rather sinister men, Captain. Who may well know by now exactly where I live.

His brows converge. He leans into my ear, speaks in a stage whisper.

—She some kind o' criminal, Tim?

—No, Captain. Just an orphan.

—Not one o' them Belgian girls, is she?

—Italian, actually. Which does make conversing with her a trifle sticky, but I'm expecting to bring in a translator tomorrow.

—An' she won't steal nothin', will she?

—If anything, she'll offer you all her copper nails.

He nods, then raises himself to his full height and fixes Philomela with an interrogatory stare.

—See here, young miss. Has you ever been to Majorca?

Whether it is the name itself or his tone of voice that flummoxes her, I cannot say, but she takes some time before shaking her head. And Gully, far from accepting this denial, appears to find in it some positive assertion of the highest order. For he winks at her and nods very slowly and says:

—Ahh. Ahh.

And then he is thrown back in his chair as a screeching blur of orange flies up his front and vanishes over the top of his head.

—We'll skin you from head to tail! Just try us if you don't believe it!

The girl is up on her feet now, not in alarm, as I first think, but only to survey her surroundings. The Dutch clock and the tiny coal scuttle and the teetering column of atlases. (The captain these days travels mostly by armchair.) And there, over the door, a bedraggled rope of privet—Gully's best approximation of mistletoe. I believe she is even smiling a little by the time she sees that.

I touch her on the shoulder.

—Do you think you would mind staying here for a few nights? Until we can find you something more permanent?

She makes a second perusal of the privet, considers a while longer, then says:

—I was having the cat once.

To which Captain Gully mutters:

—Cats, my eye. Spawns of Beelzebub, that's what.

—And perhaps tomorrow we can talk about those men, I say.—The ones who were chasing you.

How familiar it is already, this closing down of her face, like a bank on holiday. *Come Again Tuesday.* But rather than sending me on my way, it makes me want to rap on the glass.

—You must tell us who they were, Philomela.

Nothing.

—Were they with the police? What did they want from you?

More silence. Deeper silence. And behind me, Gully's voice, softened.

—Leave the bitty thing alone, Tim. She's done in, we're sure of it. My dear . . .

He cups a hand to his mouth, until his already penetrating voice is cannonading off the walls.

—*Would you care for a bit of washy-washy?*

At a loss, she whirls back to me.

—He means a bath, Philomela.

To this she consents. Within a minute, Gully has set the water to heating, and he and Colin have dragged up a washtub and placed it behind the fireplace screen (only briefly arrested in their labour by a tortoiseshell thunderbolt). Looking dazed and fatalistic, Philomela disappears behind the screen. We hear a brief dappling sound and then a wholehearted plunge, followed by the smallest of exhalations. And then nothing for a good ten minutes but hands ladling water, and then only silence. And when our calls go unanswered, Gully, peeking round the screen, finds the girl asleep in her bath, head lolling against her arm, hair spilling over her shoulder.

Between the two of us, the captain and I manage to lift her from the bath, dry her off, and wrap a couple of blankets around her, and then, with Colin's help, we lay her on Gully's turnup bedstead. She makes barely a stir, opens her eyes only to close them again. And as soon as she is prone, she rolls over on her side, draws her knees up to her chest, and drops back into sleep.

Colin gives a whistle.

—She *were* a bit knackered, weren't she?

—'Course she was, wee poppet. Now, Tim, don't you go a-frettin' on Gully's account. The chair's bed enough for us. Many's the night we've slept in it, anyways. Reminds us of some of our old berths, it does.

He stops himself in the act of throwing another blanket over Philomela.

—Something wrong, Captain?

—No. No, indeed, Tim. It's just she looks very like the gal Gully left behind in Majorca. We've told you 'bout her, ain't we? Drambusca was her name. A few years older than this one, but built along the same planes, no mistake.

And where is Drambusca now? I wonder. Longing for Gully as he for her? Chasing little Drambuscas through the olive groves? It matters not, she dwells forever in the captain's heart. Still unravished bride of time, as the poet says.

—Have no fear, Tim. Anyone so much as tries to board this little ship, they'll get themselves a broadside from yours truly, make no mistake.

He punctuates this with the fiercest of glowers, which expands to include Colin.

—See here, young fellow, we don't want no beasts of hell a-wakin' this girl afore she's ready, now do we?

—S'pose not.

—What say you and Gully goes on a cat expedition?

—Can I keep one if I catches it?

—You can keep 'em all, lad, God shield you. Kill 'em, too, while you're at it.

They close the door behind them. A minute later, I hear the muffled howls of Gully's quarry, the scraping of claws and shoes on wood, and the ostinato of the good captain's voice, calling down a lifetime's worth of oaths. And it may be the instinctive need for counterpoint that draws the song from my mouth, and places it in a lower octave than I was once used to hearing it. Something, something about this new register transforms the music, so that it becomes as remote in my mind as Majorca.

> *O, slumber my darling, thy sire is a knight,*
> *Thy mother's a lady so lovely and bright;*
> *The hills and the dales, and the tow'rs which you see,*
> *They all shall belong, my dear creature, to thee.*

—Not bad, says Colin. Bit sharp on that last note.

—Oh.

My face is still smouldering as I walk to the window.

—Something my mother used to sing, I say. Some years back.

—She about, your mum?

—No.

—Dad?

—Gone, too.

—Huh. Wish mine was. Always turnin' up when you least wants him. Mr. Badpenny, I calls him.

—We'll talk again tomorrow, Colin.

—Oh, yes. Regardin' the dress for this here whorefest at which I am to shine—

—Here's some money. Find something suitable.

—Squeeze out another pound, it'll be even more suitable.

—Good night, Colin.

—Good night, then.

The door closes softly after him, and with him goes most of the sound. Nothing beyond the final protest of a cat in the distance, and the captain's low humming as he pours himself another glass of Madeira, and the patient respiration of the Dutch clock.

As good a time as any, says the clock.

First the blankets: peel them carefully from the shoulder, one after the other. Then the sheet. The obscuring fronds of hair, they must go. And now, in short order, we arrive at the bared skin of the shoulder.

Except it is no longer bare; it has company.

A remarkable creature, only superficially resembling the letter *G*, but glimmering through it, a pair of piercing eyes and an undeniable animal intelligence.

The rudiments of a snore rise up through Philomela's throat. And behind me, the strand of Captain Gully's humming broadens into knots of language: *Rest ye . . . dismay . . . saviour.*

It's eleven o'clock by the time I let myself in at Mrs. Sharpe's. Peak working time for the staff, so it's a bit disconcerting to find the good madam tending not to patrons but to me. Sitting in a bare wooden chair in the foyer, in a nightgown and shawl that look calculatedly dowdy, her arms folded, her face sectioned into frowns.

—Good evening, Mrs. Sharpe.

The frowns carve themselves deeper.

—I trust you're well.

The eyes are hard as cherry stones.

—Well, I think I'll retire now, if that's all right with you.

I get as far as the stairs before her voice stops me.

—I waited for you.

It's the aggrieved voice of a young girl, and when I turn around, I see there's a pout to match, the upper lip swallowed entirely by the lower.

—Ohh. Your lesson. . . .

—Maybe your *other* women don't mind being jilted, Mr. Timothy, but I run a *business*. A great many people depend on me.

—Please accept my—

—I can't be wasting half the day waiting for an employee to, to condescend to . . . why, if you must know, people wait on *me*, never the vice versa.

—I promise it won't happen again.

Unmollified, she gives herself a shake, glares at the hall clock. She says:

—Mr. Crusoe has just saved a Spaniard from being eaten.

—Oh! So you've . . . you've read ahead.

—It wasn't the same, doing it myself. It lacked something.

—I imagine it did, I'm very sorry.

She fiddles with the drawstring of her nightgown.

—Well, I know how the world works. A young man can't be expected to do an old woman's bidding, not forever.

—Oh, well, it's . . .

—He must follow his heart, mustn't he?

—Heart, yes.

She studies me as one might study a cloud formation.

—You're not yourself, Mr. Timothy. These past few days, you have most certainly not been yourself.

I lean against the banister. Very tired, all of a sudden.

—A friend of mine is in some difficulty, Mrs. Sharpe. That's all.

—Perhaps there's something I can do?

—No. I don't think so.

—I am, after all . . . *known* to a few personages. I'd be glad to *speak* to them if you—

—It's most kind of you, but not just yet. Thank you.

If she feels rebuffed, she gives no sign of it. Rises to her feet, adjusts her shawl. Honours me with a seasonal smile.

—Well, we're sure to be busy as goblins the next few days, so I thought I might give you this now.

It has been hiding under her chair all along, a tiny bundle in embossed forest-green wrapping. Inside is a casket, which opens to reveal a silver horse the size of a fingernail, so small it nearly vanishes into the folds of my palm.

—It's very nice. It's . . .

—A charm, Mr. Timothy. For your watch chain. Merry Christmas.

Stricken, I look up at her.

—I haven't . . .

—No matter, Mr. Timothy.

—I've been fully meaning to get you something. I've been strapped for time of late.

—There's no *need*, you've, you've already . . . I mean, it's been lovely, the lessons and . . . and all of it.

I have no idea what to say, and Mrs. Sharpe contents herself with brushing a spot from my waistcoat.

—Look at you, such a state. What, have you been sleeping in a sawmill? And where's your hat? We'll let Mary Catherine have a go at the jacket, it's a horror.

It does bring back Mother, I won't deny it. The whole performance: impersonal inventory, flurrying hands, deliberately brusque tone. All that's missing is the concluding "Get on with you now."

And then Mrs. Sharpe says:

—Get on with you now.

The sight of the smile drifting across my face must alarm her, for she takes a couple of backwards steps and clutches her shawl even more tightly round her.

—And don't forget the party tomorrow night, Mr. Timothy. I won't be stood up twice.

—I'll remember.

—And my poem? You won't forget that, either?

—Of course not.

—Good night, then.

—Good night.

Coming back from Gully's, I confess I envisioned an uninterrupted line straight from the front door to my bed. But once I have cleared the obstacle that was Mrs. Sharpe, a new one confronts me: George. Waiting in the hall by my bedroom in list shoes and a rather natty flannel dressing gown, scanning the inflammatory headlines of the *News of the World*. How long he has been there, I cannot say, but when he spies me, he contrives to look as startled as if we had collided in a Chinese pagoda.

—Why, Mr. Timothy! A bit late for you to be turning in, isn't it?

—The holidays are rather a full time, George. As I'm sure you appreciate.

—Full, that's it. Why, things have got so *full* even the police have stopped in. To partake of the fullness. Did you know that?

—Can't say I did.

—Odd, they were looking for some sort of dangerous criminal, but I don't know how dangerous he could be, since he sounded a bit like *you*. From the description, I mean.

—I'm a fairly nondescript sort, George. I imagine there are any number of people who resemble me.

—Imagine so, yes. All the same, this *particular* description was quite close to the mark, right down to the . . . oh, well, *limp* is such an un-Christian sort of word, isn't it?

—I have heard worse.

—Well, why go on? I mean to say, even if this fellow, this criminal . . . even if he *looks* like you and . . . and *limps* like you . . . well, London's spilling over with nondescript cripples, is it not? Turn over a rock, I mean to say, and you'll find one.

—Very true.

—So I suppose we'll just have to stay on the watch for this dangerous criminal.

—Naturally.

Smiling, George takes a step towards me. Wriggles his fingers down the center of my waistcoat.

—You see, the thing is, Mr. Timothy, we're on very favourable terms with the police, the missus and I. It's something we take pride in, if you must know. I'd hate for all that to be jeopardised by someone who doesn't . . . oh, let's be charitable and assume he simply doesn't know any better. Insists on doing things he oughtn't.

—You may depend on me, George, never to lower the moral tone of this establishment.

His fingers linger on one of my waistcoat buttons.

—Just thought you'd care to keep these things in mind. Please do keep them in mind, won't you, Mr. Timothy?

By the time he's gone, I am so exhausted I barely have the power to undress myself. I lie there in bed with Father's old comforter round my neck, but when I close my eyes, the creature is still there—that carnivorous *G*, branded inside my lids. I give my eyes a rub, I try to blink it away, but it only transmogrifies into something else: a man in a carriage, tracing a line along his lips.

I know you, he says.

No. No, you don't.

We carry on the argument for some time, well past the bounds of consciousness, until the flapping of wings sends us both scurrying.

———— ❧ ————

20 December 1860

Dear Father,

Have I described my bedroom to you? It's ugly, but it has its fascinations. For instance, there's not a right angle in the whole space. The walls meet at acute or obtuse angles, and the ceiling line ripples like water, and the floor slopes downwards, so that, lying in bed, I feel the faintest tug of gravity on the soles of my feet. Some mornings, that pull is the only thing that gets me out of bed.

Not a bad place for a bachelor, but all the same, I'm rather glad Philomela hasn't seen it; she might not approve. I don't know why I should be jealous of my standing in her eyes; I can't honestly say I have any. All the same, better she should imagine something a bit grander than this.

We were talking of narrators the last time we spoke. No; I was talking of narrators.

When I was still young, Father, I assumed yours was the only story that could bind me. But that was before Uncle N introduced an entirely new version, one that is still unfolding in directions I can't predict.

Now, if I were to compare the two texts—yours and Uncle N's—I would say that yours was exclusively present-tense, while his was oriented almost entirely towards the future. Also, his had a guiding metaphor—rather an exhausted metaphor, but there you are.

Are you ready for a story, Father?

A young boy—roses blooming in the hollows of his cheeks—is deprived by cruel Fate of the use of one limb. He is clasped in the bosom of a warm, distracted family, who dote upon him but fail to understand his intrinsic worth. For this boy, the reader soon learns, is nothing less than a changeling, a prince of nature whose birthright was stolen from him in infancy (even as his leg was robbed of its motive force). The infamy might have stood uncorrected were it not for the intervention of a kindly family friend who detects something unusual in the boy, something no one else can see, the boy least of all. An effluvium of gentility that burnishes the very air around him. And so this kindly old gentleman resolves to restore the changeling to his proper place in the cosmic hierarchy—to raise him up, as it were, to the life for which he was originally destined.

This ambition will, of course, be realised through the means closest to hand: relentless philanthropy. And so there are doctors—galloping hordes of doctors, from every point on the medical spectrum, and a few from far off the spectrum. There are trips to Bath and Brighton, and there are accompanying wardrobes, for what passes in Camden Town will not always do elsewhere. There are incidental gifts, tokens and knickknacks and party favours, unaffiliated with any holiday or celebration.

The child is grateful for these attentions and not, perhaps, as puzzled by them as he ought to be. He assumes only that his medical condition has sparked the gentleman's latent Christian sentiments. But as the months pass, and as the attentions increase, another possibility dawns on him. Perhaps this gentleman has divined something in him—some germ of potential waiting to be cultured.

And in this way, the boy becomes slowly acculturated to his own mythos, and over time, so does the rest of his family. With mysterious unanimity, they accept the central premise of the story—that great things are expected of this boy, and so great things are to be given—and they none of them bat an eye, with the possible exception of the eldest brother, who is left to moulder away in the local grammar school while the young changeling is offered his pick of Charterhouse and Harrow and Rugby.

In the end, of course, it is decided the boy isn't up to outdoor sports, and so various tutors are co-opted in the great work of making him a gentleman. Quite dreary, these tutors, and as itinerant as apple peddlers. The boy runs through four or five of them a year. Whether this is his doing, no one can say, but it is clear that the prospect of spending months in a North London garret whipping a cripple's vowels into shape and quizzing him in cognates does not excite the ambitions of the average educator.

And here comes a break in the narrative: Mr. McReady.

Oh, you must remember him, Father, I don't care how long you've been dead. He had furnace-red hair and a gold-tipped cane that he held like an épée, and outsized russet cravats that spilled halfway down his chest, and a new flower poking from his lapel every day—not simply the petals but the entire stem, winding down his torso like an extruded vein. The first time he saw me, he tilted his hat to one side and cried:

—Up, up and quit your books, or surely you'll grow double!

I was thirteen at the time. I had no idea he was quoting someone; I took it simply as a call to action. That very day, we marched out of the garret and into London's waiting arms, and we never really came back.

Days would go by with neither of us opening a book; we chose instead to tour the city (in a landau, usually, leased for us by Uncle N). Sometimes Mr. McReady would order the carriage to stop and would drag me out to inspect a floral display or to meet an especially eloquent shoeblack or racetrack tout or to make covert study of the profile of a recruiting sergeant at Westminster.

We did eventually get round to the books, but only the right sort of books. Mr. McReady had no use for Latin, you see; Greek was the language for him and Hellenism his most exalted theme. He would speak at great length on Plato's Symposium and Lacedaemonian beauty, on Castor and Pollux, Damon and Pythias, Heracles and Hylas. And even the non-Greek passages tended to follow the same line. We read long excerpts from Li Amitiez de Amis et Amile, and the first hundred or so of Shakespeare's sonnets, over and over again, and everything by Marlowe and nothing by Jonson. And on occasion, Mr. McReady would gladly abandon his role of tutor, would actually plant himself at my feet *and demand to know what I thought of a particular strophe, and he wouldn't relent until I said something, and at first I had nothing to say, and then finally I did have something, and as I gazed down at Mr. McReady, sitting rapt at my feet, I thought perhaps I was different—different from you and Mother and everyone else.*

In the end, Mr. McReady lasted only a little longer than the others, although he would have stayed for the rest of his life. That, at any rate, is the vow he made me in his letter, the one he sealed inside a perfumed envelope and slipped into my coat pocket. A fascinating document—I wish I still had it with me. Disjointed autobiography, for the most part: the salad days of Oxford and Professor Jowett and Professor Pater and the Newdigate Prize and then some shadowy ellipsis and Eden gone like smoke. None of it made much sense to me, but the closing peroration was extraordinary. A hymn to the love of Jonathan and David. And yes, a pledge of undying fealty. Most embarrassing to a thirteen-year-old; it seemed an act of kindness not to mention it. But as luck would have it, Mother found the letter—probably smelt it during her daily house rounds—and complained to Uncle N, and that was all for Mr. McReady.

You probably didn't notice his absence, Father. He was just another tutor.

Back to our story. Having witnessed the dismal progress of the tutoring profession, the kindly old gentleman resolves to take the boy's education into his own hands. Pedagogy is not his natural bent, but what's to be done? He's the only one who can be trusted with this precious cargo. And so the boy and the gentleman travel to the Crystal Palace (the old man grumbling the whole while at the profligacy of it, the foreignness). They attend operas and plays. The boy is especially struck by Charles and Ellen Kean in Much Ado About Nothing *at the Princess's Theatre. The dazzling intimacy of their exchanges—the boy flushes and looks away, as though he has blundered into someone's boudoir. At some point in the middle of the third act, the old gentleman leans in to him and says:*

—That chap had a father, I think. An actor like him. Can't recollect the name offhand, but quite good in what was that play, the one with the Jew?

He is trying his best, this old gentleman. It isn't his fault he isn't Mr. McReady.

They go to see the Keans many times after that, and the boy grows quite comfortable in their boudoir. The trouble is he must always leave it. He must come back to Camden Town. Not to the same house as before, no: the father's salary is enough now for moving up in the world—a few blocks, at least—and the family now has a maid. (The mother follows the poor thing round the house, making sure she has emptied the ashes properly and hasn't singed the bread or beaten the rugs upwind.) It is not the castle in which the boy almost certainly began life, but it is, all in all, a fine bourgeois establishment, with bay windows and railed areaways and, most miraculous of all, a bedroom for each of the children.

But it still has a garret, almost indistinguishable from the one the family left behind. And this is where the boy finds himself most afternoons and evenings. Reading, reading. The once-banned Jonson and the second half of Shakespeare's sonnets and Keats and Sterne and Hobbes and Kant. And Hume, under whose spell he spends each day refusing to believe his family will necessarily be there the following morning. This is fully in accord with the mythos into which he has been indoctrinated.

The boy reads in the garret because it is the one place where he can be sufficiently alone—and of course the one place that most accentuates his aloneness. Staring through the narrow grid of the window mullions, he sees able-bodied boys and men striding past, jaunty and crowing and charged with animal promise. Striding into their future. Creating their own boudoirs. While there he sits, still dreaming, still waiting for The Event, which is his private term for the public realisation of his destiny. He envisions it as a carriage, a grey brougham pausing at the curb in front of his house, opening its door.

The carriage never comes. And that is when the boy begins to get well. Because it is either get well or stay in that garret for the rest of his life. And he believes, still he believes, that he is meant for better things. He just doesn't know what they are. Down to the present day, he persists, not knowing.

Chapter 12

I FIRST MET SIGNOR ARPELLI three summers ago. He was selling half-penny ices from a barrow in Saffron Hill, one of about ten Italian gentlemen crowded into the same small court for the same unremunerative purpose. For reasons I have yet to define, Signor Arpelli stood out from his colleagues. The curled brim of his hat, perhaps. A certain mingling of gravity and levity—I thought the masks of Janus had merged in his eyes.

In any event, I bought ices from him whenever I was passing through, and one day, I stopped a pair of boys from running off with his barrow, a small act for which he was lavishly grateful. It was then he sketched for me the impressive downward trajectory of his life: artist's atelier in Pisa, doomed romance with a *contino*'s daughter, duel, hair's-breadth escape across Lake Geneva, portrait painting on the Rive Gauche, half-voluntary servitude to a Montmartre *charcutier*, steerage across the Channel . . . halfpenny ices.

Since then, his fortunes have improved somewhat. A banker in Portland Place hired him to teach Italian to his three corvine daughters, but that ended abruptly when the banker absconded to Honduras with a mess of securities. More recently, Arpelli has gone into business with a French card dealer: the two of them earn a modest income replacing signs and tickets for linen drapers and small merchants. Each morning, M. d'Antin scours the windows of Regent and Oxford Streets for some especially dingy specimen of lettering, then rushes into the offending establishment with a flutter of handkerchief and a trailing moan: "But this thing in your window! It is too awful!" Caught dead to rights, the guilty merchant atones for his aesthetic crime by commissioning a new work.

It is Arpelli's job to carry out the commission, in a small attic in High Holborn—a hot, close space, even in the dead of winter. And yet when I come knocking, he is sporting the costume he wears all year round: a weathered woollen jacket pulled up at the collar, as though to keep off a north wind. He holds his paintbrush as casually as a fountain pen, and periodically breaks off work to toss morsels of bread to a pink mouse that sits obediently by his elbow.

—Good morning, signor.

—Mr. Cratchit! What a surprise. And how kind of you to visit me in my studio.

—Business is good?

—It is. . . .

He gestures towards the square of cardboard that has been occupying him for the past half hour:

Try our own dripping at 6d. a lb.

—The masterpieces must wait, Mr. Cratchit.

—It was ever so.

—May I offer you some cocoa?

—No. Thank you, no.

He pulls a tangle of hair from his forehead, brushes a crumb from his moustache. Smiles.

—There is something I may do for you, Mr. Cratchit?

—I'm very sorry to trouble you. I wonder if I might borrow an hour of your time.

—An hour?

—I'm in rather urgent need of an interpreter.

The truth is, I am prepared to take any of several tacks with him. Flattery. Pathos. The call of the motherland, the spirit of Father Christmas. I am prepared to argue, propitiate, bribe. None of that proves necessary. All it takes is a brief perusal of my eyes, and Signor Arpelli is opening his hands and saying:

—I am a happy man, Mr. Cratchit. I may at last repay my debt to you. You will please wait while I leave a note for M. d'Antin.

Minutes later, we are strolling arm in arm down Chancery Lane, as companionable as school chums. I have always wondered at the transformative powers of personality—Arpelli is the most signal exemplar I know. His clothes are not conspicuously new, his shirt linen is too thick to be elegant, the boots rather too square to be fashionable, the greatcoat too heavily fondled by its previous owners. And still he carries himself like a manor-born dandy. Walks on the outside of the sidewalk, sidesteps the coffee stalls with practised ease, smiles benevolently on the newsboys, the wall workers, the chimney sweeps.

And when he sees me glance over my shoulder, he mimes the same gesture, as if it were the gentlest of pastimes. And with an air of utmost tact, he murmurs:

—I think perhaps we are being followed, Mr. Cratchit.

—I'm inclined to agree, signor.

—Followed most inadequately, I should add. By a tall man in a velveteen jacket.

—And a blue-check waistcoat.

—The same.

Arpelli removes two purses from his coat pocket, tucks one into an inner compartment, and pats it back to sleep.

—This gentleman is an acquaintance of yours, Mr. Cratchit?

—No.

—Perhaps you know his employer.

—In a manner of speaking.

—And you will forgive my asking twice, but where is it we are going?

—Craven Street.

—Very good.

Arpelli snaps up the brim of his hat and gives his moustache a quick caress.

—If you please, he says.

Just the barest pressure on my arm, and we are moving. Not forwards, as before, but on a tangent, and with all deliberate speed, so that the Strand is soon left behind, and before I can get my bearings, we are passing into a narrow alley, musty and unregarded. The backsides of flats rise up on all sides, and whatever light the day once offered is gone, and a vague claustrophobia gnaws at my stomach as I whirl around just in time to see the man in the velveteen jacket pause at the alley's entrance, then continue past.

—He will return, says Arpelli. Don't you agree?

A flight of steps carries us into Strand Lane and then to an old watch house, in whose archway Arpelli pauses. Leaning on a rusted iron railing, he makes a show of consulting his timepiece.

—An ideal time for a plunge, wouldn't you say, Mr. Cratchit?

It has taken me this long to realise where we are: the old Roman bath.

But then, it's been twelve years since I was here last. Dragged by one of Uncle N's religious enthusiasts, who was convinced the waters were fed by the Holy Well of St. Clement and had curative properties. Cold is the only property I can recall at present: the ague I contracted here kept me in bed for three days.

That memory rises in me now like a foreboding, but rather than wait for my protest, Signor Arpelli skips down the stone steps into the brick vault. And as I follow him, it seems we are dropping into another time altogether. The sulphurous tendrils of air, the tingle of rot, the faintly overlapping slaps of water in the crucifer-shaped plunge pool—everything breathes a spell of antiquity.

And the bath attendant himself is the very image of Charon: a hairless, toothless, almost jawless man, rasing us from his memory even as he hands us our towels and robes.

—They'll be no undue splashin'. And please to keep the voices to a pleasin' murmur.

As we pass into the changing room, I feel Arpelli's hand once again in the crook of my arm, drawing me back with him into a tiny niche. And there we wait, hidden from view, eyes fastened on the entranceway. We wait.

Not for long, as it turns out. The footsteps announce themselves like a judgement, echoing with unnatural volume against the arched ceiling. The man in question arrives a full minute later, scratching the lapel of his velveteen jacket and offering Charon the most tentative of smiles.

—Excuse me, we hear him say.—I was meaning to meet a couple of friends here.

I whisper in Arpelli's ear:

—You should know, I'm not the fleetest of runners.

—I am relieved to report that running will not be necessary, Mr. Cratchit, I myself being too old for such games. This way, please.

We never do make it to the changing room. A yard or so shy of the entranceway, Arpelli draws me off to the left into a region of pure darkness. The hand now leaves my elbow, and Arpelli disappears without a word.

Paralysed, unable to see more than an inch in front of me, I wait there in the blackness, listening for some report of my companion: a shuffling footstep, the tiniest grunt. But the only sounds come from the region of light. The churning of the Holy Well water against the brick. The pensive footsteps of the velveteen man, converging on our hiding place.

Riveted there in the darkness, I suck in my breath, willing myself into invisibility. My muscles quiver from the combined impulses of holding still and jerking into flight, and just when I think they will explode from the contradiction, Arpelli's hand reappears—like light made palpable—drawing me even further into the dark.

As if to compensate for the loss of sight, my other senses prickle into full maturity. My lips taste whale oil. My nostrils pick out a wafting trail of salt. The hair on my skin dances to the music of magnets.

And my ears discern a voice, Signor Arpelli's voice, impossibly distant.

—Close it behind you, if you would.

It takes some groping before my hands find what he means—a flat abraded stone surface that yields with surprising ease. As it swings back, it herds the sound before it, so that even the footsteps of the velveteen man enter a realm of memory.

—Take my arm, Mr. Cratchit. We haven't far to go.

Slow is our pace, a half-step at a time. The smell of salt intensifies as we pass through the darkness, as if to season the other smell that gathers around us, thick and vegetative. At one point, seeking an anchor, I lean against a greasy sponge of wall, which quickly gives way, swallowing my arm all the way to the elbow before I am able to pull it out again.

The claustrophobia ebbs, and after a few minutes, my eyes begin seizing on shapes—dim and bleary-blue—and none blearier than Arpelli, leading me onward. His steps are so sure, his manner so calm, I am tempted more than once to ask how he came to know this causeway so intimately. There is a map, perhaps, some fragile parchment passed down through a lineage of Italian spelunkers, dating all the way back to the Roman centurions who dug these channels out of the earth. But the shroud of arcana in which Arpelli is robed admits for no explanation, and so we pass on in silence.

And now the path rises very gradually beneath our feet—the gentlest of inclines—and the darkness opens out into dimensions, and for the first time, I am able to walk unaided. But Arpelli, far from consigning me to my fate, hoops his hand all the more protectively round my elbow, and as we walk the final yards, we assume a constitutional gait. There is one last barrier—a heavy oaken door with no handle—and Arpelli gives it such an indolent kick one would think this was the most natural ritual in the world.

—After you, Mr. Cratchit.

One last flight of stone steps, and the day rears up before us, its pallor lambent now to my dark-adjusted eyes. Compassless, I squint up at an enormous

Doric column . . . a span of granite . . . seagulls and pigeons wheeling in mad circles.

—Waterloo Bridge, says Arpelli.—Not the accustomed angle.

I check the coordinates. Somerset House to the east. The handsome Roman arches of the Adelphi Terrace. And directly before us, the river, with the high, belching chimneys of a passing tug, and a colony of gulls floating placidly as ducks. And an oncoming front of amber fog, nullifying everything.

—We will stay by the river for now, Mr. Cratchit. And we will take the precaution of doubling back, in the unlikely event we are still being followed.

From here, it is a leisurely fifteen minutes' walk to Craven Street, and having assured ourselves twice over that we are unescorted, we slip into the topsy-turvy lodging house and clamber up the stairs. I am already raising my hand to knock when I notice a tiny splinter of light coming from the room inside.

The door is ajar.

Arpelli's eyes meet mine. We pause for a moment to gather ourselves and then, on a silent count, push the door open.

I can't say what it is I am expecting to find—no particular nightmare has imprinted itself on my brain—but this is not even in the realm of possibility. A family tableau, shocking in its completeness. Colin by the window, whistling a sea chantey as he buffs his shoes. Philomela on the hearth rug, applying a damp calico cloth to the Captain's headless elephant figurine and pausing just once to stroke the tabby that has coiled itself round her feet. And the benign paterfamilias of Captain Gully, camped in his chair, with the *Times* streaming across his lap, and on his face a look of genial abstraction that turns apologetic the moment he sees me.

—Christ! Did we forget to lock it again?

His spirits swiftly restored, he hoists the newspaper like a sail.

—Suicide in Shadwell, Tim. Jumped right off the pier. Care to go for a bit of dredge tonight?

—I can't, Captain.

—Come now! Gully was thinkin' we could make a reg'lar party of it, us and the boy and the lass. Reg'lar family outing.

—I'm afraid I'm already engaged for a party. Colin, too. Some other night, perhaps.

His spirits are too abundant to be doused completely. Rolling his eyes, he allows as how there are always going to be folks itching to kill themselves.

—Specially round Christmas, he adds with a knowing look.

And then he rattles the paper back into place and rejoins the tableau, and I feel much the way I felt on entering Mrs. Sharpe's drawing room that long-ago night. The interloper. The chord that won't resolve.

—Philomela, I'd like you to meet Signor Arpelli.

She has replaced her dress with a pair of trousers, a fustian plasterer's apron, and a cambric shirt that, unless my eyes deceive me, belong to her host. No denying it makes for a comical costume on her, but she carries herself with equanimity, never once trips as she crosses the room, even though the trouser legs have wrapped themselves under her feet, and she inclines her head very nicely and extends her hand to Arpelli, who studies it with merry-melancholy eyes.

—*Buongiorno, signorina. Come sta?*

What is it like, I wonder, hearing one's native tongue spoken again after a long absence? All I know for certain is that Philomela waits awhile before disgorging her reply:

—*Bene, grazie.*

And that is as far as I am able to follow, for very soon they have lapsed into intonations and inflections that resonate as strangely in my ear as the call of falcons, and before long their entire bodies have entered the conversation—arms, hands, shoulders—a kind of streetside theatre as riveting as it is unintelligible.

And then Arpelli breaks off and opens his arms to me.

—It is very delightful. This girl and I, we are both of us Calabrese.

—Is that . . . oh, I see. . . .

—And now I am going to propose something distinctly un-Calabrese, Mr.

Cratchit. I am going to ask you and your friends to step into the hallway, if that will not be too dreadful an imposition. I think it might be best, you see, if Philomela and I enjoyed a short spell of privacy.

The hallway is indeed large enough to accommodate the three of us, but the captain seems deeply reluctant to quit his own lodging. And as the door fastens after us, I understand why: we have thrust him into the belly of the beast. As the minutes pass, his nostrils dilate, and beads of perspiration well up along his neckline, and his eyes dart in all directions, scouring every niche and crevice of the stairwell for predators.

—That was a purr. Damn it, we heard us a purr.

Colin, already bored by the cats, uses the interval to go over his recital program.

—Start in with "Cherry Ripe," that's always good for a hand. But not knowing the crowd or anythink, maybe "The Tartar Drum" or "The Banks of the Blue Moselle"? Not sure. Save "Isle of Beauty" for later, I expect, people need to be a bit stewed for that one, then finish with "The Mistletoe Bough"—that's fetched me many a dinner in my day. What I don't know is, should I insert a character song—somethink along the lines of "Sam Hall" or "Jack Sheppard"—or is that too racy for this bunch?

The program is still in flux when Arpelli emerges from Gully's flat, and everything else is suddenly in flux, too, because there's something about the way he closes the door behind him, something about the clipped demeanour, the smile curling into a frown . . . yes, I'm back in the old house, I'm standing outside Mother's room, and that Harley Street physician with the hairy brow is resting his hand on Father's shoulder, speaking in that low, resigned tone perfected at a million bedsides: "Won't be long, Bob."

Curious, I can't even remember the look on my father's face. All that comes back is the indignation I felt on hearing my father addressed by his Christian name, as though he were the hostler or the groom.

Signor Arpelli, by contrast, gives me the most deferential bow, then pauses to assure himself of my attention.

—It is a fine thing she is Calabrian, Mr. Cratchit. We grow very tough there. Like thistles.

—Did she tell you anything?

—Not much more than she has told you. Her father, Signor Rotunno, came here to start a business, the framing business, with his cousin. But this cousin, it turns out, has gone to America, perhaps to avoid arrest, no one knows. Shortly after coming here Signor Rotunno fell ill—with what sounds to my ear like typhus—and the tale ends therein. Very sad, I'm sure.

—No other relations?

A shake of the head.

—What about the man in the carriage? Did you inquire about him?

—Of course.

—Did she know his name?

—No. Just that he was—how would . . . ?—someone with rank and title. A lord or a duke, this was her thinking. Of course, there is no being certain of that.

Yes, there is: I saw the carriage, the coat of arms.

—Did she offer up anything else about him?

—She knows very little, Mr. Cratchit. He introduced himself to her soon after her father's funeral.

—How did he find her?

—She believes he was directed to her by . . . by a missionary, I believe? Could that be?

—It could very well be.

—This man never told his name, but he claimed to be most sorry for her and asked if she would like to come stay with him in a very nice home. And be a servant in his household. She did not . . . you understand, at the time she did not have any . . . which is to say, she said yes.

—And then?

—This is where I cannot penetrate, Mr. Cratchit. It appears this . . . I will not use the word *gentleman* . . . this *person* had other ideas. It appears he fancied our young girl, in a great way. And indicated that many of his friends would do the same.

At this, Colin, previously absorbed in the mechanics of his recital, looks up for the first time. The churning of his mouth becomes a mirror for his revolving brain.

—Christ! Sounds like a bloody ring.

—A ring?

Arpelli turns to me for glossing.

—A sort of organized community, signor. In this instance, employing many women for the same purpose. Did she—would she say whether other girls were involved?

—That was the implication, yes.

—And what happened to those girls? Did she tell you anything else about them?

Arpelli gazes at me for a moment without speaking. Then:

—I'm afraid, you know, when I pressed the matter . . .

He waves his hand in front of his face, but he needn't bother re-creating it: I know that look of hers quite well by now.

—And did she say whether they had harmed her in any way?

—She did not.

—Not even, you know, marked her with a brand or anything?

—A brand? She did not say.

—Or mention anything about the police?

—No.

—And that gesture, signor—the one I told you about, in the carriage?

—That she *did* mention. It seems that the man in question was signaling to her that if she ever breathes a word to anyone, he will cut out her tongue.

The silence that falls over us appears almost to embarrass Arpelli. He shrugs and says:

—That is what it means.

It's too much for Gully. He slashes a vent through the air, then waves his box wrench in such violent circles that one might think he was trying to refashion it into a hook by sheer force of friction.

—Let 'em try! We'll cut their fuckin' hearts out first!

Arpelli extends a placating hand.

—All good and well, my stout fellow, but it seems to me there are questions more pressing at the moment. For instance: Who will look after this girl? Knowing her story, I myself would be happy to offer, but what space I possess, I share with M. d'Antin. As a consequence . . .

—I know a woman in Southwark, Colin says.

—And I've a brother in Oxford Street, I say.

—No need, interposes Gully.—Not to worry. She can hunker down here as long as she bloody likes.

And with a meaningful glare at the floorboards, he adds:

—We don't care who raises no ruckus over it.

All of us, in our own way, convey our deepest respects to the captain, who shakes each of our hands before blustering into silence. I turn one last time to Arpelli.

—You are quite right, signor. We do need to find a home for this girl. But I couldn't in good conscience leave her anywhere until we have arrested the men who have so cruelly used her. It seems to me as long as they are at liberty, she is in danger.

—An excellent point, Mr. Cratchit, and a laudable aspiration, but how do you expect to accomplish it? You are, I hasten to say, one man.

—And a man with no plan, I confess it. But I expect to conjure one up soon.

—Then I will remain at your service until such time. In the meantime, Mr. Cratchit, may I consider my debt discharged?

—Many times over.

—Only there is one more thing. The girl was quite insistent on a certain point.

—Yes?

—That point being that she is still pure. She said this over and again: she can still be someone's wife.

Scratching his big, round head, Gully mutters:

—Well, 'course she can, young missy. Why, in Majorca they marries at seven or eight, never looks back, more power on 'em.

Narrowing his eyes and speaking more distinctly, Arpelli continues:

—She especially wants her papa to know this about her. She asked me to tell him when I see him.

—Her father?

—She believes he walks still. As a spirit, you know. A ghost.

I have to suppress my first reaction, which is simply to laugh, as well as the next, which is to pose a rather obvious question:

Does he ever bump into Bob Cratchit?

It's at least conceivable, isn't it? The pair of them squaring off each day over cards, or sharing a cup of grog before bedtime. Boasting of their children. It is all quite possible, and it raises another, more urgent inquiry:

Why isn't Signor Rotunno doing a better job of watching over his daughter?

That's how I come to notice that the door to Gully's flat has been pulled open, just a fraction, and that the girl inside, rather than pressing her face to the opening she has created, has fallen back, the better to dramatise her indifference to our proceedings.

All the same, she is there, framed in the crevice, watching us. Watching *me*, in particular. And on her face, a full palette of tones, from which a few hues emerge: dread, anticipation, the prickings of conscience, and (here I read more deeply into the canvas) an undisguised resentment.

And something else, too: an open challenge, as if she were bouncing back the question I just posed to the air.

Who's watching over you?

Chapter 13

MRS. SHARPE'S GIRLS STILL TALK about the night the King of the Belgians came (though none of them was around to see it). They say he arrived in a coach-and-six, wearing a Pierrot mask and smelling of hollyhocks and bacon. His servant introduced him as a Mr. Gluwid from Wales, but no Welshman ever sounded like Mr. Gluwid, nor sported such a large signet ring. He stayed but fifteen minutes, long enough to be bound in a bell rope and half asphyxiated with Mrs. Sharpe's unwashed chemise. Before he was released, the recumbent gentleman was heard to moan:

—May Heaven take me now, for this earth has nothing left to yield.

Well, that was ten years ago, and it is fair to say that Mrs. Sharpe's clientele has fallen off a bit in the interim. At tonight's function, there will be no Belgian kings amidst the bowls of trifle and the ropes of privet and the Tom Smith Christmas crackers. No princes or dukes, no ministers of the Crown, not even a rank-and-file Tory. According to Mary Catherine, the only guests of real note are a Viennese surgeon, a clergyman from Exeter Hall, an editor of the *North London Press*, and a retired colonel from the 13th Light Dragoons rumoured to have been somewhere in the vicinity of Sebastopol either shortly before or shortly after the famous battle.

For all the paucity of titles, though, there is a superabundance of facial shrubbery: great topiaries of whisker, woollen and baroque, running in an uninterrupted line from one jaw to the next. And Mrs. Sharpe's strictures remain in force. No medical students will be found on the guest list (too poor by half). No soldiers or sailors below the rank of captain. No one under the age of eighteen, and most of all, no lawyers, it being Mrs. Sharpe's contention that the Inns of Court have ruined more girls than all the brothels of London combined.

This is not to say that the interests of the Law go unrepresented here. Three members of the Metropolitan Police, still in uniform, have arrayed themselves round a giant bowl of negus. By the looks of things, they have been at their station for some time, for they are all of them three sheets to the wind, and have taken to using their hats as ladles. Whenever Mary Catherine passes by with a platter of food, they make elabourate shows of snatching an oyster or a leg of mutton and then pointing accusing fingers at one another.

—Officer. Someone has gone and pinched a meat pie.

—It were you, Officer.

—No, I swear. It were the other officer.

And to think, last night, with Bowler on our heels, we were searching for someone just like them. We failed to appreciate how easily a public trust can be breached. A bowl of negus, a toothsome ham bone—that's all it takes to look the other way. And if I'm not mistaken, the rewards are just beginning for this lot: later tonight, they will have their pick of Mrs. Sharpe's girls.

> *Cherry ripe, cherry ripe*
> *Ripe I cry*
> *Full and fair ones*
> *Come and buy. . . .*

Bizarre, isn't it, to hear that pure treble welling up from these climes? It must be said that Mrs. Sharpe's parlour, with its strange cross-hatching of respectability and sex, is not the best venue for Colin's talents. His timbre is swamped by the flood of conversation, and the wreaths of cigarette smoke tend to catch in his throat. Still, he carries on as though he had the room's undivided attention—stands on a piano bench, one foot slightly in advance of the other, and glows with justifiable pride in his knickerbocker suit. The short jacket, with its fashionably roomy sleeves, has been fastened at the neck with a single button and hangs open to reveal a grey cloth waistcoat, to which Colin has attached a miniature watch chain, sans watch. His face has been scrubbed, his sward of curls slicked and parted—all in all, he looks quite the little man. Mrs. Sharpe's girls swooped down on him when he first arrived, and Colin took these attentions so personally that he has spent the entire recital scanning the room for his nymphs and giving each one the most salacious of winks. Whether the girls wink back is unclear, but Colin seems to derive fresh assurances from each new contact, and his voice swells with confidence.

Where my Julia's lips do smile,
There's the land of Cherry Isle. . . .

—He's lovely, Mr. Timothy. I can't thank you enough.

Mrs. Sharpe's fingers graze my wrist. It's a gesture I normally equate with proximity, but when I turn, I find her at a great remove, her torso bent and her right arm extended to its full length. This is the closest she can come to anyone tonight, for her dress makes anything nearer impossible. Other women her age might have made do with a bonnet and a modestly flounced skirt. Mrs. Sharpe, in defiance of propriety, has encased herself in the roomiest of crinolines, and whirls about the room like a miniature planet, blowing others out of her orbit. More than once, she has knocked ceramic bowls off tables, and in one particularly alarming manoeuvre, she swept a spadeful of flaming cinders onto the hearth rug. (Mary Catherine had to throw the piano shawl over them.) How many horses must have forfeited their hair, how many whales their bones, so that Mrs. Sharpe could occupy this sovereign space.

The dress is somehow in keeping with her personality, for all night long, she has been exerting a kind of reverse magnetism on her guests. Not twenty minutes ago, I watched her repel with great success an audience of monarchists.

—Oh, the Queen! Poor dreary titmouse. Forever mourning the loss of her chin. Well, at least she can comfort herself with the father of her children. Oh, no, I'm talking about the royal physician. Please don't look shocked, you *must* know, *everyone* does! That Hun she's married to couldn't impregnate a dairy maid. Oh, my, no, the only people in danger from him are the footmen. Why, if equerries could have children, we'd have a whole new royal lineage to contend with!

Perhaps it is the influence of the hock, but with me, she exchanges her provocations for a more benign style of impishness. Smiling now, she points her elbow towards the corner, where the lovely Minnie and her swain, the second son of the Bishop of Exeter, sit on a dos-a-dos, spooning frumenty into each other's mouth.

—Aren't they positively oozing, Mr. Timothy?

—The very word I was looking for, Mrs. Sharpe.

—I'm afraid we shall lose her before long. At least for a few months.

—Well, perhaps he will make an honest woman of her after all.

—Oh, yes, look at my friend Skittles, very happily married to the Marquess of Hartington. But you know, Mr. Timothy, I think pigs fly only once or twice a century. In any event, this does not bear on the real question, which is why have you been standing off to yourself all evening, tiresome wretch?

—I am only listening to the music, Mrs. Sharpe.

—Ha! The best way to distinguish a bore. He will tell you he is listening to the music. Come. You can't still be worried about your friend?

—Not at present.

How could I be? When I left her, she was sitting on the arm of Gully's chair, watching him unveil the wonders of his scrimshaw collection. Each fragment of whale evoked a different destination—Tunis, Lisbon, New Bedford—and each destination called up a new story, and I couldn't be sure how much of it Philomela understood, but her response was something deeper than politeness. At one point, leaning over to inspect a particularly diminutive figurine, she placed her hand on Gully's shoulder, and the hand stayed there, to neither party's consternation. I left them in a daze of wonder. Who would have thought that Gully's warren would so easily admit a visitor? Or that Philomela would burrow in with such a native air? See how quickly a family can be assembled, from the least auspicious ingredients.

—Well, if you are not worried about your friend, Mr. Timothy, perhaps you can tell me: *Where is my poem?*

Oh, dear God.

I clap my hand over my eyes. The beginnings of an apology, of many apologies, form in my throat, expire on my tongue. All that emerges is a small, helpless gasp.

—Never mind, young man. I have taken the liberty of preparing something of my own.

And with a tap of her Chinese fan on my arm, she turns and gives a quick signal to George, on the far side of the room. Whereupon George, brimful of what might pass for Christmas spirit, sets to rapping a spoon on his glass.

—Oyez, oyez! he calls.

The voices die down, and the white-whiskered faces swerve towards the center of the room, where Mrs. Sharpe is even now advancing in her crinoline armour, one hand pressed against her breast, the other frozen in a mime of royalty.

—Dear friends, a merry welcome to you all. George and I and, of course, the girls—we mustn't forget the girls—are all so piqued and pleased to see you masticating our humble Yuletide repast. It was a wise man who wrote, *I was exceedingly surprised with the print of a man's naked foot on the shore.* And I may add that far from surprising us, the naked feet we have housed in this establishment have been a source of great and well-nigh overweening pride to us. How *enchanté* we have been to cater to so many distinguished members of society. And now in this holy religious time, we sacredly lay ourselves at your feet in meagrest thanks and devotion. And we echo the saying of a very fine savage who once said . . .

Here she steals a covert glance at the square of paper secreted in her palm.

—*Me die when you bid die.*

She delivers this last remark at such a high volume that the ensuing silence is like the plunge from a cloud. The room grows smoky with confusion. Every face in the crowd peers at Mrs. Sharpe, waiting for a cue that will never come, and she peers right back, all words exhausted, and it looks to be something of an impasse, possibly eternal, until Mrs. Sharpe, shaken, whips her face round, searching for mine. Her lips form a mute entreaty:

Did I say it right?

And rather than answer, I start clapping. And George takes up the cue on his side, and the silence soon gives way to a round of huzzahs and hear-hears and scattered outbreaks of she's-a-jolly-good-fellow, and Mrs. Sharpe is ushered out of the room with the full blessings of a relieved populace. Pausing once in the doorway, she blows a kiss to the still-applauding room, flutters her hands in farewell and, with one last lethal swirl of her crinoline, exits. I bid fair to say that the applause that follows her into the hallway is, by this point, almost sincere. Mine is, at any rate, and I might even go on applauding were I not presented with the beaming face of Squidgy, only a few hours past his most recent whipping, and wearing a black frock coat as negligently as if it were a towel.

—See here, Timothy. I was wondering if you wouldn't mind too awfully doing me a favour of sorts.

—Of course not.

—Might be best if we stepped down the other hallway. Not so inhabited. Oh, and there's George, give him a little wave. Looks quite bothered about something, doesn't he? I shall have to make it up to him. By the way, I've been reading the most peculiar book lately, can't recall who . . . all about species and whatnots and finches and quite a lot on pigeons. Lovely drawings, but I can't make head nor tail of it, I'm afraid. That's a pun, you see, bit of a play on the bird business. . . .

His conversation is the barge that floats us out of the parlour and down the hall towards the back of the house, where he stops just shy of the cellar door, leans in to me, and murmurs:

—Most embarrassing. Seems Pamela was off duty tonight. Home with her mother or some such creature. For the holidays.

In fact, Pamela will be spending the holidays in the infirmary, getting a couple of buboes lanced, but that is not for public bruiting.

—Don't mistake me, Squidgy adds.—I'm not in the least put out. Girl's obliged to steam by the old homestead now and again. But you see, the replacement girl, Sadie, lovely thing, but not quite so experienced with the old lasheroo. As a consequence, I believe some of it may still be lodged in the back, for I don't mind telling you, I've got the most horrible itchies.

—I'm sorry to hear it.

—If it's not too much of a bother, would you mind, you know, giving it a bit of looky-look, pokey-prod?

Before I can assent, before we have even fully ensured our privacy, Squidgy is peeling off the frock coat, whipping off his braces, undoing the studs of his shirt, and stripping to the waist. It is a sight I never expected to see again: that naked white back with its topography of torture, the pink ridges of flesh running up and down his spine like telegraph wires.

And Squidgy's voice, breezing through:

—Lovely woman, isn't she, Mrs. Sharpe? Absolutely lovely. Never serves the port chilled, always puts out the best vintages for the guests. Don't know where she keeps them all, the cellar, perhaps, but the only person I know who's been down there is Iris, although who can believe a word Iris says, nothing against her, mind, just not airtight. Oh, yes, right there, do you see anything?

—There seems to be a . . . horsehair of some kind. Still lodged in the skin.

—Very like.

—Shall I . . . shall I pull?

—If you would.

The hair comes clear after just three tugs and produces in Squidgy a lingering shiver that leaves me wondering if I have just unwittingly pleasured him.

—Oh, dear. Oh, my, yes. Infinitely better.

—I'm glad.

—Stay a minute, Timothy. Some token of appreciation?

He reaches into his trouser pocket, jangles a mess of coinage. Feeling exactly like the servant he takes me to be, I tell him it isn't necessary, sir. Anyone would have done the same, sir. Really, couldn't accept it.

—Are you quite sure? Well, then, do accept my thanks, Timothy. I shall always remember your kindness. And now, if you'll excuse me, I'm in the most dire need of a catnap.

The only proper thing to do, I suppose, is wait for him to reclothe himself, but it turns out Squidgy has no intention of reclothing. Still topless, he gives me a brief nod and a smile, then ambles back down the hallway, trailing his coat, tie, and shirt after him. What I wouldn't give to see him dragging his scarred carcass across the parlour, like Banquo's ghost, startling the punch out of everyone's glasses. But my attention now has shifted to a small wine table, where sits the parrot of the house. Banished here because his featherless appearance was judged too discomfiting for the guests, he shivers now in his enamelled cage, balancing on one foot and greeting me with soft, convivial eyes.

I am more struck, though, by what lies under his cage: a large green-leather volume, with a cracked binding and a front cover so nearly detached that I must pull it open with the greatest care, in millimetre increments. And once I see what the book is, I read with even greater care. I read it front to back, standing there by the cellar door, with the squawks of the departing guests and the final strains of "The Mistletoe Bough" trailing down the hallway, and just this silent parrot for company.

George hooks his hand round my elbow as I make to climb the stairs.

—Well, now, Mr. Timothy. Where've you been closeting yourself all evening?

—Just exchanging small talk with a lonely bird, George. Nothing that need concern you.

—Oh, well, you should know by now. Everything concerns me.

—What a great vexation that must be for you.

—Vexations are made to be dealt with, Mr. Timothy.

At night, the door to Mrs. Sharpe's inner chambers feels infinitely larger and denser to the touch. I wouldn't have guessed it, but then, I have never been here at night.

—Mrs. Sharpe?

I rap a little more forcefully, but there's no response, and I have just about given up when I hear a wobbling voice.

—Is that you, my pet?

She looks amazingly slight now, stripped of her crinoline fortification and sitting bolt upright on her daybed. I couldn't imagine sleeping a minute in such a vertical position, but with all the pillows and cushions and shams and coverlets that surround her—and with the columns of rag dolls rising on either side of her—lying down might well be even more difficult. And having additional company would be impossible.

—Mr. Timo . . .

The last syllable is lost in the daub of cotton wool she presses to her lips. A nip of brandy, I'm thinking, to take the edge off a toothache. But then I see the brown half-ounce bottle, with the word POISON written across it . . . I inhale the sickly opiate tang . . . and it takes me straight back to Mother, to those last few weeks when she was downing laudanum like shandy. Of course, she was dying at the time, wasn't she, so no one said anything. Mrs. Sharpe, by contrast, has enough vigor to outlive all of us, and for all that, she is spending the aftermath of her social triumph drugging herself half blind.

—Very sorry to bother you, I say.—I know it's late.

—Scrumptious, wasn't it?

—The party, you mean.

—De-lect-*til*-ious.

—Yes, it was.

—My remarks.

—Yes.

—Next time a poem, Mr. Timothy.

—I won't fail.

—No, you won't. My pet. My pretty pet.

Hard to say how long she's been going at it. An hour or so, judging from the hard, white, reflective surfaces that have replaced her eyes. She brushes something from her flannel gown, waves off a band of invisible mist. She says:

—You're still there.

—Yes.

—Well, all right, then.

It's so quiet in the room that the voice inside me sounds almost deranged in its force. It is shouting at me to stop. Stop.

For I have other cares to attend to. I have Philomela, stowed away at Gully's—how safely? for how long? I have an emissary of Scotland Yard on our trail. I have a member of the British peerage whipping him on. I have a retinue of ghosts dogging my every footstep.

And don't forget, Tim, the blank slate of your own future, bearing down with new force each passing day.

Oh, you're already rich in worry. Why get greedy?

—Mrs. Sharpe. If you would, please, reflect on the initial terms of our arrangement—I mean, the official capacity in which you first engaged me, which was, you may recall, as your bookkeeper.

—Did I do that?

—Yes, you did. Now, I understand this was intended only to cloak the true nature of our arrangement, but owing to your kindnesses and your . . . well, owing to all that, I do feel some kind of obligation to look into your, your financial affairs when the occasion presents itself.

—Awf'lly nice of you.

—And tonight, the occasion has presented itself.

A slight crack in the opaque surface of her eyes.

—Yes?

She unties, then reties the drawstring of her gown.

—The news will not be welcome to you, Mrs. Sharpe. We may discuss it tonight, or we may discuss it tomorrow. But it can no longer be ignored.

—Why? Why why?

—Because I have reason to believe your friend George has taken advantage of, of your educational deficits. And now that those deficits have been overcome, I beg you to take matters into your own hands.

I draw the green volume from behind my back, set it on the edge of her bed.

—If you read carefully, you will see that over the past year, more than a few business transactions have taken place without your knowledge. The precise nature of these transactions has been left deliberately vague. What is manifestly obvious is that significant sums of your money are being diverted to a man named Frig.

—Frig.

It takes hearing the name on her own tongue, it takes seeing the wriggle of amusement in her lips to understand the joke of it. A trap for the unwary, perhaps. George's idea of a trip wire.

But the humour soon vanishes from Mrs. Sharpe's face. She cocks her head and stares at the accounts book as though it were a green python crawling towards her toe.

—Well. I suppose it's . . . d'you think serious? A bit?

—Men have been imprisoned for less than George has done, Mrs. Sharpe. But this is not an orthodox business, and that judgement is not mine to make. I leave it in your hands, that is all.

Neither of us moves for quite some time. *Her* reluctance I can well comprehend, but what is mine? Am I waiting to be dismissed? Or is it something else I'm after? Some tiny morsel of gratitude, perhaps?

Well done, my boy. I always knew you weren't a total waste of breath.

But when at last she breaks the silence, Mrs. Sharpe sounds only like someone speaking to herself. And she speaks in someone else's voice. The voice of that old woman in Peter's photography shop.

—I was just on the edge of the most marvellous dream.

Chapter 14

Next morning, I come down to a surprising sight: the breakfast table, generally empty, has been occupied. Sadie, spurning her normal practice of sleeping till noon, has risen with the sun (or close thereto), wrapped a plain cotton blanket round her tiny frame, and bowed her head over a rum-and-water tankard nearly as large as she. Worked through the night, that's my first thought. But when I search her face for the usual dissolute glaze, I find instead a pair of shrewd blue eyes, grown even shrewder in the morning light.

—You're up early, Sadie.

—Oh, as if anyone could sleep, with such a rumpus going on.

—What rumpus?

She hesitates, more for formality's sake than anything else.

—The madam and Mr. George.

—What about them?

—Why, they've been having at it in her office upwards of an hour. The madam's positively livid. I'm sure I've never heard her go on so long.

Just then, the kitchen door swings open to reveal the harassed form of Mary Catherine, bearing down on us with a tray of devilled grill and kidneys. Her face, as she sets the tray in front of us, is a study in reproach.

—I don't believe it's any of our business, Miss Sadie.

—But you must have heard them. You'd have to be deaf as a stone not to.

—It may be there was some voices raised in the general vicinity, but what them voices was a-saying and who was a-saying what to who, I'm sure I don't know. Having better things to do than stand about busy-bodyin'.

Sadie laughs.

—You mean the kitchen's too far away to hear. Well, I was standing just outside the madam's door, which, as you know, is normally too thick for eavesdropping, but I could almost swear on oath I heard the words *swindler* and *pig* being used. Oh, and your name came up as well, Mr. Timothy.

And with that, Mary Catherine abandons any show of detachment.

—Oh, now, *that* I heard. There was Mr. George screaming your name like it was Judgement Day. If I was you, Mr. Timothy, I'd make myself scarce. You never know what—

Her mouth freezes in place. Her eyes freeze, too.

George is standing in the doorway.

In his usual costume—white shirt and waistcoat, collar unbuttoned, sleeves rolled up—his face wreathed in an ecclesiastical smile. He takes two paces into the room, gives us a courtly nod.

—Good morning. Would you two ladies do me the favour of leaving Mr. Timothy and me to ourselves? For just a few moments?

Not a murmur of dissent from either of them. Mary Catherine slinks back to the kitchen, and Sadie makes a straight line for the stairs, as stiff in the shoulders as a schoolgirl on her way to the headmistress.

George pulls out the chair opposite mine. Brushes specks of soot from the table, rearranges a bowl of golden chrysanthemums. Then speaks.

—My leaving the books lying about, that was careless. You *reading* the books . . . now, that was worse than careless.

—Embezzling funds, George. What would you call that?

The look in his eyes isn't something I would have expected. From someone else, I might call it pity.

—Oh, me, he says softly.—I'd be embarrassed if I knew as much nothing as you know.

Rising to his feet, he begins a leisurely circuit of the table, studying his watch the whole way. His eyes never once leave it, and mine never leave his—at least until he passes behind my chair, where he pauses for a tantalising moment before reemerging on the other side, still locked in his slow orbit, still studying the watch.

—I'm staggered, Mr. Timothy. Did you truly think you could hand me my walking papers? You?

—It never crossed my mind.

—Or maybe you were just hankering to take my place, was that it? Worm your way into the old gal's confidence?

—You needn't worry, George. I leave the whore trade to you.

He almost laughs then.

—Listen to him. The trade's done all right by you now, hasn't it?

—I haven't bit the hand that feeds me.

—You don't even know whose hand's feeding you. I should enlighten you sometime.

—Tell the police, I'm not interested.

—Oh, the police.

His voice, his eyes, the very tips of his fingers are flooded with a rich tributary of irony, and it's impossible, at this moment, not to recall the three policemen who caroused last night around Mrs. Sharpe's negus bowl. On George's payroll, for all I know. On anyone's payroll.

—Yes, indeed, George says.—We must certainly take it up with the police.

He's standing directly behind me now. His hands, suddenly liberated of the watch, are running the length of my shoulders, taking their measure as a tailor might, except their touch is more caressing.

—Really, Mr. Timothy. You make me almost regret it was me who first sent you here. I remember thinking at the time you looked quite harmless. You *are* quite harmless, aren't you, Mr. Timothy?

If I didn't know better, I would assume it was a woman's touch. Slow and cool and lingering, passing from the shoulders to the clavicle and then to my waistcoat, pausing on the way down to toy with each button. A soft, sliding motion, impossible to reconcile with the row of raw knuckles sliding down my abdomen, stopping now just above the wasitband of my trousers and then, after a brief consideration, plunging into my crotch.

I start backwards, but George leans his weight into the chair, pins me against the table, and his hand bears down with a geological force, tightening and contracting round the mound in my trousers, even as his voice eases into a whisper.

—You can't even put it in a woman. You think you've got enough to take *me* on?

Unspeakable, this pain. No longer localised but radiating down every neural corridor. The only response I can make is to deny it, and even so, my body betrays me. The shoulders twitch. The eyeballs quiver. Tongues of sweat run down my cheeks.

And George, seeing it all, speaks in a loving lilt.

—Repeat after me, if you please. No one hands George his walking papers.

Another squeeze. A new infusion of pain, rising up through my ribs, pounding at the walls of my chest.

I close my eyes, but the voice keeps purring in my ear.

—George leaves when he's bloody well ready.

A gentle, reasoning tone, as though he were addressing a child. Why should I be surprised, then, to hear a child's voice answering?

—Maybe you'd like a kick in the balls yourself.

I recognise Colin's voice before I recognise him. Over the last twelve hours, he's unravelled into a creased and dangling shirt, a matted tangle of curls, pillow-mashed eyes . . . he must have spent the night on Mrs. Sharpe's divan. And there's still a bit of sleep clinging to him now as he wavers in the doorway, straining for the right note of truculence.

George relaxes, then releases his grip on me, and, with an affable smile, turns his attention to Colin, *advances* on him, eyes appraising, right arm raised as if for a blow. Only when he sees the telltale flinch on Colin's face does he lower his arm to his side, and even then he darts it out one more time for a brief tousle of the boy's hair. The reaction this produces is so entertaining he repeats it. Then, grinning broadly, he returns back to me.

—The newest word in bodyguards, Mr. Timothy.

I'm standing now, one hand braced against the table to keep me from tottering.

—Are you Mr. *Frig*'s bodyguard, George? Or just his little thieving boy?

He looks at me for a few moments, then wraps his arm around Colin's shoulders, hugging the boy to him like a nephew. A font of human kindness is our George.

—I'd hate to see you lose such a fine young bully, Mr. Timothy. Or anyone else belonging to you.

One last squeeze of Colin's shoulder, and he is gone.

Neither of us moves for a good half minute; we're both, I think, trying to resurrect our dignity. Colin's is restored before mine. He pulls back one of the chairs from the table and sits in it side-saddle. Shakes his head and, to my surprise, pulls out a cigarette—palmed, no doubt, from one of last night's guests—and holds it in the flame of a candle.

—Christ alive. You must've fucked 'im but good, Mr. Timothy.

—I wish I had. I think I've only startled him awake.

Colin takes a long, professional drag, exhales in two forked streams of cloud. He rubs the smoke into his hair and takes another drag, even longer.

—What put him in such a fury?

—I can't say.

—Anything to do with that naked old cove running up the stairs last night?

Oh. Oh, I'd quite forgotten that.

—No. Squidgy's quite benign.

—Happy to know someone is.

I am walking now, and it feels so good I find myself circling the table, just as George was doing a few minutes ago, but without the same confident stride—just my own interrupted cadence.

—Listen to me, Colin. I've been giving some thought to our, our little business relationship.

—Oh?

—I've come to believe that it might be in everyone's best interests if we . . . if we *concluded* it. For the time being.

—What for?

—Well, I think you'd have to agree it's exhausted its usefulness, in a sense. For now. Which isn't to say you haven't been helpful—far from it. You've been, you've been *indispensable*, and I don't know what I would have . . . really, I can't tell you how—

—Is it George? Coz he's all air, that one. He don't scare me a bit.

—It's not George. It's just that the stakes have got a little higher than any of us expected, and I'm feeling, I suppose, *answerable* in a way I wasn't before. And as a consequence, I think it might be time to call in some institutional help.

—You mean the police?

His tone is every bit as scornful as George's was.

—Perhaps the police. I'm not sure.

Colin jams the cigarette back into his mouth and sucks on it until his whole face is fuming like a smokestack. Then he allows himself a luxuriant cat stretch.

—Well, so fuckin' be it. We had us a good run, didn't we, Mr. Timothy? But a man has to know when his time is up, don't he? You won't see me wringin' my titties over it.

—I'm glad you—

—Anyways, I got me a date with my old mum.

—Your mother?

I don't know why I should be so astonished. He's already mentioned a father, and all humans have *mothers*, don't they? Did I think he'd sprung full-blown from the brow of London?

Well, yes. In a manner of speaking, I did. My surprise must be writ across my face, for Colin quickly adds:

—Oh, she's still about. Somewhere. We got this arrangement, see. Every time I come in to a bit of change, I stop in and give her some. It's a little like tithing, ain't it?

—I didn't . . . well, I mean to say, that's very good of you, Colin. To think of her.

He waves me off with his cigarette.

—She gets a better class of gin for a few days, that's all. Not that she notices.

Even this tiny glint of revelation is too much for him. He bounds to his feet, cocks his head towards the doorway.

—You making for Captain Gully's? he asks.

—For a while, yes. Then I'm off to see my uncle.

—Uncle who?

I don't answer. I just tap him lightly on the shoulder and point to the door.

On our way out of the dining room, we encounter another early riser, and not a welcome one. Iris stands by the banister, already in her morning dress, with her arms folded across her chest like a harem eunuch and her face frozen in an attitude of suspended relish. There seems nothing to say but:

—Good morning, Iris.

To which she has a riposte already prepared, it is clear, but it never materialises, for Colin chooses this moment to grab a healthy chunk of her arse. Whether he molests anything beyond several layers of petticoat I cannot say, but Iris is sufficiently put out to swing her right arm in the general direction of his face. Foreseeing this, Colin has already ducked and squirmed his way through, and when next I see him, he is skittering towards freedom, half crawling, half skating. The door slams behind him before Iris has even realised he's gone.

And with that slam comes an odd twinge in my gut. Absurd. Absurd to expect a formal adieu from Colin the Melodious. He sees his chance, he moves on.

Iris, too, is moving on. It takes her a few seconds to recompose herself, but when she turns back to me, the air of triumph has returned, and so has the arch smile, biting hard at the corners of her mouth.

She presses the backside of a playbill into my palm.

—What's this?

—What does it bloody look like? An *invoice*. You don't suppose you could pinch something of mine, and me not know it?

It's not what I would have expected from her, and I have enough presence of mind to note that the handwriting is not Iris's, nor is the language:

Iris Tulliver hereby demands £2 in remuneration
for the theft of one red ribbon from complainant's dresser

How could I have forgot? The ribbon. The one I gave Philomela back in the graveyard. Still adorning her hair, last I checked.

—Two pounds seems rather dear, Iris. Even by your standards.

—The sum in question takes into account the lost hours of sleep, not to mention the disturbance of having a strange man prowling about, howsoever unthreatening he may be.

I fold up the invoice, tuck it neatly in my waistcoat pocket.

—Thank you, Iris. I'll give it the most careful consideration.

—You'd best do more than that, lest you want the madam knowing of your perverted ways.

—Mrs. Sharpe has seen far worse perversions than ribbon stealing.

—Oh, the ribbon is the least of it, I'm sure.

That last remark will haunt me more than perhaps even she could have guessed. I leave Mrs. Sharpe's house, I pass down Pall Mall, I sidestep an overflowed water plug, I drop a coin in the cup of a blind violoncello player, the muffin man's bell rings out—and it all might as well be a painted back-drop from Peter's photography salon, I barely hearken. I am too engaged in the cataloguing of my sins.

A dismal registry, now that I look back on it. Nothing remotely cardinal. Only a chain of malices and fancies and foreshortened desires.

Pinching Jemmy in the neck once when she complained about having to carry me to the table.

Finding Sam's body in the canal and not telling anyone.

Wishing sometimes that Mr. McReady would come back.

Telling Martha her new husband looked like a boil.

Copulating with a black-toothed woman in a St. Giles mews.

And hating my parents for having the temerity to be my parents. And for keeping me in Camden Town, when there were boy pharaohs to see and racetrack-card vendors to meet and Greek myths to be conned and a whole world waiting to wrap its arms around me.

Well, that's the best I can come up with on short notice. Not a hanging offense in the whole bunch, just the slow, steady attenuation of a soul.

So here I stand, prematurely aged on a young day. Yesterday's wind has blown in the sun, and a gentling hand has been laid over the Strand's commotion, granting a quality of reprieve to one's knuckles and toes and ears. Even the fog has ebbed to half its normal density. Trees, seen up close, reveal their full complexity. It is only farther off that their outlines begin to soften and blur, until the very notion of outline loses its meaning, and one could imagine that the whole world was at sea and these trees were simply the masts of ships, and the sounds of dead leaves chattering around the lampposts the rustle of surf.

In a fog such as this, shapes don't just appear; they seem to be forming on the spot from the materials of one's own mind. Behold! a coster's donkey. Lo! a woman with a parasol. A billboard advertisement for Foster's Vintage Ports. An abandoned brazier.

And Father. Mustn't forget Father.

Today he has metamorphosed into a dealer in fancy-ware, stationed near St. Martin-in-the-Fields. A rather fashionable location for your common swag, and the merchandise is pitched accordingly high. Lovely scarf pins and display vases and gilt frames. Leather and bead purses, plated jewelry. A pair of coloured-glass sleeve links in the shape of mastiffs.

Father takes justified pride in these goods. Note the gently proprietary pose of his hands as they rest on the barrow. I would recognise those hands anywhere. The face, too, for that matter, even if it is disguised in a chest-length beard.

The voice, though, is foreign. So unalterably foreign it stings.

—Ah, I see you got your eye on the eardrops, sir. Take my word for it, they makes a lovely lady even lovelier.

And in this manner, Father vanishes as abruptly as he appeared. And just when I was ready to pepper him with questions:

How is the post where you are?

And have you bumped into Serafino Rotunno?

And just what are the dead afraid of?

I shall have to write them all on a piece of paper next time, and hurl it straight into his ectoplasmic heart.

—Why, we never knew we had so much grime about us, Tim. Boggles the mind, don't it?

So says Captain Gully, standing fully erect on his chair while waves of domestic industry wash at his feet. Philomela, sporting yesterday's trousers, has just swept under the chair, having already beaten the hearth rug and swept away the ashes, and now, without a moment's respite, she throws herself onto all fours to swab the metal surfaces of the fireplace with blacking. In between the rubbings of the rag, I can hear her brief exhalations; I can see her pinked complexion and the lines of sweat leaching through her temples. Going at it with every fibre of her being, is our Filly, and I know enough of her not to be surprised. She has to earn her room and board somehow, doesn't she?

The amusing part is how Gully keeps pointing her out to me—with his whole arm extended, as though she were a comet or a zoological specimen.

—We'll have you know, Tim, before dawn, before we was even out of bed this mornin', this'n was heating the copper and scrubbin' the bejeezus out of our shirts. Look at 'em, Tim! They're positively holy!

It's true. Gully's still-damp shirts billow in the open window like the suspended bodies of priests. They have left a film of perspiration over everything in the room: tabletop, chairs, globe, scrimshaw, even Gully's upper lip.

—We says to her, we says, "Come away, lass, there's no need, so early in the day." And she gives us such a look as though to say, her English not being what ours is, *Why, what better time is there?* And Gully knows he's a beaten man, he does, so he gives her free rein, don't he? And blessed if she don't take to the work like a hog to shit.

—Well, it's delightful, Captain, to see the two of you getting on so famously.

—Oh, we're boon companions, that's what we is. Ain't we boon companions, now, Filly?

A slow, abiding nod from the scrubbing girl. She must have been asked this question many times in the past twenty-four hours.

—Last night, we was playin' a bit of casino, Tim, and it took her maybe three rounds to get it down. To the point she was slaughterin' us by the end of the evening! And then, 'fore that, we had a go of backgammon. Natural genius, Tim. There she was, just a few particklers of instruction, and lo and behold and never say die, she was a-leapfroggin' over us 'fore the hair could even settle on our head. Weren't you, now, Filly? A bloody prodigy, weren't you?

Another nod.

—Not that we lets her out of our sight, Tim. Oh, perish the thinkin'. Why, if there's water to fetch, it's Gully as does it. If there's cold pork 'n' beans or sherry to be got, why, Gully's your man. Never goes out but by the back way. Always looks both directions lest he's being shadowed.

He demonstrates it for me. Swivel, swivel.

—And mind you, every time we comes back, don't you think we uses a Secret Knock? So she knows it's Gully and not some malfeasor? Look, we'll as good as show you.

He disappears into the outer hallway. A pause of five seconds and then a gentle tattoo on the door, recognisable (from its metre alone) as the opening bars of "Pop Goes the Weasel."

And then, on cue, Philomela's voice, articulating with the greatest care:

—Come in, please.

At which invitation the door swings open to reveal Gully, beaming from his soles on up.

—You see, Tim? Works like a charm, every blessed time.

The next hour passes like the most benign of factory shifts. Gully hums his fragments of Christmas carol and scans the paper for corpses ("Oh, now this'n looks promisin', a leaper off Blackfriars. Can't have drifted far, can he?"). Philomela dusts the globe and the scrimshaw collection and the pile of atlases and plumps herself down by Gully's chair to clean her boots. Rotating divisions of cats brush against the furniture, leap from the windowsill, or simply gaze about in a fog—perplexed, I imagine, by the peace that has dropped on them like mercy.

And Timothy? He leans against the wall. Lets his thoughts rove at leisure.

Invariably, they come back to the same place, to the fancy-ware dealer outside St. Martin's. My mind keeps stretching, elongating itself, as I try to remember if there was anyone else in the picture. Anyone I should have been on the alert for.

—What did your father look like, Philomela?

She looks up from her polishing. The word lolls on her tongue:

—Look . . .

I point to my face.

—His features. What did he look like?

She shrugs, makes a sketching motion with her hand. That's all it takes. Within seconds, Gully has procured the necessary items: a quire of paper, a pen, an inkwell. Philomela seats herself at the table, cautiously dips the pen, makes a few preliminary scratches, then abruptly crumples the sheet and begins again.

From there, it is a largely unhindered progression of short, sharply etched lines. Occasionally we hear her make a muffled cry over an errant mark, but for the most part, she works steadily, and as the minutes pass, her wrists loosen and her hands range with greater freedom across the paper, and before we know it, Serafino Rotunno is reborn, in all his Calabrian splendour. Fairly bursting from the page, he is: the round, wide-set eyes, made all the more watchful by the receding brow; the half smile, with its uneven rows of teeth; the tiny dimple in his chin, like a thumb pressed lightly into peat.

—My father, says Philomela.

No particular inflection in her voice. Simply stating it for the world's benefit.

Gully, entranced, leans over the table, whispering into the paper.

—Oh, me. She's got the gift, though, ain't she?

It is impossible to deny, and impossible to define. Working without charcoal or paint, she has nevertheless created her own shading, her own colour. An alchemy of ink. How mysteriously her subject emerges from the paper. And how pleased the subject would have been to build a frame for it.

—Tell me, Philomela. Can you draw the man who was chasing us? The one in the bowler hat?

She frowns, then sets to work. More false starts this time, more sheets sacrificed to her displeasure, and even when she is finished, she must hold it up to the candlelight for another minute before she is ready to part with her creation.

The sight of it sends a shard of ice through me. She has caught him in the moment of our first meeting. The roundish face, with its narrow brown eyes and the barest glimmer of a grin. The hard topknot of the hat.

And the wood-carver's blade, agleam and almost afloat—an obelisk of steel.

—Excellent likeness, Philomela. May I keep it for the time being?

She nods.

—And now . . . what of the man in the carriage, Philomela?

Oh, I should have expected it. The old eraser, wiping her face clean before anyone can stop it.

—The man who wished to take you away, Philomela. I need you to draw him.

She shakes her head.

—I may not.

—It would be a great help if you could.

—My hand. It won't . . .

But her hand looks quite purposeful as it descends into the pocket of her newly acquired trousers, clasps its small bundle, and reemerges with fingers fluttering.

The rosary beads.

Amazing how the sight of them enrages me. I don't trust myself; I have to walk almost to the other side of the room.

—It's all right, Philomela. You don't have to draw him.

She is calmer when I turn round; the litany has done its work. Indeed, I would go so far as to call her completely serene at the moment she looks up at me and says:

—We kill them.

The contrast between those words and the holy relic in her hand is so pronounced it fattens my tongue, numbs my lips. A line of bluster trails from my mouth.

—Well, no, we may . . . we may bring them to *account*, yes, but we cannot presume to . . . that is for the ministers of justice and . . . and for God. . . .

—Or they kill us.

And what is there to say to that? So many things. Nothing. I sink into Gully's chair, and he takes the chair opposite Philomela, and the three of us lapse into silence—broken only at intervals by the plaints of cats, circling the furniture and snagging threads of rug and brushing against our trousers.

And then, in a quick hot burst of empathy, Gully reaches for Philomela's shoulder, strokes it gently.

—There, there. Won't be no need for a-killin', dear one. Not while Gully's in the crow's nest.

The look she gives him then produces an instant echo in my mind. It is an exact replica of the look George gave me earlier—that strange, fleeting pity, but with a new element this time: consolation. *Poor man*, she seems to be saying. *I don't have the heart to tell you.*

And so she goes back to polishing her boots.

Chapter 15

SOMEONE HAS TIED A WREATH round the gargoyle on Uncle N's door, but this has in no respect limited the creature's omnipotence. If anything, it is simply the tribute a downtrodden world pays its conqueror, and even Mrs. Pridgeon, opening the door with her usual ponderousness, is, in this setting, nothing more than a handmaiden to the great gargoyle god. A lifetime of submission is stamped on her stooping shoulder.

—Good afternoon, *Master* Cratchit.

—Is my uncle about?

The barest of shrugs, as though to say, *When is he not?* She leaves it to me to close the door and immediately makes for the stairs.

—Am I at the head of the queue today, Mrs. Pridgeon?

No response. The funeral march has begun. As I follow my fellow pall-bearer up the stairs, I sneak a look at the sitting room, expecting to find it empty, and thus all the more startled to find another visitor, yielding place to me. A man of perhaps fifty years, hat in hands, observing me with the keenest interest. How familiar he seems: that theatrical bearing, the fine wounded eyes with their deep-revolving plans. It is the very man who was studying me last time I was here. No more inclined to part with me now than he was then. Even after he has passed from view, I can feel the ray of his gaze striking me between the shoulder blades. It prickles, this gaze—unmans—and it is a decided relief to stand finally on the first-floor landing, in the half light, with nothing but the prospect of Uncle N's bedroom door before me.

—Knock first, says Mrs. Pridgeon.

The fire is still roaring in the bedroom grate, but the bed itself is empty, and the bedclothes have been tossed off like gift wrapping, and I'm just beginning to wonder if this is a form of holiday prank when I catch sight of Uncle N's robed form by his converted dressing table—bent over a microscope, oblivious to outside distraction.

Who would have dreamt? Uncle N, back to his collecting.

For many years, of course, he collected nothing but mammon. But his friends having long pressed him to take up a hobby suitable to his station and time of life, he, after due consideration, hit upon one that, in some peculiar way, expressed his inner nature. Which is to say, he became an amateur naturalist, specializing in fungi. A small collection at first—mostly mushrooms from the local market—gradually expanding to include rusts, smuts, and mildew. Now and again, Peter and I would bring him a fistful of brewer's yeast or a particularly mouldy loaf of bread that the Cratchits had given up on. One might have thought we'd brought him Arabian perfume: he would sweep his booty into his arms and, with a distracted smile and a promise to return presently, make a headlong dash for the microscope. We might not see him again for an hour.

I once plucked up the nerve to ask him what he found so very appealing about fungi.

—Oh, but they're ingenious, Tim, don't you see? They grow in soil, water—wherever they *can* grow, they grow. Perfect little opportunists.

Much as you used to be, Uncle: that was the un-Christian thought that first seized me. Over time, however, I came to appreciate the exemplary qualities of fungi. As proof, I offer you Uncle N himself, grabbing the first opportunity to grow out of bed, colonising the surface nearest to hand. Ingenious in his own right.

—You look much better, Uncle, I tell him now.

He draws away from the microscope, rubs his naked eyes. Smiles faintly.

—I find myself at one of those strange crossroads, Tim, between illness and health. Trying to glimpse the signpost, as it were.

—To health?

—To home.

And in that moment, it's as though the air were being drawn open like a drape: I see this same house as it will be not so many years hence. The microscope abandoned in a corner, the fungi scattered to the winds. Strange hands filling and cleaning the lamps. Strange feet resting by the downstairs grate, strange voices commenting on its old-fashioned Dutch tile, the scriptural tableaux. "What sort of person would have kept such a grate?" they will ask, and will not stay to answer.

Uncle N exerts himself to rise from his chair, then abandons the effort halfway. Making a virtue of necessity, he crosses his legs and leans back in an attitude of boulevard ease.

—Well, this is a lovely surprise, Tim. I hadn't expected you back so soon.

—I am as surprised as you, Uncle. I will not keep you long.

—You may keep me as long as you like, I have no objection. Time is bizarrely irrelevant at my stage in life. As are pastimes.

He has taken the room's one chair, and so my only recourse is to sit on the edge of his still-unmade bed. The feather mattress collapses gently beneath my weight, virtually soundless in its protest.

—I have come because I need your help, Uncle.

—You shall have it, if it is mine to give.

—I hope it is. I am looking for an honest policeman.

Carefully, he wipes his spectacles on the sleeve of his robe.

—Why, that shouldn't be so difficult. There must be dozens, surely.

—Be that as it may, I have reason to be skeptical.

He returns his glasses to their original perch and peers at me over the rims, and in that instant, his face assumes the shrewd mercantile air my parents used to speak of. It passes, however, before I can fix it for posterity. All that is left is a straightforward query:

—Does it relate to that business of yours? The one you alluded to last time you were here?

—Yes.

—And is it fair to say that in the course of pursuing this business, you have encountered some less-than-sterling representatives of the Metropolitan Police?

—Yes.

—And you are looking for someone who would not be beholden in any way to these aforementioned persons?

—In a manner of speaking.

One long, knobby finger taps the bridge of his nose in a rigid pendulum beat. He starts to speak, stops himself, starts again.

—I know of a man.

And as though to reassure himself that yes, yes, he does know a man, he nods several times over and says:

—Surtees is the name. Detective Inspector Graham Surtees. Curious sort of fellow. Assisted me with a rather tricky embezzlement case some years back. One thinks he's not quite attending at first, then it turns out he's attended far more than one could have imagined. Quietly dogged, no matter how he behaves on first acquaintance. If there's any of them to be trusted, he's your man.

—I will remember, Uncle. And now, would you be so kind as to write me a letter of introduction?

The ink and paper are easy to procure, and within two minutes, he has written, in his tight, sharply angled hand:

I herein commend to you my de facto *nephew Timothy Cratchit. Would you have the goodness to hear him out with all due kindness and deliberation? He is*

most awfully bothered about something, and knowing him as I do, I can assert
with conviction that he is seldom bothered without cause. Please assist him as
you would me, and you shall have my
  Everlasting thanks and gratitude,
  EBS

Smiling mostly to myself, I fold the letter in half, turn it into an unsealed
envelope, and tuck it inside my jacket.

—Thank you, Uncle. I shall see him this afternoon, with your blessing.

—You have it. Only stay a moment.

—Yes?

—I have promised, I *know*, not to pry into your affairs, and I am bound
and determined to keep that promise. But remember what I told you, Tim. If
in these next few days, you need anything, anything at all, you have only to
send word, and I'll rouse myself from this bed and tear down rafters and . . .
and . . . oh, that line, Tim. The one we used to laugh about.

—Spirit-calling, you mean?

—Yes, tell me how it goes.

—*I can call spirits from the vasty deep.*

—And the other fellow, remind me what he says.

—*But will they come when you do call them?*

—Ha! That's it. Excellent, yes, very fine.

For nigh on another minute, he speaks the line over and over again to the
square of floorboard between his feet, chuckling after each iteration and
muttering:

—Oh, fine . . . deuced fine, that.

Whereupon, seemingly replenished, he looks up at me again.

—Tim.

The briefest hesitation then. And in that interval, I feel a roiling inside him
and all round him, and I have to fight the impulse to quit the room without a
backwards look.

—I was only wondering, Tim, if you still see your father.

—Yes. Here and there.

A great expanse of air issues from his throat—more air than I would have thought that shrunken chest could hold. His head tips to one side, and it looks as if it might keep tipping all the way to the floor, but then, like a flat, bony pillow, his hand rises to meet it in a trembling stasis, and it is from this nearly recumbent angle that he gazes at me and says:

—I used to see spirits, too, Tim. Terrible things. How I miss them.

At the age of eleven, I was persuaded, for about ten minutes, that I was destined to be a bobby. It was Peter who informed me, as gently as he knew how, that even were I able to walk someday without a crutch, I would very likely fall short of the height requirement. In fact, that would indeed prove the case—I tapered off just shy of sixty-eight inches. And so to my adolescent mind, the members of the Metropolitan Police came to seem like another race altogether: stiff-lipped, fat-necked giants, bestriding our narrow streets like colossi.

So here I am at last, in the colossi's den, stepping into this disreputable cluster of buildings off Whitehall Place and finding not giants but a hive of discombobulated bees: sergeants in top hats and swallowtail coats bustling past on no discernible trajectory, vaulting over piles of books, tripping on stray saddles and blankets, smacking their knees on balustrades. The air sings with din and velocity and confusion, and with the crackle of my own foreboding.

This is Scotland Yard. . . .

Inspector Graham Surtees, to whose office I am ushered, bears as much resemblance to the rest of the constabulary as a salmon does to a school of herring. He is not so much bigger as more concentrated: tall and stretched thin, with eyes at once stern and watery, and a chin that slopes imperceptibly into his neck, and long, skeletal fingers that he interlaces across his chest. This last gesture gives him the air of a slumming don, and even so, the donnishness seems rather carefully constructed. Squint hard enough, and you can see the vowels and consonants and inflections and mannerisms piled atop one another, brick by brick, according to someone's blueprint. Piled, perhaps, too high. The air is thin where Inspector Surtees now lives.

He asks me first if I would like some licorice, and looks chagrined when I decline. He compensates by jamming a piece into his own mouth and clamping down on it with all the force of a bear trap. Through clenched teeth, he asks after my uncle.

—How is good Mr. Drood? Still slaving away at the law?

—Banking, actually. And the name is—

—Ah yes, the counting house. Getting and spending.

—And the business, such as it is, has been handed over to his nephew. His blood nephew, I mean.

—Blood, yes.

He snatches up a piece of paper just to the right of his elbow, reads it with a show of great interest, then crumples it and tosses it over his shoulder, where it joins a great cairn of paper snowballs by the grate. All of them apparently waiting to be consumed by fire, although the strands of cobweb across the grate testify to months of disuse.

Without warning, Inspector Surtees slams down a hand on the desk.

—Well, Mr. Cratchit, you profess to have urgent business. Will you do me the kindness of proceeding? But stop . . . you're quite sure you won't take some licorice? No? Well, proceed then, by all means.

He looks me square in the eye to begin with, but as the tale unfolds, his eyelids grow swollen and listless, and his head sinks very gradually towards his chest, and one would think him asleep were it not for a curious galvanic current, which manifests itself in an agitation of the fingertips and in jerks of the head that leave me feeling, each time, like a burglar caught with his fingers in the eaves.

It takes me longer than I expected to finish, and perhaps in deference to my labour, the good inspector allows a cloud of silence to build up round us before he offers his thoughts.

—I wonder, Mr. Cratchit. I sometimes wonder if papist blood runs in my veins.

—Sorry?

—I'm so enormously attracted to trinities, you see. I simply dote on them. And here, as a kind of early Christmas gift, you have given me the most remarkable trinity. Three girls, Mr. Cratchit. Compellingly triangulated, but each intriguing in her own right. And so we take them, for no good reason, in sequence. This first one . . . you found her body where?

—In an alley off Jermyn Street.

—Ah, Jermyn. Did you know—why this should come to mind, I can't say—Newton lived there.

—Did he?

—Can't think of the house number right off. Hardly matters, does it? Now this aforementioned girl. If I recall correctly, there were constables on duty at the time.

—Two of them. I assume, as a consequence, there is some record of the crime.

—Record. Mm.

He flutters his fingers towards the wall behind him. My eyes take in the half-open cabinets, all of them vomiting paper—paper of every colour and thickness, poking out at all angles and sprouting long tendrils of dust. On the floor behind me, still more paper, crammed pell-mell into biscuit crates and flowerpots and already yellowing with antiquity.

Inspector Surtees gives his fingers another flutter.

—For economy's sake, let us move with lightning speed to the second girl. The one you and your friend found downriver. May I ask where you left the body?

—With the coroner's office in Rotherhithe.

—Did you stay to make a report?

—No.

—How peculiar. Why ever not?

—I don't know. My friend wanted to. I don't know.

His eyes fog over.

—Friends, yes. They . . . redoubleth joys, and they . . . and they cutteth griefs in half. Something along those lines. Bacon, I think. Neither here nor there, but tell me, if you please. The name of your wise friend?

—I'd rather not say just now.

—It would be most helpful to have corroboration.

—I know it would.

He pulls down one of his grey eyes, regards me for a cool half minute.

—Your friend is perhaps engaged in an unorthodox profession. You'll note I do not say "illicit," I say only "unorthodox."

—He is a retired seaman. How he earns a wage currently, I couldn't say.

—And how do *you* earn a wage, Mr. Cratchit?

—I am a tutor.

—In what subject?

—Reading.

—And whom do you instruct?

—That is not for me to say.

This draws from him the most amiable smile of our brief acquaintance.

—It is vexing, Mr. Cratchit. You come to me for assistance in prosecuting a crime, and yet you decline to answer any of my questions.

—Because the questions do not pertain to the crime. If I may remind you, Inspector, we are talking about three girls—at *least* three, quite possibly many more—all of them, by my reckoning, abducted, branded in the most horrible fashion, almost certainly cozened into prostitution, and in some cases murdered. If you would care to direct any inquiries to me on *this* subject, I should be delighted to answer them.

For whatever reason, he chooses that moment to dive behind his desk. An angry rattle, the scraping of a drawer—more licorice?—and from the same general vicinity, the inspector's disembodied voice, asking:

—How old were these girls, Mr. Cratchit?

—I can speak for the one who is alive. She is ten.

—You mean that is what she told you.

—I mean that is what she is.

His head reappears above the horizon of his desk.

—And the ages of the other girls? The ones you found?

—I have no way of knowing.

—Your best guess, then. Have a go.

—Ten or eleven. Twelve at most.

His eyebrows pinch together; his lips push outwards.

—I ask only—why do I ask? Oh! Because the age of consent, you see, is thirteen.

—I wasn't aware that murder victims needed to tender their consent.

—Ah, but we don't know that these are murders, do we? You said yourself there were no marks other than . . . bloody hands, was it?

—Yes.

—A certain look of terror in the eyes, was that it?

—Yes.

—Anything else?

—No. No, that was quite enough.

And now he is up on his feet, strolling through his office as though it were a village common. Sniffing the air, pumping his arms. Sliding his boots through the drifts of snow-paper.

—You mentioned a man in a carriage. With rings and whatnot. Let us fasten on him for a moment.

—I don't know who he is, Inspector.

—Not a clue?

—I have . . . I have a frustrating sense of having seen him somewhere, but I can't recall where.

—Perhaps there's something else you recall. A stray nuance. I adore nuance.

—I've told you everything. There was . . . there was a coat of arms on the carriage.

—Can you describe that for me, Mr. Cratchit?

—I didn't get much of a look.

—Anything at all.

—There was, I think, a lion in it.

—A lion.

—It seemed to be a lion. A lion's tail, at any rate. Haunches. That kind of thing.

—Ah, yes, haunches.

It doesn't matter how often I come back to that coat of arms. It's always muddle. And the muddle never clears, although it does brighten. Indeed, it becomes extraordinarily vivid in my mind, and this vividness is somehow indivisible from the muddle, as though the image acquires, in the act of breaking down, a prodigious and supernatural power. Can things do that, Inspector?

—There was another man, Mr. Cratchit. The one who pursued you with the blade.

—Yes.

—Perhaps you could describe him for me.

—I can do better.

The drawing looks quite small, spread across the expanse of Surtees' cherry desk. It seems almost to be shrinking before my eyes—awaiting the fate that must come to all paper in this place.

—Did you sketch this yourself, Mr. Cratchit?

—My young friend.

—And is it a good likeness?

—An ideal likeness.

He pushes his face to within six inches of the paper. And there is something about the way he holds his pose, something about the way his eyes fix on the image, rather than glancing away, something that makes me say:

—You recognise him.

He studies it awhile longer, then raises his head.

—Sergeant William Rebbeck.

And as he speaks the name, his eyes dart towards the doorway, in a rush of expectancy, and I swivel round in my chair, fully expecting to see Mr. Bowler himself, bearing down with his gleaming blade, and I am already heaping curses on myself—the credulity of you!—and my arms have crossed in front of me, bracing for the blow, but they are not braced for *this* blow, which is simply a gale of surprise. For the doorway is empty, empty.

And from behind me comes the inspector's soothing voice.

—My apologies, Mr. Cratchit, I have led you astray. Sergeant Rebbeck is nowhere in the building. Indeed, he no longer bears the title of sergeant, being no longer affiliated with Scotland Yard.

I fix him with my best interrogative glare.

—Was Sergeant Rebbeck employed by the Detective Department?

—Like most police, he regarded this department with an implacable hostility. In which I take a sort of morbid pride.

—And when did he leave the force?

—Three years ago this past September.

—And was he asked to leave?

—That, I'm afraid, is confidential business, Mr. Cratchit. Not for idle bruiting, I'm sure you understand.

—I *would* understand if he hadn't taken to chasing people with woodcarvers' blades.

Eyes shining, Surtees jabs an index finger into the air. A quality of childish gloating suffuses his face.

—Primitive Methodist.

—I'm sorry?

—Willie's late father. Methodist minister. Don't know why I should recall that.

Why indeed? I find myself gripping the arms of my chair just to cram down the anger. Uncle N's words rattle in my ear:

One thinks he's not quite attending at first. . . .

—You refer to him as Willie, Inspector. Am I to presume you are friends?

—Oh, that's just the fragment of an old nickname, Mr. Cratchit. Not one I coined. But here you are, in need of assurances, so may I offer you one? This very day, I promise you, I shall do everything in my power to locate Mr. Rebbeck and call him in for inquiries.

—Inquiries?

—Why, yes. If in fact there is some larger criminal enterprise at work—a point I don't necessarily concede, but for argument's sake—and if certain malfeasants are indeed preying on young girls, then surely we should begin by questioning the one man who is known to have some connection to them.

—In the hope that he will confess on the spot? Is that the presumption?

—I have learnt never to presume anything, Mr. Cratchit.

—And whilst you are posing polite inquiries of your friend Willie, his employer will simply take on a replacement and continue his operation unimpeded.

—Mr. Cratchit, as soon as I am persuaded that such an operation exists, I will move like an Arabian steed to close it down. I've never seen an Arabian steed, but I fancy it moves very quickly indeed.

He is leaning back in his chair again, his hands once more interlaced across his chest. He gives a soft little whistle.

—Oh, me, you are still not satisfied, Mr. Cratchit.

—No.

—You believe . . . I am merely speculating here, forgive me . . . you believe that even were we to take Mr. Rebbeck into custody, this young friend of yours would remain in danger.

—I do.

—Then by all means, allow me to put your mind at ease. Simply tell me where she is, and I shall do my best to see to her safety.

Odd. When I left them this morning, I couldn't have imagined her any safer. She was sitting on the arm of Gully's chair, leafing through his atlas. He had asked her to point out her native town, but the town itself was not shown, just a blur of topographical green, and even this was enough to draw names from her mouth: Rossano . . . Policastro . . . Paola . . . Acri. . . . Whether these were neighbouring villages or people who inhabited them, I couldn't have said. But Gully listened in a trance of respect, the way one might listen to a Latin mass, understanding and not understanding. He was filled with the sacredness of his obligation. And as I think back on that, I ask myself: How could a peeler ever feel the same?

—He who hesitates, Mr. Cratchit.

And still I linger over that tiny tableau, and it takes the jagged edge of the inspector's voice to scatter it for good.

—I trust your faith in Scotland Yard has not been unduly tainted by your experience with Mr. Rebbeck.

—Faith in general is in very short supply with me these days, Inspector. I have become quite miserly with it.

—In other words, you wish to take sole responsibility for this girl.

—Until the men who seek to harm her are in Newgate. Or swinging from a noose.

—And failing that?

—Failing that, I must declare myself an independent agent. With all due respect.

His eyes seem to narrow and widen at the same time. He clears his throat.

—Well, in my official capacity, Mr. Cratchit, I cannot, of course, sanction the path you have chosen. But as a private citizen, I am bound to wish you well.

—I should be glad of more than good wishes.

—And I hope to offer you more. Once I have learnt anything of import, you may be sure I shall be in touch. May I ask you to do me the same courtesy?

—You may be sure of it.

And with that, he jumps to his feet—frankly relieved, I think, to have this tiresome business put behind him. He rubs his hands together with unmistakable relish.

—So there is nothing left, Mr. Cratchit, but to bid you a very merry Christmas.

—I think you are being ironical.

—Not a bit.

He takes my hand. And if there is an unexpected warmth in that clasp, and a flash of solicitude in his mild grey eyes, those sensations pass so quickly as to cast themselves into doubt.

I am nearly in the hallway before I think to turn round again.

—How did the rest of it go, Inspector?

—Rest of what?

—That nickname you mentioned. The one coined for Sergeant Rebbeck. How did the rest of it go?

—Oh, it was just one of those jesting epithets the locals give a chap. I shouldn't worry if I were you. I myself was known as—

—Indulge me all the same. What was the full name?

It is his turn to hesitate. And as though to override his initial reluctance, he says the name at a higher volume than is strictly necessary, and with the crispest possible diction:

—Willie the Slasher.

Merry Christmas. A very merry Christmas indeed.

Yet there must be a measure of genuine holiday spirit welling up inside me, for my first impulse on leaving Scotland Yard is to return to the toy shop that I first passed with Philomela and Colin. For the strange purpose of buying Philomela a gift.

There are many items to choose from: a toy carousel in the shop window, and inside, rows and rows of hobbyhorses, cricket bats, tops, boats, drums, bows and arrows, miniature prams. I settle on something obscure and plain: a rag doll with a swollen, mottled head and legs that corkscrew around each other. Paltry creature, to be sure, but the sales clerk cannot find enough superlatives for it.

—Absolutely charming. Exquisite. The little girl will love it.

I don't have a little girl.

And the mere act of repressing that thought drives me into a pique, which the rest of the world conspires to extend. A viscous puddle materialises beneath my left boot. The right boot is crunched by a young boy swinging himself round a lamppost. (This has the odd effect of reintroducing me to my knee, unusually querulous today.) Even a makeshift group of carolers, stationed along the Strand, decides to wander far from its original key and then aggravates the damage with ill-timed flings of handbells.

The only thing to do is keep moving, in the circuitous path that has come to seem native to me. East for a couple of blocks, checking the reflections in shop windows. North for a block, south for two more blocks, zigzagging, changing tempo, and whirling about . . . avoiding any semblance of a pattern.

And then, finally, down the river. Only here, amidst the barges' grumbling and the gulls' flapping and the jetties' slow rocking, only here do things feel completely visible. The wind blows hard from the west, and the salt from the river has scrubbed the air clear, and a strange vitality sneaks into my limbs. The knee ceases its singing, the arm tingles with unspent force. I think, if I were inclined, I could hurl this rag doll halfway across the river.

But when I reach the bottom of Craven Street, the doll is pressed even more tightly into my midsection. I make one last check of the periphery—Gully's patented swivel-swivel—and then forge up the avenue, straight into a ten-knot wind. A starling totters past me in the general direction of the Hungerford Pier. Rising up in its place is a bird of another kind.

—Hello, dearie.

She stands there with her hips thrust to one side.

—What a fine pack of man you are.

The words are coarse, yes, the voice a pawnbroker's squawk, but what explains this attire? Better suited to Grosvenor Square, I'd say, than to Limehouse. An almost perfect cone, from her high-crowned, bell-shaped felt hat to her grey jacket hanging full from the shoulders to her even fuller skirt of purple wool, braided at the hem. A structure of Euclidean purity, with that exquisite little hat dancing on top like virtue's ensign.

—Care to taste some of Sweet Sally's candy?

Lest I mistake her intent, she unbuttons her jacket, inserts two fingers into the line of her bodice, and pulls it down to reveal a ribbon of white flesh.

In my short time on earth, I have been approached by enough gay ladies to feel quite calloused on the subject. Why should this particular band of flesh have the quality of a summons? Well, she is lovely, for one thing. Terribly lovely, in her highborn weeds. Lacking the prostitute's usual swath of paint, her face has found its own lustre. It fears no more the light of the sun.

I take a step forwards, another step back. Her body writhes in a pantomime of desire. She grips the hem of her bodice and pulls hard, until the fabric at last gives way, ripping downwards in a jagged scar to reveal a translucent swath of camisole. But there is barely time to enjoy the view for, after one final smile, she erupts into a sky-shattering cry:

—Rogue! Villain! Help!

Other sounds come hard upon it. Cries and footsteps, thundering down the street, merging with the percussion of my heart. I have the raw sense that all of London is converging on us, and still the woman keeps baying, in the ripe tone of a Coburg melodrama.

—I am undone! Villain!

Her speech gives way then to wordless sobs, punctuated by shrieks. Someone, an elderly man, is drawing her away, throwing his coat around her, murmuring in her ear. Someone else is running for a constable. (*But I was just talking to one.* . . .) And in this frenzy of motion, there is one peculiarly still point: a woman standing under a sage awning with a black parasol and smiling on me with an entire Sunday's worth of benevolence.

I recognise her immediately. The missionary who tried to take Philomela away.

Not one for grudges, though, is our Miss Binny. Nods to me in the most pleasant fashion. I think, if the context weren't quite so awkward, she would have no compunction in saying how nice it is to see me again. But then, her whole purpose is to see me again. In this very context.

—Here's your man, Officer.

A low voice, from a region just behind me. A stubby hand on my shoulder.

Back in Inspector Surtees' office, of course, he was no more than an imminence. Now he is as real as breath, hard as macadam. And he is grasping not the blade I remember from our last meeting but something that, on first sight, seems less threatening. A small leather bladder, shaped like a petrified tear.

And it seems he has trained at the Coburg himself, for he raises his hand in a gesture of pure declamation, and his voice reaches all the way to the back of the gallery.

—Scoundrel!

The leather sap descends. My right temple bursts into flame. And the last thing I see is Philomela's rag doll falling to earth.

———❦———

23 December 1860

Dear Father,

I can't be entirely certain of the date. There are no windows in this particular establishment, and for all I know, it is still the twenty-second. But the air has an early-morning rawness, and the gentlemen with whom I share the space are deep in alcoholic stupors, except for one, who is having brief and distinct conversations with an invisible interlocutor. He's the only one I recognise, oddly enough. Lushing Leo. Used to make a habit of throwing himself into the Serpentine in Hyde Park, so that passersby might fish him out and carry him off to the Humane Society, where he would be restored only with copious quantities of brandy. Four, five, six times a day, our Leo was being rescued, until the good folk of the Society caught on. Whereupon Leo took his dodge to St. James's Park, waiting, on any given night, upwards of two hours to be saved. He used to say, with a shake of his head, that people wasn't as Christian as they once was.

He slumbers now, five feet away. Quite damp, as you might expect: the stone floor has grown fairly mossy beneath him, and the air is swampy with his evaporations. Dead to the world, but more than able to hold up his end of the conversation.

—Uncommon parched, sir. Uncommon parched. Oh, God bless. Lord have mercy. . . .

In some respects, he is having a better time of it than I. Speech is virtually impossible for me just now: my mouth is numb, and all available sensation seems to have concentrated around my right eye. This head of mine, Father, has swelled like an exotic gourd. It feels freakishly large, larger even than myself.

And yet, in the troughs between the throbbing, I have located deep recesses of lucidity. I find myself ranging with great confidence over the facts of past and present.

Gully and Philomela, for instance. I believe them to be safe. For you see, I was waylaid before I could give them away. And if Gully is true to his vow, Philomela will never stir out of doors until I have given him word, and how can I give him word when I am a tenant of the station-house cell? So for now, I believe them safe.

What else can I say with certainty? The jailer is fat. I infer this from hearing the tread of his feet against the stone, the way his keys jingle and then go instantly silent, as if they were being smothered in a great orifice. I seem to recall, too, a pair of porcine hands diving into my pockets, but perhaps I say that only because my purse has been confiscated. One of my purses. I have adopted Signor Arpelli's practice of keeping a separate purse in an inner compartment. Ha!

Gully and Philomela, safe. Jailer, fat. Money, here. What else?

It is raining. Of that I am almost certain. Raining quite violently, to judge from the tiny cataract of water spilling down the wall behind me. Also, there is a periodic tremor in the floor that suggests thunder. In my mind, Father, it is one of those titanic gales—the kind that split tombstones and bowl down villages. I can hear it battering Mrs. Sharpe's casement windows, I can see the long fingers of water snarling down the joists of my bedroom ceiling. Drip drip. Drab drab. I hope your comforter will stay dry.

Well, that about exhausts the present, so what remains for an intermittently lucid mind to do? Lacking better exercise, it must turn to the past. Why it should fix upon Sam, I cannot say. I almost never think of him any more, although there was a year or so when I thought of nothing else. But he was still fresh in the ground then.

One thing I never told you, Father: I was the first to find him. You see, I'd wanted him to take me down by the tracks with his friends, to race the Birmingham parliamentary, but Sam said I'd only embarrass him, which was almost certainly true—I could never have competed with the other boys—but still a bitter thing to hear put so baldly. So I resolved to follow him, at a safe distance. Quite the detective I was, hobbling along, ducking in and out of niches and mews. I lost him somewhere by the Railway Arms and wandered about for close to half an hour, seeking him in eating houses and office houses and the goods yard. No sign. By that point I was all done in—following people was exhausting work for me then—so I sat on an embankment overlooking the canal and closed my eyes, and when I opened them again, there was the most extraordinary thing billowing in the water: a great flower, practically a whole new phylum. Brown fronds and white petals and pistils that looked very much like boots.

I don't think I understood what it was—not completely—until I went into the Excavators' House of Call and asked them for a hot lemonade. And when the alarum came half an hour after, I was reluctant to leave; in fact, I didn't want to leave ever again.

But I did, somehow. And I remember how startled you were, Father, that I'd made it to the scene so quickly. Or perhaps you were just twining your brain—even then, in that first numbing shock—around the inscrutable workings of Fate. Because it wasn't supposed to be Sam, was it? The child you lost too soon.

He never even made it to the Birmingham train. As best anyone could tell, he snagged his foot crossing the bridge, tumbled headfirst into the canal, and struck his skull on a submerged stone. Precious little water in his lungs, the doctor said. He never had a chance to drown.

And that was all for Sam, except memories, and what is left even of memories? Yours and Mother's are interred with your bones. Mine are founded on perhaps six years' acquaintance and bent through the prism of childhood; I scarcely trust them. If I think of Sam at all now, I think of him as an absence . . . or else a different sort of presence. A timbre that could be lightened or darkened as needed, and which spoke more directly through some of us than others— through Mother more than anyone. Never left her entirely. I remember her telling me, about a week before she died, that she'd seen Sam peering through the front window, waving his dirty little hand. Just wanted her to know he was all right.

—So thoughtful, said Mother.

That was the first sign, I think, that Uncle N wasn't going to make things all right. We were all under that spell, weren't we? The money. The money. It would make me well again, make my brothers and sisters prosperous, it would float you and Mother into an honourable retirement, with rabbles of grandchildren to carom off your plump knees.

But when all was said and done, there wasn't so very much money, was there? Uncle N had been too frugal to court great wealth, and what with all the philanthropic gestures and the subsidies for his nephew Fred (now with five children of his own) and the armies of doctors and religious healers poking and prodding my right leg—well, we shouldn't have been astonished to find so little remaining for the other Cratchits. A better salary for you, yes: sixty a year by the time you were played out. A nicer house and a series of maids. And monthly remittances for Peter and me, once we came of age.

But what of the Cratchit girls? In retrospect, I think they must simply have grown tired of waiting for something to happen. They must have reasoned that if they couldn't have remittances, they could have dowries . . . and so they seized the first chance to be gone. That's why Jemmy married that engineer, whose sole qualification was that he promised to take her to Canada. This he accomplished, and he was quite punctilious, wasn't he, in notifying us of her death? I recall the phrasing quite well: "Lost her life in giving life." Nice sentiment, that, although the life she bore barely outlived her. I still have the letter somewhere.

I've kept Belinda's letters, too: the weekly marginalia of a country curate's wife. She might be writing them still if the goat fever hadn't taken her husband.

I like to think that the rumours that have since trailed after her are a kind of compressed correspondence on her part. Last we heard, Father—Uncle N made inquiries shortly after your first attack—she was either fashioning bonnets in Cheltenham or keeping house for a rector in Monmouth or living somewhere in Herefordshire with a sawyer who was not certifiably her husband. Gone, in other words. As surely as Sam was gone.

It's strange to think how soundlessly it can happen. I never imagine that middle-class children will drop from view so freely. I always think they will make some great noise on the way down—drag their fingers along the parapet, pound the wall, rage, rage.

But there is always pride to consider, isn't there? Look at Martha, Father. Your eldest. You never knew how things stood with her, because she took such pains to keep it from you. We knew, though. We knew all about that husband of hers, the drunken rover—never one to leave a pub vertical when he could leave horizontal—and all the more eager, when he did come home, to reassert the household sovereignty he had forfeited. Peter once pounded him a new eye, which helped matters without exactly improving them.

Martha never told you that, Father. Nor did she tell you how the money ran so dry once she had to run to Uncle N to plead for a remittance of her own. Two months later, she was back, pleading for him to cut it off. The law, you see, doesn't protect a woman's income from her husband, and Martha said she'd rather go without a penny than watch it all be flushed down that human sewer of hers. By then, she was making excuses not to visit or be visited. Rather unpersuasive excuses—sudden illnesses, mysterious errands—anything, I suppose, to keep from enduring witnesses. The last I saw her, Father, was at your funeral. She came alone, offered a large show of affection towards me and Peter, and left without a word to anyone else. Held herself the whole time with outright defiance, as if to set the world's judgement to scorn. I'd never seen that head of hers raised to such an altitude.

Ah, yes, pride. I fear that Martha and Peter and Belinda must have divvied up my allotment amongst them. Of all the Cratchit progeny, I am the only one left on Uncle N's payroll. Much good it is doing me at present. If, for example, I were to move my arm just a few inches to the left, my hand would be resting in Lushing Leo's urine. It has spilled out over the top of his trousers, and even now, the tip of his waterlogged penis hangs in plain view, looking pinned and severed, like the head of a martyr.

I could move to a safer remove, but I find it more agreeable just now to lie perfectly still. There is a strategy to my asceticism. I have the sense—call it a hope—that I am husbanding my powers for a great calling. For something, anyway. For something. It glimmers out there in the dark. Or is that just you again?

Chapter 16

AT TIMES LIKE THIS, I wish I hadn't parted with Colin quite so precipitously. What an admirable errand boy he would have made me, dashing through crossings, slipping between carriages, leaping puddles—fully enlarged by his own importance. As it is, I have to make do with the jailer's son, a sausagey, slack-bodied child, either eight or eighteen, with dull brown eyes that turn to treacle when I flash him a half-crown.

—Them's so lovely, them coins. I like 'em ever so much more than florins.

He is, inevitably, a dawdler. It is nearly an hour and a half before he returns with the following dispatch:

—Nothin' doin' nohow.

It takes all my self-control to keep from reaching through the bars and grabbing him by his sausage nose.

—What do you mean? Did you go to Mrs. Sharpe's?

—She warn't in, sir.

—Still abed, you mean. Did you explain why I needed her? Did you say it was pressing?

—Yes, sir, that I did. To a Miss Iris. Who said as how Mrs. Sharpe had gone and went away for the foreseeable future, and who was to say when she'd be a-comin' back?

Ah, Fate, how you use me. The one person who bothered to answer the knocker this morning: Iris.

—Never mind, I have another errand for you. Here is the address. You are to tell this gentleman I need him urgently, and you are to bring him back with you. Ten shillings in advance, and another ten if you're back within the hour.

It can't be said he moves with alacrity, but the profit motive does impart a mild spur to his bovine disposition. At least it brings him back before another hour has passed, bashful with triumph, his pudgy hand already extended for his candy. Following close behind is Peter, who takes in the surroundings with an expression that I soon recognise as mock astonishment.

—It's come to this, has it, Tim? Who'd've thunk it?

Hard on his heels is Annie, not a wife who trucks with idle banter. She whips off her hat and gloves and surveys the alien terrain like a regiment colonel, seeking the breach points. Her mind, I can see, is aswarm with strategies and counterstrategies and contingencies, and the only thing that arrests her warrior momentum for even a second is the sight of my face.

—Lord above, Tim, what have they done to you?

—No, Annie, don't touch it.

—It's downright criminal!

—I didn't mean for *you* to come.

—And who would dare keep me away? As soon as I heard, I said to Peter, "Why, Tim would sooner cut off his head than go near a woman." In that way, I mean. And if they need some *other* woman to testify to that effect, why, here's one ready to be sworn. And you can tell *that* to Mr. Magistrate, with my compliments.

I ask them who's minding the shop, but rather than answer, they stand to either side of the barred door and pepper me with assurances.

—You mustn't worry about a thing, Tim. Listen.

—We've engaged a lawyer for you, Tim. . . .

—Not the usual procedure for a police magistrate case, but one can't be too . . .

—And he came highly recommended by the friend of a . . .

—And he was just leaving his office when . . .

—And he was most optimistic about . . .

—And he's coming right behind . . .

—Ten minutes, no more. . . .

—So you mustn't worry.

—You really mustn't.

In fact, another half hour passes before Augustus Sheldrake squeezes his way through the station-house door. A stout, whey-skinned man with a decamping hairline and advancing whiskers, soldierly red on both fronts. The hand he presents to me is quite damp, and there is a prevailing humidity all about his person: wet eyes, wet lips, wet teeth . . . and, exhaling from his pores, an effluvium that, unless my nostrils deceive me, represents the final gaseous iteration of imported Jamaican rum. I think I might have done better with Lushing Leo.

There is no doubt, however, that Mr. Sheldrake exudes confidence. He greets us individually and severally and treats us to so many cunning variations on the same smile that one feels constantly on the verge of applauding him.

—Never fear, my dear friends. The battle is joined, and our triumph is ordained. We shall pummel our opponents from heel to toe. We shall bung them with the fist of logic. We shall jab them with the elbow of truth. We shall crumple them with the knee of righteousness. Oh, my friends, we shall carry this day.

So persuasive is his rhetoric, so lustrous are his teeth, that I feel quite churlish in positing an alternative outcome.

—Supposing, in spite of all your efforts, Mr. Sheldrake, I am still found guilty. Can you tell me what sentence I might expect?

—Oh, yes, well, this particular magistrate . . . well, you see, he's known for being a bit of a stickler. P's-and-q's, letter-of-the-law codger, you know the sort. Even so, I shouldn't expect more than . . . what? . . . two months' hard labour.

—Two *months*?

—One, perhaps, if he's feeling generous. Or else a good hearty whipping and have done with it. Never mind, Mr. Cratchit, I am fully prepared to invoke the holiday spirit. I wish you could have heard me just yesterday arguing the case of Bawdyhouse Bob. 'Christlike-mercy this, seasonal-clemency that.' I carried all before me, Mr. Cratchit.

Annie can bear it no longer. She has jammed her tiny fists against her sternum, in an effort, I think, to keep her heart from bursting through.

—They'll get hard labour from *me* if they start in with the whipping or the two months, and you can tell *that* to Mr. Magistrate, with all my blessings.

Mr. Sheldrake looks discomfited by such sincerity. Collapsing into the nearest chair, he fumbles in his coat pocket for a silver flask—lime-and-seltzer, he explains—and drains it in half a second. This has the contradictory effect of reanimating and clouding him over, so that it is never clear how deeply the details of my case have penetrated his miasma. The only certain thing is Mr. Sheldrake's smile, which streams forth so relentlessly it could set the sun to school.

—Carry all before us, I tell you. We few, we happy few.

A scant ten minutes later, we are ushered with bare ceremony into the magistrate's office. Not an office at all, really, but a kind of morning room, with a large window and a fire grate and there, at the reading desk, the redoubtable magistrate himself, playing a game of patience. So engrossed is he in this work that I begin to wonder if we haven't inadvertently broken into his home, disrupted his most cherished postprandial ritual. I look for some acknowledgement of us in his expression, but the calf pen in which I've been deposited permits me no view beyond the lank hand that screens the left side of his face.

The screen stays in place even as the magistrate, with evident regret, raises his head to confront the roomful of petitioners.

—Good morning to you all.

A strangely occluded voice—buried under generations of neglect—and yet it stirs something familiar in me. I labour in vain to find my connection to it, but the voice keeps sliding from my grasp.

—Oh, and good morning to you, Mr. Sheldrake. We so seldom see you in our environs. Then again, we so seldom see *any* of your ilk.

There is no mistaking the gratitude with which he regards his deprivation. No mistaking it, I mean, unless you are Mr. Sheldrake, who rises and, with a protracted bow, announces:

—Your worship, think of me as a mere conduit for the disinterested liquid of the law. As such, I pour myself humbly into your august cruet. You may imbibe me as you will.

—Thank you, Mr. Sheldrake, I shall. Now, with respect to the matter at hand, may I ask who took the charge?

A police officer steps up. A particularly tall specimen, full in the waist, proud in the chin.

—It were me, your worship.

—Swear him, please, Fairweather.

The clerk is a wizened, furious man, with a scowl carved all the way down his short, bent frame. He holds the Bible like a banker, and as soon as the oath is complete, he retracts the loan with a violence born of equal parts revulsion and satisfaction.

As for the policeman's tale, it is notable only for its brevity. An unconscious woman . . . an unconscious man . . . a vague and general suspicion that something was amiss . . . an arrest. He looks embarrassed, frankly, at having so little to impart, and the magistrate's voice, though still encrusted, sounds quite consoling during the ensuing interview.

—An excellent accounting, Officer. Truly a *credit* to . . . to . . . now, if you wouldn't mind my asking, why was the accused struck down in such a fashion?

—I believe it were to keep him from escapin', your worship. However, the person as done it was not on the scene when I arrived.

—And correct me if I am wrong, Officer, but you did not actually see the crime in question?

—No, your worship, I did not. Whatever as happened happened, and there's an end to it.

—And were there any witnesses?

—Yes, your worship. A lady saw it all as it was occurrin' and has very kindly stepped forwards.

—Ah. Call her, please. And swear her, my good Fairweather.

Miss Binny's uniform is squarely in place: the plain white bonnet, the misshapen black dress that gives her the look of an inexpertly wrapped parcel. Intact, too, is her wheedling manner, that way she has of inclining her whole body towards the dignitary in question. She even performs this obeisance with Mr. Fairweather, whose satisfaction is abruptly cancelled by the sight of a rival Bible smothered in her armpit. *Bigamy*, his startled expression seems to say. But Miss Binny, for her part, appears to relish the superfluity, hugs her own Bible all the more tightly to her as she strokes Mr. Fairweather's. Sails through her oath and even adds a closing benediction:

—May God's mercy guide us all!

She then moves on to the divine work of burying me. A tale of sorrow and pity, and to her credit, she never looks too eager to tell it. Indeed, under the courteous questioning of the magistrate, she gives the impression of someone being dragged, against every instinct of her nature, towards a dire and unavoidable conclusion.

—I couldn't, of course, say exactly what was happening, your worship. By which I mean, I saw the gentleman in question tear the young lady's dress, but I could not tell you what he hoped to gain by it. I rather hoped he was plucking a burning ember from her person, but not seeing any fires in the immediate vicinity . . . why, I didn't know what to think.

—And was it then you screamed, Miss Binny?

—Yes, your worship. I blush to admit that the weakness of my sex overcame me in that instant, and not feeling fit to settle judgement myself, I preferred to leave it to minds wiser than my own.

An especially pronounced bow in the direction of the magistrate, and then a final homily:

—I must say, your worship, the good Lord has more than once seen fit to use me as His instrument in averting unspeakable crimes. I only pray that today, we may also be an instrument of salvation for the wretched gentleman who stands accused before us.

With that, the magistrate ends his questioning, and Miss Binny settles into a silence as impervious as steel. It is enough to quell my good lawyer, who remains rooted in position, breathing labouriously, until nudged into action by Peter's elbow.

—Well, now. Well, now, your worship. My young client here seems to believe that Miss Binny is not, perhaps, the person best suited to appearing against him.

—And why is that, Mr. Sheldrake?

—On account of the fact that he and the aforementioned Miss Binny, the emissary of that admirable organisation, the Bible Flower Mission . . . on account of the fact that he and Miss Binny had an altercation of sorts.

—Yes?

—This altercation having to do with the welfare of a young girl of Mr. Cratchit's acquaintance.

—Is that true, Miss Binny?

The missionary's hand flutters to her chest.

—Oh, your worship, we come across so many girls in our mission work. They droppeth as does the gentle rain from heaven. Twice blessed.

—It was a particular girl, your worship. By the name of Wilhelmina. Sorry, *Philomela*.

—Why, I'm afraid I don't recall such a girl, your worship. By either name. Perhaps this gentleman has confused me with another of God's handmaidens.

And with that, the tether of Mr. Sheldrake's brain snaps taut. Nothing now but dribbling expostulation:

—Yes. Well. Be that as it may. Yes. . . .

But he has reserves, does Mr. Sheldrake. Enough, at any rate, for one last burst of advocacy.

—Your worship, I ask you to dredge up the deepest wellsprings of seasonal charity and regard my poor client here. *Behold* him in yon godforsaken pen. Behold him, as the steadfast Christian you are, and tell me true. He don't look so dangerous, does he?

To this, the magistrate has no response. He never even drops the hand that screens him from view, or clears away the gravel that obscures his voice. Miss Binny seizes this moment to deliver her own verdict.

—It may be that the good Lord has seen fit to fill this young man with a cleansing spirit. In which event, your worship, I hope that the punishment you see fit to bestow will but further him along on the path to full redemption.

And now Mr. Sheldrake really is done. All done. Although that doesn't stop him from sputtering on for a few seconds more:

—Redemption, yes. All very fine, but there's . . . there's . . .

A long stretch of silence then. And over the course of this interval, I am cognizant of two things: the undisguised contempt with which everyone, the clerk above all, regards my lawyer; and the kindly disposition of the magistrate when at last he interposes.

—Thank you very much, Mr. Sheldrake. And thank you, Miss Binny. You may stand away.

He lowers his head, and I fear we are once again on the verge of losing him to his game of patience. His hand surreptitiously places one card atop another, another card on that . . . and then he looks up, shocked to see the room still occupied.

—Yes, yes. Helter-skelter, lickety-split. Please call the young lady who is preferring the charge.

Seldom has a wronged woman made so triumphal an entrance. Her hair has been swept back into a virginal chignon. Her head is arranged at an angle of virtue. Her eyes fix on a point in the upper ether as she advances with tiny, brave steps. To my mind, the one thing that spoils the effect is her decision to wear yesterday's dress. The rent has been ostentatiously fastened with pink ribbon, and from time to time, her hand flies to it, as though it were a scabbing wound.

—Your name, please.

—Miss Sally Grenville.

—Please state your complaint against this man.

—Well, it were like this, your lordship. Picture it, if you will. A young girl, out for a stroll on a brisk December afternoon. Walkin' 'long the thoroughfare, takin' the air, hummin' a bit of seasonal ditty to herself. . . .

—Evocative, thank you.

—Well, if you were her—and believe me, I *were* her . . . well, then, wouldn't you be surprised—I mean, taken all the way aback—to see this particular gentleman comin' right alongside you?

—In fact, why *were* you surprised?

—Well, he were a stranger, weren't he? And then, your grace, it weren't so much the comin' up, it were what he said *after* he come up. If you must know, he made an indecent suggestion. Actually whispered it in my ear in broad daylight, if you can stand it.

—And what was his suggestion?

—Oh, I couldn't *speak* it, your grace. Not in front of all these good people.

—Why don't you whisper it in my ear, then?

With a rueful smile, she shuffles to the magistrate's desk, drops a most becoming curtsy, and cups her hand around his right ear. A brief pause, followed by the magistrate's dry voice:

—Very colourful. You may return.

How vexing not to be able to gauge his expression. All I can detect is a slight tilting of his head, but whether he is appreciating her effect or trying to assay it, I cannot determine.

—And after this suggestion was whispered in your ear, Miss Grenville?

—Why, I let him know I was not the sort as would take him up on a proposition like that. My sainted mother never raised such a girl, is what I told him. And that's when he grabbed a-hold of me. Grabbed with all his force and tore at my dress. Which you can see it yourself, Your Grace, is tore clean all the way down t'here.

—Yes, I do see.

—Well, that's when I started in to screaming. And the horror must've grown so upon me, why, I fainted dead in the street. Which is not my custom. And after I come to, they told me the man in question were in custody, and Lor', was I grateful! Preying on defenseless women such as myself, it's a wonder anyone can walk the streets these days, may God defend us all!

Until now, Annie has stood with great forbearance against the back wall, arms folded across her chest. But this pious oration is more than she can abide. Ignoring Peter's restraining hand, she takes two strides forwards and, in her most trumpeting tone, declares:

—Your worship, this is the ripest form of nonsense!

—Silence!

The sheer volume of the clerk's voice sends veins of bright purple shooting across his bald crown. Annie presses on as though he were living in another county.

—My brother-in-law is the gentlest man alive, your worship, and anyone who says else is a barefaced liar.

The clerk is beside himself now.

—Turn this woman out! Clear the office!

—You shall not turn me out. I will be sworn.

From there, matters get quite out of hand, and the wonder is that in the midst of all the cacophony, something so quiet as the magistrate's clearing his throat should even register. And yet register it does, for the assailants disarm at once—subsiding into dagger looks—while the magistrate carries on in the same unruffled tone as before.

—Mr. Fairweather, with all due respect, I believe the decision to clear the office is mine to make. Good Mrs. . . . . .

—Cratchit.

—I must beg you, please, to be silent for the time being. Otherwise, I really shall have to turn you out, and that would distress me to no end. As it is, I have just a few more questions for this young lady, and until I am finished, I must beg everyone's kind indulgence. Thank you very much. Now, Miss Grenville.

—Yes, your lordship?

—If I'm not mistaken, you and I have met before. In this very room, in fact, on at least two or three previous occasions.

—Have we? I don't recall, your holiness.

—I nearly failed to recall it myself. You were dressed rather differently then.

—Was I?

—It is fortunate I have a tolerably good memory for faces. And for names, too. Yours, if I remember correctly, was Sweet Sally.

The eyes enlarge ever so slightly. A titter, a swatting of the hand.

—Oh, I've had coves call me lots of different names. They meant no harm by 'em, I'm sure.

—No, indeed. Although on your last two visits here, I believe you were charged with annoying passersby.

—Well, that's as in the eye of the beholder, ain't it? It were my contention they was annoying *me*.

—As it is your contention today. Let me see—before that, there was a charge of public drunkenness. Public lewdness prior to that. And beyond that, I lose track. The mists of memory and all that. . . .

Oh, this is not part of her intended effect, surely. That heavy lower lip, that drooping jaw.

—Of course, we are always happy to see you, Miss Grenville. But I am afraid your past conduct has not left you with a sterling reputation for veracity.

Visibly quivering now, eyes flashing from side to side, Sweet Sally wheels about and, in one last beseeching gesture, points towards the black-garbed missionary.

—*She* saw it, too!

—I'm sure she did, Miss Grenville. Handmaidens of God are always seeing something, aren't they?

And now it is Miss Binny's turn to express surprise: a reeling motion that evokes the (now dear) memory of Colin feinting a punch to her head. The magistrate pauses, wondering, perhaps, if water or smelling salts are in order, and then bears onwards.

—As it happens, I myself have some personal acquaintance with the accused, and I can testify to his character quite as well as his admirable sister-in-law. I therefore declare these charges groundless, and I herein discharge him.

It is the first crack I have seen in the formidable Binny facade: a slackening of the face, like a wax doll left too long in the sun. She has poise enough, however, to give a peremptory shake of the head to Sweet Sally, who, thus chastened, shoves one fist all the way into her mouth to stifle her outrage.

But no one is more put out than the clerk, Mr. Fairweather, who turns grape from crown to collarbone and begins leaping up and down like a splenetic troll.

—Your worship! This is peculiar, this is *erratic*. . . .

—Clear the office, Fairweather. There's a good chap.

Only one thing keeps me from quitting the room posthaste: the desire to know my saviour. But the way to him is still blocked, and when I try to crane my head, I am met by the incoming tide of my lawyer, who is already jacking my hand.

—Sheldrake came, Mr. Cratchit. Sheldrake saw. Sheldrake conquered.

He must take my mumbling for agreement, for his chest swells as he says:

—None of that, Mr. Cratchit, justice is my reward. Dame Justice, in whose temple I am but a lowly hierophant. Now then. To whom shall I send the invoice?

I am just about to suggest a proper receptacle when I am interrupted by the voice of the magistrate.

—Oh, Mr. Cratchit! One word, if you please.

And still the hand refuses to budge. And as I come round the desk, I half expect to find additional screens sprouting up on all sides, hand after hand, a palisade of fingers. But after a few paces, the vista is clear, and the view that opens before me is of an elderly, heavy-eared man with a pickled grin and a nod of practiced affability.

Squidgy.

Squidgy's face, at any rate, and his voice, too, shedding its disguise now and addressing me once again like a fellow clubman.

—You'll excuse my not hailing you ex officio, Timothy. One does have these pesky protocols to follow.

I stand before him, dredging for words, and the only candidates that emerge are:

—Is your back feeling better?

—Oh, my, yes.

—Not still . . . not still itching or anything?

—Hardly notice it now. But see here, Timothy, you really must stay away from the Sweet Sallys of the world. Mrs. Sharpe's girls are of a higher order, if that's what you're after. And while you're at it, stay away from the Sheldrakes of the world.

—You may be assured of that.

—And do have someone look at that eye, it's a fright.

—Yes, thank you. Thank you, Mr. . . .

Squidgy. That's what I want so desperately to call him: Mr. Squidgy. But if there is an alternative name, the gentleman in question is not saying. He hunches his shoulders over his game of patience; he proffers a half-salute.

—Off you go now. Trotty-trot.

Peter and Annie would prefer me to come home with them, but I have other errands to attend to, and so, apart from my profuse thanks, the only reward they receive for their pains this morning is the prospect of my retreating back. And still they follow me, in my mind: a pair of invisible rebukes on either side, mutating block by block into something slightly warmer.

I have need of warmth. In my confusion, I seem to have left my greatcoat in the station-house cell. Too late to go back for it—Lushing Leo has by now claimed ownership—and too cold to go entirely without. So I stop in an old-clothes shop and, for want of anything better, grab a tattered green comforter, which the dealer is willing to part with for a few shillings. And as I wrap it round my neck and shoulders and bear it down the street, its weight becomes indistinguishable from the weight of memory. For this is how Father used to travel, isn't it? Every working day, from the Royal Exchange all the way home to Bayham Street, he kept that moth-chewed comforter wrapped round him like ermine.

Surely now, at this moment of unexpected doubling, surely this is the time for him to reappear. But he is scrupulously absent as I make my way back to Craven Street. Or else I am less able to see him. My right eye has closed up almost completely, leaving nothing but a slot the size of a coin, and my left eye, by way of compensation, pulls too hard to port, dragging me off course, and as I stagger along the pavement, tracing my usual roundabout path, it dismays me to think I have become a spectacle, something that passersby must account for. As I climb the stairs to Gully's chambers, the apologia is forming in my throat:

There's a reason, you see. It happened like this. . . .

And in my eagerness to explain myself, I nearly blurt everything to the brindled cat that has settled itself by Gully's door. A fat and lolling cat, even by this house's standards, enjoying the new amnesty, licking the puddle of milk that someone—Philomela, no doubt—has poured along the floor there. Licking so hard that the milk has turned clean red.

Chapter 17

THE DOOR SWINGS OPEN WITH A PUSH, and the trail of rust-coloured milk ribbons into the near distance before coagulating round the sprawled figure of Captain Gully.

His left arm lies crushed beneath him, and his stubby right arm is extended as though he were hailing a cab, and his eyes look straight at me, daring me to blink.

He is still, still as fallen snow. Even his blood has ceased to agitate, and over the gaping flap of his neck, there remains only a dull red matte, which the cat gives a few disconsolate licks before moving on.

All the other cats have vanished. Life itself has abandoned this space and left behind only husks. A pair of inert arms. A compacted torso. Two staring eyes.

I'm on my knees now, with no memory of having knelt. I'm on my knees, and from my closed mouth issues a long, keening moan, the sort the wind makes when it scours round a chimney crown. The sound rises and falls, and my body rises and falls with it, until my hand, grasping for a brace, closes round something hard and wooden: a strand of beads, mashed in sections, with the paint nearly chapped off from fingering.

Hail, Mary . . . Hail, Mary. . . .

No, it's Philomela who knows the words, and she's not here. My only litany is the sentence that flies round the circuits of my brain, in endless loops, forestalling the inevitable:

O forgive me. O forgive me.

The horror comes on all the same. The horror of that small definite incision across the carotid artery. The clean flat sharp blade that made it. I know that blade. I have seen it, I have seen the man who wields it. Nothing can shut them out.

Minutes pass . . . years pass . . . the truth becomes only less assimilable. I lower my head towards Gully's, I rest my forehead on his. The chill is almost enough to make me pull away, and yet there must be a residual heat, too, for I find I can linger there, at least until I look into his eyes, which are another story altogether—colder than any other part of him, and further away. It is the eyes that send the doleful news. Gully is gone.

Best, kindest of men: gone.

And now the fury gathers inside me, gathers and rises, hisses through my skin, and my mouth opens in anticipation of the scream to come, but it is only the same old litany, mumbled in Gully's cold ear.

O forgive me. O forgive me.

Too bad: Gully's power of dispensation has vanished with him. The words bounce off him like bent arrows.

And yet, as I kneel there on the floor, I begin to feel, against all odds, a kind of benison at work, casting the room in a new slanting light, illuminating the mournful procession of Gully's belongings. One by one, they pay their tribute: the Dutch clock, the tiny coal scuttle, the rope of privet over the door.

And there, on the floor by Gully's chair, one of his dog-eared atlases, still open.

Why I should take the trouble of picking it up I can't say. I already know what page it's opened to. I can hear the good captain himself, invoking the olive groves and the stone towers and the coffee-skinned women . . . as if he were whispering in my ear. Just as he was whispering in her ear, probably, when they came for him.

Majorca. You'll see. Changes a man forever.

The page tears off easily, and it rolls up even more easily, into a fife-size scroll. From there, it is simply a matter of turning Gully on his back—avoiding the face for the time being, avoiding the cambric shirt, with its strange diagonal sash of red, avoiding everything but the box wrench protruding from the cavity of his left arm.

Into that wrench's orifice I insert the scrolled-up map. I kneel, I murmur in Gully's ear.

—You may go anywhere you like now, Captain. The world is yours.

But, as always, I am too late with my tidings. For Gully has quit this world, that becomes only more definite with each passing minute. Gully has flown to the next place, and left his chrysalis to rot here on the floor.

And still some of him remains. It is oddly comforting to look down at my hands and find them smeared with the sticky residue of Gully's blood. Not even the comforter will wipe them completely clean. In this way, in this way, I will carry Gully with me. And the longer I kneel by him, with one bloody hand on his brow, the more I believe I am travelling with him, escorting him into the next world.

They will be glad to have him, I know, but what of me? What will they make of me? Nothing to do but send me back, to the ground of my sins.

And already I hear the old world calling to me. A mewling sound that I attribute to Gully's cats until it acquires a more human dimension, a plaintive timbre.

Rising to my feet, I follow the sound—in circles, for it seems to be coming from all quadrants. And then, as my ears sharpen, the sound does, too. It settles in the far corner of Gully's chamber, and as I approach, it concentrates into form: a small huddled shaking figure, head between its knees.

Colin the unmelodious.

To a true Christian gentleman, I know, this would be an opportunity for solace. Why, then, does the sight of him inflame me with the whitest rage? Why, instead of laying a gentling hand on his shoulders, do I haul him straight up in the air and slam him against the wall?

He is too far gone, fortunately, to be shocked. His eyes have winced shut, and his head drifts to port, and even the sound of my yelling cannot make much of a dent in him.

—How long have you been here?

I shake him, shake him hard, until the words come coughing out.

—Don't know.

—Did you see it happen?

—No.

I grab his chin, force his head up. I glare into his waterlogged face.

—You're lying.

—I stopped in, that's all. Same as you.

—You're lying.

—Honest, Mr. Timothy, I was—

—What? What?

—I was bringin' 'em gifts.

And then, from his limp hand, two bundles fall to the floor. A white handkerchief, trimmed with violet lace, and a miniature globe, two inches in diameter—the earth writ small.

—They was for Christmas, like.

His voice has a dying fall, and on any other day, I think, seeing him this way—so wholly stripped of his customary armour—would have thawed me. But not today. Today I am a column of ice.

—Did you *steal* them, Colin?

And this, oddly enough, is the very thing to prick him back into volubility.

—It were my own money, I swear. I got lucky yesterday, bet on a prize cock with the money you gave me, and I was meanin' to have a bit of a lark, it's not often I get two quid. . . .

Such is the pitch of his hysteria I'm sure he would go on talking, all through the night and clear on to New Year's, but for the realisation that stops his mouth in midmotion.

—I didn't need to go to that cockfight, Mr. Timothy. I oughta have come here 'stead. I oughta have been here. . . .

He sinks back to the floor, gouging the tears from his eyes.

—God help me, I oughta have *been* here.

—Why? So they might have killed you, too? How would that have served Gully?

The mere mention of his name draws our eyes back to that figure on the floor—even smaller in death, I think, than he was in life.

I bow my head. I say:

—He is on my conscience, Colin. Not yours.

On my conscience forever, I should add. But that hardly seems necessary. Once again, I kneel by that squat form. From behind me comes the tentative shuffling of Colin's feet, the soft hiccoughing of his chest.

—He were a good sort, the captain.

—Yes. The finest.

He pauses for a few seconds, then asks:

—What they done with Filly?

—I don't know, Colin.

—Kilt her, likely.

With a raw wonder, I unclasp the fingers of my left hand. The rosary beads rest in my palm, like a dowager's stolen necklace.

How quick they must have been. She would have reached for these before anything else.

But if they did kill her, why didn't they leave her body with Gully's? Dragging a corpse down to the pier would have served no purpose. If all they wanted was her silence, it would have been easier, surely, to leave her here.

No, they didn't kill her.

—She's still alive.

I say it under my breath, but still Colin must hear, for he draws a little closer and, in a small voice, asks:

—What they want with her, then?

—I don't know.

Rising to my feet, I give Philomela's beads a final worrying, then shove them into my trouser pocket.

—We shall find her, Colin. You and I.

And then kill them.

But that hardly needs voicing, does it? It's what she asked us to do, after all: *We kill them.*

And you, you overcivilised fool, upbraided her for her presumption. Wasted your time with Scotland Yard and licorice, with Sheldrakes and Squidgies, when all along you should have been following that simple injunction.

Kill them. Or they kill us.

How does arriving at such a determination change a man? I don't feel any different. The room itself hasn't changed. And yet the air is stiller, and Colin is quite noticeably shrinking from me.

—You sure you're all right, Mr. Timothy? Coz from the looks of things, they banged you but good, and you know how a fellow can get when he's had the senses knocked out of him. . . .

I motion him towards me. And in the ensuing seconds, every misgiving that Colin has ever entertained seems to roll across his face, and it is probably a tribute to Gully that he does eventually come, that he assumes this attitude of submission, so contrary to his nature.

—Listen to me, Colin. I need you to do something. Can you do it?

He nods, briefly.

—You're to go to Scotland Yard. Do you understand?

Another nod.

—You're to ask for Inspector Surtees. Not another living soul will do—it is Surtees or nobody. And if he is out of office, then you are to wait for him. As long as it takes. Can you do that?

—Yes.

—You're to tell him everything that's happened since last I saw you. That's all you need to say, he is acquainted with the rest.

—I'll do it.

—And tell him from me, Colin. Tell him that Sergeant Rebbeck's latest artwork is on public view here in Craven Street. Free of charge.

Colin grimaces, sets to scratching his head.

—But, Mr. Timothy, he'll want to talk to *you*, won't he?

—It's too late for talking. If I have need of him, I'll let him know.

—But you can't just . . . I mean, there's inquests, Mr. Timothy, there's, there's funerals 'n' burial expenses. . . .

—All in good time, Colin.

Finding no redress with me, he falls back a step and exhorts the ceiling.

—And then what? I mean, Good day, Inspector, jabber jabber, and then what? You know, it's . . . it's . . .

He's spinning in circles now, and the words spin with him, and as best I can make out, he's trying to ask me something but can't. And then it occurs to me that this is in itself a form of asking, and so I speak to him in the gentlest voice I have yet been able to muster.

—Would you like to stay with me, Colin? For the time being?

His eyes dart back to the ground. The mask slides back into place.

—Well, that's an interestin' notion, Mr. Timothy, for a free-roamin' cove such as myself. 'Course, if you was lacking for company and all, you and the captain bein' mates and all, well, that would be, that would be another think altogether. . . .

This is as far as he will come to meet me. It is far enough. I say:

—Meet me back at Mrs. Sharpe's when you're finished.

He shrugs and nods and then, with a flurry of mutually cancelling gestures, bids me farewell and slips through the door frame. He stops for one last backwards glance at Gully and appears to take fresh assurances from it, for he then leaps down the steps two at a time and propels himself through the front door like a cluster of grapeshot. And it is only when I peer out the window and see his tiny figure dash down the street that I realise he has failed to ask for money.

Likely, he took one look at my disarray and pegged me for temporary impoverishment. But in fact, the coin purse is still there, in the deep recesses of my waistcoat. Kneeling one last time by Gully's still form, I roll down the lids of his eyes and dot them with copper pennies. Instantly, his face clouds over, assuming the very myopia I remember seeing on Father's face. I remember thinking it was a form of mercy.

Speaking loud enough for Gully to hear, I say:

—We shall meet again, Captain. Very soon, perhaps. And I shall repay my debt to you a hundredfold.

Unlike Colin, I don't take a last look. I simply close the door behind me. And as I pass down the steps, I think: They came this way, too, Rebbeck and his minions. With Gully's blood on their hands.

But how did they get in? That's the question that will haunt me to my grave. *How did they get in?*

Did they pull some confidence game on poor, credulous Gully? Was that it? Rebbeck wouldn't have been above using his old police uniform. He might easily have supplied some tale, something with a flash of verisimilitude—poor Tim, perhaps, rotting away in a cell.

No, getting Gully to open the door would've been the easy part, but *finding* the house—how did they manage that? All of Gully's precautions, all the care I took in coming here, the circling and doubling back and the sidelong looks and darting trajectories . . . and still they were waiting for me when I reached Craven Street. Already preparing their strike, I've no doubt, and needing only to hold me off to keep the way clear.

But that part of it is history now, fast receding, and Craven Street is once again a fairground for lawyers. Only two days left till Christmas, and still they are locked in their ant-rounds: buzzing and jostling, humming and chattering, skittering off to Lincoln's Inn and scuttling back again. There were probably a good two dozen of them trolling for business when Rebbeck came knocking on Gully's door. Two dozen lawyers beetling past when Gully's arms were pinned behind him. Two dozen lawyers clutching their sheaves of parchment as Rebbeck, smiling courteously, advanced with his wood-carver's blade. Two dozen lawyers stopping their ears to a man's gargled scream, to the thunder of a body falling to earth.

Oh, Gully.

My resolve gives way. I sink to the kerb—a squelch of mud. I wrap my head in my hands. And now, at last, that tide of feeling is ready to crest. It roars up my throat, it wrenches open my mouth, it flings itself into the December air, an unwavering line of sound.

—Aaaaaaaaaaaaaaaaaaa!

No one stops. The only response I elicit is the small gilt-edged piece of cardboard I find resting in my lap when I open my eyes again.

> BRACEBRIDGE YOUNGBLOOD, ESQ.
>
> *Solicitor*
>
> Reasonable terms. Speedy dispositions.

Mr. Youngblood has long since swept on, like every other tenant of this street. Every one but me, that is, and the miniature waif abandoned a few yards down the way. It is swathed in mud and jammed against the kerb, nearly lost in a pile of orange peels and peanut shells, and only its distinctive corkscrew shape recalls it to me. Philomela's doll. Mashed and squashed and soaked through, but curiously hardy all the same. It would outlive London, if it could.

*—M*rs. Sharpe said . . .

Funny thing about having only one eye available to you: the people who pass across your field look both nearer and impossibly remote. Mary Catherine, for instance. I might be looking at her from the wrong end of a telescope, and yet her face stands as intimately revealed as one of Uncle N's fungi. I can see the way it crimps and unravels slightly at the sight of my blood-smeared comforter, and I can see her mouth catching at the thread of message on her brain's bobbin.

—Mrs. Sharpe said (Lord above, Mr. Timothy!) you were to knock on her door as soon as (shall I fetch you a compress?), as soon as you come. And how she heared all about the goings-on from Iris (oh, that eye!), and it's a bloody travesty, she says, and a sacrilege, too (are you sure I can't?), and what's more . . .

I put out my hand.

—Tell Mrs. Sharpe I won't be able to see her today.

But the mistress of the house comes knocking, anyway, about ten minutes later. A tiny rapping on my bedroom door.

—Mr. Timothy? Are you feeling poorly?

A low, even voice, much more attractive than its public version. And a part of me, I will say this, would like nothing so much as to open the door. The very largest part of me, it may be, but I dare not trust it. And so I let the words die on my lips, leaving nothing but cold, deep silence.

—All right, you rest, then. There's a good boy.

And with her voice goes my last connection to the living world. I collapse onto the bed, I burrow down into a pudding of wool: Father's comforter below, the bloody comforter on top, and me somewhere in the middle. The fire grate is empty, but I'm too weak to get up and tend to it, so I just lie there, shivering like Lushing Leo. My hands shake, my teeth rattle . . . every part of me is atremble. And as the afternoon wears on, the shaking becomes almost comforting, a kind of ostinato line beneath the teeming melodies of my brain. So many motifs. Gully on the floor, hailing his cab. Philomela disappearing into the sewer. The girl in the alley and the girl in the river. The gentleman in the carriage. Discrete images at first, and then, imperceptibly, they merge. Gully's coin-eyes stare out from the river girl's face, Miss Binny's weeds wrap themselves about Philomela's doll, Sergeant Rebbeck screams as the brand sears his flesh.

And glowering over everything else, a flapping *G*, with falcon eyes and lion haunches, dousing us in shadow. I hear the beating of wings . . . a high, strangled call . . . and now the shadow parts, and through the vent, a head emerges, and I am running, my hands have curled into talons, but the creature is not fooled, it draws ever closer, I can feel its hot breath on my neck, the tickle of its feathers. It is close enough now to call my name, a mocking stage whisper . . .

—Mr. Timothy. Mr. Timothy.

A soft voice, and yet so insistent that it drags me from my stupor, drops me back in my bed. The dregs of afternoon pour through my bedroom window. The crack in the ceiling smiles its toothless grin, and the shivering in my body has passed to the rest of the room, for even the door is shaking.

—Mr. Timothy.

Someone is knocking, very lightly, so as not to wake the dead.

—Mr. Timothy.

I'm not sure from where I derive the strength to get up from the bed, to cross to the door and slide the lock. I think I must still be riding the wheels of my dream.

And behold. It is Colin. Hand raised for one more knock.

—Jesus Christ, Mr. Timothy!

Helpless, I fall back before him. With a nurse's ruthless instinct, he claps a hand across my forehead.

—You're all aboil.

Yes. Yes, I knew that. How silly of me not to mention it.

—Quiverin' like Saint Vitus. What say we lay you back down again, eh? There's a good fellow.

He wraps me back in my comforter pudding, then sets to laying coals in the grate. Within minutes, a robust fire has sprung up. I turn to it in admiration—greedy for a new sensation. I watch Colin stoke the fire, boil a pan of coffee, smear a film of vapour from the window, and I am conscious, even in the midst of my tremors, of the reversal in our positions. In the normal course of things, surely I ought to be consoling him? That is my bounden duty, is it not? As the elder. . . .

—Well, it was . . . it was a shocking business, Colin. You know, if you'd like to . . .

What am I offering him, exactly? He's not buying, whatever it is. His voice is keyed to a domestic hum, and if now and then a quaver tips the balance, it never lasts long enough to betray him outright.

—It'll come as no surprise, I'm sure, Mr. Timothy. Colin the Melodious has done the job once again. Don't you think he went and sallied into Scotland Yard, not taking no guff nor nothink? Don't you think he told them peelers, "You give me Surtees, or you give me nobody"? And don't you think they as good as rolled him straight in? Lord, though, that Surtees is an odd sort o' mackerel. Wouldn't keep to the subject, always askin' if I wanted for candy. Talked more of licorice than anythink else. D'you think it were a code, Mr. Timothy?

Gradually, very gradually, the fire's heat takes over, and the shivering dies away, leaving behind only crucibles of ache, dull pinpricks scattered across my body. It's as if the old pain in my leg has borne children, a dozen generations' worth, sliding down the banisters of my bones, digging their heels into my sinews.

I raise myself to a seated position. I run my hands through my hair.

—Well, that's the spirit, Mr. Timothy. Lookin' a bit more human, ain't you? Should I send for a potboy? A little ale'd get the piss movin' again.

—That would be lovely. But first . . .

—What?

—Would you be so good as to take down that glass from the wall? I'd like to see myself.

—You sure about that, Mr. Timothy? Coz you're not lookin' your best, you don't mind my—

—All the same.

It turns out to be the face I deserve. I am altogether pleased with it. People spend many months in Marshalsea striving for just this sort of pallor. But the eye is, of course, the primary attraction: a soufflé of deep purple, well nigh perfect except for that seam of sealed eyelid running beneath it. I poke the bruised flesh: it makes barely a murmur.

—Colin, would you pass me that pin?

A quick lance is all it takes. The blood pours out in a thin wash, dribbles down my cheek, curves around my jaw. My lids, relieved of their weight, begin to pry themselves apart, and through the widening crevice, my eye starts back to life. A sea of red, in which Colin's face swims like a flounder.

—Christ, Mr. Timothy! At least wipe your face, will you?

The potboy brings two pints, and Colin and I settle by the grate, him on the floor, me in the chair with a blanket wrapped round me. Locked in our parallel griefs, we stare into the fire. No escape but the far corner of the room, and I don't trust myself to cross even that short distance without escort.

The air grows cold on our backs; the sun drops out of the window frame; twilight creeps near. And perhaps it is the spell of darkness that unties Colin's tongue, or perhaps it is simply the coaxing of ale and fire, but before long, he is asking me about Gully. What sort of career he had, where he hailed from, where I first met him. I tell him everything I know, and in telling it I realise how little it is. No family that I can attest to. Only one friend I've ever met: an elderly ship's outfitter down in Radcliffe. How unfit I am to bear his memory into the next generation.

Colin raises his tankard.

—To the captain, then.

—To the captain.

But it is too soon for elegy. Too soon, with Gully's body still unburied— stretched out in a police waggon, for all I know, or lying in a morgue. Too soon, with that infamous assault still playing out in my mind, more violent with each iteration.

And so, as night comes, grief turns ineluctably to rage. Rage is the heat that courses beneath the other heats. Those coals in the grate, they will crumble; the fever may well be gone tomorrow; but *this* heat will rival the sun for longevity. It will burn on until it has been answered, until Gully's spilled blood has been requited.

Strange, that my rage should take as its main object not Rebbeck, not the men who abetted him, but the man who sent them. That silent man in the carriage, with his obscene gestures and his obscene jewellery. The man who sends young girls to their deaths, who means to do the same to Philomela, if he hasn't already. This, *this* is the man who must be removed from the earthly vale before anything else can be set right.

And once again, the sensation of having seen him before—of having, somewhere in my possession, the *clue* that will solve him—is like an electric nettle in my skin. I find myself wanting to reach into my own brain, scrape his image free of every other integument, answer the question that tasks me so cruelly.

Where? Where have I seen him?

In my mind, I retrace my steps over the past few weeks, to no purpose. I scan the streets I have walked, the rooms and hallways through which I have passed, the chance encounters on random street corners . . . and still the face eludes me.

Here I sit, ready—oh, ready—to avenge, and my quarry dances quicksilver through my fingers. One of your better jokes, God. Oh, yes, an excellent joke you've had at my expense. If only . . .

What?

If only you hadn't made me choose Gully's flat.

If only you'd forced me to listen to Philomela.

Oh, why leave it there? Why not extend the regrets into the realm of fantasy? If only you'd given me one of Peter's three-legged cameras, had it follow me through the streets like a hunting dog, searing into my cortex every face I encountered, the exact circumstances of each meeting.

One of Peter's cameras. One of . . .

Wobbling, trembling in every limb, I rise to my feet. The tankard in my hand tips to one side, pours out the rest of its ale in a smooth, even stream.

—Bloody hell! says Colin, leaping to his feet.

—Come with me.

—Where we headin'?

—Come.

Night has fallen quickly on Oxford Street, but the plate-glass storefronts are still aglow with candlelight. Even this establishment, with its thyme-coloured awning and golden scrawl, even Cratchit's Salon Photographique burns bright. And there in the front window, Father's face stands proudly illuminated; his anxious squint has never tasted more of beatitude.

As I raise my hand to knock, Colin grabs me by the sleeve.

—They're closed, Mr. Timothy. I'm sure of it.

—They're at home.

It's just a matter of pounding and then pounding more fiercely, that's all, and before another minute has passed, Peter is hustling over, rolling down his sleeves, and Annie is one step behind him, making quick reparations in her hair, and all the adjustments cease as soon as they see who it is.

Peter wrenches the door open. His mouth forms my name, but Annie is the only one who speaks.

—You look like death, Tim.

I feel a bit like Death, too. Merciless and unstoppable. Even Annie is too cowed to block my way. I stride into the shop and march past the souvenir case and the seashells, past the entrance to the studio, past the painted backdrops of Mont Blanc and the Parthenon, only half listening to Colin's bleating voice as it trails after me.

—I *told* him he weren't well enough . . . head like a furnace . . . no weather for bein' out of doors. . . .

And still I keep going, until I have reached the wine table at the shop's western end. The table with its pocket-sized prints on thin paperboard mats—the *cartes de visite* that have become the last word in fashion.

And there, rising from the maelstrom of imagery, is an upright, swarthy man, on the far side of forty but dressed like a smart twenty-fiver, in a full-sleeved frock coat and a crossed tie and high collar. And wearing on his index finger a very heavy Spanish ring of carved rose gold, with an inset gem, large and square and perfect.

I snatch the card from the table. I dangle it in front of Peter's astonished face.

—Who is this?

—What's the matter with you, Tim? It's one of our patrons.

And that's when I start to roar. I wouldn't have thought I had the strength for it, but I do, I indisputably do.

—*Tell me his name! Tell me his damned name!*

Chapter 18

ANNIE IS THE FIRST TO SPEAK.

—What are you going on about, Tim? That's Lord Frederick Griffyn.

She tilts her face towards mine, awaiting, *demanding* an explanation, but she will have to wait, for only now are things being explained to me. Explained not in words but in a whirligig of associations: an incised *G* with raptorial eyes . . . the sound of flapping wings . . . a lion's haunches on a coat of arms . . . all coalescing at last into a single coherent figure. A name.

Griffin.

The image that has eluded me for so long, the image that breaks down every time I contemplate it, is now freely assembling itself in my mind. It is as if Mr. McReady had torn the frontispiece from one of his mythological compendia and dangled it before my eyes. I see the eagle's head and wings, tapering and blending almost imperceptibly into the body and hind legs and insouciant tail of a lion. I see it all so clearly I can almost breathe on it.

The griffin, Tim. Common decorative motif in ancient Asian and Mediterranean tombs and sanctuaries. Mythological function not clear. Perhaps there was none; perhaps it laid a purely visual claim on the viewer. What claim does it lay on you?

A ripple of dread is all I remember. The puissance of a lion, expanded unimaginably by the addition of wings. There would be no stopping such a creature, surely. The entire world would have to bow down.

—Shall we have some tea? asks Peter.

And, at first hearing, it is an indecent suggestion, it is perfectly appalling. A good man has been brutally murdered, a young girl may well meet the same fate unless something is done now, there's no time. *There's no time for bloody tea!*

This, at any rate, is the remonstrance I am prepared to make, and then I see Annie striding forwards, with a heavy green tome pressed against her collarbone. A book as large as a bank box and as freely consulted as an almanac, judging from the ease with which the dog-eared pages pry themselves apart.

—Annie?

She drops the book on the nearest table, blows out a cupful of air.

—*Debrett's Peerage and Baronetage.* You wish to know about Lord Griffyn? Here is the place to start.

While Peter serves the tea, she bends her head over the gilt-lettered volume. Five minutes later, the head is still bent, and a low grumbling rises from her throat.

—Oof! I can't get anywhere. Llewelyn of Llanishen, Williams of Llangeinor—they must *invent* these names. The only thing . . . well, what do you make of this? *The family returned to Denbighshire in eighteen thirty two and very shortly afterwards Lord Thomas Griffyn*—that would be Freddie's grandfather—*sold the Llanbradach estate; why, no one can tell. The estate had been in the family for nearly 600 years, and Lord Combermere told me upon the authority of Lord Griffyn himself that no Welshman ever boasted greater pride in his lineage.*

She scans the succeeding paragraphs.

—I don't see . . . no, there's no sign of their acquiring another property in Wales. All one can assume is they hoofed it straight to London.

—Very sad, says Peter.—Landed gentry with no land. The heart cracks.

—Not much in the way of money, either, remember, darling? He hasn't been able to pay for the cards. That's the reason they're still sitting here.

Peter looks up from his teacup.

—I do remember! Most of our patrons would sooner die than admit to money troubles, but he was unusually frank on the topic. Quite disarming, really.

—I'm sure.

—Of course, I told him he was welcome to have them on credit, but he said not to worry, he had no need of them just yet.

Peter's cup pauses in the air.

—And he said something else.

—What?

—He said he would be coming into additional income by Christmas.

—Christmas?

And with that, all the urgency, all the dread that drained off with the tea return a hundredfold.

For Christmas is less than thirty hours away. Lord Frederick Griffyn has less than thirty hours to come into money.

There, next to Peter's elbow, lies the *carte de visite*. There lies the author of Gully's death, with his annealed face, his squirrel's nest of light curls. And there, on the back, his gracious inscription:

> LORD FREDERICK GRIFFYN
>
> presents his compliments

Just so. Mr. Timothy Cratchit is about to send his compliments right back.

Starting up from the table, I reach for my coat and motion to Colin, who makes ready to follow me. We have not reckoned, though, on a superior force: Mistress Annie, the reigning monarch of Cratchit's Salon Photographique. A full head shorter than me, and for all that as unassailable as the Tower.

—You're not to go anywhere, Tim, do you hear? Not until you tell us truthfully. Has Lord Griffyn done something terrible?

—Yes.

—What is it?

—I can't say.

—Why not?

Because the people I tell get killed for their pains.

I can't bring myself to say it, and perhaps Annie divines it anyway, for she passes with all due speed to the next question.

—The police won't do anything about it?

—I doubt it.

—And you mean to say you are the only man alive who can remedy this . . . this crime?

—Apparently.

—And you won't let anyone else help you?

—No.

At an impasse, finally, Annie stalks off to the far end of the room. Peter, for his part, never leaves his seat, only lowers his cup of oolong to the table.

—And just what do you intend to do, Tim?

It is my obligation, I know, to answer him. It is my full intention. I do everything within my power to summon the necessary words, but they don't come when I call them, and so the silence lengthens, and Peter after a while turns away.

—Mother'd never forgive me. You know that, don't you?

—I know.

—Father, too. He'd haunt me to the end of my days.

I nearly laugh then.

—I promise you, Peter. He won't be haunting *you.*

And because he looks so thoroughly unconvinced, I add:

—As soon as I can, I'll get word to you.

—In another sixmonth, you mean.

—No, you'll have news sooner than that. Much sooner. I promise.

And still he won't look at me, not for love or money. It is left to Annie to tie things in a bow. Advancing on me at her usual brisk clip, she slaps a piece of paper into my palm, folds my fingers over it.

—What's this?

—The address, Tim. You'll find Lord Griffyn in Portland Place. And if it will help you at all, you can always say you're making a delivery from us.

—Thank you, Annie.

My gratitude makes not the slightest impression on her. Wrapping her arms about herself, she gives her lower lip a pensive chewing and turns away again. And Peter, rising slowly from the table, transfers his attentions directly to Colin.

—Now see here, young fellow. You're to look out for my brother, do you understand? He won't let anyone else do it, so it'll have to be you.

—Yessir.

—And tell him for God's sake to keep warm. And tell him I'll be looking for him Christmas Day. At Uncle N's. Tell him he's expected.

And with that, Peter turns away, too, so that my parting glimpse of the Cratchits is of two eloquently slumping backs. Eloquence enough to make me pause there on the threshold, draw my lips apart for some final valediction. But words are scarce for me these days. Best to hoard them.

And what, anyway, could I say that would make it better? No, let them begin the necessary work of erasing me. Just as Sam was erased, over time. Belinda and Jemmy . . . Mother . . . each of them less legible with every passing hour. Father, too, one day. Perhaps.

The door whispers shut behind us. Above us, the moon drives its sickle through the encumbrances of cloud. Beneath us, veils of mist blossom from the pavement, weave through the ochre day-fog, and bind it tight. The world is falling away. My feet have vanished from view, and the madman's comforter I wear about me has become indistinguishable from the air that surrounds it, and my companion, not two feet away, is dissolving into a palette of greys and browns and tans.

—Colin.

—Hm?

—I'm sorry my brother spoke to you that way.

—Oh, he were right gentle, Mr. Timothy. . . .

—No, the point is, you're not accountable to me or responsible *for* me or . . . or *anything*, and given that I can't answer for what happens from here on out, I can't . . . I suppose what I'm trying to tell you is I can't, you know, in good conscience subject you to the dangers.

—'Course you can.

—No, Colin. We parted friends once before. We may do so again.

Through the mist, I can just make out the glimmer of a wry smile.

—Well, yes, we could part right easy, Mr. Timothy, if it were but the two of us. But there's Filly to think of, now, ain't there? And the cap'n, too, leave us not forget. I mean, if you must know, this is what he wanted I should do.

I squint at him.

—Oh, it's hard to wrap a mouth 'round it, Mr. Timothy. All I can tell you is when I left the cap'n—him a-layin' there on the cold, hard floor—I don't know, it were like he were speakin' to me. God's truth, Mr. Timothy, he came to me strong and clear. "Now, don't you worry over me," he were saying. "Acoz I've gone to a better place. But *you*, young fellow, you got yourself a great labour to perform. And you make sure it gets done afore you take up anythink else." So that's how it stands, Mr. Timothy.

Colin sidles away just then, disappears into the mist, and for a few seconds, I lose track of him entirely—and then that sward of wavy black hair swims back into my ken. The cheeky, coal-eyed face climbs towards mine.

—And look at it this way, Mr. Timothy. You can't run worth shit, you don't mind my sayin'. You want a healthy pair of legs, you do. And a cove like me don't often get a chance for real live Ad-ven-ture, now do he? Not like this. So lay on, Mr. Timothy! That's what I got to say to you. Lay on!

I nod, very slowly.

—Cat got your tongue, Mr. Timothy?

—No. I was only wondering if your parents know about you.

—'Course they do.

—I mean, do they *know* you? As I do?

—Oh, Gawd, no. Better that way, ain't it?

Colin procures the clothes: pilot's trousers and oilskin caps and a pair of black pea coats purchased from the patrons of a public house in Coventry Street. (Colin's coat is too large for him by half; he has to roll up the sleeves almost to the elbow.) I am in charge of the gear: a rope ladder and a butcher's hook, secreted in a tartan knapsack.

And a butcher's knife, filched from Mary Catherine's pantry.

The cab we engage from a taxi stand in Piccadilly Circus. It is a little down at the heel, as hansoms go, with doors that sag and sigh, and ratty curtains over the side windows, but even so, it is positively sprightly in comparison with the cabman. He is as grim, as bedraggled, as mournful-looking a gentleman as ever sat atop a carriage, and rather than give our mariner's garments the suspicious eye they deserve, he seems to derive from them fresh evidence of the world's perfidy. *Oh*, he seems to say with every crevice of his being. *It's come to this, has it?*

—What's your name, driver?

With a long, trailing groan, he confesses:

—Adolphus.

—Very well, Adolphus. I wish to engage your services for the rest of the evening. Is that acceptable to you?

Job, at his deepest ebb, never took things so hard as Adolphus. He cups his hands and raises them to the heavens, as though he were pleading his case with the Great Celestial Mediator.

—"Acceptable!" He asks if it's acceptable! As if a fellow had any choice on a night such as this, with a wife and three young 'uns home abed, and who knows where I'll be when they wakes up? "Acceptable?" he asks!

—You'll be paid liberally for your time. And your discretion.

—Oh, "discretion!" It's *discretion* he wants!

This invites yet another discourse on the absurdity of free will (at least as practiced by one Adolphus the cabman), a treatise that carries on even after Colin and I have taken a seat inside and closed the door after us. The roar of the city dies down, but the dirgelike cadences of Adolphus continue pelting the roof of the cab like so many dirt clods. *Dame Fortune's grindstone . . . family obligations looped round a man's feet like an anchor . . . rentin' a cab and horse no better than slavin' on a sugar plantation, and that's a fact.* Our cabman, it turns out, is a bard of despond, and now and then, when the vehicle comes to a halt and the wind quiets, his lyric odes chime out in the chill night air.

—And he wants me to be *discreet*, does he? Why don't he ask me to be wealthy, too? That'd be summat. Adolphus with money in his pocket! He could afford to be discreet *then*, couldn't he?

The longer I listen, the more pleasing the sound becomes—as fixed and reiterative as a lullaby. Adolphus's children, I think, must go to sleep to this every night. Even now, I can imagine the sound worming its way back home to them, through the extinguishing blanket of fog that lies all round us. Although it would be hard to imagine anything penetrating this, for we are in the grip of a real London particular: whole buildings not so much hidden as excised, monuments decapitated, light swallowed entire. The fog doesn't roll in; it pushes outwards with a hydraulic force. It boils like the sea, burns in our nostrils, and eats at our skin.

And under its influence, my shivering fits return, like old family. I sit there in the corner of the cab, in the darkness, with Father's comforter wrapped round, a finger inserted between my teeth to keep them from chattering. And even still, my body shakes for all it's worth, and whenever a streetlight manages to bleed through the mantle of fog, it illuminates the look of wavering consternation in Colin's eyes.

Danger is one thing, those eyes say. *A companion unfit to meet danger . . . that's another.*

The church bells strike the nine o'clock hour, and still the fog rises, muffling the very tongues of the bells, and as we continue northwards, the city itself seems to fall back before the wall of tawny grey. But here it is not the fog that has pushed the buildings away, for this is Portland Place, widest and grandest of all London avenues.

At least by repute. There is not tonight a great deal of grandeur on display, or if there is, it has been wiped clean by the fog. A sepulchral quiet reigns, and that quiet is not so much dispersed as reinforced by the orderly clatter of hooves, the creaks of waggons, all dying in the uttering.

—Driver! Stop here, if you please.

The cab lurches to a halt. From above comes the aggrieved timbre of Adolphus:

—What's he goin' on about? We hain't reached the address yet.

—We'd prefer to walk the rest of the way, if that's all right with you.

—Oh, if it's all right with *me*.

The reins are thrown down, and with a polysyllabic sigh, Adolphus lowers himself to the ground, jerks open the carriage door, and stands there, glaring at our feet.

—No doubt you'll expect me to wait.

—Why, yes, if you would be so good.

—As if it were up to me. As if *I* had any say in the matter.

Not even the coin I place in his hand will brighten his mood; it is simply one more shackle in the chain that binds him to earth. With a gesture of martyred resignation, he pockets the copper and hauls himself back up to his box.

—Oh, driver, one last thing. We may have an additional passenger when we return.

—Additional? There's but room for two in this cab.

—And we may be in something of a hurry.

—"Hurry," he says. More freight, he tells me. It's all the same to him, I'm sure. Don't worry hisself 'bout Adolphus, shiverin' up on his box, coldest night of the year. . . .

We leave him there, inveighing against his fate. And whether he leaves off for want of an audience, or whether his sound goes the way of all sound, his voice does, in fact, dissipate after a few paces. How I miss it! With nothing to attend to now but the sound of our boots scuffing against the pavement, and the occasional shrouded carriage trundling past, it becomes all the harder to stave down this feeling . . . this feeling of what? Of being alone, I suppose. Irrevocably alone.

For that is what we are, Colin and I, with our threadbare disguises, our knapsack full of tools, our barely concealed infirmities. By our own design, we have ventured into the griffin's lair alone. May God guide us out again.

Ah, yes. The bravado of two hours past has seeped away and left behind only loose fringes of possibility, unravelling even as I contemplate them. Perhaps, I think, perhaps it really would have been better to fall back on the vast institutional presence of Scotland Yard. And yet even at this moment of deepest doubt, I cannot trust men like Inspector Surtees with my holy work. For Inspector Surtees never knew Gully. He can never know this rage, this *heat* . . . scalding me through and through.

O, Gully. If you could but reach down from whatever aerie you now occupy, part the fog before my eyes and show me all the things I long to know. How many of them came at you? Did you have time to cry out? And was *he* there? Lord Griffyn? Baring his golden fangs? Did he offer his card?

And what of Philomela, Gully? Tell me why they spared her. Tell me what end they have in mind for her. *Tell* me.

—Mr. Timothy?

Colin's hand is on my arm. He peers into my face, waiting for something to dawn.

—What is it?

—You can stop now. We're *here*, ain't we?

We're here.

But Griffyn Hall registers to my dazed eyes as nothing more than an absence. Only after standing for some time before the front gate, only by letting my eyes relax into the mist, do I realise that this absence is, in fact, Griffyn Hall's intention. From its very genesis, perhaps, before even the Griffyns arrived, the house was doubling back on itself, sprouting an arcade of beeches on each side and sequestering itself behind a short lawn. Forming itself into a tiny citadel of secrets.

—You two! Move along!

Standing before the gate, like a pair of Myrmidons muscling away the fog, are two representatives of the Metropolitan Police. Not on their usual rounds, that much is clear. They have been engaged to a specific purpose: to guard the citadel through the night.

Old drinking mates of Rebbeck's, very possibly. Or just as likely, two random specimens of corruption, plucked from the streets. Amazing now to think that in my weakness, in my dread, I contemplated calling in Scotland Yard. When they have already been called in.

—What, deaf and dumb? I said, move along! Smart now!

One of the Myrmidons takes a step forwards, jabs the air with his baton. Colin tips his cap and grabs my arm.

—We was just leavin', Officer.

Passing from their range of vision, I murmur a prayer of thanks that Rebbeck himself was not manning the gates. God, it seems, has granted us this one favour. And a second favour, too, in the fog, which thoughtfully conceals the eastern side of Portland Place from the western. Simply by travelling on for ten paces and then crossing the street, Colin and I are able to retrace our steps without once being seen by the constabulary. And as we creep back towards our starting point, it occurs to me that the Myrmidons' presence is the best possible sign. It means—doesn't it?—that something is happening tonight at Griffyn Hall. Something the rest of the world isn't meant to see. And unless my intuition plays me false, Philomela lies at the heart of it.

Chapter 19

WE ARE MORE CAUTIOUS ON OUR SECOND PASSAGE. Rather than broach Griffyn Hall from the front, we come at it sideways, through a neighbouring estate. Easy enough at first, just a quick hop over a low wrought-iron fence, a plunge into a high yew hedge . . . and then a new obstacle confronts us: the hedge itself, too dense to be breached. We feel our way along the branches, grasping for openings, the tiniest gaps, but they are too few and too small. In a panic, Colin seizes the butcher knife from the knapsack and begins hacking a passageway of his own. But the branches fight us at every step, scratching and clawing, retreating only to surge back again. It takes us ten minutes more to carve out an opening—an illusory one at that, for though it bids fair to admit us, it changes its mind once we are admitted, and only by crawling and scrabbling our way through do we at last emerge on the other side, roughly halfway down the lawn to Griffyn Hall.

We crouch there, in our torn trousers, staring at a house that looks no closer than when we began. Indeed, from this vantage, it seems altogether more distant, an heirloom from the age of Palladio. Through the miasma, we see, some thirty feet away, a high flat white facade as sheer as a chalk cliff, topped by a dome one twentieth the size of the Pantheon's and yet conceived on a grand enough scale to lend the entire building a colossal impression.

Dismal to report: Griffyn Hall is no less a citadel on closer viewing than it appeared from the street. The only access I can espy is a flight of stairs running parallel to the house and climbing towards what looks to be a pedimented Greek-temple portico. Before we can apply ourselves to those stairs, though, we must first make peace with Griffyn Hall's advance patrol: a row of statues running perpendicular from the house to the street. Greek nymphs, each a perfect duplicate of the others, all in flowing robes, with eyes that pierce the fog . . . and gaze directly at us.

Fortunately for us, their marble enchantments have denied them a voice, so they make nary a peep as we crawl across the grass to them, and when we reach the middlemost maiden, she even presents her stone heel to us as a kind of good-luck charm (Colin takes the liberty of rubbing it) and her stone tunic fans round us, concealing us from both the Myrmidons on the street and the house itself, which now lies perhaps fifteen feet off.

—Stroke of luck, whispers Colin.—I'll take statues over dogs any day.

And just then the curtain of fog parts to reveal not a dog but a far more fantastic sentry: an Indian peacock in full regalia, dragging its long train of turquoise and bronze feathers, each feather tipped with an iridescent eye, and each eye peering up at us with a baleful interest.

The anomaly of him is almost too much. He should be mewed up this time of year, shouldn't he? He shouldn't have this profusion of feathers, not with the mating season so long past. Just our luck: a hothouse bird, following his own season. His train of feathers spills forwards, vibrating and shimmering, sending ripples of light into the grey.

—What's it doin', Mr. Timothy?

—He's . . . I believe he's courting us.

Just then, the fog gives way to another cock—irresistibly drawn by the commotion and exploring us with the same degree of priapic interest as his companion. And then, right behind, yet another peacock, and then another, and still one more. An alien race, inexorably crowding in, with not a hen in sight, and no other end in view but us.

Or rather, no end in view but my young friend. It is Colin whom the birds circle with their frank, appraising air. It is Colin for whom they flutter and flash and make their lovelorn entreaties.

I whisper:

—*Do* something.

But their rustling is so loud by now that the boy's appeals are barely audible, even to me.

—Here, you got the wrong impression—I'm a bloke, I tell you . . . God's truth, I'm a bloke. . . .

And still the birds close in, craning their heads, thrusting out their chests, sweeping their feathers higher and higher, and now Colin draws on a new fund of rashness. Jumping backwards, he claws open his trousers and, with wildly scrabbling hands, drags out the nearest available evidence of his sex. Holds it there in his hand like a pickled eel, freshly wrapped.

Circling their inamorato, the cocks take turns inspecting the offering, and as they gaze, they draw back again, widening their circle as they go, and before another minute has passed, the first peacock has angled off onto his own tangent, in search of more promising love objects, and within another minute, the others have followed his example, ducking their heads and retracting their plumage and vanishing into the fog.

Colin is the last to know. His eyes are welded shut, and his hand trembles beneath its pale cargo.

—It's all right, Colin. You may put that away now.

—Oh. Thanks.

And so we are alone once again. Alone in the mantle of night, afraid to draw breath, pricking our ears for the faintest reports of our discovery. But the silence only thickens and deepens round us as the night broods on, and this silence becomes to my ear more appalling than anything else. Huddled there by the hedge, I find myself longing for the scrape of a heel or the groan of a door.

And at last, after a wait that feels like many days, I am met with a quick burst of sensation: a blaze of light in the portico.

It is the former Sergeant William Rebbeck, holding a match to a cigarette. Long after the cigarette has been lit, he peers through that corona of light while the flame works its way down to his thumb and nestles against his skin and then, exhausted, blows itself out.

A mere fifteen seconds of illumination, twenty at best, but enough to determine that the famous bowler is gone, replaced by a top hat of medium distinction and supplemented by a frock coat, a velvet collar, a large bow tie, and gloves of the downiest white. Willie the Slasher is hobbing with nobs tonight.

Wonder enough, but there is an even greater wonder: apart from Rebbeck and the two policemen in front, not another soul is afoot, either at window or out of doors. Where is the butler? The liveried footmen? The hostlers and grooms? Can Lord Griffyn's economizing have extended to ridding his house of help?

Or have the servants of Griffyn Hall simply been given the night off?

They were delighted to have it, I've no doubt. Seized their unexpected gift and never, in deference to their employer, taxed themselves wondering what would happen in their absence.

By my watch, it wants only a few minutes to ten o'clock. Griffyn and his men will have many hours yet of protective cover. Many hours before dawn claws away the night, more hours still before the fog lifts.

But there's one thing to be said for this fog: it is too fickle to be yoked to one master. Even as it shields Griffyn Hall from the world's scrutiny, it shields us from Griffyn Hall. We need only bivouac behind one of the marble maidens to be effectively hidden from view, and in this position, we might bide all night long, if necessary.

Let us hope it won't be. The air is frosting our bones, and my comforter is back in the cab, and the effort of sitting back on my haunches has set my chronically ailing knee to a rare pitch of protest. The only comfortable attitude, after a time, is to sit squarely on my buttocks in the damp, smeary grass and feel the cold steal its way up me.

Just like the old dream. The paralysis, as the doctor foretold, rising through me, up the thigh and hip, through the lower vertebrae, the breastbone and lungs . . . all the way to the heart, vainly protesting. . . .

Colin nudges me, holds a flask to my mouth. It is a labour, prying these lips apart, but I am soon rewarded with an infusion of fire, and under its influence, I experience one last fit of shivering before the paralysis departs. All that remains is this throbbing purple ache, not comfort exactly but a kind of expectancy, faintly underlaid with hope—all I need, apparently, to weather the dogged passage of hours. That and the silent witness of Colin, who, though half obscured, is yet close enough for our breathing to coalesce.

It is ten minutes to midnight when the sounds reach us. A carriage. No different at first from the usual clatter of hooves, but for the slow deceleration of wheels against slick macadam.

Shaking off our listlessness, Colin and I rise to our knees. We hear the cry of a coachman, the answering cries of the Myrmidons. A carriage door opens . . . a pair of descending feet. . . .

And then, like a hand pulling away the fog, the voice of Willie the Slasher.

—Good evening, your grace.

Colin grabs my sleeve.

Him?

I shake my head. *Not him.* Only dukes are addressed as "your grace."

—'Evening, Rebbeck. Is Freddie receiving yet?

—Waiting in the library, your grace.

The front door is opened; a fusillade of feet issues forth. Griffyn Hall, it turns out, is not the abandoned hive it proclaimed itself to be. The bees have merely been biding their time, and here they come, a horde of drones, with droning voices to match—the flat, half-respectful monotones of clerks.

—In here, if you please. That's right. Bernard will take your coat, your grace. You know the way to the library, I expect?

Four, five men—it is hard to disentangle their voices, and before long, new sounds are added to the welter. More carriages, each following hard on the last, each paying homage to the Myrmidons, each disgorging a new gentleman. And each gentleman receiving, from Rebbeck's lips, his due honourific.

—'Evening, Sir Reginald . . . Dr. Earnshaw! So nice of you to come. . . .

Lord Northdown, Baron Keble, Sir Leicester—Rebbeck's old colleagues would be astonished to hear him so at ease among the gentry.

The church bells strike the midnight hour—a symphony of chime—and still the carriages keep coming. I can hear them now, backed up halfway down the block, the horses quiescent in their harness, the coachmen impatiently tapping their crops. The delay is enough to goad some of the gentlemen into the heresy of letting themselves out of their own carriages. Converging at the front gate, they stroll up the front walk together, filling the air with their banalities.

—Beastly business!

—Not a night to be abroad.

—Dog of a driver nearly struck an omnibus.

—*Mine* will be given his notice before the year is out. One can't go on like this. . . .

Rather than stay to hear themselves maligned, the coachmen, as soon as they have discharged their loads, tear off down the lane, clearing the deadlock as quickly as it formed. The street empties out again, and within another few minutes, the lawn, too, has emptied.

Griffyn Hall, however, has sparked into life. Candles now burn from the front windows, shadows flit across the curtains, and through the ancient stones creep the sounds of holiday revelry: halloos of recognition, muffled shouts, a tinkle of glass.

Screened by the marble maidens, Colin and I steal towards the house, feeling our way through the mist until we reach the staircase. There we crouch beneath a huge globe of a stair cap and peer up the stone steps. But the fog has thrown up a wall so dense that an entire cavalry might be sequestered there in the portico, and we would be none the wiser. And so we linger there by the base of the stairs, frozen by irresolution or, more accurately, by cer-

tainty. For I know, as sure as the breath on my hands, that Rebbeck is out
there somewhere. Waiting.

Have another cigarette, damn you!

And in direct response to my prayer, a match flares up once again to reveal
Rebbeck's blunt, dogged profile—uncomfortably closer than last time—and
the fixed outlines of two other men, likewise dressed beyond their station,
and spaced on either side of Rebbeck before the portico entrance.

No question of trying to slip by them. What, then, is left?

Nothing, proclaim the frowning, implacable stones of Griffyn Hall. But as
I gaze up into the murk, I discern for the first time a purchase: a cornice or
ledge, about ten feet over our heads, running along the front of the building.

Not much, but something. It seems to me if we can gain that modest
height, we can lift ourselves out of Rebbeck's ken and, more to the point,
gain access to one of the windows—and if God so chooses, a stolen view of
Philomela.

But the ledge is quite high up, and reaching it will take some ingenuity.
The best course I can see for us is to climb onto the stair cap at the bottom of
the steps and haul ourselves straight up.

I mime my plan as best I can to Colin, and then I hoist myself onto the
smooth stone globe. It is no easy task, finding my balance with a knapsack
wrapped round me, but when I stand on my toes, I find I can just clasp my
hands round the ledge, and after several trials, I can even swing my boot
onto it. Several more trials later, I have prised my torso up, and soon thereafter, my fingers find a tiny crenellation in the house's wall, which affords
me enough leverage to lift myself to a standing position.

Perched there on the ledge, I feel a ripple of pride. *Hark the cripple boy*. All
those years of plying a crutch, not wasted after all.

Colin is just barely visible below, poised on the stone cap and swinging his
arms like an organ grinder's monkey. Clearly, the gap between the staircase
and the ledge is too great for him: he will have to make up the difference by
leaping.

And leap he does—hurls himself at the stone face. His fingers land just to the left of my boot; his body slams into the building. A grunt of pain breaks free from him as one hand clamps down on his bruised face, and the other lingers on the rim of the ledge. Four tiny fingers, clutching for all their worth and already losing their grip on the cold stone, sliding with agonising slowness towards the edge.

They have given way altogether by the time my own fingers lock round them. The weight of him jerks my arm taut, nearly pulls me from my perch. It takes a pair of scarifying wobbles before I can regain my balance, but Colin has no balance to regain. He hangs suspended now, twelve feet from the ground. Gravity drags at his boots; blood smears his chin. And his free hand—I have just enough presence of mind to notice this—is shoved in his mouth to stifle the pain.

From this charged silence emerges the sound of footsteps, passing down the portico and advancing down the steps towards us. Leading the way, that minute corona of match-flame, nestling against the callused skin of former Sergeant William Rebbeck.

The fog has closed round us, but that oncoming light leaves little doubt: Colin's hanging figure will be in full view once they reach us. Closing my eyes and uttering a silent orison, I draw three breaths . . . and then I haul upwards with all my might. My shoulders tremble with their burden; my chest swells with spent air; but Colin does begin to rise—in spasmodic hitches, like a piece of rickety scenery—and my labour is eased by the sight of his blood-smeared face heaving into view, his blood-smeared hand clutching the ledge with renewed authority.

Another hydraulic surge with my left arm, and Colin's feet at last find their foundation. Trembling, he lets go my hand and throws himself against the stone wall as though it were a nursing breast.

Below us, the match-flame flutters out, then starts back into life—hovers now directly below us. We stifle our panting, we flatten ourselves against the wall . . . and we wait, in an agony of suspense.

A full minute passes before we hear Rebbeck's flat, hard voice, calling:

—Fetch me a lantern.

Which is to say, we have not escaped; we have only purchased time. Time enough, anyway, to examine our options, which, on closer scrutiny, dissolve into one. We must follow this ledge away from the portico entrance . . . plunge into the mist in the hope that we can take ourselves out of the range of Rebbeck's search party.

From the direction of the portico comes the next wave of light, larger and more assertive and moving more rapidly than before. A prod to our own feet, which take longer, quicker steps and carry us with relative ease along the stone ledge, even as the light bears down on us.

I can't say how exactly the equilibrium shifts, but at some indefinable moment, we look down and realise, with a salutary shock, that the light is falling further behind, dropping lower and lower as the search party descends the steps towards the lawn.

Before much longer, the light has come to a complete halt, and now only a single conclusion is possible: they have reached the bottom of the stairs. Some five minutes pass before the light streams back up the stone stairs to the portico entrance, where Rebbeck and his two minions, to all appearances, take up their old vigil.

Liberated for the moment, we unclench our bodies and move along the front of the building in an easier rhythm, until we have attained something approaching relaxation. A little too close to relaxation, as I discover when my leading foot, expecting more ledge, finds nothing but wobbling air, and my torso, weighed down by the knapsack, makes ready to follow. It is Colin's turn to grab me.

—Bleedin' corners, he whispers.—Get you every time.

Fortunately, the ledge, like the building, makes a ninety-degree turn to the west, and we follow it round, resuming our single-file pilgrimage. Ten feet along, we are slowed by something new: an amber vent in the fog, diffusing and then disappearing entirely, only to resolve again as a plain double-hung window, smouldering with refracted light.

Here, before we even expected it, a vantage point on the house's interior, and yet whatever germ of excitement opens inside me is at once smothered by the instinct for caution. Signalling to Colin to wait, I sidle over and tip my head into the outermost part of the window frame.

The room inside is dark and uninhabited, a sealed box, with the exception of a door that has been thrown open to admit the light from a larger room. It is this farther sanctum to which my eye unavoidably turns. Convex walls festooned with looking-glasses and torchères and ancestral portraits of varying sizes, all of them dreary with soot. Unless my internal compass deceives me, this is Lord Griffyn's front hall.

There is precious little time for confirmation, for even now, tonight's guests are strolling across the patterned marble. The sight of them, not twenty feet away—presenting, in their limpid definition, such a contradiction to the murk in which I crouch—makes me start back from the window.

I go on watching nevertheless, as they pace back and forth across my aperture of light, extravagantly bearded men in their forties and fifties, with the same agonised rehearsals of gesture that one associates with court presentations. But they are not dressed for court, any more than they are dressed for evening: black trousers have given way to white and pale grey; cravats are turquoise and crimson. Only one accessory binds all the gentlemen in their separate agitations: a red geranium, inserted with unnerving regularity in the buttonhole of each waistcoat. And this, too: in the midst of their pacing and pivoting, they each give evidence of some larger purpose, larger than all of them, and preparing to breach.

A breath in my ear, a touch on my elbow. Colin has stolen up behind me.
Do you see her? he mouths.
No. Not yet.

Just then, the gentlemen, operating on some unheard command, begin to fall against the wall in a crooked line, standing with tight shoulders and downcast eyes, like schoolboys about to be arraigned before the headmaster. In fact, no headmaster in the land would be a match for the personage who next appears: Miss Charlotte Binny, her missionary raiment exchanged for a lace bonnet and a black mantilla, her pious attitude traded for a far more redoubtable mien. Scowling, she claps her hands and calls over her shoulder, and though I cannot hear them, her clipped words might be wired straight into my ear.

—Come along, now. No dawdling. You there! Pick up the heel.

Give Miss Binny a regiment, and she will have it storming the enemy garrison within two hours. Tonight, however, smaller wonders are asked of her. The company over which she presides is a squadron of gawky girls—all between eight and twelve, I would reckon, and whipped into strict formation, staring straight ahead with a rigidity that would put dragoons to shame, and wearing uniforms that no cavalry officer would dare sport.

Bridal dresses. They are all, to a girl, wrapped in bridal dresses.

Miniature replicas, at least, of the most striking kind: white satin, lace, and silk with matching shoes and long, translucent veils. Garlands of white narcissi in their hair and bouquets of white pansies and snapdragons in their gloved hands. Everything so gleaming in its newness that I half expect to see the seamstresses and their apprentices still at work, their bent figures scurrying amongst the brides, adjusting bodices and trimming veils and pinning back stray hems.

But aside from Miss Binny, the girls stand all to themselves and betray no sign of the strangeness of their condition—or even the irregularity of an evening wedding. Indeed, they look as though every nerve had been scourged out of them. Their arms swing with no purpose; their heads loll so markedly to one side that Miss Binny must step in now and again to knock them back into position, as one might realign a set of ninepins.

How to describe the effect of this masquerade? How to limn the contrast between the men, in their jittery wallflower formations, and the girls, half the size of ordinary brides, but with a lifetime of obedience already drummed into every fibre? One might almost confuse them with actual women were it not for the occasional telltale gesture: a crossing of the ankles, an uncensored case of the fidgets—random unsocialized motions. That young girl halfway down the line, for instance. Mark how her hands fuss inside their white gloves, how they insistently bend into a shape I recognise quite well: the shape of a bird's talons.

Is Miss Binny speaking now? Has a trumpet sounded? Something it is that snaps the gentlemen to attention and reassembles them, according to pre-arranged order, in a line parallel to that of the girl-brides. With a long, froggy smile, Miss Binny extends a beckoning finger to the first gentleman, a jowly, snow-haired man playing ostentatiously with a buttonhook.

How pleased he is to make the first girl's acquaintance! With what deep gravity he bows to her, presses her hand to his lips. How he trembles with the momentousness of his own act as he tickles his fingers beneath the girl's veil and draws it up and away. There is a moment of arrested reckoning. And then, reassured by what he finds, the gentleman breaks into a half grin and casts a relieved look round the room.

His reaction is nothing, though, compared with the hard, frozen look on the young girl's face. She has anticipated this moment, I think, so intensely that the actual experience of it is redundant. She is forearmed against it, she is helpless against it. So that when the gentleman offers her his arm, she takes it with the absent-mindedness of a woman reaching for a fan, and when he leads her away, she lets slip her bouquet without a backwards look or a tremor of regret.

The expression on that face is virtually duplicated in the next girl, and the one after that. So alike are they, once their veils are lifted, that I find myself doing all within my power to commit their features to memory, so as to claim some distinction amongst them. A dark brow, a high, knobby forehead: I seize on every idiosyncrasy I can, but each one disappears into the nullity of that collective gaze.

They go, these girls, without a thought or pang, without any hope of reprieve. Only one, a moonfaced redhead with a mole on her chin, she alone hesitates in taking her groomsman's arm, hesitates for the briefest interval. And then Miss Binny makes a move towards her, and all hesitation disappears.

It is quick work, as you might imagine. Ten girls are paired off in half as many minutes. Only one remains—a shrouded white island in the middle of the parquet floor, waiting to be claimed. But no one steps forward. The gentlemen who were standing against the wall have marched off with their prizes, and as the seconds pass, I begin to wonder if perhaps the formidable Miss Binny has miscalculated and left one of the brides without a groom.

And then, as if to stifle my doubts at their very inception, Miss Binny steps up and derogates to herself the privilege that has previously fallen to the grooms. She lifts the bride's veil. Lifts it to reveal the stone-cold features of Philomela.

It is no surprise. It is, to some degree, everything I expected. And yet the sight of her, marooned in the middle of that checkered floor, is akin to a steel beam in the stomach. I deceive myself, perhaps, in thinking that some particle of her has survived the trials of the past twenty-four hours. But who is to say?

By my watch, it is precisely forty-two minutes past the midnight hour when the door frame is suddenly filled by a tall, curly-haired man in a blue frock coat and lilac waistcoat. Bowing to Philomela, he extends his left arm in a smooth, sweeping gesture, the kind of unhurried munificence that comes easily to Lord Frederick Griffyn.

Other girls, perhaps, might be overwhelmed by such a gesture, but she is as fixed as the portico of Griffyn Hall, and even when the good lord offers her his right arm, she refuses to acknowledge its existence. That elegantly attired arm simply hovers there until it becomes, to my eyes, incontrovertible proof of the very thing I was seeking: Philomela's will, beating quick inside her.

It is with the utmost reluctance that her hand at last breaks the plane of its isolation. It is with unconcealed revulsion that her small white fingers rest on Griffyn's arm.

None of these small signs of rebellion, however, disturbs the self-possession of her host. With a seigneurial nod, he clamps his hand over hers and leads her, in long, dreamlike steps, down the checkered floor. And as they pass from view, the riddle I posed to Gully's departed spirit cracks open, and I understand at last, I *understand* why Philomela has been spared. Tonight, she is the intended bride of Lord Frederick Griffyn.

Chapter 20

—WE'VE NO TIME.

No point in whispering any more; I use the flat, declarative tone the situation seems to demand. Colin, though, insists on whispering back.

—Where've they taken her?

I have only my intuition to guide me—that and a scatter of images. The expressions on the brides' faces. The way the grooms shifted against the wall, like boys at a ball, screwing up their courage. And above all else, the cast of Griffyn's face, that look of virtual consummation. Everything draws me on to the same conclusion: the ceremony is over. The wedding night has begun.

—She's in Lord Griffyn's bedchamber.

Acting on a common impulse, Colin and I drop our heads back and gaze up the face of the building. If Griffyn Hall follows the customary plan, the master's bedroom is almost certainly located on the upper storey. And if that's the case, then an immediate change of altitude is in store for us.

This one, I can already see, will be harder-won than the last. The architecture has, like the fog, turned against us. No gargoyles, buttresses, or casements, not a single Gothic excrescence to fasten on to. Just these time-sanded Palladian walls, rising into the blankness.

And then Colin whispers:

—The window.

Strangely enough, my eyes are already converging on the same point: a protruding stone lip, perhaps six feet over our heads. What else but the sill of an upper-storey window?

Without another word, Colin drags the length of rope ladder from the knapsack and fastens it to the butcher's meathook with such deftness I am left to wonder if loitering by the Hungerford Stairs might not be a more educational experience than I had reckoned on.

Gathering the ladder in his arms, Colin flings the hook towards the windowsill. It takes him several tries before the hook catches, and several more before it holds. Moments later, he gives the ladder three harsh tugs and pronounces it fit for climbing. And indeed it is: we ascend to the upper window with a near-magical haste, as though some giant's finger were hauling us up in its crook.

Here, though, another obstacle. The upper storey provides not a single ledge to lead us round the building, and so we are forced to hook the ladder round the balustrade above us and make straight for the roof. The sky rushes towards us, and for a few moments, I lose Colin entirely in a bank of fog that sweeps round him. Then, through a slot in the murk, his hand materialises, already hauling me in. A scrape of stone against my shins, and all at once, I am standing atop Griffyn Hall.

Not so impregnable as it once seemed, but not yet ready to give up its secrets. No enchanted doors open before us, and as far as I can see, there remains but one way to reach those upper-storey windows: we must climb down to each one in turn, repositioning our ladder each time, until we have found Philomela's bower. Arduous labour, to be sure, and bound to consume more time than we have to spare.

—Colin.

—Yes?

—Please tell me if you are desperately afraid of heights.

Only after he has assured me several times to the contrary do I tell him what I have in mind.

—By the *feet*, Mr. Timothy?

—Yes.

—And then what?

—Well, then I'll lower you to each window in turn. You'll look inside, give me some sign—yea or nay—and I'll raise you up again. And then we'll move on to the next window. Until . . . until we find her.

Colin's eyes are still widening to admit all the implications.

—And it's . . . you mean to say head*first*, like?

—If you're up to it.

He peers over the balustrade—sounding the depths of the grey sea into which he will be submerged. Then he clears his throat and gives his chest three quick taps.

—Colin's your uncle.

—You needn't fear, I shan't let go.

—I ain't feared.

Nevertheless, as we position ourselves over the first window, we are subsumed in an awkward idleness. It breaks, finally, when Colin claps his hands together and perches himself on the edge of the balustrade.

—Heigh-ho and off we go.

—We needn't, Colin, if you're—

—No, I'm for it. Truly.

Once I have my hands round his ankles, it is a fairly simple matter to let gravity take him earthwards. And as he passes down the face of the building, he finds ways to anchor himself—tiny niches that give him at least the illusion of control. But what an eerie spectacle he must present! A little pea-coated bat, crawling blind down the weathered brick, resting his feelers on the stone lintel and then, with a panting ardour, lowering his head into the frame of the double-hung window. A moment of silent inspection, a hitch of his little bat-thumb, and up he comes again.

—Sorry, Mr. Timothy. Nothin' but dark.

The next descent likewise ends in disappointment, and as we edge round to the back of the manor, my mind teems with doubts. *Have they repaired to some other bower? Departed through the back?* But the next foray yields more reassuring results.

—*Live* ones, Mr. Timothy. I could see 'em, coupla monkeys by the door, lookin' into the hallway.

—Guards, do you think?

—Dunno. But there's got to be a reason for 'em, eh? Couldn't be just dawdlers, now, could they? Not tonight.

And so we make our next descent with renewed purpose, Colin navigating the building's facade as if it were his natural medium. All the more strange, then, to see him pause at the very instant his head drops beneath the window frame. I wait for the sign, but his signalling arm remains pressed against the building and then, after another minute, swings all the way over his head.

Hauling with all my might, I drag him back to the roof, where I lay him flat out and wrap my hands round his face, ready to slap him into consciousness, to *breathe* the life back into him.

But his eyes are still blinking, and the only change in his face is its absence of colour.

—Philomela? I ask.

He shakes his head, covers his eyes.

—Someone else, Colin?

A long pause, and then the smallest of nods.

—One of the other girls?

—He were . . . he were right on top, Mr. Timothy. He had his . . . his arm all crammed, like . . . in her mouth. So she couldn't . . . she couldn't . . .

Colin looks up at me, wonderingly.

—An' there were blood. I could see it. She couldn't move, not a hair, and she were bleedin'. On the sheets.

Of course, I think. *There* must *be blood. Lord Griffyn's patrons must be assured of the quality—the purity—of their merchandise.*

—I'm sorry, Colin, I should have warned you.

—I wish . . .

—Yes?

—I wish we could take 'em all with us. I wish there were more on us, and we could take 'em all.

—Yes. Yes, I wish that, too.

It doesn't pass, exactly, this period of mourning, but it dissipates enough that before another minute has passed, Colin is back on his feet and, if anything, more eager than ever to make the next descent. The only difference I note this time round is a slight flinching of his head as it passes into the window frame—a gesture superseded, within half a minute, by a violent upwards jerking of his thumb. By the time I haul him up again, he is bursting with the news.

—It's his dressing room!

—Lord Griffyn's?

—The same.

—How do you know?

—I don't. I mean, I *do*. Well, it's got boots all in a row and brushes and what do you call 'em? Po-*maids*. All thrown about, ain't it? Shoehorns and bootjacks, them what do you call 'em *snuff*boxes, all tossed in the slop. It's got to be *him*, don't it? A guest wouldn't make such a muck of his kit, he wouldn't have time.

—The dressing room . . .

There's no need to complete the thought. We both know.

The next window. The next window will almost certainly take us into Griffyn's bedchamber.

I suppose that knowing this should quicken our pace, but for reasons I can't define, we are more deliberate than ever in preparing for the next descent, and Colin is visibly reluctant as he crawls once more down the building face, rests his hands on the lintel, protrudes his trembling head into the waiting space. His head, craning for a view, darts from side to side—whether to see better or to avoid discovery, I can't be sure—and his body actually swings in my hands, like the pendulum of a kitchen clock, before going still again. And then it arches with such a violent motion I have no choice but to pull him up straightaway.

—It's *her*, Mr. Timothy!

—You're sure?

—'Course I'm bloody sure! The blinds was open, and there were . . . well, fuck it, you don't think I knows Filly when I sees her?

—And are they . . .

—What?

—Are they . . . ?

I can't speak it.

—It were just *her*, Mr. Timothy. Sittin' on the edge of the bed.

Philomela. Directly below us. Ten feet from deliverance.

—Wait here, Colin.

—We can both on us go, Mr. Timothy, there's a *balcony*, ain't there?

This I wasn't expecting: an unadorned piece of masonry, the length and breadth of a coffin, extending three feet on either side of the window and catching us in its grip like a soft stone glove. The good fortune of it is almost more than I can bear. Here we stand, shielded from below by the fog, shielded from above by the sky, Philomela but a few breaths away, and our cab (God willing) just up the road.

As Colin advertised, she is sitting on the edge of a canopied four-poster, her head bare but the rest of her bridal raiment intact. Her face is only slightly averted—we might easily rap on the window and persuade her to open it—but now there is another, larger barrier to consider.

Lord Frederick Griffyn. Standing just a few feet off.

His coat has been shucked. The collar round his neck has been loosened. The red geranium has been plucked from its buttonhole and laid gently on a chiffonier. And at this very moment, with infinite care, Lord Griffyn is divesting himself of his waistcoat.

Precious little of the wedding night about him. He sheds his outer clothing and tugs at his shirt frills with the banal, ritualistic air of a man married forty years. And Philomela takes so little notice of him one might think they were occupying two parallel daydreams—until Lord Griffyn draws a penknife and charges her.

Colin's hand jumps to the window; my own hand closes round the carving knife in the knapsack; but these are the mere tokens of our impotence, for we are no better equipped to assist Philomela than we were an hour ago, a day ago. We can only watch, with a sense of violation that must be nearly equivalent to hers, as Griffyn removes her shoes, caresses her feet, and, with his knife, scissors the silk stocking from her leg.

But when I see Philomela's head jerk away, when I witness the tiny, myriad ways in which pride and rage and fear contend within her, then I know that the violation is hers alone to bear. We cannot possibly share it.

There is, however, a chance of reprieve. Griffyn has abruptly left the bed and made for his dresser, and he is reaching for something . . . I can't quite make out what . . . pinkish gold in colour, the size and shape of a fat orange, with sprouts of hard green leaves at its top. He weighs the thing in his hand as if preparing to hurl it, but what he does next fairly steals my breath away. With slow, surgical precision, he drives his knife straight into the thing's heart—cuts it clean in two, to reveal a beautiful tracery of cream and brilliant red.

A pomegranate.

Ever the good host, he offers half to Philomela and seems not in the least offended when she refuses. Smiling gently, he takes up his half of the fruit and, with his knife, scoops one of the seeds from its casing and mashes it against the girl's naked foot until the red pulp bursts free. He then pops the stripped seed into his mouth and from there repeats the procedure again and again, seed after seed, until her entire foot is dyed the same ruby colour as the fruit's flesh. A stain like blood, seemingly ineradicable, until Griffyn begins the slow work of licking it off—his tongue working in darts and feints, his eyes shuddering, his entire face relaxing into a look of deep and bottomless satisfaction.

I cannot look away, any more than I can interfere. Only prayer is possible, and the words go dry on my lips.

But perhaps the mere intention of prayer is enough, for Griffyn, once he has finished his occult mysteries, declines for now to pursue them further, instead moving back to the dresser to extinguish the candle still burning there. He does the same with a candle on a buhl tray, and now a crepuscular gloom settles over the room, liquefying each object and imparting to the air a new solidity.

It also emboldens Colin and me to press our faces against the window. And by some miracle of simultaneity, it sparks Philomela out of the bed and onto her feet. A protective instinct on her part, feeble in itself, but with this added effect: it draws her closer to the window, until only her own preoccupation can keep her from seeing what is so palpably there, not five feet away.

Frantic, we wave our hands in mad orbits, hop up and down in a private trapeze act, but her eyes persist in turning inwards . . . until Colin, despairing of everything else, falls back on the simplest possible gesture, lays his hand flat against the window like a starfish pressed against the wall of an aquarium.

The very thing. Philomela's eyes draw in, her head pops back. Her mouth forms a word or a name, or perhaps just a bubble of astonishment.

There is barely time enough even for that: Griffyn has now wrapped his arm round her waist and is guiding her back to the confines of the four-poster. If he were to glance out the window—or even take a single survey of her face—he would realise that something was amiss, but he is far more concerned with the positioning of her body between the immaculate white sheets. Takes great pains to get it right, arranges the tresses of her hair on the pillow, extends her arms, tilts one hip towards the ceiling, parts her feet. And then, like an artist perversely intent on shrouding his own work, he begins to close the organdy bed curtains.

The heavy crimson fabric drags along its cumbersome track, smothering the light, transforming the bed into a glade. It swallows Philomela's head, then her torso, then her feet.

And the only reassurance I can take is that she knows, she *knows* that once those curtains are drawn, we are lost.

No way of being sure, really, what words or intonations she uses. All I can say for certain is that with just a few feet of curtain left to draw, Griffyn pauses in his work and inclines his head towards his bride's.

Ten seconds . . . twenty seconds . . . my heart pounding away the intervals, Colin's heart pounding right along . . . and finally Griffyn's hand drops to his side. He takes a step towards the window.

Colin and I lurch back to our respective corners, press ourselves against the balcony's perimeter. We hear the sounds of a window being dragged open against its will. An ancient set of blinds, jerked upwards. And then a voice, at once fluty and grainy, shot through with amusement.

—There you are, *petite gamine*. Fresh air aplenty.

I close my eyes. I draw in my breath, and at the same time, I draw in Griffyn's words:

—Do you remember, *jeune fille*? Do you?

And when I open my eyes again, the window stands open, and the blinds are all the way up, and Griffyn has turned his back on us and is, at this very moment, stepping towards the bed.

—Do you recall what happens to naughty girls who make naughty noises?

It may be the window, so shockingly open. It may be the sight of that long, wagging finger. Whatever it is, it's too much for Colin. Not pausing for a signal, he squeezes his little body through the opening and, before I can even make to follow, hurls himself at Lord Griffyn's elegant back.

The good lord topples in stages. First to his knees, in an attitude of mock piety. Then, as the full brunt of Colin's weight makes itself felt, he collapses belly first on the Indian matting.

What an anticlimax is this! The man we have spent an entire day hunting offers no resistance whatsoever when I roll him onto his back . . . barely blinks when I press the butcher's knife to the brown skin of his neck—not even when a tiny petal of blood blossoms forth.

—Not a word, Lord Griffyn. Not a word, or I'll slash you from ear to ear.

If he is astonished, he gives no sign of it. Every possible reaction has been so speedily absorbed that he looks only as though he has been expecting us for a very long time.

—Tie his hands, Colin.

Our rope ladder, of course, is already spoken for, so Colin must make do with the silken cord of Griffyn's dressing gown, which has been draped over the doorknob to the adjoining room. The sash serves its new purpose admirably, and I think Colin takes special pleasure in forcing Lord Griffyn into a sitting position and yanking the bonds as tightly as he can round his wrists.

Nothing, however, disturbs the composed features of our host's face. He merely cocks his head to one side and, with a quiet twinkle, says:

—I should have been only too delighted to include you on the guest list, Mr. Cratchit.

My name. My name, coming from his mouth.

—Although I'm not sure *girls* would have been quite to your taste.

The knife draws back from his throat.

—But why quibble when you have brought such a darling little boy with you? Good evening, my dear! Would you like me to show you round downstairs? I know some frightfully rich men, simply sneezing with loot. I could introduce you to all of them.

—I could interduce you, too. Blokes as would peel the skin off your bones, inch by inch.

—Ooh, delicious.

One can't always tell, with well-bred people, whether they are seriously entertaining a suggestion or simply being polite. But there is in His Lordship's smile some answering chord—some presumption of affinity—that, more than anything else he could have done, recalls me to my rage. Everything now is fuel for it: Griffyn's long, oddly shaped body, swelling at the hips; Colin's bruised face; the pink residue on Philomela's bare foot, the ivory obscenity of her costume.

I raise the knife. Higher. Higher.

And then, like ligatures, Colin's slender fingers wrap round my belt.

—No, Mr. Timothy. Come away.

—It's what Philomela told us to do.

—No.

—Kill them before they kill us. And I didn't listen, and now Gul—

Most embarrassing: I can't even voice the last syllable. It is out of kindness, perhaps, that Colin assumes the role of speaker, raising himself on tiptoe and whispering in my ear:

—You ain't the one to do it, Mr. Timothy. It ain't in your nature, is it?

But it may well be in Philomela's nature, for as I step back, she is coming hard on, and before anyone can stop her, she has snatched the knife from my hand and driven it in a clean, sure line towards Lord Griffyn's face. The knife halts a mere inch from his mouth and then begins to inscribe a slow circle around his bulbous lips. A bizarre, almost religious gesture—I can't make sense of it until I remember, in a flash of second sight, the scene by Lord Griffyn's carriage. This was the very sign he made to her: *Breathe a word to anyone*, it said, *and forfeit your tongue.*

The knife goes round and round, scoring the darkness, but the steel of that blade is nowhere near as hard as Philomela's eyes. Her brown irises have contracted into something black and impermeable—incapable of admitting light—and the breath steams from her nostrils in fierce bursts, and her fingers tighten round the handle of the knife.

And then, gradually, the fingers loosen again, and her breathing subsides. She takes a step back. She lowers the knife to her side. She says softly:

—Nothing.

And which is more remarkable? That she should have come to such a conclusion, or that I should have reached it at roughly the same time? The conclusion, I mean, that killing Lord Griffyn would be an act of purest futility—fatuity, even. You may plunge a dagger through him, drive it straight to the other side . . . you will find nothing to kill.

Philomela hands the knife to me. Wipes her hands along her flanks. Then, looking back at Lord Griffyn, she murmurs:

—More.

—More what, Philomela?

—*More.*

Helplessly now, she grabs a fistful of bridal gown, shakes it at me.

—More *girls*, you mean?

A long, pained silence.

—Where are they, Philomela?

And now comes the mask, woefully familiar, rolling down her face and clouding everything from view, as impenetrable as the fog that hovers just outside the window. And once again, I have the strongest urge to barge through it—drag every last secret into the light—but I feel Colin's chastening hand on my sleeve.

—Time to go, Mr. Timothy.

And he's right—of course he's right—but how much harder it is to let her slip away this time. She has turned her face to the wall now, adopted a maidenly attitude that puts me in mind of the assurances she gave Signor Arpelli: *I am still pure. . . . I can still be a wife to someone.* Quite an aspiration, that. After tonight, why should she wish to be anyone's wife?

I touch her, lightly, on the back of her head.

—Say good-bye, Philomela. Good-bye forever.

At this, Lord Griffyn, locked for so long in enigmatic silence, finds his tongue again. His voice swells with a rhetorical fervour.

—You put me off, my girl. You put me off, and you know it binds me to you ever tighter.

We turn away, but the voice only rises to new heights of declamation:

—Take pity on your poor knight at arms! *Belle fille sans merci*, release me!

It is, in the end, Colin's decision—or more precisely, his inspiration—to take the uneaten half of pomegranate from Griffyn's dresser and drive it straight into the good lord's mouth until all further speech is impossible.

—May he choke on it, Colin mutters.

—Amen, says Philomela.

Chapter 21

THIS IS OUR PARTING GIFT TO LORD GRIFFYN: we use one of his bed-posts as our anchor. The four-poster holds firm as I lower myself down the western face of the building to the ground-floor cornice. Philomela follows right behind me, moving with surprising agility, for all the encumbrances of her bridal gown. Not, perhaps, the best costume for absconding, but it does impart a certain comical air to the proceedings. More comical still: Colin, bounding down the side of the building like an alpine Eros.

Our rope ladder, we soon learn, will not take us all the way to the ground. And so we must leave it dangling and retrace the path that Colin and I took earlier, walking single-file along the stone ledge. The fog is still dense as por-ridge, so every few feet, I find myself stopping to be sure my companions are still behind me. And as the glimmering ovals of their faces squint back at me, I am tempted to confess the bald truth to them.

I have no notion of how we are to get down.

We can't simply jump down the same way we came up: the stone stair cap that served as our launching point is far too small for landing. Our only hope is to find some other route of descent, one that won't lead us straight back to Rebbeck and his men.

This is the conundrum I am pondering when the branch of an ash tree reaches through the mist and slaps me across the face. Far from being affronted, I grasp the bough with a faintly amorous intent. I press my chest against it, then set a single foot on it. It yields but a few inches.

Nothing to do now but trust it with my full weight. I hear a sharp intake of breath from Philomela as I leave the comfort of the ledge and wrap myself in the tree's embrace. I sway there for some time before finding my equilibrium, but nothing breaks or cracks beneath me, and so as soon as the rocking has ceased, I motion for Philomela to follow. After some deliberation and a suitable arrangement of her dress, she does.

It is this new freight that begins to tax the tree's capacity. The branch rocks more violently this time and sags quite noticeably where Philomela is straddling it. It's clear I will have to find another perch or risk having the branch give way altogether beneath Colin's weight.

Fortunately, my feet, bobbing in the dark, find a heavy, knobbed beam, just a yard below the one on which I'm sitting, and as I shift my weight to that lower branch, my boot glances off yet another one, another yard below. In short order, I have descended a good fathom, but then my feet, searching for the next rung down, find only vapour.

Nothing else for it. Against all the tenets of our respective upbringings, we must leap before we look.

That, at any rate, is the intention that slides me off the lowermost branch and suspends me over the grey void. But the intention soon vanishes . . . leaving behind nothing but cold, hard panic.

Above me: the spectral form of Philomela, unsnagging her dress from an outcropping of bark. Just above her: the descending outlines of Colin's feet.

And below me: freedom. Or nothing at all.

I can't say how long a time I hang there. Long enough, in any event, that I begin to experience a certain upswelling of shame, which is strangely exacerbated by the arrival of one of Lord Griffyn's peacocks.

The bird, disturbed in its roosting, has wandered down the branch and squatted by my right hand, from which position it glares at me with a pestilential rage and pecks an angry circle round my knuckles. The plumage has been retired for the night; all the bird's colour and force are distilled in its glinting eyes, which, even through the fog, resonate with the plainchant of Griffyn Hall:

Nothing. Nothing.

It must be the simple desire to escape that sound that at last pries my fingers loose. I drop. I drop without a thought or care or hope, without a sound, and the earth rushes pell-mell to meet me, and it is over sooner than I could have imagined, I am flat on my stomach, my face daubed with frost and leaf-paste, my hands twitching by my side. Everything, everything still in working order.

Philomela is considerably more graceful in her dismount. Only the complications of her dress keep her from staying upright, and even as she lands on her backside, there is an almost musical element of surprise to her.

We both of us jump to our feet and stare up into the canopy of fog, waiting for Colin. A half minute passes, another half minute . . . no Colin.

And then, from some upper region, comes his stifled cry, and shortly thereafter his body, plummeting to earth. A transformed body: arms aflail, hair bristling with feathers.

Lord Griffyn's peacock, outraged by our presence, has exacted its revenge by fastening itself to Colin's head. These are no longer the overtures of a lover but the predations of a schoolyard bully, and as the boy struggles to free himself, the bird points its beak towards the sky and issues a squawk of triumph. A rallying cry, as it turns out, for within seconds, the rest of the platoon has arrived, and the air is exploding with blues and purples and greens, and our ears ring with screeches and flapping wings rising to an ungodly crescendo, and now the portico stirs with sounds of its own—*human* sounds—and there is no time for cogitation, nothing to do but tear the peacock from Colin's head . . . watch the tufts of his hair fly free . . . and hurl the creature at the rest of the colony like a cannonball scattering a horde of infidels.

I grab Colin's and Philomela's hands and sprint for the yew hedge. The birds, howling with fury, rush after us, and from the front of the house comes an unmistakable cry:

—A lantern!

No hope of eluding them this time. We must simply outrun them. Squeeze through the hedge and back to the safety of our cab before they have mobilised their forces.

But in our brief absence, the hedge has become unutterably foreign. Only after an endless interval of searching does Colin find our original path, now even less passable than before. The branches claw with a vengeance this time, and a stream of robust Italian oaths pours from Philomela's mouth as she drags her dress through the brambles. By the time we get to the other side, the dress has been slashed nearly in half—nothing below the waist but petticoats and dangling shreds of silk—and as she pauses to survey the wreckage, an almost tactile relief emanates from her. She has shed her charmed skin.

Through the lattice of the hedge comes the now-familiar nimbus of the lantern, growing larger and larger, and alongside the light, a voice—Rebbeck's voice—shouting:

—Fetch the carriage!

No need to hear more. We're running: Colin in the lead; Philomela, barefooted, right behind; and me, as usual, trailing a yard or two back. We scale the wrought-iron fence and dash down the street, whipping the fog before us. As our feet echo against the pavement stones, a new litany resounds in my head:

Let Adolphus be there. Let Adolphus be there.

At first he is nothing but a bit of effulgence in the fog. Only when we draw nearer does the shape of a lantern resolve from the gloom . . . then a hand . . . and finally the doom-laden features of our cabman himself, regarding us as the confirmation of every dark prediction he has ever entertained.

I call up to him:

—Put out your lantern!

—What's he goin' on about?

—Your lantern! Snuff your lantern!

It is as loud as I dare speak, but as soon as the three of us have clambered inside and pulled the door shut after us, Adolphus obliges us by summarily expunging the light.

I rap on the roof of the cab and call up to him:

—No words now.

Some reflexive grumbling, to be sure, but in the end, Adolphus does hold his tongue and leaves us to crouch there in the darkness of the cab, a welter of arms and knees and rocking hearts.

We need not wait long. First comes the sound of a carriage—a forest-green brougham with salmon filigree, if I recall correctly—hurtling past in the darkness, the flash of lantern sweeping from side to side. This is followed by a pilgrimage of ambulatory light, coursing down the far side of Portland Place: lanterns and candles, bobbing in the miasma. The scraping of boots, the muttering of men, and rising above it all, in raspy descant, the tones of Miss Charlotte Binny:

—They can't have got far. Not in this weather.

Beside me, Philomela stiffens, and a part of me, too, freezes over at the sound of the missionary's voice. Better to say it calls me back to a true understanding of our position. In our haste to elude our pursuers, we have allowed ourselves to be encircled. To the north stands the impassable citadel of Griffyn Hall. To the south, a search party, busily combing the avenue, no doubt waylaying each vehicle and pedestrian in turn. How long before the noose closes round us?

We have, as I see it, but one weapon: surprise. And we have but one chance, which is to do the very thing they least expect us to do.

Opening the door, I creep round to the back of the cab and incline my head towards the driver's box.

—Adolphus, can you hear me?

—As if I got any choice.

—I want you to light your lantern again.

—Oh, it's on with the lantern, is it? Off again next minute. No consistency, no principle. . . .

—Adolphus, do be quiet a moment. I am going to entrust you with a task, and if you repay my trust, I will place enough money in your palm to buy your own damned horse, do you hear?

Adolphus says nothing. Leaves it to the horse to nod assent in a snort of steam.

—We are going to part company with you now.

—Well, that's a—

—But only for a short time. In the meantime, I want you to drive up the street. Northwards.

—North.

—In a hundred yards or so, you will pass a place called Griffyn Hall.

—Griff—

—You shall know it by the cluster of men in front. Amongst those men will be two police officers.

—Christ! Oh, Christ!

—You needn't worry, Adolphus, so long as you follow my directions to the letter. As you pass, they will almost certainly hail you. They will ask you if you have seen anyone. Specifically, three people answering to our general description.

—Go on.

—You will tell them you have seen no one of the sort. You will tell them, quite truthfully, you have been off duty for the last two hours and are now wending your way home. Do you understand?

—Hmff.

—Repeat after me, then.

—Off duty. Wendin' home.

—Very good. Now, they may insist on looking inside the carriage. Allow them, by all means. A single glance should be enough to persuade them you are telling the truth, and in that event, they should have no choice but to let you pass.

—No choice.

—That accomplished, you are to make directly for the next intersection, is that clear? That is where we will be waiting for you.

—Waiting.

—You needn't fear, Adolphus. If you keep your head about you, you'll be a richer man in ten minutes, and we'll all be in our beds within the hour. Just give us a moment to gather our belongings, then off you go.

Philomela has used the interval to wrap herself in the comforter I brought along—Father's comforter. Not too far removed from the garb in which I first saw her, prowling through the courtyard. But tonight . . . a function, perhaps, of her newly coiffed hair and scrubbed face . . . the way she listens, without falter or flicker, as I delineate the plan . . . tonight she has the air of something antique and vanished.

She stumbles slightly on the shreds of her dress as she quits the cab, but she rebuffs our proffered arms, pulls the comforter a bit closer round her neck and waits as Colin gathers up the knapsack.

We are about to set off when a new thought occurs to me. I run round to the back of the cab. I tap the driver's boots and whisper into the air.

—If you were to have a notion to turn us over to the police, Adolphus, I'm afraid I should have to name you as our accomplice. It would be unfortunate, it would be disagreeable, but you would leave me with no choice.

Shades of the prison-house gather round his already shrouded face. He nods roughly and, with an irritable jerk, strikes a match to light his lantern. That task discharged, he takes the reins and grunts:

—Off we go.

It is hard to say who moves at a more rapid clip, the cab or the three of us, darting down the far side of Portland Place. Alongside us, the horse's hooves sound strangely muffled against the pavement, and around us, the fog grows heavier and heavier with our breathing. It is as if we were all respiring from the same lung, and this lung oscillates faster and faster as the cab inches down the road ahead of us . . . works faster still as the cab slows . . . then squeezes shut entirely as Adolphus's voice, strained to an unnaturally hearty pitch, rings through the night air.

—Sorry, Officer. Off duty.

A rough voice answers back.

—Wait a bit. You taken any fares recently?

—Not for two hours past.

—This is official business, now.

—'Course it is.

—We're looking for three persons: man, boy, 'n' girl. The girl'd be in a white dress.

—Ain't seen 'em, officers.

That last statement sounds, to my ears, a bit too rushed, too prepared, and the ensuing silence seems to crackle with suspicion. There we stand, the hunted party—frozen on the opposite side of the street perhaps thirty feet from our pursuers—and the only thing still pulsing is our skin: our chapped hands, the puckered pomegranate surface of Philomela's bare foot, all of it prickling with dread.

The policeman clears his throat, a long, luxuriant rasp.

—All right, carry on, then.

That's as much as Adolphus needs to hear.

—'Night to all!

We hear his fierce "Gedya!", we hear the cab's wheels turn half a revolution . . . and then we hear another man's voice.

—Stay where you are.

A sickeningly familiar voice. The silence stretches round it, and in this anticipatory moment, the smallest expressions stand out as clearly as the most florid oratory: Colin's teeth grinding in rhythm; Philomela's hands reaching for her absent beads. . . .

And now, of a sudden, it seems intolerable, worse than intolerable, to stop here for another second. We must run. We must run and keep running until the last dram of oxygen has leached from our blood.

It is a hard matter, though, to convince the other two. Without benefit of words, I can only tug on their sleeves—with a gentle persuasion at first, and then a brute force when that fails to answer. And even when they are at last tramping alongside me, their heads keep wheeling back towards Adolphus, as though they might by dint of concentration rescue him from his plight.

In short order, we arrive at the promised intersection. A true crossroads, if ever there was one: Colin and Philomela, still inclining their heads back; me casting my eyes forward; everything else compassless.

And then, like the alighting cry of a raven, comes Adolphus's high, nerve-strangled call:

—Thank you, Officer. Good night, I'm sure, Officer.

The relief of it is almost more than we can bear. Colin's mouth twitches upwards, and Philomela's shoulders unclench, and even the cab itself, as it approaches us, seems to move at a lighter, easier clip, its iron wheels slicking across the wet stones, its lantern bouncing for joy.

Only Adolphus fails to enter into the general merriment. His head is bowed sulkily over the reins, and he is mumbling truculent sentiments to his knees, and when I ask if he will take us back to Piccadilly, he waves us in with a fretful swipe of his hand.

—*Grr, blff, mmrr.*

This is what we have reduced him to. No remonstrance, no litany—just consonants. It will take a handsome sum indeed to restore those soliloquies of woe.

But that, after all, is the least of our worries. We are back in our cab, with Philomela perched rather awkwardly on our knees, and every hoofbeat takes us farther from Griffyn Hall and closer to our future. And as Adolphus bears right and then right again, back towards the center of town, all of London seems to clear a path for us.

It scarcely matters now that the seat chafes, that Philomela's elbow is jabbing my ribs, that Colin's knee knocks against mine. An uncanny serenity has stolen over me, as if we have left this city altogether and passed onto a smoky plain that grows more expansive the more we consider it.

And in this new environment, the whole prospect of the future loses its sinister air and begins to assume entirely new forms, forms not yet fully decipherable but enticing nonetheless. This much is evident: in some fashion, and half against our will, Philomela and Colin and I have thrown in our lots together. And if tonight is any indication, we are more powerful jointly than singly, and that being the case, why need we ever part again? Better, surely, to join hands against all obstacles, spurning Society's outstretched arm, drawing only on our native craft and will.

And if this prospect be a dream, why, pray, does it resonate more powerfully than the phantom obstacles raised against it?

Income. Behold, I have two strong arms. My companions, the same. Among us, we may certainly scratch out a sufficient living in the modern economy. We may even be the engine of its transformation.

Food. Every corner of London teems with meat and fish and produce. What we cannot procure through money, we will procure otherwise. What we cannot procure, we will do without.

Shelter. Why, that is the most easily arranged of all: Mrs. Sharpe's. And if her lodgings fail to satisfy, we will move on to the next place, even if it means residing on God's green earth. The stars will be our lantern, the sun our clock, the grass our pillow. We will wake with the dew on our lashes and the wind's breath in our nostrils, and we will give thanks for each new day that drops in our laps and for the strength to embrace it in all its plenitude.

In all *our* plenitude. That is theme that resounds most clearly in my mind. We have no need of anyone else. *There is no need!* We will fortify ourselves. We will hold the world at bay, till the end of our days, if necessary. Welcome to the Cratchit family, present and future.

Ah, it is pretty, yes? My little soothsaying vision—most pretty and most fragile, too! See how quickly it evaporates at the first touch of reality: Colin's head flopping back against the seat; Philomela's unnaturally hard face, her dry, sleepless eyes.

And this, too. This square of white lace, protruding from the India-rubber matting beneath our feet.

Unmistakable in its provenance: a fragment of Philomela's dress, torn off as she left the cab. We were in too great a haste to notice it, of course, but surely no one else—no one who gave the cab even the most cursory inspection—could have failed to see it. Or to guess its origins.

And just then, Colin's voice filters into my ear.

—Mr. Timothy.

—Yes?

—Ain't we back in Portland Place?

Strange to think we are *anywhere* at present. The fog has transformed every house-front into a fading fresco. And yet there is something direfully familiar about this *space*—this feeling of grandiloquent silence on all sides. Either we have left London altogether or we are back again on London's widest street.

And that nugatory patch of grey—just ahead on the left—is either an empty parcel of land or the commanding front lawn of Griffyn Hall.

I don't know why it is that every sensation of alarm should be smothered in its rising. I think it must all go back to Adolphus. The notion that *Adolphus* could turn the cab all the way round and bring us straight back to our starting point, without our ever noticing: that's quite beyond his capacities, isn't it? And what better proof than this? The first figure to emerge from the fog is Adolphus himself—slumped on the kerb, shorn of cloak and hat and whip, his face tilting upwards at the sound of our approaching wheels, and a curious lightness enveloping his features: not relief but a kind of diabolical corroboration. Everything he most feared is at last coming true with a vengeance. He couldn't be happier.

I bolt upright in my seat, I leap out onto the dashboard and hoist myself up by the brass rein guide and pop my head above the compartment roof. And there, in the chiaroscuro of lantern light and fog, sits our driver—head no longer bent, eyes now fixed on a point just to my right, his voice calling out in that loud, unutterably familiar timbre:

—Now!

From every side, gesticulating black shapes swarm towards us, but in this frozen interval, they are but shadows, and only two things impress me with the fixity of truth: the terrible, erect form of Willie the Slasher atop our cab,

and the flying, quicksilver form of young Colin, who, understanding our circumstances better than I, has already abandoned the comfort of his seat and
hurled himself straight onto the horse's back.

It is the rashest of all possible acts—so crazed, so foolhardy that the converging shapes halt in a kind of stupefied admiration, and even Rebbeck
loosens his grip on the reins.

—Hee-yaa! cries Colin.—Hee-yaa!

Seizing the horse by its harness, he pounds its flanks, kicks its arse, and
heaps curses in its ear . . . until the horse pushes through to the other side of
its confusion . . . whinnies and stomps and half rears and then bursts forth in
a stream of outrage.

The acceleration is so sharp I am thrown back into the cab's interior, and
as I scramble to my feet, I can see, on our periphery, the black shapes shouting and falling back—all but one, a small man with a bare head, pumping his
arms manfully and staying abreast of us for a good ten or fifteen yards until
the horse, goaded beyond endurance by its human gadfly, lets loose with
another burst of speed and leaves our pursuer sinking to his knees in the
street.

Past Griffyn Hall we fly, past all the neighbouring houses, past every intersection in turn . . . our horse no longer hewing to any particular route but
flying as fast as the atmosphere will allow, and Colin lying flat as a jockey,
chiding the animal on in a remorseless rhythm—the two of them now a
compound organism, punishing and responding in equal measure—and the
cab behind them rattling like loose teeth against the cobblestones, tossing and
buffeting its passengers so violently that the normal laws of physics seem
indefinitely suspended.

The wheels jump and kick against the stones, straining against their own
axles. And in some demarcated realm of my mind, I ask myself if any hansom cab has ever gone quite this fast before and, if so, for how long.

Then I hear the crack of a whip, and I look out just in time to see Colin
clutch the back of his leg: a simple act that costs him all his precarious balance. Groaning, he slides off his mount—tips half over—and were it not for
the last-minute interference of the harness, he might tip off altogether, and

even so, he lies there, trapped on the horse's side, a mere three feet from the pavement, hooves thundering in his ear.

From above, another lash descends, and though Colin ducks clear, the horse is not so lucky: the whip lands with an audible slap on its rump, and the animal, stung to the quick, unleashes yet another burst of speed, dragging the cab after it, and Colin can do nothing but lie pressed against the horse's side, his hair frothing with wind, his arms and knees drawn to his chest, waiting, with agonised resignation, for whatever may come next.

At that very moment, the solution to Colin's plight presents itself to me: we must give our driver fresh game.

And who better than I?

Simply managed, as it turns out. I need but push my head through the reins until I am squarely in Rebbeck's line of vision.

The first lash takes my cap clean off my head. The second catches me in the shoulder, and as I put out a remonstrating arm, the third bisects the palm of my hand.

The pain is indistinguishable from the sensation of wetness: a slow leak of blood, seeping down the wrist and burning as it passes, so that I am perfectly astonished to hold my arm aloft and find my hand still attached to it.

The relief will be short-lived, I can tell. Once again Rebbeck has raised the whip, and his face has acquired the stoniness of an idol, and his arm pauses at its apogee as if it were gathering all its powers for one final, apocalyptic blow. I shut my eyes to the doom, but the sound that jars them open again is something else altogether: a tiny explosion in the roof of the cab, as a trap door—never before suspected—bursts open to reveal Philomela, defiantly interposing her head between me and Rebbeck's whip.

—*Vaffanculo!* she cries.

A pretty rage indeed, but what impresses me most is how coolly she has calculated her risk. She understands, doesn't she, the dilemma she has created for our man Rebbeck. He may strike Colin and me as long as he likes, till there is not a lick of flesh left on our bones, but Philomela? Mar that head, and he will be answerable to his employer.

And so, as the seconds pass, the impulses of rage and self-preservation vie within him for possession and, in their tussle, produce only agitation—a headlong dive from the driver's box that succeeds in forcing Philomela back down and slamming the trap door after her.

But that moment's distraction is all I need to clamber onto the roof of the cab and throw myself at Rebbeck's prone figure, and as he rocks back towards me, I raise my elbow—the one part of my right arm that is yet free of pain—and smite him on the side of the head.

The whip flies free . . . the reins jump clear . . . and now, whatever constraints our horse was operating under are gone, and the animal speeds unencumbered down the lane, sprinting as though its very soul depended on it, relieved of any care . . . until the fog parts to reveal an oncoming carriage.

With a screech of terror, the horse jerks sharply to the left, and the whole cab shifts with it—Rebbeck and me included. With no purchase, no axis, nothing but our scrambling hands and legs to aid us, we both slide inexorably towards the edge of the roof.

And when at last we are disentangled, we find ourselves in oddly parallel predicaments, each of us hanging from the rein guide and kicking his legs madly to keep clear of the wheel. How peculiarly liberating it feels to put Rebbeck out of mind for the time being and devote myself to nothing but my own survival.

The muscles in my upper back gather their forces, the shoulders take up the call, the arms answer back . . . and the whole cogged, geared apparatus of me hauls itself back onto the roof.

The effort is sufficient to leave me sprawling on my belly, gasping for air. And there ends my reverie. For in the square of space just before my eyes lies the cold black promontory of Rebbeck's boot.

It is instinct, pure instinct that makes me draw up my head, not quickly enough, for the boot, missing my chin, glances off my left temple, and the force of it knocks me flat on my spine and drops my head over the side of the cab's roof, and suddenly the entire world is flipped on its end—our horse is galloping through the clouds—and the buzzing in my head is so profound it becomes quite an easy thing for Rebbeck to pin down my arms and to reach, with all deliberation, into his coat pocket.

Out it comes. That gleaming band of steel with its two beveled edges. So vividly emblazoned in my mind that my every new encounter with it has the quality of memory.

And in a way, I *am* remembering. I am seeing Gully's last moments—through the medium of Rebbeck's mild hazel eyes.

And in my heart I am saying:

You won't. You won't kill me as you killed him.

And then, from my upside-down vantage, I see Colin. No longer pinioned on his side, he has somehow managed to climb back atop the horse, and even more remarkable, he has gathered up the errant reins and is grasping them to his chest with sacramental care . . . and as Rebbeck lowers the blade to my neck in a soft, caressing declension, I scream:

—Pull, Colin! Pull!

The boy needs no further exhortation. Bracing himself on the traces, he leans back with all his might, and as the horse's head snaps backwards and the wheels screech against the pavement, the world is once again knocked on its ear. Colin is thrown against the horse's shoulder, and Philomela thumps against the dashboard, and Rebbeck, still holding his knife, vaults right over the top of me and lands with a sharp *thwack* on the running board below.

I alone remain where I was—prone atop the cab roof—but for how long? Our horse, far from stopping, has simply shifted its course onto new tangents. And although Colin is still yanking on the reins for all he's worth, the horse is beyond minding now. It swerves back and forth, taking up every last square inch of the road, sketching out acute angles and half circles and parabolas—a fit of insane geometry.

No one is moving now, least of all Rebbeck. We are all of us, I think, braced for disaster, but there is at least another minute of mad careening before the cab, swerving to avoid a streetlight, tips onto a single wheel and then, after a suspenseful hiatus, turns over altogether.

From there, everything goes dark. I am conscious only of being hurried through the upper air—swiftly, silkily. My body goes limp in anticipation, and every nerve in me ceases firing . . . and then, after a short interval, those same nerves sharpen and quiver tenfold as a sensation like a thousand switches invades my legs.

It requires some investigation to discover the source of this new pain. I have been thrown into a hedge of boxwood—the border of someone's lawn. And here I stand—in the thick of it, as it were—fully erect, like a tin soldier carefully set back on its shelf.

And as the report of my survival trickles back to me, the abrasions of these branches become a source of indescribable joy, and it is with some lingering regret that I must leave their embrace and step back into the road.

Adolphus's cab will not be going out in service again any time soon. It lies collapsed on its side, in a posture of terminal illness, on a bed of shattered glass and splintered wood. One of its wheels, broken off in the crash, has rolled down the hill in a trance of terror, and ten feet off stands our now-becalmed horse, cured of its madness, trailing its broken harness behind and surveying the wreckage with a kind of professional pride.

And there, clamped as tightly as a lichen to the horse's shoulder, lies Colin, barely stirring when I tap him on the shoulder.

—Come down, Colin. It's over.

I don't stay to help him, for I have already glimpsed, next to the broken cab, two other recumbent forms, impossible to separate in the fog. Only upon closer scrutiny do they reveal their identities. First Rebbeck, flat on his belly, back heaving. And then, crouching close behind him, Philomela, her comforter wrested away, her bridal raiment in tatters, her arms working in a small, industrial flurry.

I am just on the verge of hailing her when Rebbeck's eyes jolt open with an electric surge, and before I can make another move, he has jumped to his feet and thrust forward his blade—a slightly altered blade, unless my eyes deceive me, stained at its very tip with blood.

My blood, I assume. But my hand, reaching for my throat, finds only uninterrupted flesh, and after making a quick canvass of my companions, I am ultimately led back to Rebbeck's own leg, to the gash in his trousers and the sticky rill of blood coagulating above his knee. He sways there, trying to fix me in his sights, and his self-inflicted wound, far from deterring him, seems to goad him on. Eyes wobbling, head listing, he holds out his blade like a sabre and comes for me.

And, truth be told, he is such a mesmerising spectacle it doesn't even occur to me to run; some part of me wishes to be here when he arrives. It is Philomela who chooses this moment to act. She runs to the horse, slaps it on the haunch, and, in a voice of uncompromising power, cries:

—*Su! Come andiamo!*

Stunned, worn out, the horse nonetheless jerks in what's left of its harness and, for want of any clear direction, canters off the same way it just came. Not even noticing its latest fare: one Willie the Slasher, who, much to his own surprise, is arrested in the act of charging me, pulled to his knees, and then, with a howl of frustration, dragged back across the cobblestones.

Here at last Philomela's cunning reveals itself: she has fastened the reins round Rebbeck's ankle.

And the horse is moving too briskly now for any of her work to be undone. Each time Rebbeck succeeds in righting himself, the reins pull taut again and haul him earthwards, and as the poor blinkered horse draws him back up the hill, back to Griffyn Hall, the only way he can stay upright is by alternately jogging and hopping—hopping backwards, on a single foot, like a senile rabbit.

Strange that in such a situation, a man's first thought should be of his dignity, but that is the case with Sergeant Rebbeck. His face might be fairly considered a model of composure in the midst of mortification, and on any other night, under any other circumstances, the dichotomy of that solemn mask and that ludicrous hopping gait might be good for a guffaw. But as Rebbeck disappears round the corner, the only emotions we three can bestow on him are a certain dry resignation and a small degree of gladness.

Everything else is swamped in exhaustion. Colin is planted on his arse in the middle of the road. Philomela leans against the toppled cab, wiping her brow smooth. And I . . . well, the only acts of which I am capable are kneeling on my haunches and knotting a handkerchief round my lacerated hand.

All round us, the fog begins to wear away, like the napping of an old towel. And in this new interval of clarity, an old imperative reawakens inside me. I reach into the inner pocket of my pea coat. I draw out Philomela's rosary beads and the rag doll. I lay them in her unresisting hands.

She examines them a bit, examines me a bit longer.

—I know, Philomela. It's a bit early for gifts.

Just then, Colin looks up. It has taken me this long to see the full extent of the damage to his face: a smear of dried blood across his forehead, another bearding his chin; a black eye, nearly as florid as my own; and that tiny nose now leaning slightly to one side, as though it had tumbled over in a kiln.

He turns up one of the corners of his bruised mouth and, in a thickened voice, says:

—It ain't early, Mr. Timothy. It's Christmas Eve. Near three hours now.

cᐳ

24 December 1860

Dear Father,

Have you been to the Regent's Park lately?

It's not, as they say, what it used to be. The oaks and planes and maples have grown quite stunted, and the grand allée of Broad Road is pocketed with ruts and stones, and even the willows look to be weeping more extravagantly than usual. Any day now, I expect, they'll bring in new gardeners to spruce up the place, but I rather like it in its current condition: stifled and longing.

I'm not quite sure how we ended up here. Our cab took so many spins and swerves before we had done I shouldn't have been surprised to be hailed by the mayor of Liverpool. But in fact, once the dust had settled, we found ourselves just a mile or so north of Griffyn Hall, with the Regent's Park just up the road. Not exactly beckoning us onwards, but not completely averse to the idea of us, either—willing to try us on for a few hours. Under the circumstances, it seemed a safe bet.

We found an elevated glade next to a swan-laden moat, with a commanding view of the park's eastern end. And as soon as we were persuaded that we were truly alone, we began to scare up as many dry leaves as we could find—no small task, given the prevailing damp. Wrapped in our foliage, we dropped straight to sleep, not even stopping to disport our bodies in conducive postures. You may see the result now. Colin is bunched against a tree stump. Philomela never made it off her knees, simply balled up your old comforter, Father, into a pillow and collapsed. And I, upon waking, realised that I had spent the whole night with my left arm wedged beneath my breastbone. The feeling is only now returning.

It is quiet here. The only sound that breaks through the trees is the rumble of a carriage, too far removed to be a source of alarm. It sounds like my *carriage, if you must know. The one that was to take me out of Camden Town. No surprise: it has come too late.*

What amazes me, in retrospect, is how long I waited for it. Day after day, in that dank garret, with the smell of curdled dust everywhere, and those diamonds of strained light . . . day after day, waiting with a dogged constancy, the way a woman waits for her husband to come back from the sea.

And still no carriage. No grey brougham stopping in front of our house. No door admitting me to my future.

And then one day, a few weeks after my seventeenth birthday, Uncle N invited me to a dinner party at his home. And in that one stroke, the waiting was ended. The golden quince of opportunity dangled from the bough. I knew, as surely as I knew my name, that once I had sat down at Uncle's table, I would shine like a newly minted sun, I would fling my sparkle carelessly, profligately, in every direction, and society would be left with no alternative but to snatch me up. I would be lionised by hostesses across the West End, I would be the envy of bachelors, the prize of heiresses. The toast of the season, the wit of the age.

And it was all to begin with Uncle N's dinner party.

I think I must have spent half a day preparing, Father. Combing bear's grease through my hair, brushing my coat, the nap of my hat. Inserting your prized enamel links in my turn-back shirt cuffs. Stringing my watch chain horizontally, the way I'd seen Prince Albert do it. And through it all, rehearsing an infinite array of conversational gambits, gleaned from the Times *and the* Morning Chronicle *and* Punch.

Did I even stop to say good-bye to you and Mother? Well, there was no time, you see. My destiny was rushing to meet me. I couldn't be late.

The cabdriver engaged by Uncle N spoke to me in rapid bursts of Hungarian; it was the sound of acclaim. The elms and lilacs dipped their branches as I passed. Even the knocker on Uncle N's door smothered its usual grimace in deference to my prospects.

I know what you're thinking, Father. I should have guessed. I should have guessed that no one really distinguished would be there. Second- and third-tier bankers, mostly—colleagues or passing acquaintances of Uncle's—and the usual moth-eaten complement of charitable emissaries. All moving and speaking with alarming slowness, like residents of a private aquarium, and imparting such a heaviness to the proceedings there was no staying afloat.

The one aberration in the guest list was a large, sweating woman with a terribly forward manner . . . the founder of the Pure Literature Society . . . who patted my cheek over pie and cried out to my uncle:

—He is the sweetest little creature I have ever clapped eyes upon! I shall take him home and dress him up like a Dresden doll.

If she had called me a lily-livered knave and swatted me with her fan and bathed my face in spit, she could not have insulted me more grievously. But all I heard from the other end of the table was Uncle's halting, shambling reply:

—Yes, capital little fellow. Awf'lly, you know, yes.

And after that, the sparkle—what little I possessed, anyway—went out of me. Why expend any more, here or anywhere? I was still the protagonist of Uncle N's story, and there was no breaking free.

I needn't tell you how the evening crawled into a corner and expired, although it's worth observing that the ride home was, if anything, slightly worse. Uncle N, you see, had engaged a grey brougham for me . . . and this brougham did, in fact, stop in front of our house, but only to disgorge me into the past.

Herewith my predicament, Father: I no longer possessed a narrator. Uncle N had abdicated the role. And you . . . you were willing, yes, but your story had finished. I was well now, wasn't I? I no longer needed to be Good. For you or for anybody. And so that left me free to be otherwise.

Oh, yes, I sat down to breakfast and dinner at the same time every day. I answered when spoken to; my voice never wavered from its tone of mild acquiescence. But in my deepest, most private recesses, Father, I was on fire with a hard true clean resentment.

Why the bulk of it should have been directed towards you, I cannot say. I know only that it became a kind of pastime of mine to enumerate your failings. Your dirty gloves, your dirty handkerchiefs. The way you smacked your lips over jam or dunked your toast in your tea or cried "Huzzah!" every time someone pulled out a deck of cards. All those times you couldn't find a proper scarf and had to make do with that bloody comforter, wrapping it round you and saunter-ing down Crowndale Road as though you were Beau Nash.

These were, all of them, crimes. Crimes against me. And there was no tribu-nal to plead my case to. There was only you, with your soft, pliable, anxious face—ready to please, perfectly incapable of pleasing.

I remember one night in particular, a few months after Mother died. You were listing all the various routes by which you came home from the office. Looking back, I can see that even then you were failing, in some indeterminate way. Uncle N had by then taken the unusual step of engaging an additional clerk, and while there was no question of letting you go, there was less and less for you to do, and so you were channelling all your remaining mental energy into the task of identifying the optimal escape route.

—The key, Tim, the absolute key to all this is to leave the office via Cornhill. Don't even think of Lombard Street, because everyone on the 'Change is travelling by Lombard that time of day. Cornhill's your man. And this way, you'll catch the Kentish Town omnibus before the masses get there, and you'll nearly always get a seat down below, which in cold weather, I don't mind telling you . . . but there's a catch, you see. There's a catch. You must get off at Bloomsbury, and then you must walk for two blocks, so that you may catch the Hampsteads bus. Why, you may ask? Because the Kentish Town, depending on the driver, will at times make detours down Paddington, round Euston Square, Clarendon Square. But the Hampsteads, why, that's a straight shot up Tottenham Court Road, and once you're on it, the only thing you need remember, Tim, is to get down at the next-to-last stop, not the last one, else you'll have a longer walk home by way of Plender. . . .

It was something to behold. You had spent months, apparently, determining this configuration—poring over maps, consulting with omnibus drivers, timing every leg of every day's journey. Had I been older, I would have realised: here is a man who wants to come home. But all I felt at the time was a hollow reverberation . . . because you no longer had anything to say to me, Father. Nor I to you. And that was the point at which you began to lose me, or rather I began to be lost.

I thought it was for the best. I had left you behind, hadn't I? And so rather than dwell on our difference, I thought it best to erase it.

Perhaps you came to understand what had passed, I don't know. We were still together in the same empty house, and I was doing my best to keep up appearances: I put my room tidy every night, I made the occasional supper, and when your birthday came round, I ran down to Hobhill's Bakery to buy a cake—some German-chocolate confection, I think, which I remember our eating in perfect silence in the parlour in the twilight.

And I was there, in your bedchamber, when you finally slipped free. Remember, Father? That was me, by the door with Uncle N.

It is a curious irony, Father, a not altogether unwelcome irony, that in the act of dying, you forced me once again to be a Good Son. I had forgotten how strict were the requirements. I was the one, for instance, tasked with carrying the news to Peter and Martha; the rest of your children were beyond telling. I was the one who received the well-wishers, dispensed the necessary Christian consolations, saw to all the logistics of mourning. It never occurred to me to complain. If you must know, it was a strange relief, this whirl of doing, for beneath it was only more hollowness—the kind that comes from missing an opportunity, the nature of which one cannot ascertain. What was it, this lost chance? Was it lost for good?

One of the pallbearers never turned up, Father. (It was Mr. Dyer from round the corner—sleeping off a rather long toot, I was later told.) No recourse but to offer myself for the position. I duly took my place under the coffin and gave the signal to the other bearers, and up you went and up we went—the slow, rising grade to the cemetery.

Even for June, it was humid; the rain was constantly threatening, never breaching. And what with all the encumbrances and the weight of the pall and the scratch of my mourning scarf, I was perspiring inside of a minute. What a *weight you were, Father! Who would have thought such a reedy fellow as you could attain to such bulk? And as we groaned beneath your coffin, as we ground our way up the hill, my muscles seemed to bristle with a new and human consciousness, as if they were flinging memories, still aflame, into the coals of my brain.*

And before I knew it, I was six again, and I was back atop your shoulders, borne aloft through the streets of North London. Miles and miles of street, every kind of pavement, every degree of inclemency, and me stuck on the whole way like the cock on a weather-vane. And now and again you would stop and let me off because, you said, you needed to scratch your back. But all you did, really, was rub the hurt out of your neck and shoulders and then hoist me back up as though nothing had happened. That was as close as you ever came to protesting. And so I never once suspected how much I was taxing you—you laboured on and pretended it was sport.

How fitting, then, how fitting that in the act of shouldering you, I should come to see how much larger you were than I.

Oh, yes, Father. Large enough to march me round London without a care for your own comfort. Large enough to go hungry so the rest of your family would not. Large enough to keep your cheer when there was nothing left to cheer for. Large enough to spend your entire life scratching out figures in a small, draughty office, in the service of a changeable and all-mastering man, so that your children—your children, Father—might aspire to something better.

But there was one thing you didn't count on: we could never be better than that. We were too compromised—too addled, too egoistical—to match you gesture for gesture. And here is the final proof of our unworthiness: we thought you were dragging us back. When in fact, you were just leaving us behind.

And so if we do meet again, you must stop and let me catch up to you. And tell you all. For there is so much love in me, Father. Love for you, most dreadfully deferred, and no avenue for it now. Nothing but these words—insufficient—the barest, the meagrest of tokens—all I have. Accept them, and know that your son loves you still. And forgive, so that he may one day extend the same benediction to himself.

Well, Father, there I was, assuring you we had found the most isolated spot in all of London, and I have now discovered persuasive evidence of a nighttime visitor. A small fleet of rain, too soft to wake us but enough to leave smears of frost on the tree trunks and slicks of black ice on the walks. The fog, which last night had the quality of something permanent, has receded into a long ribbon across the green. Hanging just over the northern horizon is the scar of last night's moon. A troop of ducks is scattering across the boating pond, and somebody's dog, or nobody's dog, is wrestling himself silly in the damp grass. I have been up for close to an hour, still awakening.

Chapter 22

IT IS WELL PAST TWO IN THE AFTERNOON when Philomela wakes with a start. Clawing her eyes open, she swallows a spadeful of air and swings her head from side to side . . . looking, I suppose, for the creature that has chased her out of her dream.

From a remove of several yards, I call out:

—It's all right. All right.

Hard to say if she believes me. Her face does not clear so much as it concentrates. She jumps to her feet and swipes the mud from Father's comforter. Frowns and mutters:

—Food.

—Yes, well, Colin's run off to fetch us something. He's not exactly a hunter, but he's quite resourceful.

Rather than reply, she twitches away. It doesn't matter; I am in no hurry to talk. Truth be told, I have been conversing all morning. Not half an hour ago, I was having the most intense discussion with a flock of pigeons. One thinks of them as eternally ambulatory, and yet they are altogether lovelier in their rare bursts of flight—bodies darting in perfect synchronicity, wings flapping in and out of shadow. They toss the light amongst them like a rugby ball. I wasted no time in telling them that.

—Are you cold, Philomela?

She shakes her head.

—I was thinking perhaps we might build a fire.

She shrugs. And because she shows no further inclination towards speech, I resume my silent colloquy with the air, until the resolution that has been gathering inside me all morning clamours to the fore.

I press my bandaged hand against my belly. I clear my throat.

—See here, Philomela. It's occurred to me that . . . what with all the proximity we've enjoyed . . . may still enjoy . . . it seems but fitting that you should, should *know* certain things about me so that you might, I was going to say *understand* me a bit better, and inasmuch as I know something, a very little something, of *your* past, why should I begrudge, as it were, providing the same courtesy to you?

If she is attending, she gives no sign. Her back is turned; her hands are busy rubbing the warmth back into her body. Not a single outward show of encouragement, and even so, I am undeterred. I speak of the first thing that comes to mind, which is to say, the first thing I remember. Which is to say, Christmas.

And as I speak, I find there are not enough words any more to tell everything. The chestnuts shovelled into the fire. The goose, fresh-cooked from the local bakehouse, and the sage-and-onion stuffing, and Peter mashing the potatoes, and Father's hot gin-and-lemon and the steam from the coppers, and everyone beating on the table, and Sam dousing the candles. And the pudding, yes. Bodied forth on a brandy pyre.

And as momentous as the pudding itself: the pudding postmortem, led as always by Mother.

—Too much flour, that's my considered opinion.

—But my dear, it's pure magnificence.

—Be that as it may, there's a touch too much flour, and a fraction too little treacle. And if you were to haul me before a court of law, I would have to confess that the potatoes were wanting for pepper.

It is Mother who, more than anyone else, seems to preside over these memories. She is central to them, and if I were to summon one image to evoke the holidays of old, it would be the sight of Mother's commodious posterior bent over a saucepan of potatoes or a bowl of apple sauce.

Is this perhaps too intimate a memory to share on such short acquaintance? Philomela gives no indication one way or the other. Merely sits propped against a willow tree, exuding a great cloud of weariness.

—Funny thing about Mother, she always believed in the dignity of extra syllables. My father, you know, he was Bob to the world, but with her, it was always *Robert*. And with me, it was *Timothy* from the time I was ten. My brother used to say if Mother had got her way, we'd all have been called the Cratchitmagillicuddywhatchamacallems. But you see, she had a great-great grandfather on her mother's side who was said to be the bastard son of a Staffordshire baronet, and she was always wishing the Cratchit line would cough up more than a few poor, honest tradesmen and perpetual curates. I'm sure even a pirate might have been preferable, provided he had a nice house in the country. . . .

Oh, I could go on for days, couldn't I? I have become quite profligate with memory. Watch me spend it down.

But the vault of reminiscence abruptly snaps shut in the face of a rough, buzzing *sound*, emanating from the direction of Philomela's larynx.

She is still snoring ten minutes later when Colin returns, his cheeks slapped red by the morning air, his arms heavy laden. A marvel of resilience he is. Here am I, still working up the gumption to stand and shake off the various contusions and abrasions, and Colin was on his feet the moment he awoke, hunting down food as diligently as a mother bear, returning in triumph with . . . with . . .

—What are these, Colin?

—Crusts of bread. Some biddy as was feedin' 'em to the ducks. Wouldn't give me none till I promised to give 'em to a bird. So I says to her, "Word of honour, ma'am, I got two coves just up the hill, they'd like nothin' better." So she let me have 'em. This one still asleep, then?

With his foot, he taps Philomela on the flank.

—Actually, she *was* awake, but I bored her straight back to insensibility.

—Best thing you could've done. She were right tuckered, I expect.

—And what of you?

—What, me sleep? With a grand old bloody Ad-ven-ture still a-rollin' on? Fuck off.

The bread, it turns out, is just about right for ducks—no taste to speak of but a fairly pleasing texture, a bit like dry toast left too long on the hob. It contracts the moment my teeth touch it, then dissolves and slides down my throat so quickly I lose all memory of it.

Colin chews his portion in a slow, ruminative fashion, as though he had days to devote to each crumb.

—Mr. Timothy.

—Yes?

—What d'you reckon's to happen? Once all this is done with?

—How do you mean?

—Well, Filly, for an instance. What's to become of her?

—That's a good . . . yes, that's a good . . .

—Not that it matters, but we'd hate to think of her . . .

—What?

—Well, in some workhouse or other. That ain't no life, you ask me.

—No, it's not.

—Now nobody'd call me a hexpert, Mr. Timothy. God forbid, I ain't no hexpert. But it seems to me she'd be better off—so far as she'd be willin' and all—better off with someone who's taken a real interest, like, in her welfare. Some nosy bugger who's gone and mucked about in her business without so much as a by-your-leave. That's the fellow for her. 'Course what do I know, eh?

He stretches out his legs, wipes his lips free of crumbs.

—And what if this someone, Colin, were barely old enough to take care of himself? And possessed of a deeply melancholy disposition, let us say. And a questionable set of acquaintances. And not a penny to call his own.

—Well, it ain't like the civil service, is it? A sod don't need any qua-li-fi-cations. You think *my* dad had qua-li-fi-cations? Just a prick is all he had.

I have not laughed in some time. How strange it feels.

—And what of you, Colin?

—Me?

—What happens to you?

—Why, nothin', that's what. I go back to what I was a-doin'. And I mean to tell you, Mr. Timothy, after my blazin' triumph at the whorehouse, the sky is the bleedin' limit. I mean to say, the career of Colin the Melodious has just *begun*, Mr. Timothy.

—And you don't sometimes . . .

—What?

—Nothing.

—What?

—Never mind.

A flock of seagulls, grounded, has colonised the nearest expanse of grass. Two black-necklaced swans sail down the moat, and there, on the hill just above, a duck works its way down to us with a pinched, peeved expression—annoyed, very like, at having its breakfast pinched. Its implacably officious walk brings to my mind the ravening strut of last night's peacocks, and I shiver and turn instinctively for Colin, but he is staring quite peaceably at Philomela's propped-up form.

—Mr. Timothy.

—Yes?

—How come she run like that?

—Like what? When?

—When you was takin' her home the other day. There she was, a-lookin' the place over like she were the bloody Queen. Next minute, it were like some ghost come along and pinched her up the hoozummy.

—Yes, I know.

—And that look she gave you, Mr. Timothy! Evillest eye I ever saw.

—I don't . . . I can't explain any of it.

It gives me a twinge of shame to admit it, for I have had three days now to consider the matter, and I am no closer to having an answer.

Why, Philomela? Why did you run?

Miss Binny was there, yes, but you had already contended with Miss Binny. Griffyn and Rebbeck were waiting round the corner, but you didn't know that, else you wouldn't have run straight into their waiting arms.

It was someone else—some*thing* else—driving you down the same trajectory of flight on which I first beheld you. Perhaps only a memory, and yet how can a memory hold terror without having at its nexus an event? Or a person?

Here is where I fall back on the feeling that has been tasking me for the past twelve hours. The feeling—it's too slight to be termed an intuition—that some human connection lies between us and Lord Griffyn.

I felt it first, oddly enough, in the presence of Griffyn himself. All during our brief interview, I had the tantalizing impression that someone had done more than simply warn him about me. Someone had actually gossiped in his ear.

Why else that absurd taunt? *I'm not sure girls are quite to your taste.* Baseless and, at the same time, eerily familiar—a chord of insult.

—Colin?

—Mm.

At first I don't know how to frame the inquiry. *I say, do you recall anyone impugning my manhood of late?* But then the answer comes to me without my even needing to form the question. It comes not as a word or a name but as a pair of connected sense-memories.

An excruciating viselike pressure on my scrotum. A breath in my ear.

You can't even put it in a woman. You think you've got enough to take me on?

And now I am seeing George once again, not as he was then but as he'd looked days before that, on the front stoop of Mrs. Sharpe's establishment.

In that frozen late-afternoon moment when Philomela had just broken free of us, and Colin had disappeared after her, and I was taking up the chase, and *there*, coming out the front door, was *George*, with his collar open and his sleeves rolled up and that air of middle-class entitlement. A man on an outing.

And here is the curious part. That memory of him has become indivisible, in my mind, from the bells of St. James, tolling now, the half hour and still tolling, days later, in the campanile of my memory.

Ding dong ping *dong* . . . *Ding dong* ping *dong*. . . .

That's what it takes, finally: hearing the bells. That's when I know. I know why she ran. I know everything.

And now *I* am the one running. Straight to Philomela. Grabbing her by the shoulders, rattling her back into consciousness.

And as her eyes straggle into focus, I lower my face to hers, and I say:

—The bells.

She gives me a vexed shake of the head.

—The *church* bells, Philomela.

She sits up now, and as the import of my words seeps through, she begins very slowly to slide away from me. I follow, as unappeasable as an inquisitor.

—Foolish of me not to see it. You'd only ever been to Mrs. Sharpe's at *night*, hadn't you? It was still daylight when I brought you there, and you couldn't be sure, not completely sure. That's why you were studying the house so intently. The gate, the alleyway . . . even the lamplighter . . . I thought you were just being particular, but in fact, you were on the verge of *recognising* the place, weren't you? And then you heard the bells. And you knew for certain.

Ding dong ping *dong* . . . *Ding dong* ping *dong* . . . .

—Such a distinctive chime, isn't it, Philomela? One could never mistake it for any other. As soon as you heard it, you knew precisely where you were. The very place you'd been trying to escape all along.

She stops moving now, bows her head over a patch of leaves. So buffeted, so still: in the act of contemplating her, I hear my own voice sink into a dry, leafy rustle.

—And *I* was the one who led you back there. Delivered you right to them, didn't I? Lord Griffyn and all the rest. Couldn't have done it better if I'd been in league with them. And of course, that's why you looked at me the way you did. You believed I *was* in league with them.

Her eyes flick towards mine, then glance away. It is all the confirmation I need. And with that, the rest of the puzzle slips quickly, neatly, irrevocably into place, like the shells of a Russian doll.

First George. Then George's account book. Then the name inscribed therein.

Mr. Frig.

Oh, Lord, have mercy.

Invert the first four letters of Griffyn's name . . . transpose the *i* and *r* . . . and meet therein the mysterious receptacle of Mrs. Sharpe's profits.

From somewhere on the near horizon, I have the dim sense of Colin circling us, discreetly skimming his feet over the tops of the leaves. Commendable tact. I would congratulate him, were I not diverting all my remaining powers to this girl. To this moment.

—What happened in that house, Philomela?

More silence.

—Why can't you tell me?

She never once lifts her eyes from the ground, and yet there is a quickening about her, a mounting urgency. It infects me to such an extent that I find myself staring *through* her . . . through time . . . to my first glimpse of her, floating through the courtyard beneath that white tarpaulin. . . .

Through the courtyard.

And now it is no longer an image that claims my attention but a chain of sounds, the blithe word-stream of Chief Magistrate Squidgy.

Always puts out the best vintages for the guests. Don't know where she keeps them all, the cellar, perhaps. . . .

I pass a hand across my face.

—It's the cellar, isn't it?

Perhaps the word is unfamiliar. Perhaps her own recollection of it is already dissolving. But when at last she raises her head, she imparts only fresh mystery. Her features ripple, her lips part and close again. She looks to be translating, in fits and starts, from the language of another planet.

—Philomela.

She shakes her head, four times in rapid succession. Then at last she speaks:

—More.

The same word she used in Lord Griffyn's chamber. Chilling in its brevity.

—More *girls,* you mean?

A quick nod.

—In danger, Philomela?

—I am not . . . it may be. Yes.

—Where are they? In that house? The one I was taking you to?

Another nod.

—Then . . . then we must go back there, mustn't we, Philomela?

And for the first time since I roused her, she actually finds my eye and holds it. She says:

—Yes. We go.

It is, as I expected, an acute disappointment to Colin not to be accompanying us. But as I explain to him, *someone* has to go to Scotland Yard, and who better than he? Who more experienced? Who more accomplished?

No amount of flattery will win him over.

—It ain't right, Mr. Timothy. You're a-goin' to have some more Ad-venture, and she'll get my piece of it.

—If all goes well, there won't be any more adventure to speak of.

—But why don't we *all* go and fetch the police?

—Colin, if others are in danger, we can't waste another minute.

—Well, fuck, whyn't she say somethink afore, then?

—I don't know. I suppose . . . I suppose she *couldn't* before.

A bitter guffaw escapes from his lips.

—So she goes and gets herself a conscience, and *you* go and get yourself kilt.

—Colin, if anyone can remain safe in such a godforsaken place, it is I. Do remember, I *live* there.

But he is not persuaded. Nor is he mollified.

—S'pose this Surtees mug ain't in his office?

—Then wait for him.

—It's Christmas Eve! What if he's on holiday, like?

—Then come straight back to us. You know the way.

And so this is the result: we hail *two* cabs just south of the New Road, in Baker Street. Colin, without a backwards look at us, hops into the first carriage and slams the doors shut after him. I offer him a coin for the fare, but he crosses his arms and slouches out of sight.

—Keep your damned money.

The second cab is rather elegantly turned out: a blood horse with polished brass fittings on its harness; a dandyish cabman, ablaze with a red ascot; two small looking-glasses inside, and a tray for cigar ash, and a box of lucifer matches. And in the blind on the side window, a silk narcissus, a perfect replica of the flower woven into the horse's mane. I can't help thinking of Adolphus's sad little equipage, collapsed on its side . . . Adolphus himself, dispossessed on the curb, with no way to get home. . . .

I'll see to him. When it's all over, I'll see to him.

On the corner of Jermyn and Regent, a small, ragged brass band is playing "The Coventry Carol" over a blind busker's accordion. An old man is selling Christmas punch for tuppence a pint, and the air is quick with pea soup and cloves and hard sauce and burnt dung, and a woman with a shit-smeared baby tugs at the hem of my trousers. But I pay heed only to the figure of Philomela, still wrapped in Father's comforter and hurtling down Jermyn Street as quickly as she once fled it. Part of me, I confess, expects her to keep running, but when she reaches the house in question—the house that has haunted her into silence—she stops by the gate and waits for me with ill-disguised impatience. Her way of acknowledging, perhaps, that she can no longer run.

—Ready, Philomela?

—I am ready.

Less than twenty-four hours have elapsed since last I crossed Mrs. Sharpe's threshold; it might be three years, so alien does the place look to me now. The cramped vestibule and the tiny looking-glass and the small wine table with its cracked porcelain pitcher. Everything wreathed with cut ferns.

And strangest of all: Mary Catherine, caught in the act of dragging a rug outside. She puts a hand to her clavicle, as though she has just discovered a missing locket.

—Mr. Timothy! My heavens, you look more of a fright each time I see you!

At a loss for words, I dive into the knapsack and draw out the butcher's knife.

—Yours. I'm sorry. I had to—

Normally, I would do my best to provide an explanation, but on this occasion I am stopped short by the scant residue of blood on the blade's tip. From Lord Griffyn's throat. And remembering that, I am all the more reluctant to part with it. Some curatorial instinct in me wishes to file it away for future generations of scientists.

Mary Catherine, though, is gently prying the knife from my hand.

—Let me take that, Mr. Timothy, shall I? Put it in the scullery, shall I?

—Mrs. Sharpe . . .

—She's in her office with Mr. George. Shall I fetch her?

—That's all right.

Her eyes drift towards Philomela—still sporting that damned comforter, with her petticoat still in shreds.

—Funny sort of costume she's got.

—Never mind that.

—A bit young for working here, isn't she?

—She's not in that line, Mary Catherine. Please remember that.

—Oh, it's no affair of mine, I'm sure.

With an exaggerated shrug, she gathers up the rug and turns to go.

—No! Please, Mary Catherine. We're in need of a favour, I'm afraid.

—I'm very busy, as you can—

—Yes, I know. I need you to procure some keys for me.

—Keys?

—To the cellar.

—Oh, but I don't have them.

—You know where they're kept, though, don't you?

Poor thing. Couldn't dissemble to save her life. Mouth twists out of alignment, eyes blink: the game is up.

—I was told never to go down there, Mr. Timothy. On pain of I don't know what, I'm sure.

—You won't have to.

—Why, it's got all Mrs. Sharpe's best vintages. One breath of upstairs air could ruin 'em, that's what was told me.

—I will bear all the consequences, I promise.

—But if they found you, they'd know it was *me* as gave you the keys. They'd *know*, Mr. Timothy!

—I'll simply say I stole them. It's not a hanging offence, is it?

—But Mr. George . . .

—Mr. George will know nothing about it. Didn't you say he was engaged with Mrs. Sharpe?

And still she hesitates. The time has come to take a new tone, a *higher* tone. Not an easy task, given my battered face, my torn trousers, but I make the best go of it. A loud *harrumph*. A squeeze of the lapels.

—See here, Mary Catherine. I wanted to spare you this, but it appears I can't. This house . . . this establishment . . . is implicated in some extremely serious business. *Criminal* business. The police have already been dispatched, and they will be here in short order. Now, I mean to protect you and Mrs. Sharpe and everyone else as best I can. And so if there's anything down there, anything at all, it's best that I find it first. You do see that, don't you?

Whether she does is unclear. But something, I think, has swelled inside her—a germ of fear, an answered suspicion—cresting slowly and overwhelming every other scruple. She frowns. She lets go the rug.

—Wait here. And don't let a soul spot you.

By which she means: *Hide*. But Philomela and I must be done with all that, for we make not a move in any direction, and as it turns out, the only intruder is Mary Catherine herself, bustling back with the contraband keys jangling in the pocket of her apron.

—This way.

We pass quickly down the hallway and then pause by the cellar door while Mary Catherine fumbles for the right key. A good dozen and a half to choose from—a regular gaoler's ring—and she seems bound and determined to try them all, and as her large, clumsy hands jam each new key into the lock, Philomela flinches . . . flinches again . . . and then nearly gives up the ghost altogether when she turns and finds, to the right of the door, Mrs. Sharpe's bald parrot, shivering as uncontrollably now as Lushing Leo.

He is indeed a disturbing sight, even for those of us who have witnessed his depilation in stages. But all he does in response to our gapes is poke out his black tongue, bow his head in a gesture of reflexive *politesse,* and cry:

—Kroo-sol! Kroo-sol!

This is followed immediately by the sound of a bolt sliding home. The door shudders but refuses to give way, no matter how hard Mary Catherine pulls against it. And even when I ply my own muscle against it, it resists . . . and then, of a sudden, abandons resistance altogether and wrenches wide open.

A cold sable light floods over us. A stream of dust and mould splashes across our faces and makes the flame of Mary Catherine's candle gutter.

Taking the candle from her, I usher Philomela inside and make to draw the door after us. But Mary Catherine puts out a hand and whispers:

—Don't be shutting it now. It'll lock on you.

And with that, she is gone—a jingle of keys and a pair of footsteps receding down the hallway—and all is quiet as Philomela and I stand on the uppermost stair, peering into this wall of cool, dusty, ventilated darkness. I take a step down; I wait for her to follow.

—We must hurry, Philomela.

The darkness has already so obscured her face I can no longer read its expression. I can only *feel* it: an eerie, paralytic pallor, waxen and faintly bilious.

—Shall I go myself, then?

—No.

One syllable, that is all, but there is in it a new note. A concern that extends beyond herself, beyond even me, perhaps.

I take her hand once more. She does not protest, not even when I draw her level with me. From there we pass to the next step and to the next, moving in a deliberate, dreamlike rhythm. After a few more steps, I lose all sense of descent or, indeed, of direction. The darkness folds us round, and Mary Catherine's candle, held straight out in front of me, does not disperse the darkness so much as carve a little redoubt from it.

—Just a few more steps, I should think.

But why make such an assumption? Absent any coordinates, we might just as easily be lowering ourselves into the earth's mantle. A damp, fetid spirit invades our nostrils. A faint dripping resonates from below. I can see no farther than the length of my arm, and yet I can clearly image, on all sides of us, dank green walls—solid on the surface but worried and honeycombed within by the constant drip of viscous fluid. An entire world, on the precipice of collapse.

And yet the stairs hold our feet quite comfortably, without even a creak. And when the steps come to an end, there is good solid stone floor awaiting us. And something else, too: a new smell, or perhaps an all-pervasive feeling. Excrement and sweat and sinew and pulsing skin. Presence and absence, all bound together.

This, of course, is pure intuition, for the darkness holds absolute. We take a step here, a step there, not from any hope of arriving somewhere but from an instinctual aversion to staying put. Stay put and be swallowed. And so we press on, in the endless circling rhythm of a nightmare from which there is no awakening.

Until something slams against my shin. An abrupt incursion of feeling . . . every fibre in my body explodes, and the candle leaps from my hand, and I watch, in dismal suspense, as it sails through the air. And in the parabola of light, I see, for the first time, the vintages that are kept in Mrs. Sharpe's cellar.

Not wine but coffins. A roomful of coffins.

Chapter 23

THE CANDLE IS DEAD ON THE FLOOR. My box of matches is upstairs, in the knapsack, next to the parrot's cage. And because no other light breaks through the Stygian gloom, the coffins, as quickly as they coalesced, revert to memory: a lightning-lit spectacle of elm-wood boxes on black trestles.

Only the throb in my shin holds me in the realm of the actual, and that pain becomes my home port as I light out into the darkness.

Within seconds, my hands have landed on a planed wooden surface. As I draw closer, its properties melt into view: a raised lid, a bevelled lip and, most disturbing of all, a row of nail heads, unnaturally burnished, glowing fiercely.

And more: an unspeakable odor, rising to meet me as I lower my face to the opening. Heavy and acrid and cloying, an *organic* odor, redolent of evacuation, so large and corporeal I can't imagine the box having room for anything else. And this somehow liberates me to plunge my arm straight into the cavity, to grub along the sides and comb every corner and crevice in search of . . . what?

It matters little. There is nothing there. An empty box.

And as I draw away, my head rocks with the futility of it.

Empty coffins. Why fill a room with empty coffins?

Then, like some provisional reply, a tiny cry leaps into the void. Almost undetectable at first—as assimilable as the squeaking of a hinge or the rattling of a window—until it repeats itself, a little more loudly. And then louder still.

Philomela.

I whirl back for her, but she is precisely where I left her—directly behind my left shoulder—and the mask of her face has altered but little in the last minute. There is no possibility of such a sound emerging from her.

Then from where?

I close my eyes, the better to attend, but the sound refuses to locate itself. I hunt it down the way one hunts a housefly, in clumsy stealth, seeking to trap it in the corner only to find it buzzing on the far wall. And so I am reduced, finally, to groping my way amongst the coffins, running my hands along their raised lids and waiting for the sound to come to me.

And still it slips away, alternately sharpening and blurring itself in my ear, until it seems to draw itself up through my fingers into the very orifices of my body. I realise then that this particular coffin—the one by which I am now standing—possesses a feature that distinguishes it from the others in the room: it is shut.

Or as shut as it *can* be, given that its lid is checkered by a series of gouged-out holes, each large enough to admit a finger.

I kneel by the coffin. I lower my ear to one of the holes. I rap gently, three times.

From inside comes a sound such as I have never before heard. Not an extension of the earlier cry but something much larger: the throes of a soul. And undergirding that, the scratch scratch scratch of fingers clawing on wood.

—Philomela! There's someone in here.

Silly of me, expecting her to be shocked. The moment I see her face, I understand: this is why we are here.

And now she is by my side, reaching under the lid with a grim purposeful-ness, fumbling for a few seconds, and then, with a sharp, wrenching motion, drawing it upward.

A latch. The coffin has a latch.

Philomela pushes . . . pushes . . . until the lid is perpendicular to the ceiling. Then, after a ceremonial pause, she gazes downward, and I follow suit, bend-ing my neck over the coffin's rim.

Gazing back at us is a pair of eyes. Eyes such as one might see on a drowned body: bluish-white, with a web of exploded veins. Eyes swollen well beyond their normal size, and so fixed and unyielding as to land upon us with the force of an auger.

The eyes of death, I am about to say. Only *these* eyes blink. From the depths of their sepulchral chamber, they blink.

Some part of me must notice the pale crust of face, the dilating nostrils, the drawn-back lips. But I am lost, I am *drowned*, in these eyes. They stare *past* me, with an expression of such abject feeling I have not the heart to look away.

And so, for want of anything else, I say:

—You needn't be afraid. We're here.

But before I can finish, the girl has found her tongue.

—I good. You say. I good. No fight. You say them I good.

A *Mitteleuropa* cadence to the words, but the terror . . . the terror is beyond language. It is bone deep.

—I good. No fight. I good.

The sound she makes releases me, after a fashion. I am free now to take in the rest of her. That plump white face. The foreshortened body. The black shoes and stockings and the remnants of a white shawl, torn nearly in two and littered with what look to be marigolds.

And most of all, the hands: claw-shaped, bloody-knuckled. These are the hands that have been following me from day to day, street to street, in and out of consciousness.

—I good. I good.

She is ten years old at most, but in this context, immeasurably aged. And in truth, lifting her from the coffin is akin to hoisting a longtime invalid from her daybed. There is no springiness in these bones, only *weight*. Philomela takes her by the legs, and I take her by the shoulders, and we lift with all our might, and I would swear we were lifting a giantess from the bowels of a pit. Gasping, Philomela sets the girl's feet on the ground, but the girl can no more keep her balance than a newborn baby. She swoons in my arms, and for a moment or two, we dance there, across the stone floor, between the coffins—a curiously intimate exchange that ends with both of us collapsed on the floor, sandwiched together like oarsmen. So close are we now I believe I can actually smell her fear, which mingles with the larger tang of shit and piss and sweat.

—Good. So good. You tell.

The girl shows no inclination to move, and it occurs to me we might profitably spend a fair amount of time in this very position—laying out our future, as it were—but that is not to be. From above us comes an abrading surge of light, and I look up to see Iris, dressed for work in a fitted bodice and long, full skirt, standing halfway down the steps and holding aloft a lantern. Her face is in shadow, but I have no doubt as to the expression it wears. And even so, I am desperate enough to run towards her, waving my hands.

—Iris! Wait!

Too late. She has hitched up her skirt and dashed for the light, and by the time I reach the bottommost stair, she has slammed the door after her.

An awful sound—lethal in its force. And yet it has the effect of opening a new door in my mind: the human connection I have failed, until now, to decipher.

Iris.

This is the curse of the male egoist: to assume that a woman opposes him out of feminine pique. When all along, she has simply been following orders.

That's just what Iris has done, from first to last. It was Iris who left me to rot in gaol by keeping the news of my arrest from Mrs. Sharpe. It was *Iris* whom Colin and I encountered the morning after the Christmas party, waiting for us in the hallway. How easily she might have overheard me dropping Gully's name. How easily she might have passed the name to George and let the hounds loose.

And how easy now for her to walk those few steps to Mrs. Sharpe's office, to summon George out of his private conference and tell him of the three people she has just trapped in the cellar.

The prospect is too enraging to consider for a moment longer.

—Philomela! Is there a back entrance?

She jerks her head from side to side, as though she were seeing the room for the first time. She mutters:

—Back . . .

And then she is off, shambling through the darkness. I see a flash of hand, a glint of bare calf. I make to follow, but the girl from the coffin circles her arm round my calf.

—I good. You see. All good.

It's no use trying to shake her off—I must pry her fingers, one by one, from my leg. Whether this causes her pain, I cannot say, for as soon as I have freed myself, she falls straight on to her back, re-creating the very position in which we found her: staring straight up at the ceiling.

I hear Philomela's low, affirming voice:

—Door.

But it might as well be counted a wall. Over eight feet tall and nearly as wide, a heavy oaken slab such as one might find in a French castle, belted with blackened iron, rotting and warped and sagging on its hinges, yet for all that, monolithic and impervious. One could scream away one's life in this room and never be heard.

—How did you open it, Philomela?

There's not a knob in sight. Only a tiny hole where the knob once was, and through this hole passes a chain, made fast by a padlock.

Philomela whispers back:

—Boot.

This is the only thing she says, and so it costs me seconds—precious seconds—to understand what it is she wants. Many more seconds before the blucher has been wormed off my foot.

From here, however, she wastes no more time—jams the toe of the boot between the door and the frame and, bracing the heel against the jamb, begins to work the thing like a lever. As soon as I grasp what she is trying to do, I make quick to assist her, and between us, we exert enough force to pry the door open a few inches. Through that aperture I crook my fingers and pull with all my force; below me, Philomela carries on her calm levering rhythm; and under our combined onslaught, the great oak slab slowly yields—another inch, another inch, another.

And then no more. With an elderly groan, the chain snaps taut, and the door grinds to a halt. Nothing will budge it even a fraction more.

A brush of wind paints my face as I peer through our little opening—barely six inches wide, not even large enough to admit my head. Philomela, though, wastes no time in sliding herself into the crevice. At first, I can't imagine she will get any farther than I, but with the deftness of a contortionist, she turns out her feet and straightens her spine and turns her head towards me and, against all known laws of physics, squeezes her way, with excruciating slowness, to freedom.

Even so, it is the narrowest of openings, and there are moments in the ensuing minute when I wonder if she will not be trapped here forever. But her body keeps pressing forwards, and this mechanical momentum has the effect of liberating in her feelings that she would otherwise have deemed extraneous. They come in a flood now: anger, of course, and fear, and relief, too, quite enormous relief, all washing through her features.

And also, I think, regret. A more adult sentiment than she is accustomed to entertaining—it leaves a crease of puzzlement across her face even as it raises us to a new level of certainty. For she and I both know I cannot follow.

And that understanding must be what causes her to pause on the other side of the door, on the very brink of freedom. She squints back at me. Her lips part.

I say:

—Go along, now.

She won't, though. She won't.

—I must see to the other girl, Philomela. She'll fit through, I know she will.

Her throat wobbles. A carpet of air passes through her lips. And on that carpet, a single word rides:

—You . . .

If there is an ensuing predicate, it is erased by the influx of George's voice, long and tall and surprisingly courtly.

—Come away from the door, Mr. Timothy.

I whisper one last time:

—*Go!*

And this time, she complies. Slips away in a cloud of lace, leaving behind only the tattered skin of Father's comforter, still wedged in the doorway.

Oh, yes, she is gone from sight, but if I shut my eyes tightly enough, I can see her at this very moment, doing exactly what she was doing the first time I saw her: running. Her native expression. And as I track her progress in my mind, I feel a terrific surge of pride, as if it were *my* legs carrying her out the courtyard and down the street, *my* lungs pressing the air through her, *my* heart beating time.

—Come away from the door, Mr. Timothy. Or we'll be dining on your brains. For breakfast and dinner.

George stands, alone, on the bottom step. The lantern swings jauntily by his side, but everything else is obscured—face, torso, feet. The only things claiming their rightful share of light are his left hand . . . and the revolver that sits there, addressing me with its astonished muzzle.

My first revolver. A milestone of sorts.

Letting the pistol dangle in his hand, George walks over to the coffin girl, still supine on the stone floor. He plants his foot on her belly, in the manner of an explorer colonising new land. Smiles softly as she mutters:

—I good. I good. You see.

—Not another word, Inge. There's a good girl.

Mysteriously soothed, she rises to a sitting position, wraps her arms round her shins. And waits.

George waits, too. There is about him no high dudgeon, no overweening urgency. He seems to be ambling through the darkness on some invisible private errand. Were it not for the weapon in his hand, one might think he'd come for a glass of sherry.

—It's devilish clever, George, I'll give you that. The coffins, I mean.

I'm struggling for the right pitch, is that clear? Essaying a tone that is dry and conversational without being provokingly sly. And beneath this affectation is a single driving imperative: to gain time. Time enough for Mrs. Sharpe to learn what has happened. Time for Colin to bring the police. Time . . .

—Now, are *all* the girls sent down here, George? Or just the ones who resist? I'm sure, in any case, after a few hours, they become much more pliable. Assuming they don't die, of course. From asphyxiation or . . . or, I suppose, the plain terror of it. Some people have rather a hard time of it in close quarters.

That first girl, probably . . . the one in the alley. It must have been fright that took her. And to think she was carried from this very spot and deposited like a broken dresser three blocks away. Not a mark on her, except for the hands, still clawing.

—And using mostly foreign-born girls, George, that's very sensible. Less chance of their telling anyone, isn't there? Less chance of anyone believing them.

All this time, George has been moving in his soft, indeterminate circles, evidently paying me no more mind than he would a cat. Now, however, he stops, turns slowly round, and, in a tone of grave courtesy, says:

—Step into the light, would you please?

I come forwards a few paces, until my feet have just entered the parabola cast by the lantern.

—Oh, Mr. Timothy, you have been an object lesson. I give you credit for that, an object lesson.

Raising the lantern to his ear, George shakes his head.

—Every time I look at you, I say to myself, "George, a fellow must *always* obey his instincts. When a fellow sees people who look like they don't fit in, why, that fellow owes it to himself to see they *don't* fit in. No matter who says otherwise."

A sigh, charmingly elongated.

—But you know how women like Ophelia can be, Mr. Timothy. Always needing their way, aren't they? Oh, and don't think they want it in half measures, oh, no. Give 'em just a wee bit of sovereignty, they want more and more. And now here we are. Look at us!

The workings of fate appear to strike him at some profound intellectual level. He screws up his brows and studies a patch of air, but if any wisdom penetrates those blue eye-pools, he cannot articulate it. He can only give me the lightest of shrugs and say:

—No one's fault, really.

Talk. Talk.

—On the contrary, George, the fault is all mine. It is my . . . my *misfortune,* really, to be always a little behind the facts. I think I have now pulled abreast of them for the first time. Shall I test a few propositions on you?

He gives me no sign either way.

—You have a long-standing arrangement with Lord Griffyn—going back many years, perhaps. I admit I was thrown off the scent by your account ledgers. You fixed them, I suppose, to make it look as if the money were flowing *out.* The truth is, you probably receive a regular retainer from Griffyn in exchange for sending him patrons. Patrons who have indicated a preference for a particular sort of love object. In addition, Griffyn compensates you for housing girls from his stable—the ones who are being a little too recalcitrant and need to be brought into line. Am I correct thus far?

Not a word from the man.

—I must say, I'd thought better of you, George. Always took you for a sharp sort of fellow, but it seems to me . . . I don't know . . . jeopardising a respectable business . . . awfully rash, isn't it?

He gives me his most affable smile yet.

—Oh, but you must consider certain premises of economics, Mr. Timothy. Allow me to put them to you, in the abstract. On one side, you have a business falling off steady over a long period of time. On the other, you have a demand outstripping supply. Under such conditions, what's the wise entrepreneur to do? Why, he must tailor the business to the demand. Simple as that, really. Oh, 'course, we can dress Sadie in pigtails and pinafores, and that's good enough in its way, but the truly . . . the truly *discriminating* gentleman, well, such a man wants the genuine article, don't he? He wants quality supply.

George swings the lantern to bring me back into the light. And in that splash of illumination, my carefully constructed disinterest nearly gives way.

—Supply, George. I'm wondering if you have actually seen the *supply*. Young girls barely old enough to tie their shoes, have you *seen* them?

—Oh, listen to him! As if it's such a bad thing. Some of 'em, it's the best thing that could happen. Catch the right gentleman's eye, it's like hitting the lottery. Makes you for life.

His face brightens at an unexpected thought.

—Why, look at Iris! She didn't make out too badly, now did she? Could have done a sight worse, believe you me.

I can't say which staggers me more: the fact that I will now have to look at Iris in a more complex light—when my hatred of her was approaching a state of incandescence—or the fact that Griffyn's line of business has been going on as long as that. Ten, twelve, perhaps fifteen years. Fifteen years' worth of girls flung headlong into darkness. Girls like Inge, coiled and cringing on the cold stone floor.

A decade from *now*, if we are to share George's optimism, this same Inge will be plying her trade in an establishment much like this one. Pleasuring the genitalia of grand dukes. Flirting with the sons of bishops. Getting her buboes lanced each Christmas.

And a decade from now, perhaps, there will be someone—someone just like me—bleating out another protest.

—It can't go on, you know, George. The police are on their way.

—Oh, the police.

—And Mrs. Sharpe will be only too glad, I'm sure, to tell all she knows.

—Ha! Oh, yes! That would be quite a lot.

He scratches his head with the revolver's muzzle. Clicks his tongue.

—Such a touching faith you have in people, Mr. Timothy. I'll miss that, I truly will.

He points towards the newly vacated coffin.

—And now, if you'd be so kind as to lay yourself down in that there bed? It's a bit cramped, I know, but I think it'll answer.

When I hesitate, he looks quite put out.

—We're not barbarians, Mr. Timothy. It's got *ventilation*, I don't care what——Oh, I see, it's this one, is it?

He nudges the girl with the tip of his boot.

—Well, *this* here is property, so naturally, it remains with its rightful owner. And the other one—well, that's property, too, and must be reclaimed. Now, between you and me, why his nibship should go to such trouble reclaiming a single item of inventory, I couldn't say. But no accounting for taste.

He stares at me for a moment, then turns his attention back to Inge. With the hammer of his revolver, he strokes a long line down her spinal column, scratches a circle round her exposed knee, rakes her stockinged shin. His voice, when it resumes, is so velvety that at first I assume he is speaking to her.

—Maybe you'd like me to take off a bit of her kneecap first. His lordship wouldn't mind. The stiller they are, the better he likes 'em.

Impossible to gauge his sincerity now that his face is averted. The only evidence I have is that becalmed voice:

—*Two* kneecaps would do just as well. Throw in two eyes while we're at it. Now let me see, that's a pair of bullets left over. What shall we do with those, Mr. Timothy?

And now he drags the revolver all round her body with a kind of sensual abandon. Under these ministrations, the girl gives a low, trailing moan and writhes into stillness.

—What if I do as you ask, George? Will you do as *I* ask?

—Meaning . . . ?

—Release her.

—Oh, now don't be insulting, that's completely out of the question. But I'm not a hard man, so . . . shall we say her time in the box is done? How does that strike you? She's learned her lesson, I daresay.

He smiles as he glances up at me, but it is not the smile that arrests me. It is the unaccountable look in his eyes. An omnipotent pity, with me as its object. I have seen, I have *felt* this look before. In Uncle N's sitting room. That unknown gentleman with the sad and encompassing eyes, fixing me with a sense of my own obligation. This is the gaze that straitens me now, that reduces, or perhaps elevates, me to the status of *character*.

—In you go, Mr. Timothy.

And at this moment, it seems entirely possible that no one will come for me. No one, aside from a helpless few, will even know I set foot in this cellar. And so I must reckon with the question that has dogged me without my knowing. Is there something else? Something that has drawn me here, neither with nor against my will, towards a final resolution?

George is standing a foot away. His revolver is pressed against my solar plexus. I can feel his breath condensing on my neck.

—Come, now, Mr. Timothy. It won't be for long.

And I am thinking: *Time. If nothing else, it will buy you time.*

I keep my eyes locked on him the whole way. For some reason, I want him to remember me as I am now, at the height of my awkwardness, reaching my arms back and dragging my legs over the side and squirming into this small, hot space. How ungainly I must look to him. How ungainly I feel.

Then again, the coffin is at least a foot too short for me—I must draw my knees to my chest just to fit inside. In every other respect, though, it is adequate to its task. Every human effluvium is here—stubborn traces of shit and piss and sweat and saliva—and every girl who has dwelt here still dwells, a legacy of terror echoing in my ears, at such a volume that my own cry, now superfluous, dies in the birthing.

—There's a good fellow.

George looks at me one last time—no pity now, only serene purposefulness. With a light, casual gesture, he tips the lid out of its axis and lowers it towards me.

The very moment I had anticipated, and yet how inadequate is anticipation next to the shuddering reality. I cannot acquiesce. My head jerks up. My hand flies towards the coffin lid, presses it back. My lips part in protest. . . .

—No.

But the weight of the wood and the weight of George's body force the lid back down.

—No!

And the moment that lid settles into its groove—the moment the latch clicks into place—everything changes. The sound dies away, and the air curls into stillness, and the cellar's blackness is transformed into a thicker, hotter, dryer blackness . . . clutching me fast, like a lover.

No. No.

My fingers fly towards the holes in the lid, but this only blocks the available light, and I *need* the light, don't I? To study the lineaments of my condition.

I see now that an entire history has been writ in this small box. The furiously scratched veneer on the underside of the lid. Blottings and blotches and divots. Swirls of dried blood. There, just above my left eye, a torn-off fingernail and—this is the sight that brings me up short—the chip of somebody's incisor, wedged deep in the wood.

She tried to chew her way through.

How desperate she must have been, whoever she was. Whereas my desperation is only beginning. Oh, yes, my lungs have begun to contract, and my eyes are blinking away the sweat, and my heart is banging on my ribs . . . but even so, I have many hours to go yet before I reach quite *that* state of hysteria. Many hours of lying here in the hot black suffocating air, with the residues of human bodies dripping down . . . my own breath clouding my face . . . every tremor in my body producing a corresponding reverberation in the walls around me . . . oh, I can stay here for many hours, if I must.

But then, in gradual stages, my condition begins to alter.

The light is the first thing to go—dimmed and then expunged. Gasping, I try once more to worm my fingers through the holes in the lid, but the way is blocked this time by the tautened web of a flat cotton fabric.

A bedsheet? A tarpaulin? There is no time to speculate, for now the air is leaving, too.

How quickly it goes! My lungs, stung with fear, bear down like bellows. Noxious tendrils of vapour ride up my throat—a long, slow cortege, keening as it passes. These are the sounds that dismay the human soul: the involuntary products of our bodies' own defenses.

—George. George!

But how can he hear me, when he is so busy making sounds of his own?

A gurgle. A splash. The steady drip of solvent . . . oh, yes, I can smell it . . . naphtha or kerosene . . . sliding off the coffin's sleek wood and pooling on the floor below.

And finally: a match, scraping against flint.

And just like that, the coffin fills with an ochre light. Bizarrely welcome, for it is instinct with intelligence—I might almost say, like my own. But before I can define the sensation, before I can pin it down, I am flattened by a wave of heat, bleeding through the wood and rolling up my frame and scalding my very breath.

It scorches my feet, abrades my chest, sears my nostrils and lips. It is deeply personal, it gouges me all the way through, scrapes out my marrow and wraps round my fibres and sinews and drenches me in sweat—an ablution so complete that I have the sensation now of sliding out of myself, down a molten-white corridor that shrinks to accommodate me.

I am not actually sliding, is that clear? I am absolutely still, laid out like Dido on her funeral bed. And I am, for the first time, understanding the nature of melodrama.

Which is to say the truest, the deepest impulses of the human organism, raised to a transcendent pitch. I have never felt so alive. Every nerve in me jangles. Every muscle grips fast. I understand now, at a biological level, the impulse that makes sopranos shriek. I understand why girls chew their way through coffin lids. Everything is possible . . . the grandest follies . . . here, at the brink of negation.

Outside, the fire crackles with a vengeance. Inside, there is only heat and light, and the heat builds and builds, and the light grows whiter and purer, until it seems to me my very skin is aflame, so brightly does it glow.

And in my head—extraordinary, isn't it?—I hear music. Songs I haven't sung in a lifetime. Clanging eruptions . . . bassoons calling at the top of their register . . . violins sawing themselves into flames. Cymbals with human tongues, ululating at insane volumes and then bursting into atoms of speech that shoot across the sky, tracing the news by starlight. . . .

I am burning.

—Help!

The coffin walls resonate with my screams, but the heat wraps me in its woollen silence, and that silence is nothing but the final expression of my helplessness. It dissolves me into my components and carves deep channels through me, and down these channels the scalding lines of smoke pass, claiming new territory with each second, smothering my body's every reflex. . . .

I am burning. I am burning.

—*Help me!*

And now . . . is it my imagination? . . . new sounds, barely discernible through the membrane of heat. Jawing and rasping. A fidgeting and a scuffling. A strange gargling.

And just as it seems that the last drams of air are being siphoned from my chest, I feel a new weight on the coffin lid, much greater than anything yet laid upon it. I wince at the impact, half expecting the coffin to splinter in two, but the wooden frame holds fast, and the light round me softens and darkens, even as the heat rises to a new fever pitch.

From without comes a fumbling of fingers . . . the rattling of a latch. I understand now that someone is trying to raise the lid. I understand, too, that it can't be raised—not with that enormous meteorite-like weight on top. Clearing that obstacle will be the work of a thousand men, labouring a thousand days.

How astonishing, then, to hear it give way so easily—a mere two or three seconds, that is all, and it is sliding to earth. I don't even have time to grasp the miracle of it, for the moment the weight hits the ground, the lid swings open, and a light of near-celestial intensity blazes through.

Shielding my eyes with one hand, I flail into the light, beating it before me. The darkness rushes back in, and as my eyes adjust to new shapes and timbres, the first object to which they adhere is the figure of George.

Coughing as I am, drenched from head to toe, I yet have enough presence of mind to see that George is lying flat on his belly, that his back is a strange confluence of solid and liquid, that his revolver rests two feet from his inert hand.

But in this moment of deliverance, I find myself fastening on known objects. Philomela, mysteriously returned, still wearing her tattered bridal raiment. And on the floor, Father's comforter, charred and smoking.

And Mary Catherine's butcher knife, dyed from tip to bolster, and resting like a sculptor's chisel in the gloved hand of Mrs. Ophelia Sharpe.

Chapter 24

GEORGE, in death, bears an unconscionable resemblance to Gully: the outstretched arm, the sightless, forward-looking eye. That sense of being interrupted in an errand. One almost longs to complete it for him.

On an impulse, I dip my finger into the platter of blood that has formed alongside him. Still warm, that's the first shock. And skinning over, like a saucepan of milk taken off the flame.

—I'm really quite strong, says Mrs. Sharpe.—For someone at my stage in life.

Only now, perhaps, is the full recognition of her act filtering through. She does not gasp; she does not sink. She only relaxes her grip on the knife, which tumbles to the floor with an eerily abbreviated clatter.

The coffin is virtually unrecognisable—oily and blackened and wreathed in smoke, its lid now held open by Philomela, who gazes mournfully into the empty space. Who is it, I wonder, she has just consigned to the afterlife?

Mrs. Sharpe takes a step towards me.

—George didn't . . . ?

—What?

—He didn't hurt you, did he?

—No, I'm quite well. Thank you for asking, Mrs. Sharpe.

That's when I begin to laugh. Not the easy, rolling laugh that gladdens a listener's heart, but a series of hard, visceral eruptions with dying falls. If I were to change their inflection by just a hair, they would be sobs.

Feeling wobbly, I sit on one of the trestles, and I seek out the roaming figure of Mrs. Sharpe, moving in triangular patterns now—labouriously, like a pack animal—rubbing her hands along her flanks and chattering half to herself.

From my trestle perch, I call to her.

—You *knew*, Mrs. Sharpe.

She wheels towards me. The cloud over her faculties blows off. A new relation lies stamped on her features.

—Oh, Tim.

She wipes her face and averts her head.

—Some of them died in those boxes. Did you know that, Mrs. Sharpe?

—No.

—Still clawing at the lids.

—No.

—They had the *brands*. On their upper arms.

I see her flinch slightly, I see her mouth reformulate the words. And then she turns away, her hands fluttering towards the ceiling.

—Things happen, Tim. Accidents . . . mischances . . .

Not her words. Surely not her words.

—The funny bit, Mrs. Sharpe. Have I told you the funny bit? When I came down here, I thought I was helping you. I told myself—it's really very funny—I told myself I was *saving* you. And all along, it was I who needed to be saved. From you.

Perhaps it really is my intention to provoke her. Perhaps I really do want her to whirl about in a swish of corded silk and cry:

—Saved from *me?*

And now, whatever instincts of caution and self-preservation still slumber inside her, these are swept aside in the rush of choler.

—You think you'd bloody well be *walking* now, if it wasn't for me? You think—oh, you damned *fool,* you think they'd have went to all that trouble, called in that hussy and trumped up those charges and . . . and clamped you in *gaol,* if I hadn't put my oar in? It'd been a good deal simpler to have your throat cut, if you must know. It's what everyone *else* wanted, *I* was the only one who said else. You owe your fucking life to me, Tim, twice over. Don't you forget it.

Her passion at this moment has a meteorological force. It blows me back a step, presses my head down.

—Very well, then, Mrs. Sharpe. I owe you my life. Perhaps you will tell me why you have spared it.

Of all the things she might have been asked to account for, surely this was the last on her list. Her face collapses into a mask of bafflement. She mutters:

—I don't . . . I don't . . .

And then the sluice gates are thrown open, and for the next few seconds, there is nothing but a flood of protestation—convulsive fragments torn from her most private recesses.

—Oh, Lord, Tim! It's . . . you've done so much . . . . really, it's . . . more than anyone's ever done . . . so much. . . .

So very much, apparently, that she can hardly bring herself to articulate it. Her face is cauterised with shame, and I feel my own tincture of shame at having elicited it.

—You mean . . . you're not referring to our *lessons,* Mrs. Sharpe?

—What else?

—But I have . . . I have had compensation enough. Room and board. . . .

—Oh, room and board! What's that next to *words?* An entire language, Tim. A *world.* How could I ever repay that? Except with blood.

She draws nearer and cups my chin in her hand, and even as I recoil from her touch, her face—importunate, trembling—presses closer.

—My boy Tim, listen to me. It's not too late. We can salvage this, can't we? George there . . . no one need know about that. *Iris* won't tell, she knows better.

And now, for the first time, she awakens to the presence of others. Her eyes widen to encompass Philomela, stationed by the coffin . . . and Inge, bobbing her head on the stone floor.

—Well, that's . . . that's all right, Tim. They won't tell, neither. How *can* they if no one asks 'em?

Oh, I could very well pity her.

—We'll get rid of the body, Tim, it's easily done! People disappear every day from London, and no one's ever the wiser. Christ, you don't think any-one round *here* will weep about it, do you?

She flings a look at George's body, as though expecting him to rise up and corroborate.

—And really, the way things have turned out . . . weren't you always say-ing you wanted to handle the accounts? Well, now there's no one to stop you. And we can go on with the *reading*, Tim. Just the two of us, every day at three-thirty. And once *Crusoe* is done with, we'll find *more* books. I've got a whole list drawn up, you know, I'm ready to read *everything*.

The glittering eye, the smacking lips—I feel quite churlish raising an objection.

—What of Lord Griffyn?

She looks at me.

—Oh, Christ, Tim. You don't think *you're* the one to take him on? We're none of us big enough for *that* job.

—I mean to try, at any rate.

And with that simple avowal, I render her, for the first time in our acquain-tance, mute. Her mouth wrenches downwards, and her hands drop to her sides as I step round her and make straight for the girl on the floor.

—Inge. Is that your name?

Her face, rising to greet mine, is wiped clean of feeling and thought. The very countenance that Philomela has presented to me any number of times. It holds almost a charm for me now.

—Would you like to come with me, Inge?

I am fully prepared to use persuasion on her, but the coffin has already worked its dark magic. She jumps to her feet and gazes up at me, plastic and obedient.

—We'll find a nice bed for you, shall we? Would you like that?

I take one of her arms, and I signal to Philomela to take the other. Together we walk the girl towards the stairs. And because her legs are still recovering their identity, we end up having to lift her from step to step, and in this slow, halting way, we ascend.

—You make me laugh, d'you know that?

That's Mrs. Sharpe, calling from below. The voice is higher now—a raucous cawing—and even easier to ignore. Our backs become a kind of fortress against it, and the sight of us must provoke her beyond imagining, for she cries, at the top of her lungs:

—You won't fucking catch him, you know!

I don't turn round. I don't raise my voice. My only concession is to inquire, in the softest possible tone:

—Why is that, Mrs. Sharpe?

—Coz he's leaving the country, isn't he?

An unmistakable note of triumph, but the voice lacks foundation, and in the very next second, it comes crashing down into a low, trailing moan. And when at last I do turn round, I find that Mrs. Sharpe has herself collapsed into a great flamboyant heap on the stone floor—her crinoline billowing up round her, nearly swallowing her whole. Only her head rises clear.

—May I never see his wretched face again!

I come down two steps. I call out to her, gently.

—Tell me what you know, Mrs. Sharpe.

And now her whole body is seized with a palsy. Everything vibrates, down to the lowliest petticoat. The very threads of the fabrics quake.

—Please. Please tell me.

She passes a hand across her face. She says:

—It's a shipment.

—You mean, more girls?

—It's a shipment. Antique pedestals. From Ostend.

Her head rocks back until she is staring at the ceiling.

—He always likes to be there, you see. To check the merchandise. Only this time . . .

A final sob shakes out of her chest. Her voice goes on, listless.

—This time round he means to leave it all with what's-his-name . . .

—Rebbeck.

—Leave it all and slip downriver. Till everything blows over.

She lowers her head until it is once again facing mine.

—It *will* blow over, Tim. I'm sorry, it will.

No crowing now. Just a blue, mournful tone.

—Where is the shipment landing, Mrs. Sharpe?

She doesn't answer, and so I repeat myself, with an asperity that surprises me.

—*Where is it landing?*

—Bermondsey. By St. Saviour's Dock.

What an effort those words have cost her. Her head sinks from view, and now it appears, the crinoline really has sucked her into its maw, without eliciting from her even the faintest murmur of regret.

—Thank you, Mrs. Sharpe.

She calls out to me a few seconds later.

—Tim.

—Yes?

—What happens to Mr. Crusoe?

In the receding light of our lantern, the insults to her person shine out for all to see. The henna wig, slightly askew on her head. The smear of rouge between her mouth and nose. And the blood, of course, spattering her glove, forming a chocolatey crust along her muslin undersleeve.

—I'm afraid you'll have to finish it on your own, Mrs. Sharpe.

By this time, we have reached the top of the stairs, and Philomela is pushing through the open door, and the three of us scurry past the bald parrot, squinting our way into the grey, twilit hallway, breathing with a special luxuriance the sweet heavy smoky aroma of upstairs.

—What on earth?

At the end of the hallway stands Mary Catherine, wringing the life out of a tea cosy. Surely this is the last thing she was expecting: Mr. Timothy descending with one girl and reemerging with two . . . George and Mrs. Sharpe nowhere in sight. What an astonishment we must be. I can feel Mary Catherine's awe wrapping me round, investing me with a new authority. *The master of the house.*

—Mary Catherine, this is Inge. I'm afraid she's been through quite an ordeal, and she'll require new clothes and a bed and very possibly a meal. Do you think you can arrange all those?

—Certainly. . . .

—I should be glad to help, but I've an important errand calling me away just now.

—What sort of—

—Before I go, I must leave a note for the police. In the increasingly unlikely event that they ever arrive. May I entrust you with that?

—Of course! But is there—

—That's all I have time for just now. If you would please see to Inge? Many thanks.

It is in Mrs. Sharpe's study that I find the pen—a shiny steel lozenge—along with an inkwell and a stack of stationery. With Philomela standing close by like a tutelary spirit, I sit down to write:

Have gone to St. Saviour's Dock. Come at once.

I place it in an envelope and convey it directly to Mary Catherine. Then I pull the shawl from Mrs. Sharpe's piano and wrap it round Philomela and guide her down the hall and out the front door. So deft am I in bustling her along, in fact, that it is only when we are standing on the sidewalk out front that she thinks to protest.

—Listen to me, Philomela. I'm sending you to my uncle's for the time being.

A frown etches its way across her face. She shakes her head.

—Please don't argue. I've endangered your life enough for one day.

Bafflement, skepticism, all the usual mélange of emotions work their way across her face and produce the usual fragment of language:

—No.

—I promise you'll be safe.

—No.

In a fit of impatience, I grab her by the arm and drag her over to Regent Street, gesticulating like a monkey. In a matter of seconds, a northbound cabman has spotted us, and when he pulls over to the curb, I hand him a piece of scrawling.

—There's the address. Please take this young lady there. Directly, if you please.

I hold open the door, but she balks.

—Please, Philomela.

She pulls one end of the shawl over the nape of her neck, tightens the other end round her waist, and, with a queenly disdain, steps away from the cab. And then, from behind me, comes a new voice:

—Looks like she don't want to go.

It is Colin. That poor bruised face of his, bathed in gaslight and hardened over with resolve. Devil take the man who gainsays him.

—The police, Colin. Where are the police?

—Ooh well, bloody surprise! Surtees were out of office, just like I guessed, and they're takin' their bloody sweet time fetchin' him, ain't they? So I told 'em where to meet us, and I come ahead on my own. And if you mean to do me or Filly out of any more Ad-ven-ture, Mr. Timothy, you got another think comin'.

Gully's boat is exactly where he left it—in the little watery alcove by the Hungerford Stairs. What a shock it is to see everything still in place: the winch and the grappling iron and the oars in their locks and even Gully's flask of brandy, resting on one of the benches, awaiting its owner's return.

Out of deference, I leave the flask undisturbed, and I take up my usual position by the oars, and as soon as Colin and Philomela have clambered in, I let slip the rope. Just as the pier passes from view, the first speculative drop of snow falls.

Nothing more than a gauzy shred, caught by the wind and blown back whence it came—but as we pass along, the snow gathers heart. The flakes hiss against the hull and boil along the crest of each new wave. Everything that is theirs to claim, they claim, and when I cast my eyes upwards, even the sky appears to be dissolving into its constituent elements—exfoliating into nothingness.

And yet what a charm it all has, despite the circumstances. The first snow of the season. Falling on me. Falling on Philomela and Colin and Mrs. Sharpe. On Gully. Falling on all of us, dead and alive.

—Mr. Timothy?

—Yes, Colin.

—You got any sort of . . . well, like a *plan* or anythink?

—Not particularly, no.

Other than to stop the world on its axis. But that's more a job for Atlas, isn't it? And I am not he.

All the same, there is something supernatural keeping my arms in motion. Something pumping the blood through my arms and shoulders and making me forget the chapping of my hands and the chattering of my teeth and the lingering fumes of burnt wood in my nostrils.

Perhaps it is simply the river itself . . . the winking lights of barges and coasters and dories . . . the chaff of men's tongues. A ceaseless highway of goods and humanity, flowing in each direction, with the three of us trundling right along inside it.

Yes, it all comes back to me now, this feeling of being absorbed into the river's own rhythm. But there is no giving in tonight, for we are absorbed in another mission entirely, and this mission is already teetering with uncertainty.

What if we're too late?

This is the possibility I cannot shake off. What if the shipment from Ostend has already arrived? What if Griffyn has slipped off in the darkness? What if his men are even now towing their cargo to the bowels of Griffyn Hall?

What if nothing has changed or will ever change?

And rather than answer one way or the other, I simply pull harder on the sculls—harder and harder, until my back clenches like a fist and my arms fall almost out of their sockets and my hands burn like firecrackers. And when the rowing fails to distract, I begin naming the bridges as we pass under them: Waterloo, Blackfriars, Southwark. And then the wharves: Grand Junction, White Friars, Scots, Dowgate. And beyond those, every random landmark I can recall—every shipyard and sailor's lodging, every custom house Gully ever pointed out to me.

It has taken me this long to recognise what a good teacher he was, for I *know* this river! Not in the way a pilot knows it, but in the way a priest knows his breviary—an understanding that precludes any large surprises while, at the same time, absorbing every small surprise, every turn and nuance and whim.

That is how I come to know—after more than forty minutes of incessant rowing—that the pier up ahead and to starboard is St. Saviour's Dock. So preordained and miraculous is its appearance that I feel as if I am the first ever to discover it.

—There!

Colin, mystified, squints into the night.

—I don't see nothink. You certain, Mr. Timothy?

But of course I'm certain. How many times did Gully draw my attention to it? How many times did he talk of Bermondsey, and Jacob's Island, and the time he saw a man killed there? And there I sat, taking it all in without even realising it, and here now is my reward: the assurance of St. Saviour's Dock.

A promising name that is quickly belied by the reality: a bleak black out-cropping of pier, ringed with snow and peopled by a few lone shivering figures—watermen, probably, waiting for the fares that have eluded them all year round.

I set down my oars, grateful for the reprieve but not yet ready for the labour to follow. The *cerebral* labour of finding Griffyn and his men amidst all this snow and mist and darkness.

They cannot have chosen the dock—too many witnesses. Neither can they have wandered too far, if Mrs. Sharpe is to be believed. Clear as a bell, the way she said it: By St. Saviour's. *By* St. Saviour's.

And what a wealth of ambiguity is contained in that single word. *By* could be a mile in any direction. We could spend days and nights exploring that *by* and be no closer to our end.

The boat, with no one to scull it, spins in slow, wobbly circles. The snowflakes flutter and whirl about us like maddened bees. We pay them as much attention as a statue would, for we are all of us engaged in the same activity: pulling back the curtains of night to find a scattered few of its denizens. Our heads wheel east, west, north, and south. Our eyes squint and expand, cutting this way as the next, as every fibre of our respective beings is assigned to this quixotic search.

Where are they?

The more I seek them, the more I am drawn back to the events of last night, to Griffyn Hall. That wall of fog rearing up, and the two of us, Colin and I, crouched by the hedge, waiting for a sign of occupancy or intent, waiting without hope but with a faint underlay of expectancy. And then being rewarded with that flaring match.

It all comes back with such a rush of immediacy that when I first see the miniature explosion of light in the distance, I mistake it for a memory. Indeed, I am prepared to pass on without giving it another thought, until I see Colin pointing in the same direction and jumping up in the boat, nearly tipping himself out in the process.

By then, the light has already vanished. Reconstructing it in my mind, I see once again the quick inflammatory burst, swelling and then shrinking down to a tiny point and then disappearing. The very flame a match would make.

And by the time I have reached that conclusion, I have already snatched up the oars, and I am rowing harder than ever—Atlas, indeed—and we are coursing through the water, fast as a steamboat, and the pumping of my arms is matched only by the pumping of my heart, and my eyes have sprung open to their farthest compass, the better to fix the sector from which that mysterious light emanated.

And then comes another light. Flaring up out of nothing and, just as quickly, disappearing.

A pair of them. A pair of smokers.

Oh, yes, I fully acknowledge there might be any number of explanations for two such lights. There might be any number of people capable of making them. But this is all we have been given; this is what we will take.

Rowing now in a perfect fury, I propel us through the water in a clean, hard line, staying parallel to the shore and steering solely by the memory of those two lights—navigating by them the way mariners use stars. The rowing is even more exacting now. Every muscle in my arms and shoulders and legs shouts in protest. My knee lodges the largest objection of all. Winter has gnawed it down to a prickly stump, and there is nothing to do but row beyond the pain and keep rowing until I can be sure we have passed the vicinity in question. Only then do I ease up on the sculls. Only then do I turn us on an angle and begin the more delicate work of bringing us to shore.

Another ten minutes go by before the shoreline presents itself, and still more time before I can find a margin wide enough to take us. The tide has risen in the last hour, and as I leap out of the boat and drag it to land, the tide keeps dragging us back. It takes all my doing, and all Colin's doing, to bring the boat to a halt on the narrow spit of gravel.

With my muscles still howling and gnashing, I permit myself a swig of

Gully's brandy . . . then another . . . and it turns out to be just the tonic: a ring of reassurance.

—Mr. Timothy! Pull the bricks out your arse!

Already Colin is stalking back down the shoreline, and Philomela and I are making haste to follow. Keeping up with him is a little easier than it was last night, for there is no knapsack to drag me down. Just my oilskin cap and my sodden pea coat, into which I have inserted the one item I would never have thought to call upon: George's revolver.

My hand closes round it now. Hard and beaded with melted snow and strangely warm, as though it had been firing itself in my absence. Its touch gives me no comfort; it only recalls me to how far out of my element I have come.

By now, the snow is falling full force, half blinding us with each sweep of our eyelashes, and yet one might think it had never existed to behold the prospect before us. The riverbanks, the waggons, the warehouses, the windows of the provisioners' shops—everything is coated in a blackness so thick that any snowflake is swallowed entire. All the colliers on the Thames, all the chimneys of London, the entire sum of England's industrial furnaces could have disgorged their burdens of soot right here and still not have attained to quite this degree of pitch.

And these smells! Glue and leather and dog droppings and the nauseating trace of strawberry jam, blurring into an indefinable, illimitable scent of rot. But if Colin notices any of it, he is in no way put off. He pushes past each building, pushes through the wind and snow . . . until at last he stops and thrusts his shoulders back and, without a word, points into the near distance.

Standing there by an abandoned custom house are two men, dressed in the manner of coal heavers. Their voices, unimpeded, fly towards us.

—Any bloody day.

—Extra wages, I *don't* think.

—Stow that, will you?

—Stow it yourself.

No different, in speech or appearance, from any pair of labourers you might find along the southern end of the river or along the Docks. No different but for this: they are holding their lanterns to landward. Shielding their light from the view of passing boats.

A detail, that is all. And rising out of it, an intuition, or else just a fond hope, that these two coal heavers are something other: the men who were keeping vigil with Rebbeck on the portico of Griffyn Hall.

But there is no means of positively identifying them. We cannot draw any closer without alerting them to our presence, and we cannot gain another angle on them without either plunging into the icy river or heading southwards into realms unknown.

And then I notice a rather striking particularity about the building next to which the men are standing: although it has been propped up in divers places by enormous crutches, the impromptu surgery has done nothing to keep the rear half of the roof from slipping away—dropping clean off the framing. This displaced sheet of tar and shingle now forms a crude embankment between the ground and the upper story, and it is up this embankment that Colin and Philomela and I, without another word, now scramble.

The detached roof holds firm beneath our feet, and within a minute, we are standing where the roof once stood, crawling along naked ceiling joists and peering down into the custom house. A tableau of arrested domesticity: one small oaken table; two chairs pushed back; a plate of cabbage, still recognisable; a single black stocking wound round a newel post.

—Look.

Colin taps me on the arm and points to the clearing below: a cramped, desolate courtyard stretching from the custom house to an abandoned mill just to the south. Against that mill's sluice gate, a broad front of Thames water has crested, creating a small inlet—fifteen feet wide and perhaps eight feet deep—entirely invisible to passing vessels. Some farsighted soul has even built a tiny dock projecting halfway across the inlet. And fate itself has so thoroughly emptied the surrounding space that the only remaining occupants are discarded pails and the strewn skeletons of dead cats. I feel, against my better nature, a tingle of admiration. Griffyn's men have found perhaps the one place on the riverfront where they may come and go unobserved.

The two coal heavers below don't seem particularly to relish their privacy. The snow has grizzled their caps; white epaulets have gathered on their shoulders. The only concession they make to the cold, though, is to bury their hands in their pockets and mutter a mild oath or two under their breath. One of them—fearful, perhaps, of being declared insubordinate—casts a quick backwards look and then, reassured, returns to his original post. But in that fleeting moment, I have time to follow the line of his eye to its logical end, to see a waggon with a quiescent horse . . . and two additional figures stationed by the custom-house door.

Of the two, Miss Binny is the more easily recognised. Her towering figure, her black cloak, as ill fitting as the dress it conceals . . . these I would know in any setting. In her mouth, shockingly enough, is a cigarette, whose lit end allows me to trace the wide, amiable curve of her mouth, as she puffs prodigiously and exchanges inaudible small talk with the smoker on her left.

This latter personage remains clothed in shadow until one of the coal heavers' lanterns accidentally swings his way, revealing the blunt features of that well-known face. Last night's frock coat has been discarded in favour of the customary work attire, and the bowler has once again been wrenched into place, although it is not quite able to conceal the swath of white bandage that has been wrapped round Rebbeck's crown. Neither is his air of studied leisure able to hide the asymmetry of his stance: he is clearly favouring one leg, a fact that affords me no small amount of satisfaction. He stands there now, in the falling snow, like the occupant of an opera box, waiting with barely suppressed boredom for the musical onslaught to begin.

We are all of us waiting—for what, I have only some small idea. Still, I cannot help but note the tics of annoyance that take hold of Rebbeck each time he consults his watch. *They're behind schedule,* I think. They should have been done and gone some time ago. And the longer they are put off, surely, the more brightly Providence will shine on my cause. God willing, the police have already been to Mrs. Sharpe's. God willing, they are even now wending their way downriver. . . .

Or else no one is coming. No one at all.

—Looooo. . . .

A long, lowing cry, rising out of the east. The sound jerks Rebbeck's head upwind, draws a relieved smile across Miss Binny's taut features, and spurs the two men into attitudes of expectancy, as they swing their lanterns, for the first time, towards the river.

In the sweep of light, I can just make out the charcoal outlines of a boat, propelled by two men, washing towards us on a torrent of speckled, febrile water. So much frothing and hissing that the vessel itself has the quality of an afterthought, rocking in the river's troughs even as it steers a steady course for the dock. It is a homely vessel, smaller than a barge, larger than a dory . . . unexceptional in every way, right down to its contents.

Boxes.

Ten boxes, to be precise. Phosphorescent with snow and arrayed in staggered tiers.

Tonight does not mark the first time these boxes have been brought to this pier, judging by the practiced ease, the air of rote with which the pilots and heavers go about their work. One casts the rope, one catches it, one slips it over the piling—and within minutes, the boat has been hauled in and secured, and all four men are hefting the boxes out of the hold and laying them in a neat row by the bank of the stream.

Pairing off, they proceed to carry the boxes to the waiting waggon. The footing is slippery, but the work is quick and methodical, and scarcely a sound escapes from either the men or their cargo. For all anyone might say else, these really are pedestals from Ostend.

From my chimney perch, I see Miss Binny rap twice on the custom-house door. And then, after a yawning interval, the door swings open, and into the courtyard strides Lord Frederick Griffyn.

In his raglan-sleeved Inverness cape and his resplendent square-toed button boots . . . the rose-gold ring squeezed defiantly onto his finger . . . he is the model of gentility under pressure. With a dreamy half grin, he steps into the center of the courtyard, careful not to meet anyone's eye, almost bashful as each eye turns to meet his. He points to the rearmost box, which has yet to be placed in the waggon, and in a softly inflected voice, says:

—That one.

The two men tasked with carrying the box lower it slowly to the ground. They look at each other, then at Rebbeck.

Still pointing, His Lordship says:

—Open it, if you please.

But the two men are too baffled to carry out the command, and so it falls to Rebbeck to stride forward, undo the latch, and pry open the lid.

By my side, I see Philomela shrink away, cast her eyes eastward. But Colin and I, in spite of ourselves, cannot help but look.

Even with our bird's-eye view, though, we see at first only inky absence, until Lord Griffyn, availing himself of Miss Binny's lantern, steps forward and, sweeping his arm round, bathes the box in an umber light. And now everything is plain to behold.

A small girl with long, limp, whitish hair and an even whiter face. She is pale enough to qualify as a corpse, but the lantern light has already pricked her eyes open, and as the night aromas rush in, she unleashes a huge wave of air, as if she had been holding her breath all the way from Belgium. She raises her head and then, under the combined scrutiny of all these onlookers, lowers it again, and as she sinks back, I can hear the faint echo of bilge water splashing against the box's inner walls.

Followed by another, even fainter echo: Colin's awestruck whisper.

—Holy Christ. . . .

Griffyn is now standing directly above the box, peeling off his gloves. With his right hand, he reaches down to caress the girl's cold, ashen face. Then, obscurely satisfied, he snaps his fingers twice. The men gather round once again, and in the ensuing flurry, we catch a glimpse of that small flaxen head, turned all the way to one side, as though it might press itself into the wood's grain. And then the perforated lid is once again shut, and the box is hoisted onto the waggon bed, squeezed into the niche left by its mates.

Griffyn carefully tugs each finger of his glove back into place, then turns a smile of raffish charm on his staff.

—My friends, now is the time for words, but my tongue fails numb before its task. I can only tender you my warmest, deepest admiration for the labour you have effected, and in the same breath, bid you adieu. For I am called elsewhere by unavoidable affairs. *Les affaires du coeur et de la loi.* . . .

A brief smattering of applause from Miss Binny, to which Griffyn lowers his head before shifting his attention towards the river.

—What a charming little vessel you have procured, Rebbeck! All it needs, I believe, is a Spanish guitar, softly strumming.

—We hope it will turn the trick, your lordship.

—I daresay there is no trick you can't turn, Rebbeck. You will wire me, of course, as the money comes?

—Yes, your lordship.

—And that other business . . .

With this, they relapse into a private conversation that concludes a minute later with Griffyn's clapping Rebbeck on the shoulder and crying:

—The very thing! Now, if these strapping young men could proffer me service as *gondoliers*? Excellent. Let us be off, then.

And so the moment I have been imagining now stands inaugurated. The moment in which my resolve will be put to its final proof.

But what is this proof? What is this resolve? There the imagination falls short, leaves off with dim possibilities, and each of the possibilities falls away in turn until at last there is just *one*, only slightly less dim, and only slightly more possible, than the rest.

—Colin.

—Yes?

—I'm afraid I'll require a bit of time. Do you think you might provide some sort of distraction?

—What sort?

—I don't know. Running about or . . . or making a commotion, that kind of thing. Anything you like, so long as you don't get yourself caught.

—How much time you wantin'?

—As much as you can supply. Just don't let them take you. If it's a question of distracting them or . . . or escaping, then by all means choose the latter.

He turns away a little as he considers my request. That request considered, he tenders me a slow, hard nod.

—Many thanks. And now . . . Philomela?

She looks up at me, tense with expectation.

—Here is what I need you to do. Go back to the boat and find the lantern. The *lantern*, yes? I want you to stand by the boat, in full view of the river, and make a *signal*, do you understand?

—Signal.

—So that the police will know where to find us. You must swing it in a large arc, very rhythmically. Like this.

—Yes.

—And mind you—this applies to you, too, Colin—once you're done, neither of you need come back. You may deem your work complete.

They both look at me for a moment. Then Colin says, as gently as he can:

—Fuck off.

It is the last thing he says. Before I can make any reply, he and Philomela have dropped out of sight—reducing themselves to nothing more than soft rustling sounds beneath my feet.

Back in the courtyard, the preparations for his lordship's departure are nearly complete. Griffyn's portmanteau has been procured and tucked away in the boat, the gondoliers are stationed, and now Griffyn himself, swinging his cape in the snow, strolls towards the dock with Rebbeck on one side and the good missionary commanding the other. Miss Binny chats in the flat, equable fashion of a passenger in a railway terminus, but Griffyn's voice rises above hers with no discernible effort.

—All the same, my good woman, what a crime. Not to be in London when Christmas comes round! Heigh-ho, we are pawns of the gods. And dare I suggest it? There is always next year.

To which Miss Binny offers the wheedling response:

—Indeed, my lord, there is. *Always* next year. And the year after as well.

More banalities, I'm sure, are queued up on her tongue waiting to be disgorged, but they will have to wait just now, for the air, at this moment, is rent by a loud cry to stern.

—Halloo!

It is Colin's voice, it could be no other. And yet it carries such an aged note of conviviality I scarcely recognise it.

The effect it produces, though, on the occupants of the courtyard is anything but convivial. To a man and woman, they fall silent, stiffening from boot to hat.

The first to break his pose is Rebbeck. He takes a few steps in the general direction of the sound, trying to scope out its origins. But when the voice comes again, it comes from a slightly different quarter—thirty yards farther south.

—Someone this way comes!

Rebbeck gives a signal to one of the men, who runs off at once, skirting round the dislodged section of roof without an upward look, then pressing on southward towards a dilapidated tenement.

But the voice, on its next pass, sounds clearly to the east.

—This way, officers!

In the distance, the man's body freezes at the news. Then he turns and skips round a pile of rubble, disappearing behind a teetering gallery.

That makes one gone. And there is this additional benefit: Colin's noise-making has produced answering sounds. The yowling of a cat. An aborted cry of protest from a neighbouring squatter. The shiver of a rotten window frame. Life is beginning to stir in these dead precincts.

But in the courtyard, all remains quiet. The gondoliers sit frozen in their boat; Griffyn and Miss Binny stand arrested at the water's edge. Only Rebbeck displays any inclination to move. His nostrils dilate, his fingers waggle . . . and then comes another cry, from along the river's edge, and he is on the move, limping his way round the custom house and vanishing into the distance.

No difficulty now for me to climb down to earth. No difficulty to creep round the house and peer into the courtyard. And from here, the signs look propitious indeed—but for one thing. The last of Griffyn's men still keeps sentry by the waggon.

Half a minute passes, another half minute; the ties of despair are just beginning to steal round me when, from some western precinct, Colin's voice once more sounds out.

—*London Bridge is broken down!*

Not even sung—*intoned,* like the Nicene Creed. And yet that refrain is just the thing to draw my sentry from his post. Half apprehensive, half enraged, he edges towards the sound, then follows it across the stones and around the inlet. He is following it still when I take my first step into the courtyard.

I will say this, I am quiet as a body can be, creeping towards the waggon, lifting myself onto its bed. It is, in fact, that very stealth that allows me to hear, for the first time, the sounds these boxes *do* make through their perforated lids: tiny scuffles and burbles and squelches and, beneath everything else, a low, humming plaint. The pedestals have come to life.

As I have no lantern, I must fumble for some time before locating the latch on the first box. Once found, it clicks right open, and after I have made a cursory check of the surroundings and muttered a brief, virtually wordless prayer, I nod to myself and raise the lid.

—Go! Free! Go!

I whisper it as loudly as I dare, and then I move on to the next box . . . and the next one . . . opening each in turn and confronting, each time, the same prospect: a still-living body with a blanched, dead face, fast-blinking eyes and inert lips.

So here I am, a would-be saviour on Christmas Eve, trying to raise the dead, but they won't be raised. Every girl remains a slave to her condition, wrapped in fast invisible cords. I find myself wanting almost to pound them—hammer them into life—but I have not time or strength enough. I have only . . .

My hand closes round the hard cold surface of George's revolver.

And through my head flashes the impertinent question: *How difficult can it be?*

Not so very. Not so very difficult. Cock the hammer. Raise the barrel straight to the sky. Curl the finger round the trigger and set to squeezing.

And still something in me resists. Until I hear Rebbeck's distant cry:

—Got him!

Colin. They've found Colin.

And that knowledge is all the incentive I need. I press tighter, tighter . . . and then . . .

Crack!

And at that moment, I could swear the charge passes not from the barrel but through my body—up my arm, out my head, straight to the stars. The air sings in my ear, and the whole world is aroar.

Of all the reactions I expected to elicit, the one I never really anticipated was the horse's. The poor beast, stung by the blast, lurches forwards about fifteen feet, knocking me flat on my stomach and pitching the boxes against one another like matchsticks. There is a cacophony of squeals as the girls fight to disengage themselves. One is carried straight off the waggon—her box splits clear down the middle and spits her out through the fissure.

I can see this girl now, staggering to her feet, all bloody fingers and sopping rags. I can see the other girls pushing themselves up in *their* boxes, beginning the arduous work of reorienting themselves.

And to my right, I can see the dark figure of Lord Griffyn, turning towards the waggon . . . and next to him, the slowly expanding cavity of Miss Binny's mouth.

This cavity becomes a source of unspeakable satisfaction to me as I brace myself against the waggon's side and discharge the second bullet, straight to the sky.

And instead of bolting this time, the horse, whinnying in terror, drops its back and rears its forelegs into the air. The back of the waggon tips almost to the ground, and in due process, each box comes sliding off, spilling out a new girl with each landing.

In the near distance, I can hear the sounds of running feet converging on us, but for now, the spectacle of these girls is preeminent. They are all of them screaming—at an unimaginable pitch and volume—and this noise has somehow become the vehicle of their liberation, the galvanic impulse that explodes them from their boxes and goads them to their feet and sends them flying. Their screams merge into a great echoing chord, so that the very heavens rock with the sound.

Only in Bedlam, I think, could one find such a frenzy of movement with no discernible purpose. Maddened by liberty, the girls rush in whatever direction possesses them, and woe to the object that gets in their way. Griffyn is transformed into a whirling dervish by one bundle of rags. Miss Binny is fairly flattened by two girls as she tries to waylay them. Demonic in their power, they push straight up and over her, leaving her stunned and heaving in their wake.

One girl flings herself straight into the nearest water, as if she were on fire. Two others heave themselves at the boat, tackling the astonished gondoliers and capsizing the vessel in a single stroke. Far from sinking in this new medium, the girls take to it like otters, kicking up great cataracts as the flailing boatmen disappear in columns of slime.

I watch . . . oh, I watch it all with an ill-concealed triumph. *Behold my work!* So it is that I am actually cackling when the men barrel into the courtyard—Rebbeck bringing up the rear and dragging Colin after him. Their faces slacken with amazement; their limbs jerk in all directions. Instinct tells them to pursue, but *which* girl are they to pursue? The one who has just dashed down the foreshore? Or the one who has yanked open the custom-house door and is even now bounding up the stairs and shouting through the walls? Or the one who, in a flight of ambition, has set herself the task of scaling the nearby mill?

Into this sea of chaos Rebbeck's two men, with no small trepidation, wade, while Rebbeck contents himself with dragging Colin towards the custom house. Before he can make it, though, a bellowing girl streaks past him like a comet—just the distraction Colin needs to clamp his teeth round his captor's arm. Stung, Rebbeck whips away the injured limb and raises the other for an answering blow. But Colin has already darted out of range and is running straight into the heart of Bermondsey. Within seconds, he has vanished into the darkness—nothing but a line of footprints in the snow.

Rebbeck makes a show of chasing him, limping across the courtyard and skidding into a slick of ice before coming to a quick halt. I see him there, silently weighing the possibilities. Then he turns round and sketches a path along the dilapidated house-front, pausing first to survey the wreckage of boxes . . . and then looking straight up at the grinning figure of young Tim in the waggon bed.

He waits.

The waiting is a bit of a surprise. I had fully expected him to charge. But then I look down and see the revolver still clutched in my hand. Marvelous toy! Why, with this magical pistol, I will rule the world, that's what I'll do!

And to seal the pact, I raise the pistol for yet a third time. And once again . . . oh, silly Tim . . . silly, silly Tim . . . once again I fire.

And this time, the nerve-shattered horse bolts for good—no stopping it now—and this time, I am not braced. The pistol pops from my hand, and the waggon slides from under me, and I am sailing through the air, straight to earth—a thump of bone on stone-cold ground.

My ears ring with the sound of hooves, and I am thinking this must be the natural end of all petty tyrants—to be hurled into the muck and mire—and that is the end of thinking, for now Rebbeck is upon me, and we are rolling through the courtyard, gouging ourselves against the stones, and Rebbeck's fingers are pressed against my windpipe, and mine are pressed against the closed lids of his eyes, and who's to say which of us will give way first?

But the first thing to yield is the custom house. Which is to say, we roll right into that crumbling hovel, and it is the building itself that shakes—shakes to its very foundation.

The force is enough, at any rate, to jar Rebbeck's fingers from my throat. I jump to my feet, panting hard, and when he leaps up to face me, I hook my right foot round the back of his leg (a trick Peter showed me when I was eight years old—eight years old, and still dreaming of being able to perform such a trick), I give a tug, and down goes Rebbeck in a satisfying heap.

Why then . . . why does the pain come shooting through *my* leg? The old traitorous knee—Christ alive!

I make to run, but Rebbeck's leg is not so bad as mine, is it? Oh, he finds it the easiest of sports to catch up with the likes of me and thrust me back against the house. And when I start to press back, it takes only a quick pop to my solar plexus to take the fight out of me. Nauseous, tasting blood, I stand pinned in place, every last atom of resistance concentrated in my out-stretched left arm.

For against that arm is pitted Rebbeck's own blunt appendage . . . and, to make the contest even less equal, the wood-carver's blade—redolent with history, garishly present.

It is this blade that advances, by the slightest of fractions, towards my naked throat, and I am conscious now not of Rebbeck's face, which has dis-appeared in a haze of snow, but of his voice, which has lightened into some-thing queerly paternal.

—Here comes a candle to light you to bed. . . .

Another knee in the abdomen. From my mouth, a tiny rill of blood spills forth; every fibre in my body quivers with pain; and still some involuntary impulse keeps my arm in place, holds the blade at bay.

And still it closes in . . . nearer and nearer it draws . . . and all the while, Rebbeck is crooning in my ear.

—Here comes the chopper to chop off your head.

And as his face inclines towards mine, his voice drops into the lightest, sketchiest of whispers—a tone so insinuating I could mistake it for the promptings of my own conscience.

—Don't be like your friend now. Go quiet. Come now, go quiet.

Ah, Gully. Was it like this? Was he whispering in your ear, too? Could you feel his breath on your eyelashes?

—Shhhhh. Shhhhhhhhh.

Behind me, the custom house's wormeaten wood crackles and crunches against our combined weight. I remember now what it was I was thinking when I was wrapped round the chimney, directly above. I was thinking: *The whole thing could give way any moment.*

And that's when I realise that my hand—my *other* hand—is curled round the downspout.

Only the fingers, though, are capable of movement, for Rebbeck has the rest of my arm pressed against the house, and he will no sooner release it than he will loose the blade that now hovers two inches from my throat. And so I instruct myself to do the thing least expected: to go limp in Rebbeck's arms.

And the moment my weight begins to drop, Rebbeck's knife draws away, and his free hand grabs me under the arm, and all his homicidal intent is shouldered aside by a perverse chivalry, as he devotes himself to the task of catching me—so that he may better kill me.

But now my right arm is free, and I am tugging with all my main on the drainpipe, and it pulls clear with only the smallest protest, and I swing it straight in the direction of Rebbeck's head. And in that instant, my own eyes squeeze shut, as though *I* were the one being struck, and when I open them again, Rebbeck is standing back a pace, his eyes unblinking, and I swing again, and this time there is no mistake. The blow hurls him straight into the house, and rather than rebounding against it, he drives straight through in a crash of splintering wood—nearly disappears inside—until there is nothing left but a pair of inert, protruding legs.

Around us, a battery of new sounds is gathering. The squeals of girls have been superseded by the shouts of men . . . loud whistles . . . the crunch crunch of indistinct shapes hustling through the snow. Indistinct, only because my eyes remain fixed on that pair of legs. I watch, with a detached fascination, as they jerk back into life and then, after a space of perhaps half a minute, crawl back into the courtyard, dragging with them the attached torso and, after that, the stunned, hatless head.

Blinking madly, breathing hard, Rebbeck steadies himself against the house's shell and hoists himself to a nearly erect position and stands there, with a look of wavering concentration. And yet some native tenacity is still at work in him, for he is gripping the blade all the more tightly, and he raises it one last time . . . higher . . . higher . . .

And then, behind him, the shadows part to reveal a tall, reedy figure scurrying soundlessly through the snow . . . raising a long, spindly club . . . no, a walking stick . . . and, with one short, decisive blow, sending the former Sergeant William Rebbeck into the final station of unconsciousness.

Leaning over Rebbeck's incumbent form, the figure murmurs:

—Oh, Willie.

And then he takes a step towards me.

I press a hand to my temple. I fall back.

It is Detective Inspector Surtees.

—So nice to see you, Mr. Cratchit.

I open my mouth to reply, but my astonishment is too great for words, and it is all the greater because Surtees is behaving as if we had just encountered each other in Leicester Square.

—I am delighted, Mr. Cratchit, that we were able to arrive in time. You'll pray excuse the delay, it's rather difficult to get men assembled on Christmas Eve.

And now my eyes, sharpening in the wet, stinging air, at last pick out the familiar blue swallowtail coats of the Metropolitan Police, weeding their way through the rocketing girls and Lord Griffyn's harried staff. One constable lays a firm hand on Miss Binny's arm; two of his fellows collar the mud-caked gondoliers.

And for each new figure I decipher, another emerges, equally distinct, from the miasma. Colin, still panting, gazing round the corner of a tenement. And Philomela, weaving through the lines of girls, raising her lantern high, like Diogenes.

Oh, yes, all of us present and accounted for. All but one.

I spy him soon enough: a shrouded shape absconding down the shoreline. A black Inverness cape melting into the night.

Not a word of explanation do I utter. Slipping past the outstretched arm of Surtees, I elbow my way through a circle of policemen and make straight for the river.

—Mr. Cratchit!

Surtees's voice slows my gait not a whit. Nor does the searing in my knee: I simply run *through* it, as though it were a set of hurdles placed at every step along the way.

A pretty picture I must make, dragging that wretched leg after me, but as I leave the shadow of the custom house, my exertions are rewarded with a second glimpse: Lord Griffyn, his cape hitched to his waist, dashing along the river's shore.

The margin is narrow, though, and the way is not even, and being without a light, he must pick his way more carefully than he would like. As I chase him down, I find I can read the path most easily by watching *him*—by noting where he pauses, where he stumbles, where he tests his footing. And in this way, I quickly close the distance between us.

Can he make out the sound of my boots? Or is there some deeper, subtler sense at work in him, some voice that spins him round and confronts him with the spectacle of *me,* this whirlwind of righteousness? The sight blows him right back round again. His feet scrabble in the snow. No caution in that tread now, no canvassing of the terrain. Escape is the only remaining principle.

—There! Him!

And here was I, thinking I was the only pursuer. I should have expected Philomela to be right behind. But when I look back, she is still hovering by the custom house, engaged in the altogether different work of sounding the alarm.

—He go! Stop him!

Failing to elicit a response from the police, she grabs two of the girls by their rags and points out Griffyn's receding form. Then grabs two more, actually spins them on their heels. I understand now what she is doing: whipping up a mob. A mob of ragged, unruly, hysterical ten-year-old girls.

How quickly they take to the work! All it requires is a couple of well-timed shrieks from Philomela and, finally, the stern finger of Colin, pointing like an arrow at Griffyn's fleeing back, and they have taken up the chase. Girl after girl, all screeching like goblins, sprinting down the foreshore and ripping up the earth as they go.

They are a terrible sight, ravening and near blind with rage. And seeing them in turn emboldens me so much so that, as I run ahead of them, I seem to draw out all their rage, all the combined puissance of the Metropolitan Police, and I know I will chase this man as long as I have legs, as long as there is ground to run on.

And so I draw closer . . . closer . . . the distance between me and Griffyn melts away . . . and from behind us, the screams of the running girls pepper our ears. They, too, draw closer.

And yet in Griffyn, some hope of reprieve must still lurk. He gladdens—visibly gladdens—at the sight of Gully's boat, pulled up on the shore. He would make an offering of thanks, I think, if he had the time. But now he must haul the boat back into the water for rowing, he must leap in and steady himself and seize the oars. And because the water is still too shallow for rowing, he must dig the poles straight into the river bottom and propel himself into the current.

And all this costs him time. Precious time. He is only eight feet out by the time I gain the shore, and I need but take a few long strides into the water to be within leaping distance.

Frantic now, he gropes under his cape and prunes out a revolver—a far more elegant specimen than George's, but how little that matters to me now. Griffyn's trembling hands point the barrel, his quivering eye draws the bead, and still I come on—charging through the water, pushing it before me—until my target is at last within reach, until I am soaring through the air, wings flapping, beak pointed, and there is no longer any denying me. A mere thing like a pistol drops away, and when at last we make contact, there is only the meeting of our two bodies: an enormous concussion, followed by a moment of pure weightlessness.

The next thing I'm aware of is the tide, drawing us ever farther from shore, and Griffyn's body, pressed against mine. Two equal wills in a single boat, fighting each other to a standstill . . . and around us, only frenzy. Shrill cries and splashing limbs, as one by one the girls quit the safety of the shore and beat a white path towards us. The tide itself recedes before them; the boat rocks with their agitation. And as I force Griffyn onto his back, as I climb atop him, I feel the boat suddenly tip as the first girl boards.

It is *her* will, finally, to which I yield. Out of sheer deference, I fall away, and before Griffyn can make a move, she is upon him—four feet of bone and muscle, demonically magnified to twice that size—pounding his chest, scratching his patrician face, tearing the pomaded brown curls right out of his scalp.

It is conceivable, just conceivable, that Griffyn could repel *one* such attack, but within seconds, another girl has pulled herself over the side, and another right behind, and each new arrival throws herself on his recumbent form, taking up where the last left off, and before long, Griffyn has vanished beneath this heaving carapace of bodies. No longer screaming, these girls; no, they are far too intent on their work, and the only sounds that reach me now are the muffled thuds of their tiny fists and boots and the stifled groans of Lord Griffyn.

—No. Please. You mustn't.

That's me speaking. I am preparing to explain to them all about the British system of jurisprudence, the importance of law and order . . . but these girls are having none of it. With a look poised between outrage and glee, one of them hurls herself straight at my chest. In a daze of surprise, I fall back as the boat slides out from under me.

And now I am thrashing in black water . . . the Thames is shouting in my ears . . . ice scalding my skin. A prickle of terror crawls up my scalp, and I open my mouth to scream, and then I feel my hands closing round the lip of the boat. Quickly, I haul my head above water, and I bob there in the river's lap like a buoy—a privileged viewer of what is playing out just three feet away.

By now, more girls, a full brace of them, have clambered on board—the boat sinks lower and lower with each new weight—they rip his shirt, pluck out his hair, pummel his groin, kick and punch and slash. One of them has even climbed onto his chest and thrust his head, his bleeding and terror-struck head, over the side and into the water.

Around this head the water forms a quick, shimmering column. Half a minute . . . another half minute . . . and the rocking in his body subsides, and then the head . . .

Goes still.

Like that.

So. This is how a man passes. After all the protest and panic, just the faintest shudder and then nothing.

And now the husk of Lord Griffyn shoots from the boat like a wad of snuff and follows a plumb line straight to the river bottom. And as it goes, it performs one act of posthumous violence. It tips the already foundering boat with its cargo of girls—tips it and finally upends it.

And as the boat turns over, my hands slip free of its rim. And now I, too, am following the plumb line.

Swallowing down my panic, I grasp for anything, anything—a piece of hull, the North Star—but the tangible world has slipped far out of reach. My head struggles to stay free, but the fennish black water climbs ineluctably upwards, smearing my mouth, sliming my ears, crawling into the deepest caves of my sinuses.

Somewhere inside me, I hear Gully's peeved voice:

Whyn't you tell me you couldn't bloody swim?

Because . . . because . . .

The cold binds my arms to my sides. I drop . . . a fathom and then a little more . . . the black water surges and roils round me, more violent than I could have imagined, buffeting and winnowing me and . . . and perfecting me. My temples push inwards, and my eyes surge outwards, seething with pain. Excruciating, this pressure, and yet it carries the additional mercy of nullifying itself, so that all memory of it disappears instantly. There is pain and then oblivion.

And still: the absurdity of it! Drowning in perhaps ten feet of water. With a good dozen people close at hand. A bubble of laughter bursts from me, and with it a belch of black muck. My heart slows to a dull, thudding lurch. My lungs swell and spike. Needles of ice drive through my brain.

All the same, there is comfort here. For is this not the old dream? The dream I first had as a child. Once again, the killing sap is rising through me. Once again, the feeling drains from my hands, the air from my chest. The heart thumps loud enough to wake the dead. Yes. Yes, the old dream at last—after so many interruptions—reaching its conclusion.

And what a surprise! Not a dream at all but an architectural plan. Here . . . now . . . the final touches on the edifice of my life, falling into place.

And all sorts of people are rushing to congratulate me. There's Sam! And Mr. McReady. Belinda and Jem. And Mother, too, moving quite expertly through the water, a matronly mermaid, with a pair of redoubtable fins.

And right behind her . . . who but Father? No better a swimmer than I, and yet look how easily he navigates. Doesn't even need to move his arms and legs, just cuts through the water, like a boy on a greased pole. Smiles that shy, placating smile. Cups his hand and beckons to me.

Home, Tim. Go quiet.

Chapter 25

THE GRAPPLING IRON. That was the specific means of my escape. Gully's final gift: a fierce black hook, attached to a long strand of iron hoops, dangling over the side of the boat and catching round my leg. My lifeline.

My *second* lifeline, I should say. The first was simply an agitation in the water above me. I knew immediately what it was: the paddling of human feet. I knew also to whom the feet belonged; I knew why they were there. And so I went to them—wrapped my hands round the grappling iron and hauled myself up from the river bottom, towards those two paddling bodies. towards the claims of a new family.

There was, in this arc, an undercurrent of regret that lingers with me still. And yet I cannot question the impulse, any more than I can question being born. It simply was. A predicate only, with no direct object.

These, anyway, are the thoughts that crowd in on me, many hours after the events in question. It is Christmas Day, bless you, and I am spending it, for the time being, in the office of Detective Inspector Surtees. We are seated by a rather tentative fire—the first fire this hearth has enjoyed in some time, it is clear. My host, discomfited by the intrusion of warmth, has absented himself to the far side of his own office and left me his chair, and so here I sit, with my legs stretched out, grateful for every speck of heat that comes my way.

Only now is the chill beginning to leave my bones. That it has not taken up permanent residence, I owe to the labours of the stationmaster's wife, who padded me down with blankets and kept the fire raging round me all night long. My second station-house stay was a far cry from my first. I slept for hours—days, possibly—and when I awoke, I was still at liberty, and there was a plate of devilled grill and kidneys on the table next to me. And before I left, the good stationmaster's wife insisted on lending me a starched white shirt of her husband's, two sizes too small, and by way of compensation, a pair of startlingly roomy woollen trousers, in one of whose pockets I found a drawing of a naked woman straddling the branch of an elm. The clothes I'll return, but I've half a mind to keep the drawing. Even now my fingers worm their way towards it, while the rest of me hearkens to the dry, high voice of Inspector Surtees.

—Well, the rest of us had quite lost sight of you, I'm sorry to say. But the boy and the girl, dear me! Never let you out of their bearings. As soon as you dropped, they went straight after you. Quite a willful pair of beasts, aren't they?

He totters on the heels of his boots, jangles the coins in his pockets.

—Oh, and I've had the most fascinating talk with the girl. Wouldn't say a word at first, but came round in the end when I mentioned how much I admired you. Had to quite lay it on, I'm afraid.

—Sorry.

—D'you know how she did it, by the way?

—Did what?

—Escaped the dreaded coffin.

—No . . . I never—

—Oh, it's too degradingly fascinating, it's the stuff of cheap fiction. One grows quite religious contemplating it.

—How's that?

—The rosary beads, Mr. Cratchit.

—I'm sorry?

—You noticed them, I daresay. Rather chapped and altogether squashed in sections? Well, there's a very good and particular reason they are chapped and altogether squashed in sections, Mr. Cratchit. Somehow, in the act of being shut in, she managed to insert the beads between the lid and the box. From there, she was able to pry her way free. You've noticed, no doubt, she's astonishingly good at creating rudimentary levers.

—I have noticed, yes.

—I shouldn't be surprised to learn that Archimedes was one of her scions. "Give me a string of beads and I will . . ." Of course, this is in no way meant to demean your other confederate, Mr. Cratchit. A most indomitable, an *indivertible* fellow.

The fire is wasting quickly, and the ashes are dropping fast, and somehow this imparts a new degree of urgency to our conversation. And so, as I rake the few coals still remaining in the grate, I pose the question that has been tasking me from the moment I awoke.

—Have they found his body?

—Lord Griffyn's, d'you mean? Not yet, no . . . what with all the melee . . . and the tides, Mr. Cratchit, you know how capricious *they* can be. He may wash ashore tomorrow, he may . . .

And then, unaccountably, he falls silent.

—What's the matter, Inspector?

—I was only thinking how unfortunate it is that your friend . . . Captain Gully . . . isn't around to help us find him.

—Gully, yes.

—Please do accept our condolences.

—Yes. Thank you.

And with that show of deference, Inspector Surtees slaps his hands on his thighs and pulls himself into an erect position.

—You know, I've never met your Mrs. Sharpe, I'm sorry to say. I am told she is something of a legend in the halls of Scotland Yard. Held in rather high esteem for her business acumen. Which makes it rather hard to fathom.

—What?

—Why such a . . . such a deuced intelligent woman would, without *knowing* . . . well, it's such a queer sort of business for that kind of woman to get dragged into. *Innocently,* I mean. Wouldn't you agree, Mr. Cratchit?

—Ah, well, there it is. Women, Inspector.

Even staring into the fire, I can feel his gaze upon me. It imparts a heat of his own.

—Yes, Mr. Cratchit. Women.

And herewith the final discharging of my debt to Mrs. Sharpe. The sin of omission. And if it be sin, well, then, add it to my account.

In the end, of course, there is only so much I can omit. The police have already been to Mrs. Sharpe's. They have confiscated the books, requisitioned the coffins. They have disposed of George's body and questioned Iris and Mary Catherine and let all the other girls go. Only Mrs. Sharpe has eluded their inquiries. The police were told in no uncertain terms that she was not "to home."

Whether this was in fact the case or whether the police, disgruntled at having to work on Christmas, refrained from pursuing the matter further, I cannot say. What I can say, with a fair degree of certainty, is that Mrs. Sharpe will not be to home for many, many evenings to come. Where she will go, how she will get by . . . those are matters for some future narrative . . . but if her story plays out as I would fain believe, she and I *will* cross paths again someday, and beyond any doubt, our first topic of conversation will be the fate of Robinson Crusoe.

In the meantime, Inspector Surtees is pulling the bag of licorice from his desk drawer, and it is as though he were proffering it for the first time. Everything has begun again.

—Well, Mr. Cratchit, my men stand at your disposal. Is there any service you require?

—As a matter of fact, there is. I have two letters I need dispatched at once. Under normal circumstances, I would ask Colin, but—

—I quite understand. Shall I send for a messenger?

—Please.

—Consider it done. And now, I believe, there are two young people waiting outside to see you. May I show them in?

The messenger boy is not so sharp or speedy as Colin, but he is a good deal
more civil, and he returns with answers to both letters shortly after two in the
afternoon.

An hour later, I am passing with Colin down that well-known street,
which, like every other street in London, has been transformed by the ablution of snow. Dollops of gingerbread icing hang lightly from the tree
branches; white-whiskered stoles stretch across the awnings and cornices and
lintels. Our boots crunch softly against the walk, and our breath turns
instantly to steam and wraps us round, as if every pore in our bodies was
exhaling at the same time.

—Bit gloomy, ain't it?

Colin is right, of course. It is a grim, sunless block in all weathers. A second generation of buildings has been built atop the first, and any infusion of
light now arrives purely by accident. The pavements are empty, the trees
gnarled and stunted, and I would wager that the now-obviated sundial in that
tiny bricked-in corner will carry its fringe of snow straight through to April.

And yet I so long ago absorbed all this intelligence that to hear the place
called gloomy is a kind of personal affront. I cast my eyes about, seeking
some recess of beauty to which I can call Colin's attention, but after much
searching, the only thing I can point to is Uncle N's knocker, which, under
the influence of snow and holly, has cast aside its usual gargoyle role in
favour of St. Nicholas.

Or so it seems to me. Something of its original character must still come
through, however, for Colin scowls and backs away a step.

—Holy Christ! Looks like he's a-goin' to eat us.

—Well, yes. He takes getting used to.

Mrs. Pridgeon has been given the week off, and so it is Uncle N himself
who answers the door. The season has had its usual beneficent effect on his

appearance. His spine has straightened, his eye gleams with snow-light, and the bluish tint of his skin has been chapped into ruddiness. He swings the door open as far as it will go and sets his feet a yard apart and stands fully revealed, a garland of tiny silver bells still tinkling from the belfry of his lapel.

—Tim.

The touch of his hand renders me mute suddenly, and so I turn to Colin in the hope of making introductions. But the boy, in a rare fit of reticence, has stationed himself directly behind my back, and so Uncle N carries on as though I were alone.

—Disappointing news, I'm afraid. Peter and Annie have just sent word they can't join us. We shall . . . we shall just have to pin them down another time, perhaps. And in the meantime, this is—ha!—*ample* recompense.

—Merry Christmas, Uncle.

Over his shoulder, I can make out a latticework of laurel leaves and, facing the doorway, a "Happy Christmas" motto on a wooden frame covered with red calico. Mistletoe hanging from the chandelier and garlands of ivy, rosemary, box and yew snaking up the staircase.

And more: the sounds of revelry. Clinking glasses and the accidental plunk of a piano key and a woman's chiming voice:

—Don't keep us in suspense. Tell us who it is!

Uncle calls out:

—Wait just a moment and you'll see!

And then, inclining his head towards mine, he murmurs:

—You mentioned . . . in your letter . . . a sum of money.

—Not for me, Uncle. For a cabdriver named Adolphus. I'm afraid we inadvertently caused him to lose his cab and horse the other night. I was hoping, with your help, to replace them.

Eager to make a clean breast of it, I add:

—He's not likely to *thank* you for it. He's not a thanking sort of man.

—Well, if you . . . if you think it would . . .

—It's the last thing I will ask of you, Uncle. No, pardon. The next-to-last thing.

And with that, I reach behind me and grab Colin by the sleeve of his knickerbocker suit and drag him, wriggling and writhing, into the naked light of the old man's gaze.

—As promised, Uncle. Your new boarder.

A second or two of gentle shock, that is all, and then Uncle is beaming from every corner and bending halfway down and a quarter of the way round and wringing the boy's hand as vigorously as he might a water pump.

—Oh, good day! Good day to you, young man!

—If you say so.

—I think I must have failed to make your acquaintance last night.

—Well.

—So nice to have you with us.

—Thanks, I'm sure.

—Now, I hear tell you are quite the musician. This is most fortuitous because, you see, my little party here has punch and eggnog aplenty, but we are parched for song. Do you think you might do us the favour of performing a selection or two?

Colin draws his hand away, smothers it beneath his arm.

—I gets half my fee up front.

—Oh, a wise little man of business, it is. Very well, then. Shake hands, and there's two pounds on it. The rest on satisfactory completion.

To see Colin's eyes widen in that extreme fashion is to journey straight back to our initial encounter by the Hungerford Stairs. Back to that first meeting of gold and palm, transfusing him through, alchemising his future. . . .

I whisper to him now:

—There's more where that came from.

He gives this all due consideration. Then he whispers back:

—What about Filly?

—She'll be well taken care of, I promise. And very close by.

He gives Uncle N one last round of scrutiny, then says:

—I s'pose, you know, as a bit of favour to you, Mr. Timothy, I could give it a couple nights. Or a week, like. But keep in mind now, Colin the Melodious is an *artiste,* and he ain't the sort to settle down, you *know* that. Saps the creative muscle, don't it?

—You know, Colin, I just caught sight of a pretty lady in the hallway. I'm fairly certain she was winking your way.

—Don't be daft.

And still he arches his head over my shoulder to get a glimpse. And still he believes.

It is this belief—the unresisting faith in his own future—that draws him, finally, into the safe harbour of Uncle N's home. And as the door closes after him, I can just make out the barely suppressed excitement in Uncle's voice as he asks Colin:

—You wouldn't have a passing interest in *fungi*, would you?

And now the door is shut. Nothing left to do but tip my hat to the gargoyle St. Nick. Who nods right back.

It is getting on five o'clock when Philomela and I turn in to Oxford Street. A day's worth of vehicular traffic has left the streets black and swilly and nearly impassable, but the snow still clings to the gaslights and frames the plate-glass storefronts and props up the old beggar, dozing on the corner with a sign that reads: I AM JESUS' SECOND COUSIN, ONCE REMOVED.

We walk in peaceable silence. Philomela has, like me, availed herself of the largesse of the stationmaster's wife. In her bonnet and dress, she looks more presentable than she's done in some time, like someone out for a country stroll with no particular destination in mind, and there is indeed a part of me that wishes we had no endpoint. But then Philomela goes and finds one of her own. Clutching my arm, she draws me to a halt in the middle of the pavement. Her hand drops away, and I disappear from her consciousness, as she stands wrapped in amazement.

—What is it, Philomela?

I follow the line of her stare . . . across the street . . . to a pair of men with fingerless gloves, sitting on either side of an inverted water pail and playing a round of backgammon.

Neither of them is known to me. Drop them into any street in London, and I'd pass right by without a second thought. The only thing I honestly *recognise* is the look on Philomela's face. I recognise that at once.

—You *see* him, don't you, Philomela? Serafino.

At a loss for any other response, she simply nods. Nods and keeps on staring, as if daring the vision to pass.

I kneel down until my head is level with hers.

—Well, funny as it may sound, I've some experience in this area. Dead fathers, I mean.

Her eyes flick towards me, flick away again.

—Now, I don't believe you can actually speak to them or touch them. But if you can . . . if you can *convey* to them that you're happy and everything's fine . . . well, then, they needn't worry about you, and they can . . . they can *rest*, can't they? Finish their journey.

Whether she marks me, I cannot say. Certainly, she is no more willing to relinquish her post now than before. If anything, she holds to it with greater fervour as the minutes pass. And so, as gently as I can, I stoop down once more and murmur in her ear:

—Serafino must have his rest, Philomela.

It is, I think, the strongest appeal one could make to a survivor. For do we not require rest as well?

And so Philomela, drawing up every last particle of resolve, drags a smile across her face. And then—in a gesture of bashful intimacy, a gesture that hints at vanished domestic covenants—she taps her nose three times in succession.

And turns at last to me. And says:

—Ready.

Cratchit's Salon Photographique is closed for the day, but the shop is still ablaze with light, and the framed luminaries still hover in the galaxy of the front window. The season has exacted only small tributes: a sprinkling of holly berries, nearly invisible among the velvet tiers, and a rosette of leaves and holly on the door, intermixed with white grasses and Cape flowers and sprinkled with flour to make it look even more snow-laden than it already is.

The rosette has the additional effect of rendering the knocker unusable, and so I find myself (once again) pounding on the door, with a greater urgency than I truly feel. Oh, but there is urgency on the other side— enough for all of us. See how quickly the door opens. The way Peter and Annie scramble into view, adjusting each other's fringes, pinning back errant locks of hair, composing and recomposing their faces. Something of great moment is in the making.

And it all begins with my saying:

—This is the gift I wrote you about.

I fully expected to find Peter stymied by the occasion. The surprise is to see Annie, for the first time in my memory, struggling to find her way. All the words she must have prepared, all the accompanying gestures—they have slipped out of her grasp and left behind only a pair of converging brows and a pair of slack lips.

Philomela herself is no more inclined than they to break the impasse. She hangs by my leg like a girl of three, refusing to meet anyone's eye, declining any show of intention. The sight of her flushes me with embarrassment.

—I don't know whether I mentioned . . . she's still learning the language, but she . . . I've found she understands almost anything one puts to her.

Enough time has passed now for Annie to mount a show of normality. She totters forwards and extends a welcoming hand.

—How lovely to meet you, dear. You must be perfectly famished. I've made some Yorkshire pudding special, and there's a . . . well, a bit of a present under the tree, you might—

Her face folds over on itself, and she turns away. It falls to Peter to fill the silence with a rush of disclaimers.

—Oh, it's nothing special, of course, is it, Annie? But just for starters, eh? And perhaps we can . . . sometime . . . clothes, you know, that kind of thing. Can't have her running about with no clothes, can we, Annie?

His wife's voice comes back in a much smaller form.

—I should say not.

Taking Philomela by the hand now, I lead her over the threshold and halfway into the vestibule. Annie and Peter fall back and, out of some unspoken tact, draw away altogether, leaving Philomela and me to loll by the door.

Pulling clear of my leg now and turning all the way round, the girl makes as if to leave and then, stopping herself suddenly, emits the most furious of whispers.

—Why *here*?

—Where better, Philomela?

Her hands twitch in the air. A spasm of irritation rolls across her face.

—With . . . with *you*.

It is as if she were listening to herself for the first time, for she says it again, in a quiet, bemused tone:

—With you.

—Well, that would be lovely, Philomela, but I'm afraid it's not possible. I told you, I'm going on a trip. A long trip.

Her mouth turns down at the corners. Her eyes flash with scorn.

—Oh, long trip.

—Yes.

—Some place. No place.

—Well, I don't yet *know*, you see. But wherever it is, I'll write you often, you can be sure of that. And when I come back, you can show me how much you've *grown* and, oh, all the things you've learnt and all the boys who've gone mad for you. . . .

She rolls her eyes at that, but I press on.

—Why, you'll have changed so much, I shan't even know you.

—I know you.

She says this very gravely.

—Well, yes, Philomela. I'm rather counting on that.

Over her shoulder, she takes a furtive measure of Annie and Peter, leaning tensely against the studio door. She turns slowly back to me.

—They are good?

—The kindest people in the world, I promise. Although rather stricter than me about bedtimes.

She casts her eyes downwards.

—When are you go?

—Not for several weeks, likely. So until then, I'll look in on you every day, would you like that? And Colin, too, if that's agreeable.

—That is agreeable.

She nods, once, quite solemnly. And then she binds her arms round her chest—binds them tight, in a protective vise—too late to avert that first wracking sob. The second follows in short order, shaking her from head to waist.

—Oh, dear. Oh, no. What's wrong?

It's disconcerting, I confess, to see her cry for the first time. And a great pleasure, too. For tears are the finishing touch on the canvas of her face. All the hard, proud angles of her features soften and harmonise; every line of rancour and resistance is purged clean. She bows her head, and a ball of air jolts her chest, and the words fly out of her mouth before she can stop them.

—I want to go home.

Oh, she speaks English quite well enough, thank you.

I draw my face closer to hers. I chuck my finger under her chin.

—You *are* home. I promise.

And still the sobs keep coming. Every compounded sorrow of the last six months surges out, hot and fast and pure.

—And someday, Philomela, when you're ready, we'll all go back to Calabria together, wouldn't that be fine? Oh, I can just *see* you, you know. Dragging us through the streets and pointing out the sights, and all the old neighbours will come running, and won't they just—why, they'll fall back in admiration. "Can that be her? Serafino Rotunno's daughter, grown so beautiful? Oh, no it can't be!"

She smears a hand across her eyes, gives her head an angry shake.

—They no no.

—Sorry?

—No *know*. No *know* me.

—Don't be silly, of course they'll know you. To see you once is to know you. Believe you me.

And gradually the finitude of her tears is reached. One last seismic tremor squeezes through her ribs, and then her arms fall gently to her sides.

I place my hand on the back of her head.

—Shall we try again?

And this time, it is she who takes the first step, without any further prompting from me. Nor does she have to venture very far, for Annie has now recovered *her* faculties and is coming towards us with that ravishing directness of hers, her eyes smiling right into us.

—Philomela, would you care to have your portrait taken?

The girl thinks it over. And then silently consents.

—Splendid. Now I happen to know before *I* get a portrait taken, I like to sneak a quick peek at myself in the glass. We can't have any hairs out of place, can we? Would you like that?

Another nod, this one more decisive. Annie takes the girl by the hand and leads her over to the mirror on the wall and rests a hand on her shoulder . . . while Peter stands off to the side, still at a loss, but finding his way, too, and listening gratefully to his wife's prattle.

—Have you ever been in a studio, Philomela? No? Well, it's quite simple, really, but you must keep very still. And there's this very alarming sort of *tongs* thing we fasten round your head to make sure it doesn't move. Oh, it's awful, but it's only for a minute or two. Can you stand it?

—Why, yes, I can.

—Of course, if we don't get a good likeness the first time out, we'll just keep at it, shall we? There's loads of time. Oh, and you mustn't mind the smell too much, that's just the chemicals in the darkroom. Now, you're not to go *in* there just yet, it's far too dangerous. Mind you, Peter said the same thing to *me,* but you know, he's quite hopeless at mixing things, so it's . . . and I seem to recall some rumour about you being an artist?

—Yes.

—Well, that's just the ticket. We're always needing new backdrops, aren't we, Peter? And it's so tiresome engaging other people to do it when there's someone on the premises. And besides, I think that sort of thing is woman's work, don't you?

—Woman.

I stand there, watching, in a daze of admiration. And in case I needed any further sign, there is this: a red ribbon, appearing mysteriously in the vicinity of Annie's palm and travelling straight to the crown of Philomela's head.

It takes only a few seconds of gazing at that ribbon . . . wrapping her fingers round it and undertaking the near-religious labour of putting it in its proper place . . . and the symptoms of bereavement begin to slough off Philomela's face. So engrossed is she in girding herself for the camera's scrutiny—so absorbed are they all—that it becomes the easiest thing in the world to leave them to one another and slip out the door. The bell rings as I go, but when I glance through the window, no eyes are turned my way.

Indeed, my privacy has rushed back to me with a vengeance. The old beggar on the corner refuses to stir. Three oblivious young boys dash past me, cuffing one another and dragging sleds after them.

And the two backgammon players on the opposite side of the street simply carry on as before. The only thing that has changed is their appearance. One of the men has traded in his scarf for a rather jaunty cravat. He has even traded in his features. Acquired a pair of round, wide-set eyes . . . a half smile and a dimpled chin . . . oh, yes, Philomela drew an excellent likeness.

The other man has his back to me, but of course, I would know that back anywhere. Just as I would know every feature of that long, wizened body: the pipestem legs, the elbows pointing in the wrong directions . . . the hectored attentiveness . . . all unmistakable.

Well, I've said it before. Ghosts must pass the time quite as much as the next fellow. Why *not* a quick round of backgammon?

The only remaining mystery is this: when did Father learn to play?

—Merry Christmas, gentlemen!

But they have ears only for each other. And so I forge down Oxford Street without another word, and it's not until I reach the corner that I think to call back after them.

—And a Happy New Year!

And this time, I don't wait for a response. This time, I keep walking.

———— ◌ø ————

16 February 1861

Somewhere west of Saint Jago

Dear Father,

It is three days since we quitted Porto Prayo, but the islands of the Cape de Verd archipelago seem loath to quit us. At sunset, the hazy envelope that sur- rounds them bursts open, and the barren plains of lava flash once more onto our eyes: the conical hills, the jagged peaks—everything, right down to the smallest grove of cocoa-nut trees, standing naked as a newborn.

And all through the day, a fine brown dust rains down on us, like manna—so fine, indeed, that you scarcely notice it at first, and then after a short while, you notice nothing else, and your eyes sting so mightily you have no choice but to go belowdecks. I had assumed the dust was a farewell benediction of sorts from Porto Prayo, but Professor Bramthwaite informs me it is composed largely of minute organisms called infusoria, many of which have blown all the way from Africa on the harmattan.

How, you might ask, did the son of a clerk wangle passage on a three-masted bark bound for New Zealand?

Well, it is all Gully's doing.

The day after Christmas, I communicated the news of his death to his one known acquaintance: a naval outfitter in Radcliffe. From this gentleman I learned that an unexpected berth had opened up on the Perseverant, an ancient ten-gun brig refitted for more peaceable uses.

The position was assistant to the ship's naturalist. An unexalted title, but was I qualified for anything better? I was not. I signed on at once, and here you find me.

The work is not, in itself, inspiring—cataloguing specimens, taking down Professor Bramthwaite's dictation, carrying his gear from one outpost to the next—and it does not begin in earnest until we round Cape Horn. Until then, the professor is, for the most part, good company, even if he does talk in rather extravagant circles. I have also made fast friends with the ship's hydrographer and with Mr. Keeling, the surgeon, who possesses a surprisingly vast collection of erotic drawings (to which I donated my one).

My best company, however, comes to me in dreams. Just the other night, I had Mother over for a visit. Such a long time it had been! You won't be surprised to learn that she came armed at all points with instruction: Put your cabin tidy, Tim, every night and every morning. Refrain from spitting whilst on deck. Take care to sit at the captain's right, never the left. And above all else, do not fraternise with the common seaman.

With this last exhortation, she was, I'm afraid, too late. Several nights back, stupefied by boredom, I wandered out by the forecastle and found a ring of sailors, playing all-fours and passing round a jug of skilly. One of these fellows was wearing a scrimshaw necklace, which prompted me—mostly out of desperation—to introduce Gully's name into the conversation. And would you credit it, Father? Two of the riggers knew Gully, too!
We all had a delightful chat about him and then toasted his health in the checkered moonlight. It was like drinking him straight into our system.

We stop at Majorca on the way home. Did I mention?

The last thing Uncle N said to me before I left was:
—Your father would be so proud, Tim.

Given that I haven't actually seen you since Christmas Day, it is a difficult statement to corroborate. I can only conclude, as Uncle himself once said, that you have gone to your rest. At last. I hope my thoughts do not pester you too much.

And if they do, then indulge me with one final memory. . . .

It was several months after your first fit of apoplexy, and a week or so before the second. A late Sunday afternoon, just spilling into twilight, and I was bringing up a pot of weak tea, and everything about this act—the creaking of the stair, the squeaking of my shoes, the tea's dun pallor—resonated with dreariness.

Imagine my surprise, then, to open your door and find you sitting straight up in bed, still in your nightshirt, with an expression of unhinged joy. I asked you what had happened, and this is what you said:

—It's coming! Any minute now. The coach to Hertford.

This coach, apparently, was to take you to your uncle Geoffrey, a dairy farmer who'd been dead some twenty years. Not knowing exactly how to reply, I asked you if you wouldn't rather take the railway. You looked at me then with such a profound lack of comprehension that I realised you had gone back to a time before the railway. I daresay you were all of five or six at the moment, and here you were, going on a journey! What better thing to contemplate?

And so, upon further reflection, I decided there was nothing for it but to sit with you and wait for the coach to Hertford. The surprise lay in how much I enjoyed it. There you were, prattling on about how long it had been since your last trip—a year, I think—and how lovely the grass smelt there and good Uncle Geoffrey and good Aunt Hilda, always letting you milk your favourite cow (Yancy), and no children of their own, perhaps they might leave the farm to you someday, wouldn't that be just . . .

And there I was, saying the sorts of things I imagine a parent would say:

—Yes, won't it? Oh, that should be quite the treat!

Yet our positions were not exactly reversed. If anything, a kind of equality had settled over us. We were both free of duty, free of regret. Nothing to contem-

plate but this journey. An eternally arrested moment of anticipation: you were never happier.

In my heart, Father, there are many other memories—to be carried down to my grave—but I can never forget how you looked that day. The years blown away. The griefs numbed into silence . . . indeed, not yet experienced. Your fingers fluttered, and your face tilted irrepressibly towards the sky of your bedroom ceiling, and you were a gift that would never have to be returned. I shall always have that. Dear Father.

About the author

About the book

Read on

Insights,
Interviews
& More . . .

Author **Biography**

About the author

LOUIS BAYARD is a novelist, reviewer, and journalist whose work has appeared in the *New York Times, Washington Post,* Nerve.com, Salon.com, and *Ms.* Born in Albuquerque, New Mexico, Bayard grew up in Springfield, Virginia. He received his B.A. in English literature from Princeton University, where he studied under Joyce Carol Oates, and his M.S.J. in journalism from Northwestern University.

He has worked as a Congressional press secretary, a communications director, and a speechwriter. His *Washington Post Magazine* article "Two Men and a Baby" was nominated for "Outstanding Newspaper Article" by the Gay and Lesbian Alliance Against Defamation. Bayard's other novels are *Fool's Errand* and *Endangered Species* (Alyson). He contributed to the humor anthology *101 Damnations* (St. Martin's), and he is one of the essayists in the upcoming Salon.com anthology *To Breed or Not to Breed* (HarperCollins).

He lives in Washington, D.C., with his partner and his son. ᵔ

© Don Montuori

An Interview with
Louis Bayard

When and where did you get the first spark of the idea for this book?

I'd always been intrigued by the idea of revisiting a famous author or work, having seen it done very successfully by people like Michael Cunningham and Gregory Maguire and Sena Jeter Naslund (and Henry Fielding, centuries ago). It just sounded like fun to take a really well-known literary artifact and put a new spin on it—and maybe, in the process, find a new register in my own voice.

What appealed to you about revisiting a well-known book and character like A Christmas Carol's *Tiny Tim?*

It was Dickens who drew me there. He's the author I loved most as a child (along with Mark Twain) and I think he's been the biggest influence in my own writing. So it just seemed natural to make him my co-conspirator. And I picked Tiny Tim because, when I thought about the whole gallery of Dickens characters, he was the one who satisfied me the least. Even as a child, I never really believed in Tiny Tim, and I began to wonder if there wasn't something that Dickens didn't tell us about him. And then I thought: Wouldn't it be interesting to turn this character inside out? Scrape away all the layers of sentiment and familiarity and see what was left? And out of that impulse came this rather dark story.

I should say it was never my intention to write a sequel to *A Christmas Carol*. I was ▶

> 66 I picked Tiny Tim because, when I thought about the whole gallery of Dickens characters, he was the one who satisfied me the least. 99

3

more interested in using characters from that story to explore themes of loss and family and belonging. But I found, as I was writing it, that it was following a redemptive arc similar to the original story. And that's I think what ultimately makes it a Christmas story, because it has that hopeful trajectory.

Was it daunting following in Charles Dickens's footsteps?

No, it was a real kick, because I was very clear in my mind from the very beginning that I wasn't going to *be* Charles Dickens or write like him. Because no one can—Dickens is Dickens. My object, really, was to work against the grain of the original story while, at the same time, looking for patches of common ground. So, in the end, it felt more like a collaboration than anything else, and what better collaborator could a guy find than Dickens?

What did you read or re-read while you were working on this book?

The first thing I did was to re-read *A Christmas Carol*. Which is an eye-opening experience, because even if you think you "know" the story, you don't. You see, for instance, how dark the story is compared to some of its later incarnations. Dickens was passionately concerned with the suffering that was going on around him, particularly the suffering of children. You also find that the Cratchit family is sketched fairly lightly—two of the Cratchit children are not even named. And Tiny Tim, for all his symbolic weight,

66 I was very clear in my mind from the very beginning that I wasn't going to *be* Charles Dickens or write like him. Because no one can. 99

occupies a relatively small portion of the narrative, and we never actually see him meeting Scrooge. So I found I had a lot of space for embroidering and inventing.

And I now had a wonderful excuse to read more of Dickens's work—books I'd always wanted to read, like *Dombey and Son* and *Little Dorrit*. And I read a lot of Wilkie Collins, who was a good friend of Dickens's and a wonderful novelist in his own right. One of my big finds was Henry Mayhew, another contemporary of Dickens. He was this fascinating combination of journalist and social scientist who just prowled the streets of mid-nineteenth-century London and produced one of the most remarkable urban compendia I've ever seen. It has everything from statistics on the amount of manure in the streets to man-on-the-street interviews with crossing sweeps and rat catchers and river dredgers like Captain Gully. I'm guessing a lot of writers have been drawing on him over the years.

Mr. Timothy's father is a powerful presence in the book. You became a father yourself fairly recently. Did the experience of having a child impact the writing of this book? What about your own father, and your relationship with him—any influences there?

Well, my father is still very much alive, so he hasn't been haunting me in the streets. But I think we're all haunted to some extent by our past. And it's true, there's nothing like becoming a parent to put the past in a new light. When you experience what it takes to get one child through one day, you get a little dazzled realizing you were the beneficiary of that, too—this long chain of giving and receiving. ▶

> 66 I think we're all haunted to some extent by our past. 99

An Interview with Louis Bayard *(continued)*

When I was writing the book, one of the images I kept coming back to was Bob Cratchit carrying Tiny Tim on his shoulders through the streets of London. Well, I'll tell you, I have a pretty light three-year-old, and after seven or eight blocks of carrying him on my shoulders, I'm needing some relief. So I wanted Tim to come to the same realization—to see that his father was acting as his "legs" and acting at great physical sacrifice. Unfortunately, his father has to be dead before Tim can see him that way. That does seem to be the way of things.

This book has been described as a "literary thriller"—do you think that's accurate? Is it the kind of book you set out to write? Was it difficult to weave together these two elements?

I didn't necessarily set out to write a thriller or a mystery, although I love both those genres (as did Dickens). But it soon became clear to me that if I wanted Tim to experience this fairly profound transformation—to become, as David Copperfield says, the hero of his own story—I would have to pound him pretty hard. And the thriller element really came out of that. I needed to put him *in extremis*. And, of course, I wanted the book to be entertaining in the same way that all of Dickens's stuff is entertaining. Dickens was a serialized novelist, so he was willing to give readers what they liked because he knew he had to keep them coming back. So his books are really hybrids, with a little bit of everything: thrills and laughs and pathos and satire and social commentary and just a lot of *life*. And that's a great model for any writer.

> 66 So his [Dickens's] books are really hybrids, with a little bit of everything: thrills and laughs and pathos and satire and social commentary and just a lot of *life*. And that's a great model for any writer. 99

What are you working on now?

I'm looking at another well-known nineteenth-century author: Edgar Allan Poe. Since Poe was, among other things, the creator of the detective story, I thought it would be fun to put him at the center of a mystery. The book is called *The Pale Blue Eye,* and it will feature a younger Poe than we're used to seeing. We pick him up when he's still in his early twenties—a cadet at West Point. He's going to be thrown in with an older man, himself a detective, and their relationship will really form the heart of the book. And this being Poe, there will be more traffic with dead folk. Once you start hanging out with ghosts, it's tough to leave them behind.

I have to admit, I had some trepidation about taking on Poe, because his sensibility is so Gothic and extreme, and I just wasn't sure I could get there. But then I reread portions of *Mr. Timothy,* and I thought: *No, you're gruesome enough. You're there already.*

A Christmas Carol Quiz

Keep in mind, this quiz is based on Dickens's *Christmas Carol,* not on any movie or television series that has been made from the book.

1. Marley's first name was _____.

   a: Phillip

   b: Geoff

   c: Jacob

2. _____ is the name of Scrooge's nephew.

   a: John

   b: Fred

   c: George

3. _____ and Scrooge were apprentices for Fezziwig.

   a: Thomas Fields

   b: Dick Wilkins

   c: John Openshaw

4. Scrooge's sister was named _____.

   a: Sue

   b: Fan

   c: Liz

5. When he was young, Scrooge was in love with _____.

   a: Belle

   b: Dora

   c: Flora

Reprinted with permission from www.triviahalloffame.com

Correct answers for
A Christmas Carol Quiz:
1/c; 2/b; 3/b; 4/b; 5/a; 6/c;
7/b; 8/a; 9/a; 10/b

6. _____ Cratchit played a joke on her father by hiding from him when he came home.

    a: Belle

    b: Sarah

    c: Martha

7. _____ were the children that the Ghost of Christmas Present showed to Scrooge.

    a: Faith and Hope

    b: Ignorance and Want

    c: William and Mary

8. The charwoman, the laundress, and the undertaker's assistant sold what they took from Scrooge to _____.

    a: Old Joe

    b: Uncle Nick

    c: Big John

9. After being visited by ghosts, Scrooge sent a _____ to the Cratchit family.

    a: turkey

    b: letter

    c: box of toys

10. And so, as _____ observed, "God bless us, everyone."

    a: Scrooge

    b: Tiny Tim

    c: The Ghost of Christmas Present

Correct answers for Know Your Dickens?: ▶
31, 31, 147, 91, 150, 129, 236, 153, 344, and 207
Extra credit: 65 and 188

Know Your Dickens?

Mr. Timothy is salted with allusions to other Dickens works and to Dickens's own history. Can you find ...

- the blacking factory where young Dickens was forced to go to work?

- the Hungerford Market, where Mr. Dick lodged in *David Copperfield*?

- Saffron Hill, a common haunt of Fagin's in *Oliver Twist*?

- the graveyard where Captain Hawdon was buried in *Bleak House*?

- The Roman bath in Strand Lane often frequented by David Copperfield?

- Craven Street, where Mr. Brownlow conversed with Rose Maylie in *Oliver Twist*?

- Marshalsea Jail, home to Little Dorrit and her family?

- the Adelphi Terrace, where Mr. Pickwick celebrated his release from Fleet Prison?

- Jacob's Island, where Bill Sikes was killed in *Oliver Twist*?

- the Camden Town railway establishments from *Dombey and Son*?

Extra credit: Find two uncredited appearances made by Charles Dickens himself.

Fun Facts About
A Christmas Carol

THE STORY

- The book's original title was *A Christmas Carol in Prose: A Ghost Story of Christmas*.

- The germs of Scrooge's adventure can be found in Dickens's own "Story of the Goblins Who Stole a Sexton," an interlude in *The Pickwick Papers*. That story was, in turn, inspired by Washington Irving's "Rip Van Winkle." Dickens was a friend of Irving's and was indebted to the American writer for his evocations of a British Christmas.

- Why does Marley wear a bandage around his head? In Victorian times, dead people often had their heads wrapped in bandages to keep their faces from collapsing into gruesome expressions. Dickens received the same ministration when he died in 1870.

- The depiction of the Cratchits' home life was almost certainly inspired by Dickens' childhood memories. Like the Cratchits, he and his family lived in a small house in Camden Town, then considered one of London's poorest suburbs.

- Tiny Tim may have been patterned after one of several real-life figures, including Dickens's brothers Fred and Alfred (Alfred died in childhood) and his invalid nephew Harry Burnett Jr.

- Medical experts have long theorized about the nature of Tiny Tim's illness. Contemporary diagnoses include spinal tuberculosis and renal tubular acidosis, a kidney disease.

* "Scrooge" was an actual English verb: a colloquial term for crowding or squeezing.

10

- By having Scrooge send the Cratchits the gift of a turkey, Dickens helped the turkey replace the goose as England's favored Christmas bird.

THE STORY BEHIND THE STORY

- *A Christmas Carol* may owe part of its genesis to an 1843 government report on child labor abuses in mines and factories. After reading the report, Dickens was inspired to strike a "sledge-hammer blow ... on behalf of the Poor Man's Child."

- Writing at great speed, Dickens completed the work within six weeks, even as he was laboring on his serialized novel *Martin Chuzzlewit*. Dickens later said he felt the Cratchits "ever tugging at his sleeve, as if impatient for him to get back to his desk and continue the story of their lives."

- Published in 1843, *A Christmas Carol* was an immediate sensation, running through an initial print run of 6,000 copies in only five days. It has never been out of print. Dickens, however, earned little money from it—partly because the book, with its hand-colored illustrations, was expensive to produce, and partly because he spent hundreds of pounds in court costs to combat British copyright pirates. The U.S. editions of the book were likewise pirated, and Dickens never earned a penny from them.

- Dickens insisted on keeping the price of the book low so it would reach the broadest possible audience.

- *A Christmas Carol* was a favored part of Dickens's public reading repertoire. Between 1853 and 1870, he read it 127 times before British and American audiences. A notably ▶

* Tiny Tim was never depicted in John Leech's original illustrations. The first known rendering of the character was an 1861 wood engraving by the great French artist Gustave Doré.

skilled performer, he often reduced audiences to tears with the imagined death of Tiny Tim.

* At least a dozen stage productions of *A Christmas Carol* sprang to life within a year of the book's release. (Dickens, by law, held no copyright on dramatizations of his work.) Interestingly, the famous words "God bless us, everyone!" could not be uttered on the British stage in that era. Producers had to make do with the more benign "Heaven save you!"

* Not all critics have been kind to *A Christmas Carol*. A contemporary reviewer wrote, "Nothing can be more absurd than the fable itself and the whole of its groundwork: it is the veriest brick and mortar, puerility and absurdity, of the idlest fairy tale." Henry James would later refer to Tiny Tim and Dickens's other child characters as "little monsters ... deformed, unhealthy, unnatural."

* Ironically, Christmas traditions were on the wane in Great Britain when *A Christmas Carol* first appeared. Dickens is credited with reviving those old customs and, in the process, helping to shape the Christmas celebration we know today.

* Christmas was not universally celebrated in the United States during the mid-nineteenth century, but after hearing Dickens read *A Christmas Carol* in Boston in 1867, a local manufacturer was inspired to close his factory on Christmas Day and hand out turkeys to all his employees. Three years later, Congress made Christmas a federal holiday for the first time.

* The first film version of the book was a 1901 British silent titled *Scrooge, or Marley's Ghost.* Since then, Scrooge has been impersonated on film, television, stage, and radio by everyone from Lionel Barrymore to Alistair Sim, to Patrick Stewart, to Mr. Magoo.

Source: *The Annotated Christmas Carol,* edited by Michael Patrick Hearn (New York: W. W. Norton, 2004). With the author's permission.

An Excerpt from Louis Bayard's *Pale Blue Eye*

Mid the groves of Circassian splendor,
   In a brook darkly dappled with sky
   In a moon-shattered brook raked with sky,
Athene's lissome maidens did render
   Obeisances lisping and shy.
There I found Leonore, lorn and tender
   In the clutch of a cloud-rending cry.
Hell-harrowed, I could only surrender
   To the maid with the pale blue eye
   To the ghoul with the pale blue eye.

LAST TESTAMENT OF GUS LANDOR

April 19, 1831

In two or three hours ... well, it's hard to tell ... in three hours, surely, or at the very outside, four hours ... within four hours, let us say, I'll be dead.

   I mention it because it puts things in a certain context. My fingers, for instance, have become interesting to me of late. Also the lower-most slat in the Venetian blinds, a bit askew. And, outside the window, a wisteria shoot, snapped off the main stem, waggling like a gallows. I never noticed that before. Something else, too: at this moment, the past comes on with all the force of the present. All the people who've peopled me ... don't they come thronging round ... what keeps them from bumping heads, I wonder? There's a Hudson Park alderman by the hearth; next to him, my wife, in her apron, ladling ashes into the can, and who's watching her but my old Newfoundland retriever; and down the hall, my mother, who never set foot in this house, died before I reached twelve ... well, she's ironing my Sunday suit. My father's ►

> **❝ Within four hours, let us say, I'll be dead. ❞**

somewhere out back, gathering kindling, or praying. None of them says a word to the others. Very strict etiquette in place, I can't work out the rules of it, no matter how long I look.

Not everyone, I should say, minds the rules. For the past hour, I've been having my ear bent—torn, nearly—by a man named Cadmus Foot. He was run in fifteen years ago for robbing the Rochester mail. A vast injustice: he had three witnesses to swear he was robbing the Baltimore mail at the time. He flew into a fine rage about it, skipped town on bail, came back six months later, crazy with cholera, and threw himself in front of a hackney cab. Talked all the way to death's door. Still talking now.

Oh, it's a crowd, I can tell you. Depending on my mood, depending on the angle of the sun through the parlor window, I can attend to it or not. There are times, I admit, when I wish I had more traffic with the living, but they are harder to come by these days. Patsy scarcely stops round anymore, the boys at Benny Haven's give me wider berth . . . Professor Quawquaw is off measuring heads in Havanna . . . as for *him,* well, what is there to call him back? I can only summon him in my mind, and the moment I do, all the old talks play out again. All those hours—hours and hours—trying to see if I had a soul. He was on the pro side of the question. It might have been amusing to hear him go on if he hadn't been in such terrible earnest. But then no one had ever pressed me so strongly on this point, not even my own father (traveling Presbyterian, too busy with the souls of the nearest flock to plant much of a boot on mine). Again and again, I said, "Well, well, you may be right." It only made him hotter. He'd tell me I was just putting off the question, pending empirical confirmation. And I would say that, lacking confirmation, what more could I say than "You may be right"? Round and round we went, until one day, he said, "Mr. Landor, there will come a time when your soul turns round and fronts you in the most empirical fashion possible. The very moment it quits you. You will clutch for it—ah, in vain! See it now, sprouting eagle wings, bound for the Asiatic eyries."

Well, he was fanciful that way. Gaudy, if you must know. Myself, I've always preferred facts to metaphysics. Good hard homely facts, a full day's pottage. It is facts that shall form the spine of this narrative, and where I stray from them, write it down as dotage, nothing more . . . a brain just this side of extinction.

"Extinction."

Oh, why wrap it in quotation marks when it lies so near at hand? When it was for so many years my *business*? Ceasing to be my business, it continued as habit. Foolish to expect anything else. One night, a full year into my retirement, my daughter heard me talking in my sleep—very distinct—welcoming a midnight caller, she thought. She came into my bedroom to find me questioning a suspect twenty years dead. *The corner won't square,* I kept saying. *You do see that, Mr. Pierce. . . .* This particular fellow had dismembered his wife's body and fed the pieces to a pack of watchdogs at a Battery warehouse. In the dream, his eyes looked pink and sad and half-flirty; he was sorry for taking up my time, such a gentleman as I was. I remember telling him: *If it hadn't been you, it would have been someone else.*

Foolish, as I said, to think the Pierces of the world will leave you in peace. To think you can slip away into the Hudson Highlands with your books and ciphers and your watercolors and your knobby-oak walking sticks . . . and leave extinction behind? It won't be left, I tell you. It will come and find you.

I might have run. A little further into the wilderness, I might have done that. How I let myself be coaxed back I can't truly say. The best answer I can make is no answer at all but, God help me, metaphysical. I mean to say there are times I believe it happened—all of it happened—so we should find each other, he and I.

Even as I write that sentence, my hand jerks to a halt. . . . Reason catching me by the sleeve, that's what my young friend would call it. "What of the others?" Reason says. "Just tools, were they, for realizing your destiny?" I have no good reply to make her, I have only a theory: Destiny belongs to the survivors. Like history. And I am (for the moment) alive. It's my last qualification. Alive, with these memories and these other lives—oh, if you must, *souls*—to account for. And since those souls were, on many sides, closed to me, I have made way where necessary for other speakers. My young friend most especially. He's the true spirit behind this poor history, and whenever I try to imagine who'll be first to read this manuscript, he's the one who presents himself. *His* fingers tracing the rows and columns, *his* eyes picking out my scratches.

It's not likely, I know that. Near impossible he will claim the authorship due him. Well. I suppose authors never know half of what they've written . . . any more than they can choose who will read them. We are the chosen ones. Nothing left, then, but to take comfort in the thought of this stranger—still unborn, for all I know—who will read these lines for the first time. To you, my beloved, dreaded stranger, I dedicate this narrative.

And so I become my own reader. For the last time. Another log in the fire, would you please, Alderman Hunt?

And so it begins again. ∾

For Further Reading
A Victorian-Era Bibliography

Ackroyd, Peter. *London: the Biography*. New York: Nan A. Talese Doubleday, 2000.

Arnstein, Walter L. *Britain Yesterday and Today*. Fourth Edition. Lexington, Massachusetts: D.C. Heath and Co., 1983.

Baxendale, Kenneth William. *Charles Dickens' London: 1812–1870*. West Wickham, Kent: Alteridem, 1986.

Life in Victorian England: The Pitkin Guide. Pitkin Unichrome, 1999.

Mayhew, Henry. *London Labour and the London Poor*. In four volumes. New York: Dover Publications, 1968.

Mitchell, Sally. *Daily Life in Victorian England*. London: Greenwood Press, 1996.

Pool, Daniel. *What Jane Austen Ate and Charles Dickens Knew*. New York: Simon & Schuster, 1993.

Thomas, Donald. *The Victorian Underworld*. New York: New York University Press, 1998.

Thomson, John. *Victorian London Street Life in Historic Photographs*. New York: Dover Publications, 1994.

Weinreb, Ben and Christopher Hibbert, eds. *The London Encyclopedia*. Revised Edition. London: Macmillan London, 1995.

Don't miss the next book by your favorite author. Sign up now for AuthorTracker by visting www.AuthorTracker.com.